Letters to a Secret Lover

Just then a nip of cold, spring Montana air rushed around her bare arms and she looked up to see another patron enter the Lazy Elk.

A tall, dark, handsome patron. The kind of patron that made her heart flutter on sight. He wore a flannel shirt over a white waffle-weave pullover and faded jeans, much more appropriate for the chilly weather than her beaded baby-doll tee. A day's stubble covered his chin and his dark hair needed a trim, but she suddenly *liked* that because it was so different from her ex. Her first thought: This would be a perfectly good guy to help her climb back on the horse.

She noticed he didn't smile, as he began talking with a couple of equally outdoorsy-looking guys at one of the tables, his expression staying completely serious and sexy as sin.

"Him," she said simply.

Avon Books by
Toni Blake

LETTERS TO A SECRET LOVER
TEMPT ME TONIGHT
SWEPT AWAY

Letters to a Secret Lover

TONI BLAKE

AVON
An Imprint of HarperCollinsPublishers

This is a work of fiction. Names, characters, places, and incidents are products of the author's imagination or are used fictitiously and are not to be construed as real. Any resemblance to actual events, locales, organizations, or persons, living or dead, is entirely coincidental.

AVON BOOKS
An Imprint of HarperCollins*Publishers*
10 East 53rd Street
New York, New York 10022-5299

ISBN 978-0-06-142988-0
www.avonromance.com

First Avon Books paperback printing: June 2008

Printed in the U.S.A.

10 9 8 7 6 5 4 3 2 1

To Robin,

for thirty years of fun and friendship.

I cannot imagine my life without you in it.

As always, I had help writing this book, and my thanks go to the following people:

To Renee Norris for her early critique of the first two chapters, and for being my trusted "first reader." I couldn't do it without you!

To Robin Zentmeyer, Lisa Koester, Joni Lang, and—again—Renee, for early brainstorming help.

To author Maggie Price for sharing her knowledge on police procedure as it relates to this story, and to attorney Glenda Edwards for answering my questions about certain legal situations pertaining to the book.

To Valerie Fox of the Hocking Hills Canoe Livery for her tips on running a canoeing facility, to Ron Meeks of the Sweetwater Travel Company for answering my questions about rainbow trout, and to everyone on the Novelists, Inc. loop who kindly shared their vast knowledge about the sport of fishing.

To my agents, Meg Ruley and Christina Hogrebe, for their ongoing guidance and support, and to my editor, Lucia Macro, and everyone at Avon Books for being so fabulous to work with!

Dear Gina,

I'm thinking of you today. It's selfish, maybe. No, definitely. But I can't help it. Not a lot of color here, and so I'm imagining you out in the bright sunshine, in some gorgeous dress—yellow, or maybe blue. I'm thinking of your hair, soft and silky in the breeze.

I carved a heart-shaped jewelry box in the woodshop last week, then stained it in dark oak, and it came out good. I told myself it wasn't for you, but it was. And I wish I could give it to you. But that's selfish, too.

I told my friend Glen about you, showed him your picture. He says I ought to just tuck it away under my mattress or at the bottom of a drawer, not look at it anymore. But the trouble is, no matter where I put it, it's still too easy to reach and keeps finding its way back into my hand. Maybe that will change over time. Maybe I'll get better at forgetting, not looking, not missing you.

All my love,
Rob

Prologue

Lindsey Brooks stood in the kitchen of her Lakeshore Drive high-rise condo wearing a pink, frilly apron emblazoned with the words *Kiss the Cook*—and nothing else. Well, except for a pair of bright red, pointy-toed stilettos.

It wasn't her usual way of preparing a meal, but then again, she didn't actually prepare many meals—so the whole scenario felt a little surreal. Yet if a little chicken cordon bleu, along with greeting her guy in the nude, would spice things back up between them, it was worth it. And the truth was, her kitchen got hot with the oven on, so the "naked chef" thing was starting to seem almost *practical* as she moved from sink to counter to stove.

She checked the pots where the glazed carrots were busy glazing and the creamed spinach creaming. The twice-baked potatoes were baking—for the second time—alongside the chicken, and she'd just slid a tray of yeast rolls into the seldom-used top half of her double oven. Now to light the candles and pour the wine.

Not that the meal really mattered. She hoped it would be

edible, but tonight was mostly about sex. Mostly about staging a sexy, wild seduction that would thrill her man, that would take the two of them back to the heart and soul of their relationship, back to passion. And she was more than ready—walking around mostly naked in high heels while she cooked had turned her on more than she'd anticipated. It wasn't easy for a girl who loved her wardrobe as much as Lindsey did to ditch it altogether, even for a night, but some fabulous sex would surely get things back to normal around here.

Which was good, since the wedding was only two short months away. And lately, things had been . . . strained. She'd been busier than usual—it wasn't easy to write a syndicated advice column for the lovelorn *and* keep up with her getting-more-popular-every-day blog *and* plan a gala wedding-to-end-all-weddings for five hundred of Chicago's trendiest, all at the same time.

Plus she had to keep up with her shopping, of course. Sometimes Garrett, her intended, didn't *get* that Lindsey just wouldn't be Lindsey if she didn't shop. He didn't get how the right pair of peek-toe pumps could make a girl feel ready to take on the world—or at least Chicago. He didn't get how a new dress with just the tiniest hint of a crinoline beneath it could make a play or the ballet a thousand times more fun.

One would think he'd understand about dealing with the pressures of a high-profile life—they were both movers and shakers, after all. Even if Garrett moved and shook in slightly different directions than she did. Since making partner at the firm, he'd gotten involved with the arts and local charities, suddenly serving on *this* board and *that* council, and he'd recently even announced an interest in running for office.

And God knew he'd be *glad* she had those peek-toe pumps and crinoline dress *then*—she was going to *need* a fantastic wardrobe if she was going to be in the public eye even more than usual. Although between her column's recent syndication and his ambitions, they'd already become Chicago's latest "it" couple, having their pictures show up everywhere from the *Tribune*'s society page to a local gossip rag called *Chi-Town Beat.*

So life had gotten a little stressful lately. And that's exactly why Lindsey felt they needed to get back to *them*, to the people—the lovers—they'd been before local fame had assailed them.

She surveyed the scene. Wine poured, candles glowing. Open bottle in hand, she tipped a sip to her mouth, then returned to the stove to take up the carrots and spinach, which she'd timed carefully to finish at 6:58, since Garrett was due at seven and the man was nothing if not prompt. The chicken came out right on time, as well.

Two minutes later the doorbell rang, and her heartbeat kicked up. Showtime.

This was going to be amazing, she just knew it. Wasn't it every guy's fantasy to be greeted naked—or nearly so—at the front door? "You're making his dreams come true," she whispered to herself, suddenly a little giddy. Then, taking a deep breath, straightening her apron, and hoping her boobs looked perky behind it, she sashayed to the door and whipped it open.

Garrett stood on the other side in his usual suit and tie and impeccably groomed blond hair, his eyes narrowing in confusion as his jaw dropped nearly to the floor.

"Surprise," she said, striking a hopefully sexy pose while brandishing a large serving spoon in one upraised hand. Then she shimmied a little and wiggled her hips, her body humming with sheer anticipation.

He blinked. But his eyes didn't change much—like into delight or arousal or anything good. "What the hell is *this*?" He looked down at her as if she were wearing a potato sack. "Why aren't you *dressed*, for God's sake?"

Lindsey took a deep breath and tried not to feel too

deflated. *This is okay. Stay cool. He just has a lot on his mind and doesn't get it yet.*

She plastered on a smile, still ready to seduce. "This is your sexy fiancée serving you a romantic dinner in the nude. After which I'm going to get *you* naked, too, and have my way with you. What do you think of *that*?" But in lieu of giving him a chance to answer, she leaned in, lifted her perfectly manicured fingertips to his face, and delivered an oh-so-passionate kiss.

Passionate—but short. Since before she knew it, his fists circled her wrists and he was pushing her gently back. "Lindsey, we need to talk."

"Talk?" Of everything she had planned for this evening, talking hadn't been on the menu.

His gaze swept down over her apron again, after which he gave a little head-shake and met her eyes. "Lindsey, I'm sorry to say this, but . . . you've changed. Or I have. I'm not sure, but either way . . ." He stopped, swallowed nervously, and the floor beneath her red heels began to sway. "Either way, I've decided I can't marry you."

Lindsey simply blinked. She couldn't have heard him right. Because they were the perfect couple. The "it" couple.

Okay, yeah, there'd been that recent strain. And they hardly ever had sex anymore. And he'd accused her once or twice of caring more about her purse collection than him. But really, other than that, they were perfect. They were the couple everyone wanted to be.

So she swallowed back her fears, convinced she hadn't heard him correctly. "I think I misunderstood you, Garrett. What did you just say?" She stepped closer and slid her arms back around his neck for good measure. And she waited to feel his snug embrace, waited for that sense of security to cocoon her, but it didn't happen.

Instead he only sighed, looked put upon. "I don't want to marry you anymore, Lindsey."

Whoa. That time she heard it. In fact, the words took her breath away.

"Oh," she heard herself murmur. "Oh my God."

She backed away, eyes focused tightly on his crisp red tie. She'd picked it out herself. She'd picked out everything he was wearing, in fact, right down to his underwear. Their lives were that intertwined. She forced her gaze back to his. "Why?" she asked, shaking her head in disbelief.

"You're just . . . too high-maintenance. Too self-absorbed. And you talk too much—usually about things that don't matter—and it drives me absolutely nuts. What it comes down to is—you're just not the woman I need on my arm to get me where I want to go."

Okay, pal, don't sugarcoat it or anything.

Lindsey barely knew how to react. This couldn't be happening. It couldn't. It was her whole life. Everything she'd built, everything she'd wanted, everything she'd planned for. Crumbling beneath her. And *oh God*, what a terrible time to be naked beneath a scant *Kiss the Cook* apron!

Unable to think clearly, she found herself backing up on her heels, wanting simply to be away from him. She backed through the foyer, to the dining area, where she finally bumped her bare bottom against the edge of the contemporary black sideboard that matched the black dining table they'd picked out together last year.

Then, at a complete loss for words, she made the only move she could think of. Working on pure instinct, she dropped her spoon, reached around behind her to pick up the strawberry cheesecake she'd set out a little while ago, and flung it at him.

Yep—met with the greatest shock and adversity of her life, Lindsey responded with the old pie-in-the-face routine.

It hit him with a tiny little *pffft*, and she watched in horror, just as shocked as he was, as strawberries and red glaze ran down his face and onto his suit and tie. Stunned eyes peered out at her from behind a creamy cheesecake mask.

Which was when they both heard the tapping noise across the room and looked toward it.

In time to see a window washer pointing his camera phone at them through the plate glass. The bearded guy in coveralls smiled, clearly pleased at his good fortune, just before the bright flash made them both moan and scowl. Talk about quick-on-the-draw!

When Lindsey could see again, the window washer was gone, the thick cables outside the window moving quickly as he made his escape. Oh God.

"Tell me that didn't just happen," she said.

"It *did* happen," Garrett snapped. "Thanks to *you*."

Her hands curled into tight fists at her side. "Hey, if you'd had the decency to be *nice* or maybe even *thrilled* by my surprise, the guy wouldn't have seen anything worth taking a picture of."

"Besides my naked fiancée, you mean."

Good point. But she protested. "I'm not naked! I'm wearing an apron." Then she gasped, lifting a hand to shield the side of her breast. "Oh God, do you think my boob was showing?"

"What difference does it make?" he yelled through his cheesecake mask. "Could this be any worse? What on earth were you thinking, parading around in front of huge windows like that?"

She gave her head an incredulous shake. "That I'm on the twenty-third floor and wasn't expecting Peeping Toms?"

Garrett raked a trail of cream cheese off his cheek, flinging it toward the windows as he motioned to them. "Well, what about window washers? Didn't the big, thick cords hanging down tip you off that there were window washers in the area?"

She bristled. "I hadn't noticed them, actually."

"Figures," he groused, his brisk nod propelling more bits of strawberry and cheesecake toward the floor. "Too self-absorbed to notice or care about anything outside your pretty little head." Then he let out a huge sigh of despair and buried his cheesecake-covered face in his hands. "God, I'm sunk."

She resisted pointing out that they were on the same sinking ship *together* and tried to look on the bright side. "Maybe he doesn't know who we are and it won't be a big deal. Maybe we could intercept him downstairs before he leaves."

Garrett simply glared at her. "Yeah, we're gonna go dashing downstairs looking like *this.* And he's probably already sent it to the papers—it only takes a phone call and a click. Everyone in this city knows who we are lately, Lindsey—even in cheesecake and"—he motioned to her again—"that idiotic apron. This'll be on the Internet before I can clean this goop off my face."

Lindsey took a deep breath and tried to calm down. This was bad. *Unthinkably* bad. So it only stood to reason that emotion was getting the best of them both.

Yes, he'd come here to call off their wedding, and yes, he'd said some *awful, hurtful* things to her.

But just minutes ago, she'd wanted to have sex with this man. She'd wanted to *marry* him, for heaven's sake, and have his *babies.* Despite his faults, she *loved* Garrett.

So as much as she disliked touching messy things, she took his gooey hands in hers and peered deeply into the eyes that held her heart, her future. She wasn't giving up on this—she wasn't giving up on four long years together. She wasn't giving up on Chicago's "it" couple. "Garrett, whatever's wrong, can't we fix this? Can't we try?"

He pulled his hands back abruptly. "Look at me, Lindsey. You attacked me with a cheesecake."

True enough.

"And look at *you.* Do you think this is what I want in a wife?" He practically spat with disgust.

After which Lindsey did look down at herself, at her apron, her shoes. She'd felt so sexy a few short minutes ago, so exciting and fun and devil-may-care. And he'd totally ruined that. He'd broken her heart and humiliated her on top of it. Her only regret was that she didn't have another cheesecake handy.

So instead, she turned and walked calmly to the dining table, where she picked up a glass of wine, came back over, and threw it in his face.

"That's to wash down your dessert."

One

She had officially been driving forever. So long that her shoulders were sore, so long that her fingers felt as if they were locked around the wheel and would have to be pried loose if she ever stopped. And she *would* stop soon, one way or another. The gas needle was dangerously near *E*. She'd failed to notice that the last time she'd passed through a town, and she'd been sure another would pop up by now.

Like maybe the one she was heading for. Moose Falls, Montana.

Which, it appeared, lay in the complete middle of nowhere.

Thick, tall pine trees lined each side of the narrow, twisting two-lane highway—and they'd been pretty for a while, so warm and green and voluminous. Then it had gotten dark, and now they were closer to scary. *Run out of gas here and you are* so *screwed.*

Thank God for the CD player—from which John Mayer kept her awake and humming along—because she hadn't picked up a radio station in a long time. And she didn't even want to *think* about cell phone reception, or the lack thereof.

She'd stayed calm so far—she'd stayed calm all the way from Chicago, across Iowa and South Dakota and Wyoming and much of Montana. She'd stayed calm and cool and determined. She hadn't been afraid of traveling such a vast distance alone, or of checking into a motel by herself the last two nights. She hadn't even been afraid when she'd driven over long, lonely stretches of road where she'd *also* known her cell phone would be useless if needed. So even as she glanced vaguely skyward through the windshield and thought, *Please, God, let me reach Moose Falls before this car runs out of gas,* she decided *this* was no time to start being scared, either.

Instead, as the strains of "Stop This Train" filled the car, she occupied her thoughts with memories of her Great-Aunt Millie and the letter she'd written to Lindsey last summer. Aunt Millie had lived in Moose Falls for over thirty years, moving there to start a new life after her husband's death back in the seventies. She'd *met* her beloved John there back in 1957, and though he'd migrated east to be with her, the little town had apparently always stayed special to Aunt Millie. Lindsey now suddenly understood the immense courage making such a big move by herself must have required as Aunt Millie's words played through her mind, where they had become branded.

John and I weren't blessed with children before he passed, and I suppose I ended up treating the old canoe livery on the lake here in Moose Falls like the child I never had. So I admit to loving it a little too much, and maybe that sounds like the babble of a crazy old woman . . . but after John's death, I found my soul here, Lindsey. You visited here once as a little girl—do you remember?

She did. Fondly.

Your mother brought you the summer you were five and you stayed for three wonderful weeks. You loved the place, although I'm sure you were too young to remember.

True, she was thirty-four now and didn't recall it clearly—just pleasant bits and pieces.

I'm getting on in years, Lindsey, and I'd like to leave the old place to you in my will. I could die in peace if I knew you would value it, make it your own, see that it's kept up. I know it's a world away from your busy life in the city, but maybe that's the beauty of it? Perhaps you could use a place to escape every now and then? Think about it and let me know.

Lindsey had thought about it—for about five seconds—and kindly turned her great-aunt down. After all, her and canoes? Could there be a wackier combination? She didn't think so, and certainly Garrett was not a back-to-nature sort of guy—in fact, he'd pooh-poohed the idea practically before she'd gotten it out of her mouth. So the whole thing had seemed like a rather ridiculous notion.

And maybe it was *still* a ridiculous notion, but when a photo of her and her apron and a dessert-covered Garrett had promptly shown up on the Internet and in *Chi-Town Beat*, when for the first time in her life she *did* suddenly feel the need to escape . . . for some reason she'd thought of Moose Falls and the vague but peaceful images stuck in her head from that long-ago trip.

Of course, Aunt Millie's letter had been stuck in her head, too. Sure, it had seemed easy to dismiss her as being dotty and unrealistic—had she really thought Lindsey would come to Montana to rent out canoes?—but when Aunt Millie had passed away less than six months later, Lindsey had been forced to suffer the sobering knowledge that she'd let the woman die without fulfilling her last wish.

Heck, it probably would have been kinder to just take the livery, let Aunt Millie pass on, and then sell it. But she hadn't even done *that*—she'd simply sent back a letter explaining she wasn't really a canoe kind of girl and suggesting Aunt Millie find someone else.

Aunt Millie's body had been shipped back to Illinois for

burial next to John, and as she'd been laid to rest beside him a few months ago on a blustery January day, a hard pit of guilt had settled in Lindsey's stomach. Lindsey's parents had been deeply disappointed in her reaction to Aunt Millie's gift—in truth, far more disappointed than they'd seemed at having their daughter plastered all over the Internet wearing only an apron. And they'd fully supported her decision a few days back to toss some clothes in a suitcase and set out by car to Montana.

None of which quite made sense to her, now that she thought about it. What sane parents wanted their daughter driving fifteen hundred miles alone across a desolate prairie? Even Lisa, her older, married, elementary-school-teaching sister, had thought it was a good idea. Despite the loving support they'd all shown, Lindsey could only conclude that her family was in as much shock over the whole debacle as she was and thought it would be good to get her out of the Chicago limelight for a while.

So she'd come to Montana to right a wrong, to fix a mistake, to do what she should have done last summer when Aunt Millie's letter had come. And now, as she glanced down at the gas needle again, she only hoped she would make it to Moose Falls alive.

Her plan: Use her savings to buy the canoe livery from whoever owned it now. She harbored no illusions that she would *stay* in Montana, but she'd hire someone to keep it well run, then she'd veg out here a little and figure out what she was going to do with the rest of her life.

She saw this as a chance to reconnect with something she'd forgotten was important for a while: family. This would provide a nice, relaxing vacation destination for them all—just as Aunt Millie had suggested—at the same time linking them to their past. And it would be some small way to say thank you, since God knew she wouldn't have made it through the last two weeks without her mom and dad and Lisa. Even her nieces, Haley and Wendy, had made cards promising her everything would be all right. She'd not had the heart to ask if they actually knew what had happened—that she'd greeted "Uncle Garrett" at the door mostly naked and been caught in the act. She sighed now, still not quite over the horror of it herself.

It was times like these, she'd quickly learned, when you had to rely upon the support of your family. Just as Aunt Millie had once relied upon Lindsey—but she'd simply brushed off her great-aunt's plea. The woman had been her mom's favorite aunt and Lindsey had treated her like . . . well, like an old lady who didn't matter. Now she wanted to repair that—as much as possible—and see if the decision would somehow guide her to the next step in a life that had recently been blown to hell.

And then, like a miracle, it appeared before her: a big wooden sign that said *Welcome to Moose Falls*!

"Wahoo!" she yipped in joy. She'd made it! No matter what happened now, she wouldn't die in the cold or be attacked by wolves—animal or human—while trudging up an endless highway! She was safe! Even if not necessarily sound, after recent events.

Which was when—oh God!—a gigantic ten-foot-tall grizzly bear appeared before her headlights, claws bared, face angry and snarling! She screamed and yanked the wheel to the right, barely missing the humongous thing, then slammed on the brakes, realizing she was—very suddenly—sitting in the heart of a tiny little town.

That's when she noticed the road had actually curved *with* her—she found herself, amazingly, on a small roundabout that circled the bear. And peering out her driver's-side window, she saw in the glow from her headlights that . . . it wasn't a bear at all, but a big carved *statue* of a bear. Sheesh. Some greeting. Welcome indeed.

Since there wasn't a barrage of traffic—as in none—Lindsey sat there for a minute, trying to regather her wits.

To the left of the road before her she could see nothing but a heavy shroud of mist and supposed it must be the lake. She remembered it only vaguely, but knew it was the focal point for weekend getaways that included canoeing and hiking. On the right sat a few quaint-looking buildings, yet the drifting mist obscured any signs other than the nearest one, jutting from the corner of a white clapboard establishment: *The Lazy Elk Bar and Grill.*

Thank God.

She'd neglected to eat dinner and the grill part meant food.

And at the moment, the bar part didn't sound bad, either.

To Lindsey's surprise, the Lazy Elk was fairly buzzing when she stepped inside. Billiard balls clacked together, U2's "I Still Haven't Found What I'm Looking For" echoed from a jukebox, and something sizzled on a griddle she couldn't see—reminding her again that she was hungry. A heavyset woman behind the bar yelled, "Add another burger to that last order, Jimmy," and a young man's voice echoed, "Got it," in reply through the window behind her.

Of course, the place wasn't buzzing so much that people didn't stop to ogle the newcomer. She supposed Moose Falls didn't get a lot of strangers on an off-season Tuesday night.

Glancing about, she made contact with the nearest set of eyes on her—which happened to belong to an older, grizzled-looking fellow—and lifted her hand in a small wave. "Hi."

He nodded succinctly, then took a swig from his beer bottle.

All the stools at the bar stood empty, so she slid up onto one, pleased when the female bartender who'd just called out the burger order stopped wiping down the wood with a damp cloth and met her gaze with a friendly smile. "What can I get you?"

"Um, how about a cosmopolitan?"

The woman's hazel eyes lit up as brightly as if someone had just given her a gift. "Are you serious?"

Lindsey wasn't sure how to interpret the response. "Well, yeah—but if you don't . . . make those or whatever, I can pick something else."

The bartender held up her hands in a stop motion. "No—I can make it. I'm *dying* to make it."

"Huh?"

"You're the first person to order a real drink in here in ages. You know, something with more than two ingredients. I *love* mixing fun drinks, but I spend most of my time serving up beer—or if someone is feeling really crazy, maybe a rum and Coke. So you're my dream come true."

Lindsey raised her eyebrows, pleased that someone somewhere in the world was actually glad to see her. "Well, that's great. Since my life hasn't exactly been very dreamy lately—more like a nightmare, in fact."

The bartender lowered her chin inquisitively. "Wait a minute. Are you about to tell me your troubles? Because if you are, you're my *double* dream come true. I've been tending this bar for nearly five years and no one *ever* tells me their troubles. So if I get that *and* a real drink to mix . . . wow—you're making my night."

Lindsey hadn't really planned to tell the woman her troubles, but she seemed nice, and so delighted by the prospect that she figured what the hell. Alcohol tended to give her loose lips anyway. "All right," she replied. "A worldful of troubles coming up. But first, I have to know." She motioned vaguely over her shoulder toward the road outside. "What the hell is that thing in the roundabout?"

The woman flipped long auburn hair over her shoulder. "Oh, the bear. Did he scare you?"

"Only out of my wits. I nearly wrecked the car."

The bartender shrugged as she reached for a shaker. "Yeah, it's a hazard, even for those of us who live here. Especially if you've had a few."

"Well, if it's such a hazard, why is it there?"

"Eleanor's ex-husband—she owns the Grizzly Inn next door—made it, for the inn. But turned out it was too big for the little rock garden out front. So the town council voted to put it in the roundabout so it wouldn't go to waste. Since the roundabout was empty except for a flower garden and people kept driving through it. And since it *is* a perfectly good bear."

Lindsey tilted her head. "No one thought about putting, say, a moose there? Given that this is *Moose* Falls?"

"We did. But no one had a big wooden moose lying around, or the money to get one, so the bear got the job."

Lindsey leaned closer over the bar. "So, the Grizzly Inn—is it nice?"

"Nice *enough*. Not new or anything—but Eleanor remodeled a couple years back," the bartender replied as she added lime juice to her concoction. "It ain't the Hyatt, but it's tidy, and woodsy."

Tidy. And woodsy. Hmm. It would have to do. "I guess it's my new home for a while."

The bartender raised curious eyebrows, clearly intrigued. "She'll be thrilled—she generally only gets weekend guests, and not usually for another few weeks—late May or June. Now, let's get to those troubles and what on earth a jet-setty girl like you is doing in Moose Falls. I'm Carla, by the way."

"Lindsey." She reached out and they clasped hands lightly across the bar. "And officially retired from the jet set, I'm afraid."

Carla's head tilted in a kindly fashion even as she shook Lindsey's drink. "Tell me all about it."

Okay, here went nothing. "Well, have you ever heard of the advice column, Love Letters? It's syndicated in over a hundred newspapers and there's an accompanying blog online."

As Carla poured Lindsey's cosmo into a martini glass and

placed it on a napkin before her, she appeared to be turning it over in her head. "The one where people write in with their problems about love or sex or whatever's wrong in their relationship?"

Lindsey nodded, then took the first sip of her drink. *Ah*, that hit the spot. "That's the one," she said. "I'm Lindsey Brooks, the advice columnist."

Carla's jaw dropped and her eyes went as big and round as . . . well, two martini glasses. "*Shut. Up.* You're kidding me! You're her? The Love Letters girl?"

"In the flesh," she answered with a wry smile.

"So are you . . . a therapist or something? Because if you are, I feel pretty dumb asking you to tell me your problems."

But Lindsey shook her head. "Nope. I took a few psychology courses in college, but I'm mainly just a journalist who was . . . in love with love, I guess. It came across in my early work. No matter what story I covered—house fire, burglary, charity event—I always seemed to focus on the relationships of the people involved, making it part of the story even when it wasn't. And rather than just fire me, my boss suggested I try my hand at a modern-day advice column, and a new career was born."

Her momentary cheer faded, however, as she explained that she'd just voluntarily stepped down from writing Love Letters. "Because even though my bosses stood behind me after what happened with Garrett, I simply don't feel I can go on with it anymore. Or my blog. Because how does a woman whose disastrous love life is front-page news advise people on theirs? I'd be a laughingstock. No, wait, I'm *already* a laughingstock. So I'd be a laughingstock who was just inviting people to laugh even harder."

"Wait. Stop," Carla said. "Who's Garrett? And what's the disaster? And why are you a laughingstock?"

Okay, so she'd gotten ahead of herself. Maybe that was a sign that she really *needed* to get this off her chest. So, taking a long sip of her cosmo, Lindsey told Carla all about her broken engagement and naked seduction. When she got to the part about the photo, Carla responded with the appropriate gasp and scowl of horror.

"The only good news in the whole thing," Lindsey went on, "is that—thank God for small favors—they blurred my breast in the photo. Which you can now even find on the *National Enquirer*'s website, and the *Globe*'s, too." She wasn't *that* famous, but a person didn't have to be much of a celebrity for a picture like that to seem newsworthy, given the pure entertainment value.

"So what happened next?" Carla asked, reaching for some peanuts from a bowl on the bar.

Lindsey ate a few, too—then washed them down with a tasty sip of cosmo. Once she got through her story, she'd order something hardier. "Well, I woke up the next morning and realized my life was pretty much ruined. No wedding, no marriage, public humiliation, and a job suddenly in jeopardy. And like I said, it turned out that the bigwigs wanted me to keep writing the column, but I told them I just *can't*. I need some time to figure all this out. And so I decided a getaway would be good." She slurped her drink a little more, the alcohol turning her more honest by the second—and making her slump her shoulders as she let out a big sigh. "Oh, who am I kidding? I ran away. I escaped. I came here to hide."

Carla patted her hand. "I think you need another drink, hon."

Lindsey glanced down. Suddenly her glass was empty. How had *that* happened? "I do. You make a mean cosmo."

As Carla started filling the shaker again, she asked, "But why here? I mean, *Moose Falls*? How do you even know this place *exists*?"

"Ah," she said, tipping her head back, then explained, "Millie Pickett was my great-aunt."

Now Carla let out *another* gasp, but this one sounded

merrier. "*Millie!* We *loved* Millie around here. We miss her so much."

Which led Lindsey to tell Carla about the canoe livery offer and how she'd turned it down but had now changed her mind. "Speaking of which, you wouldn't happen to know who bought it?"

"Sure—everyone knows. Rob Colter."

"All right then." She turned resolute. "Tomorrow I'm going to track down Rob Colter and get him to sell it to me. And it will be a major step in the right direction of reclaiming my life."

Carla only blinked, shaking the drink. "Uh, I wouldn't count on that."

Lindsey set her chin. "Why not?"

"Well, it's the guy's business, Lindsey. He does some construction stuff, too, but when he bought the place, it was pretty clear he meant to settle down here. He even lives in your aunt's house—she sold it *all* to him, a package deal."

A heavy feeling of naïveté settled around Lindsey. For some reason, she hadn't actually imagined anyone buying the canoe rental because they really *wanted* it—she'd more imagined someone taking it off Aunt Millie's hands as a favor; she'd envisioned a run-down canoe shack that no one really cared about.

Still . . . "I can be surprisingly charming. I'm sure he and I can work something out."

Carla shrugged, passing Lindsey a freshly filled martini glass. "He's not exactly Mr. Personality, so I'm not sure charm will sway him. He's more the gruff, keep-to-himself type."

"Sounds delightful," Lindsey said dryly. Then glanced down at the drink. "No lime wedge?" The first cosmo hadn't had one, either.

"This isn't Chicago—no lime wedge. And forgive me for saying so, but . . . maybe buying a business you know nothing about isn't what you need to find yourself again. Maybe it's simpler than that. Maybe what you need is . . ."

"Yes?" she prodded impatiently.

"Something more personal . . . and empowering. Like, say, sex. How about a good old-fashioned affair?"

Lindsey considered the suggestion, aware as she sipped her cosmo that the drinks were starting to go to her head a bit. She would *not* be that easily deterred about pursuing the canoe business—she truly yearned to regain that family connection now, thinking how much it would please Aunt Millie if she knew. But that didn't mean she couldn't also entertain the idea of an affair. Given that she was getting just a little tipsy—well, at the moment, an affair sounded downright . . . energizing.

"Yeah, an affair might be *nice*," she said, nodding. "I was with Garrett for four long years. And honestly, even though it's amazingly easy to hate him now, I really did love the jerk. So I'm feeling pretty wounded, frankly, and heck, maybe getting right back up on the horse—the sex horse, that is—would be the smartest thing I could do. Right?"

"Not only that," Carla replied, "but if you're out there sexing it up, having a passionate affair, living the dream, you can go back to writing your column with a clear conscience."

Lindsey sipped, thought. "Well, I'm not sure that *sexing it up* equates to living the dream—my readers are pretty invested in love, the real thing, the whole enchilada, you know? But . . . an affair might at least be a reasonable facsimile—as long as the sex is good, anyway." Then she nodded, warming to the idea. "You're smart. I like you."

Just then a nip of cold, spring Montana air rushed around her bare arms and she looked up to see another patron enter the Lazy Elk.

A tall, dark, handsome patron. The kind of patron that made her heart flutter on sight. But more than her heart. A lower part of the anatomy, actually. And the fluttering was notably . . . intense.

He wore a red flannel shirt over a white waffle-weave pullover and faded jeans, much more appropriate for the chilly weather than her beaded baby-doll tee. A day's stubble covered his chin, and his dark hair needed a trim, but she suddenly *liked* that because it was so different from Garrett. Her first thought: This would be a perfectly good guy to help her climb back on the sex horse.

"Him," she said simply to Carla, watching as he began talking with a couple of equally outdoorsy-looking guys at one of the tables. She noticed he didn't smile, his expression staying completely serious, and sexy as sin.

"Yep, that's him," Carla agreed.

"The man I'm going to get back on the sex horse with."

She was still looking at Mr. Sexy Flannel when she sensed Carla's flinch from the corner of her eye. "Wait. What? No."

She turned back to her new friend. "*No?*" Then she sighed. "Married?" Damn it, the good ones always were.

Carla shook her head. "No, not married. But he still won't want anything to do with you."

Lindsey glanced down at herself. It had been a long day of driving. Even if she still managed to look jet-setty, maybe she just appeared too road-weary. "You don't think I'm hot enough?" she asked, raising her gaze back to Carla. "Because I can look better than this."

Yet the bartender shook her head again. "No, that's not the problem—I would give my right arm to be so hot."

So Lindsey scrunched her nose. "He's not *gay*?" He looked about as rugged as a man possibly could, like a guy who chopped down trees or wrestled bears. Like Paul Bunyan—well, if Paul Bunyan hadn't been a giant and *had* been a complete hottie.

"No, not gay," Carla confirmed. "Or at least we don't think so."

"Then why won't he be interested?" Lindsey punctuated the question by taking another drink.

"He only moved here last spring and he's not the social type. He keeps to himself and, frankly, he's not very pleasant to be around—very brusque, all business."

"Well, he's talking to *those* guys." She pointed discreetly to where he stood chatting.

"Steve Fisher, the guy on the right, hired him to build a room addition onto his house. So I'm sure they're just talking about work. Trust me, he's not interested in getting to know anybody in town. People have tried. Women especially. But it's hopeless."

Huh. All Lindsey could think was: What a waste of a gorgeous guy. He had "fabulous lover" written all over him without even trying. But it didn't count for much if he didn't want to be anyone's lover.

She sighed, still studying him as she finished her second cosmo. How could he *not* want to be someone's lover? He looked . . . built for sex. "If he doesn't have a social life, then what does he do? Why is he here? What's he about?"

Carla laughed lightly at the quick barrage of questions. "I told you, he builds things. And he seems to hike a lot. And he also . . . runs the canoe livery. Afraid that's Rob Colter."

Lindsey blinked. Looked to Carla. Then back to the hot, rugged man in flannel. "Holy crap," she murmured. "I think I'm gonna need another cosmo."

"I'm way ahead of ya," Carla replied, holding up her trusty shaker.

Which gave Lindsey time to peer back at Rob Colter. The guy who'd bought Aunt Millie's business. The man she'd just decided she wanted to bed.

He might be a tough nut to crack—and the more she watched him, the gruffer he really did look—but she *had* been known to be a charmer, and trying to charm *this* guy was *not* going to be a hardship.

Whew. One too many cosmos, that was for sure. This was no time to try to charm Mr. Sexy Flannel, so when Lindsey stood up to leave, she was relieved he was nowhere in sight.

In fact, she'd be lucky if she could get to the Grizzly Inn

and drag her suitcase into a room without making a spectacle of herself.

"Are you sure you don't want me to walk you over?" Carla asked from behind the bar.

She'd offered twice already, and now that Lindsey was trying to balance on suddenly wobbly legs, the idea was tempting—but the Lazy Elk had gotten even busier and Carla was serving up drinks right and left. "No, I'm fine," she insisted, then pointed. "It's only next door, right?"

"Right." Carla pointed in the same direction as Lindsey, so that was a good sign.

Lindsey concentrated on her steps—keeping them straight, trying to look sober—as she neared the door at the front corner of the building. *Eye on the prize, eye on the prize,* she coached herself, focusing on the dull red door. Pushing it open to step outside left her feeling supremely victorious.

Only—whew—there were steps out here. She'd forgotten that part. Big, steep concrete steps—four or five of them. Or they suddenly *seemed* steep anyway. Thank goodness someone had put a handrail here.

She kept waiting for the cold night air to snap her out of it—she was suddenly freezing now, actually—but she still felt woozy. More so than she'd realized in the bar. It was one thing to feel tipsy sitting down—that was kind of a nice, happy, isn't-life-fun kind of feeling—but it was another thing entirely to be tipsy standing up. The world swayed even as she muttered, "Thank you, God," upon reaching the blacktop at the foot of the stairs.

Which was when she bumped lightly into something and glanced down to see it was her Infiniti—she was balanced against the sedan's grille. "Oh—well, this is handy," she murmured. She'd forgotten she'd parked so close to the door. At the moment, she couldn't exactly remember parking *at all.* "But maybe I shouldn't drive. Maybe I should just leave you here for the night." Then she bit her lip. "Unless the Lazy Elk would have me towed. But they don't *seem* like a place that would have me towed. Or like a place that would . . . even have access to a tow truck." She sighed. "On the other hand, Carla won't know you're my car. Or, well, she will if she looks at the plates, but what if she doesn't? What if she's not even the one in charge of towing? If anyone is."

Damn. She could only conclude that she'd officially passed from tipsy into drunk now. Talking-to-her-car drunk.

Taking a look around, she spotted someone in the shadows not far away, speaking with someone else in a pickup truck. "Okay, I'll call you with an estimate," a male voice said, and then the pickup backed away, leaving the shadow-guy alone.

"Hey," she called, "you know if it's okay to leave my car here? I'll be right over at the Grizzly Bear—I mean Inn." She pointed toward . . . the Lazy Elk, then realized that was wrong, so she swung her outstretched finger in the other direction, hoping that was right.

"Yeah," the deep voice replied. *Nice voice.* "It'll be fine."

Okay, good. "Thanks," she managed, then wove her way toward the trunk to get her suitcase.

Of course, that meant wrangling keys from her purse, but she managed it after a minute of searching, then popped the trunk. Hooray—her lime denim jacket sat on top of the suitcase where she'd thrown it after an earlier stop. "Brrr," she heard herself say as she slid it on.

Next, she grabbed on to the handle of her suitcase and tugged, but it didn't budge. So she tugged harder. It was big, difficult to maneuver, and had been a pain in the butt to get into a motel room the last two nights, as well. And she hadn't even been drinking then, so this was going to be a challenge. She yanked and pulled and huffed and heaved, and still the darn thing stayed lodged in place.

"You need some help?"

She flinched, then looked up. The offer had sounded grudging at best, though, so she automatically said, "No."

Then immediately added, "Well, maybe." This being-drunk-and-disoriented-in-a-strange-place thing was *hard*.

And it got a lot harder when she realized the guy who'd just stepped from the shadows to offer his assistance with a slight scowl was none other than Mr. Sexy Flannel himself, Rob Colter.

Two

Even though she was intoxicated and he was indeed casting a rather superior scowl, his very presence left Lindsey positively poleaxed with desire. Maybe it was the way he smelled—like fresh soap and . . . wood shavings? Pretty damn good for a guy who'd just been hanging out in a bar. Conversely, *she* probably smelled like beer and smoke. Swell.

Or maybe it was the very size of him—he was so big and broad-chested. He was the kind of man who could easily toss her up over his shoulder and carry her away if he wanted. Not that she wanted him to. Although why did the very thought of that make her feel so warm?

Or maybe it was just how darn good-looking he was. She had the urge to run her fingertips over the stubble on his jaw, or over the waffle weave spanning his chest. She'd never before been *drawn* to waffle weave in such a sexual way. Who knew thermal clothing was a turn-on?

"Well—can you move out of the way?" he asked.

Oh. Crap. She was just standing there gaping at him. And he didn't sound amused.

Just what she needed. Help from a big lug who didn't really want to give it. Worse yet, a big *sexy* lug. Worse yet, a big sexy lug who she needed to charm into selling her his business. Oh boy.

When he cleared his throat, she realized she hadn't moved yet—*dunce!*—and finally stepped aside.

She watched as Rob Colter reached into the trunk and hauled her large black suitcase out onto the asphalt with relative ease. But he still muttered, "Damn," setting it upright. "I didn't know they even *made* suitcases this big. What's in here—bricks?"

"Clothes," she answered. Then found herself expounding. "Shoes. Some boots. And purses. I like purses." She unthinkingly held up the one she carried, a cute little leopard-print clutch with a removable shoulder strap. "This is my current fave. See?"

He looked at her like she belonged in an insane asylum. "Uh-huh, sure."

Great. This was *so* not the impression she'd wanted to make.

"I'll drag this over to the inn for you," he told her, again sounding completely put out by the task. But she was hardly in a position to refuse his help.

Slamming the trunk, she patted the car softly and said, "Okay then, you'll be fine here for the night." Which meant—oh God—she was talking to the car again.

And this time, he'd heard her. He simply gave his head a derisive shake, then turned to start wheeling her jumbo suitcase toward the sidewalk that connected the Lazy Elk to the Grizzly Inn. "What kind of crazy chick talks to her car?" he grumbled beneath his voice.

And apparently, it was the straw that broke Lindsey's back. So she stomped up behind him—as much as one can stomp in heels. "You got a problem with it? I mean, I don't *usually* talk to my car—I'm just a little tipsy right now. Can't you cut me a break?"

He glanced over his shoulder just long enough for her to see the dry, wary look in his gorgeous brown eyes before he faced away again, trudging ahead with the suitcase as she followed behind like a puppy. "It's pretty stupid to drive into a strange place where you don't know anybody and get drunk. For all you know, I could be a bad man planning to do bad things to you."

Okay, so apparently he *couldn't* cut her a break. And maybe his words should have sent a shiver down her spine, but they came closer to making the small of her back ache with lust. "*Are* you a bad man?"

"No. But I could be. You should be more careful."

"Well, thanks for the warning, Officer Flannel, but I'm a big girl and I can take care of myself—*thank*youverymuch."

He paused, looked over his shoulder once more, then down at the behemoth suitcase he rolled, and simply said, "Yeah. Sure you can." Then proceeded into the office of the Grizzly Inn.

Behind the desk hung a large mounted fish of some kind, as well as a pair of antlers that had once belonged on some poor animal's head—and beneath them stood a woman in her fifties wearing wire-frame glasses, a plaid nightgown, and a hurried sort of smile. "Well, here you are," she said, looking only a tad impatient. "Carla called over to let me know I had a guest coming a little while ago. Now, if it were summer already, I'd be sitting right here, up till eleven o'clock, but tonight I'm at my place in back watching an *ER* marathon on satellite—you know, the early ones, with that hunky George Clooney—so I'll get you checked in toot sweet and get back to it."

"Sexiest man alive," Lindsey offered with a small smile.

The guy next to her rolled his eyes, which amused her for some reason. Maybe she was glad to have annoyed him. And it made her rethink the whole "sexiest man alive" thing, too. If *he* were a little nicer, he might be in the running. Everyone knew that George's personality was a huge part of what made him sexy, and she thought Rob Colter could stand to take a lesson.

Eleanor winked at Rob. "Your lady friend has good taste if she likes George Clooney."

"Lady friend?" he balked. "Uh, no—I've never seen her before in my life. I'm just dragging her suitcase in here because she's too drunk to do it herself."

"Hey!" Lindsey said in protest.

Her man in flannel simply flashed a pointed look.

"Well, maybe." She sighed and rolled *her* eyes. "Carla makes a good cosmo." Then she looked to Eleanor. "You should order one sometime. She would love that."

"Order *what*?"

"A cosmo. You know, the drink. A cosmopolitan."

Eleanor just blinked and Lindsey realized Eleanor actually *didn't* know. No wonder Carla was so excited to mix one—or, in Lindsey's case, several.

As Eleanor worked on the check-in process, she changed the subject. "What brings you to Moose Falls?"

After rummaging in her small purse for too long, finally producing her driver's license for Eleanor, Lindsey couldn't help glancing up toward Rob. Since she'd come to buy his business and he didn't know it yet. "It's a long story."

So Eleanor looked to Rob, too, as if waiting for him to explain.

He began to look irritated with *both* of them now. "I told you, I don't know her."

"Whatever you say," Eleanor replied with a wink. "Just sign here," she told Lindsey, then suggested to Rob, "Maybe you can help your friend to her room?"

He threw up his hands. "How many times do I have to tell you? She's not my friend. But yeah, sure, I'll drag her damn suitcase down there so you can get back to your TV show."

Sheesh—talk about gruff. *You are* so *not the sexiest man alive with that attitude*, she was tempted to tell him, but managed to bite her tongue. Instead she just followed him back out of the office into the chilly Montana night and up another sidewalk.

The Grizzly Inn was a classic roadside strip motel with rooms facing a little green slash of yard and the single row of parking spaces beyond. She supposed in the morning she'd have a lovely view of the lake, but right now it remained only a view of heavy fog.

When Rob stopped at door number seven, Lindsey nearly tumbled right over her suitcase—man, that thing *was* big—but managed to right herself and earned only a sideways glance from him. Sliding the key card Eleanor had given him into the lock, he turned the knob and stepped inside, dragging the suitcase behind.

Lindsey followed, keeping her eye on her caramel-colored boots to make sure she didn't trip over the threshold—which was precisely how she ended up walking into Rob Colter's chest when he turned to exit.

Her first thought: *Oops, I'm kind of dizzy.* Her second: *Wow. Big. Warm.*

She looked up at him just as his fists closed snug around both her wrists, which had also ended up in the area of his chest.

Oh my. She wanted to kiss him. Bad. She wanted to drag him to bed, in fact. Her heart beat too hard, and she was starting to sweat despite the cold air pouring through the open door, and her breasts tingled just from being so close to his hands. Plus her chest *had* just experienced the pleasure of bumping against his, which she now knew was completely as broad and solid as it looked. *Bad, bad* Carla for making such *good* cosmos.

"Whoops," she said. Even though she was thinking, *Oooh la la.* And a bizarre stab at self-preservation forced her to add, "I hope I don't stink." Oh God, had she just said that?

"Huh?"

"From hanging out in a bar all night."

He replied by simply setting her back away from him and

promptly releasing her from his grasp. "You smell fine," he said, every ounce of gruffness still intact.

Okay, so he wasn't going to kiss her. No big surprise there. "Stumbled," she murmured, just to make sure he knew she hadn't been *trying* to attack him. Not *really,* anyway.

Predictably enough, rather than asking if she'd be all right now, he instead said, "Well, you're in," and headed unceremoniously for the door.

And without meaning to, she said exactly what she was thinking, her sarcasm coming through loud and clear. "My hero."

He stopped with one black work boot out the door and looked back, his eyes narrowing slightly, his expression going even darker. "I never claimed to be anybody's hero, sweetheart."

And then he was gone.

Lindsey moaned when a bright shaft of sunlight came blasting through the window—it felt like someone was shooting laser beams at her brain. Her mouth was dry and her whole body ached.

When she forced her eyes open, lifting a hand to her face to try blotting out the pain-inducing light, she realized she wasn't at home. Unless a band of hunters had snuck in to redecorate during the night. The wall her eyes connected with was done in knotty pine and hung with a framed print of an elk. Below the picture, she spied a small table sporting a small figurine of a bear.

Kind of like a statue.

Which was when it all came back to her in a single flash of horror.

Bear. Statue. Cosmos. Big heavy suitcase. Big sexy man.

Oh no. Oh no, no, no, no, no.

The one man she'd needed to charm, and she'd completely humiliated herself in front of him. She been drunk—and possibly disorderly. At the very least, she'd bordered on rude.

She hadn't even thanked him. Or at least she didn't *think* she had. And without him, frankly, she might have ended up sleeping in the Lazy Elk parking lot instead of this bed.

Of course, he'd been kind of a jerk. Not to mention smug and judgmental. That would be enough to bring out the rudeness in anyone. Wouldn't it?

But oh, he'd looked good. And *smelled* good. The scent of wood shavings came back to mind—had she been right about that? She hadn't actually sniffed a lot of wood shavings in her day, but she sometimes put those little chunks of cedar in her closets to keep her clothes smelling fresh. Whatever the case, he'd smelled damn fine. And even now, her heart beat harder thinking of him. Even if he *was* a jerk.

Still staring at the bear figurine, she found herself overcome with battling emotions of irritation and lust. But lust was winning. And when a girl still managed to feel lusty right in the middle of a hangover—well, that was saying something.

When she realized her jaw was sore, she lifted it to see she'd slept with her face on her leopard-print clutch. Swell—she'd probably have a big dent in her cheek.

And, looking down, it appeared her purse wasn't the only thing she'd taken to bed with her—she still wore every stitch of clothing she'd had on when she stumbled in last night, right down to her fabulous boots.

When she sat up and came face to face with herself in a rustic, twig-framed mirror across the room, she let out a gasp. The dent in her cheek was the least of her troubles. Her hair looked . . . crazy. Like mice had played in it or something. Her eyes were bloodshot, her complexion like paste. The term "mug shot" came to mind.

Looking around then, she took in more of the room. A "chandelier" constructed of small antlers descended from the ceiling. The bed frame was made of artificial logs, and small silhouettes of elk, moose, and bears (oh my) covered the dark green comforter. Clothing hooks jutted from a flat wrought-iron moose hanging on one wall, while more woodland prints of bears and pine trees hung hither and thither.

Carla had been right—it wasn't the Hyatt. It wasn't even the Holiday Inn. But to Lindsey's surprise, it did possess a certain warm, cozy quality that actually began to relax her more than it annoyed her. Who'd have thought?

Praise God—a coffeemaker sat atop a little round dining table in one corner. And next to it rested a small wicker basket full of snacks you'd find in a vending machine. Peanut butter crackers! Oreo cookies! Her stomach spasmed at the sight and it suddenly hit her that she'd never gotten around to eating dinner last night.

Plus she'd been exhausted from three straight days of driving.

So no wonder a few drinks had put her under the table. Or face down on the bed, as it were.

After dragging herself up to madly devour a package of crackers, Lindsey started the coffee and stepped into what was probably the most refreshing shower she'd ever taken.

But as the water crashed down, washing away what had happened last night—well, at least in some ways—she began to rethink her whole plan. *Was* this crazy? To be here? To want to buy a business that—as Carla had so aptly pointed out—she knew nothing about?

Her return to Moose Falls had hardly been idyllic. So maybe it was a sign. To forget this whole idea.

Garrett had thought it sounded wacky from the outset last summer. And Carla had confirmed that last night, almost a year later. So maybe it was.

Yet when Lindsey stepped out of the shower naked, clean, hair wet, and caught a glimpse of herself in the slightly fogged mirror stretching over the vanity, she felt . . . oh God . . . empty. Utterly alone. Ugh.

It wasn't the first time she'd felt this way and she knew it was because so much of her life had turned out—suddenly—to be little more than an illusion. She knew it was the pain of heartbreak sifting down through her, and that she'd just have to deal with it over time. But somehow, it felt worse here, so far away from home.

If she gave up this plan, wouldn't it somehow feel like she was letting Garrett win? Like saying he was right—that she was too self-absorbed, too much of a froufrou girl to do anything that lay outside her comfort zone? And worse, if she gave up this plan—*then* what did she do? Where did she go?

Sadly, a canoe livery in the middle of nowhere suddenly felt like all she had.

And she didn't even really *have* it.

Rob Colter had it.

A thought which made her pulse lightly between her thighs even as she grimaced in the mirror.

Quit thinking about him.

But just as quickly as she issued the internal command, she was forced to amend it. *Well, quit thinking about him as soon as you talk him into selling you Aunt Millie's place.*

And maybe in the light of day he wouldn't be such an unreasonable guy. Maybe her sad tale of how she'd let her aunt down and now wanted to right the wrong would pull at his heartstrings. Maybe meeting him when she didn't seem like a total lush would help, too.

Aunt Millie had once started a new life here—and Lindsey could, as well. Not that her new life would *happen* here, but it would *start* here. That's all she asked of Moose Falls. *And* Rob Colter. For a new start.

Twenty minutes later, Lindsey felt like a new woman. She wore a bold fuchsia turtleneck sweater with dark-wash jeans and her sexy fuchsia peek-toe pumps. Since she wasn't going to be needing them for evenings at the theater or political rallies anytime soon. She topped the simple but stylish outfit with her favorite Donna Karan coat—smart, short, black, with faux-fur collar—and a leopard-print headband. Then she opened the door to her room ready to conquer the world—as soon as she located some breakfast.

And that's when she saw Spirit Lake.

Last night's fog was history—instead, the sun sparkled on pristine blue water that stretched as far as the eye could see. Hillsides blanketed with majestic pine trees rose on each side, seeming to cocoon the lake, making it somehow feel private, hidden away. She gasped in awe.

And then she noticed the small, quaint, red-roofed structure built over the water to the left side of the lake, its dock covered with a row of long, slender canoes, all resting upside down, in bold yellow, blue, red, and green. She could read the wooden sign that hung from the awning, even from here: *Spirit Lake Boathouse.*

The scene before her was like one of the paintings on the walls of her room—but better. More beautiful, and stunningly real. The cold bite of morning air only made her feel the charm of the north woods setting even more. Her stomach did a little flip-flop that had nothing to do with lack of food and everything to do with a bone-deep want of something. It was as shocking as it was profound.

Oh God, she *wanted* the canoe rental—she really, really *wanted* it. Not just for Aunt Millie, not just to please her parents, not just to show Garrett she could do something more than match shoes to a purse. She wanted it because the mere sight of it delivered an instant sense of peace she wasn't sure she'd ever experienced before. It was brand-new . . . and yet somehow familiar in an odd way, too. Like something people sought to find in their busy lives but just couldn't take the time to look for. And here it was. Beckoning to her.

Whoa.

Who *was* this masked woman? She didn't even recognize this person suddenly committed to owning a bunch of canoes. And the emotion was so unexpected that she barely knew how to process it. Who knew a person could get so excited over a few boats?

So Lindsey stopped and took a deep breath. Pushing down the strange rush of feelings—quite possibly caused, she decided, by all the emotional upheaval in her life lately—she headed up the sidewalk toward the Grizzly Inn's office. But she felt strangely . . . *happy.* Happier than she'd felt since the apron incident, now that she thought about it.

She found Eleanor inside looking much more put together than she had last night. Dressed in khaki pants and a simple sweater set, she watched *Regis and Kelly* on a mini-TV perched on the counter while rifling through paperwork.

"Good morning," Lindsey said cheerfully.

Eleanor instantly seemed in better spirits than she had last night, too. "Well, hello there. My, don't you look bright and chipper today. And what a fancy thing in your hair."

"Thanks," Lindsey said with a sincere smile. "And sorry I interrupted your Clooney-fest. I hope you didn't miss too much."

Eleanor raked a forgiving hand down through the air. "Not to worry. I got plenty of George-time before the marathon ended." Then she tilted her head to one side. "Now, tell me, because I'm curious and you didn't answer me last night—what brings you to our little town? Are you a girlfriend of Rob's? Because we've wondered about him, you know. He mostly keeps to himself, so . . ."

"Oh gosh, no," Lindsey was quick to correct her. "He wasn't lying—I never met him before last night. I'm actually here to . . . visit my aunt's place." An altered version of the truth would surely appease Eleanor's curiosity for now.

"Your aunt? Who would that be?" Eleanor's instant intrigue made it clear that Moose Falls was a town where everyone knew everyone.

"Millie Pickett," Lindsey supplied.

Eleanor lifted a hand to her chest. "Oh, Millie. My heart and soul, how I loved that woman."

Speaking of hearts, Lindsey's constricted just a bit. She was beginning to realize that she'd missed knowing someone very special. She and Aunt Millie had exchanged some letters over the course of her life, but she'd not seen her since that visit when she was five. "I . . . didn't know her as well as I wish I had. But I'm hoping I can get a better sense of her just by visiting the places she loved."

Eleanor nodded. "She left many a mark on this town, I can tell you that. You'll see Millie everywhere you go."

When Lindsey raised her eyebrows in curiosity, Eleanor pointed over her shoulder to the mounted fish Lindsey had noticed last night. "She caught this fish. Back in '88 at the Moose Falls Fish Festival and Fry. Biggest rainbow trout ever to come out of Spirit Lake, and oh, you should have seen how jealous the menfolk were. Millie just did a little fishing every now and then to pass the time, but she pulled this whopper out of the lake and put the fellas to shame. Won the Big Fish prize that year and let my ex-husband, Wallace, hang the trout up in here. Yes sirree—you'll see little bits of our Millie just about everywhere. Moose Falls wouldn't have quite been Moose Falls without her."

A smile unfurled on Lindsey's face—although she'd never had an interest in fishing, she suddenly wished she could have been there for the event.

"Of course, you want to find out more about Millie, you'll need to make your way to Rob's house." She pointed toward the left side of the lake—and Lindsey grasped on to an ancient memory of Aunt Millie's big log house in the woods, up the way from the canoe livery. "Now, you probably figured out last night that Rob ain't the most cordial of fellas, but he does live in her place and ended up with most of her things, you know. So I imagine it'll be worth the hassle to see what you came here to see."

Actually, she *hadn't* known who had ended up with most of Aunt Millie's things—she hadn't taken the time to think about it. But the suggestion certainly fit well enough with her plans. "That's what I hope to do—as soon as I have some breakfast." She absently pressed a palm to her empty belly. "Could you recommend a restaurant?" she asked. Then thought, *Please, God, let there be restaurants.*

"My daughter, Mary Beth, owns the Lakeside Café, right next door. She makes up a real nice breakfast," Eleanor replied, then pointed toward the far side of the inn, down past Lindsey's room.

After thanking her, Lindsey turned to take off—when Eleanor said, "Wait. What was it you told me I should ask Carla for?"

She stopped, looking back at the woman with a smile. "A cosmopolitan. It's a fun, slightly fruity martini. Try one—you'll like it."

"A cosmopolitan," Eleanor repeated, as if committing the word to memory. Then she nodded resolutely. "All right. I'll try one the next time I need a little pick-me-up."

Half an hour later, Lindsey had gotten acquainted with Mary Beth, a pleasant woman about her age who she learned also hosted a book club in the café on the last Wednesday of the month if Lindsey was interested. Lindsey had been *more* interested in the bacon and eggs she'd devoured, the gorgeous view of the lake out the café's front window, and the directions to Rob Colter's house that she'd wheedled from Mary Beth as they talked. Turned out her memory was correct—Rob's log cabin was close enough to walk. "Just a stone's throw up from the lake—if you got a good arm," Mary Beth said.

"Thanks for breakfast—it was wonderful," Lindsey told her host as she rose to go, buttoning her coat against the brisk April air.

So far, so good. She'd clearly charmed Eleanor into thinking she was a much more together person than she'd appeared last night. And she thought she'd succeeded in charming Mary Beth, too. Of course, there was a difference between them and Rob Colter—*they* were nice.

But she refused to be discouraged. She had a firm goal in mind, a strong case for persuading him, and a totally hot pair of shoes to do it in.

Get ready for some serious charm, buddy, because it's headed your way.

Rob sat at his kitchen table, pencil in hand, figuring up an estimate for the toolshed Stanley Bobbins wanted built. He was already planning to drive over to Whitefish this afternoon to pick up some supplies for Steve Fisher's room addition, so while he was there he could price out the materials for Stanley's project, then finish the bid.

Jack Johnson's "Upside Down" played softly on satellite radio, helping him start the day. But he was looking forward to warmer summer mornings when he could open the windows and listen to *other* sounds—birds, bees, breezes sifting through the pine boughs. He hadn't minded the long winter here—it was good for a guy who liked to keep to himself—but he was glad it was spring. It was still cold most days, but it had been good just to get outside, get a couple of new jobs started. He'd gotten down to the boathouse one day last week, too, to start getting it ready for the season since the weekenders would show up soon.

Just then, something moved outside the picture window in the kitchen and drew his eye. A little brown cottontail had just hopped into view, but now sat still as a stone in Rob's backyard. He studied the profile of the rabbit's little pinched-up face, wondering how it was possible to see so much in one simple black marble eye. Innocence. Fear. Purpose.

Or maybe he saw nothing at all but a damn rabbit resting in the grass. His past had given him too much time to think. But now, even years later, he couldn't stop, and he couldn't stop seeing things, either—really *seeing* them. The rich multi-toned fur, the soft carpet of grass greening up with spring and making him want to walk through it in bare feet, a last scattering of pinecones that had fallen after his final go at yard work last autumn—a few months before Millie had died. He'd not yet moved in then, of course, but he'd already started helping her take care of the place—although she'd been right there beside him, tossing pinecones into the wheelbarrow, still wearing the gentle smile that had first made him trust her.

If it were him, he'd have just thrown the pinecones away—it was a *land* of pine trees, where cones covered the ground—but Millie had insisted they drive them over to the elementary school in Cedarville. "The kids love to paint them," she'd said, peeking at him from beneath the brim of the little pale blue fisherman's hat she'd often worn. "The little ones just like to play with colors and paintbrushes, but some of the older children turn out fine Christmas ornaments."

Millie had taught him a lot in a short time. About nature. About business. About community. The community part, though, wasn't really for him. For Millie, he'd drive the pinecones to the school again this fall—*every* fall from now on—but that was about as touchy-feely as he planned to get with the locals.

Just then, King, the German shepherd he'd gotten from a neglectful landlord in Idaho, lifted his head from a sprawled-out nap on his favorite braided rug by the back door. He let out an audible sigh as he looked toward the window—he saw the rabbit now, too.

"Shhh," Rob said soothingly, motioning to the dog. King had been ready to start barking, but the gentle admonition kept him quiet.

Yet the slightly stirring dog, even through a window, had drawn the cottontail's attention—just enough to make it turn its little brown head toward the glass.

Rob knew the rabbit couldn't really see inside, but it felt otherwise. Like their gazes were locked. Like two solitary creatures communing in silence. He did a lot better with animals than with people. Animals didn't judge you.

When a loud knock came on the door, Rob flinched—then watched the rabbit dart away into the trees. Shit.

He scowled toward the front of the house as King leapt to his feet to let out a hardy bark. Who the hell could be out there pounding on his door? He wasn't sure anyone ever had, not in the whole four months he'd lived here. And he'd liked it that way just fine.

Maybe if he just ignored them, they'd go away. He'd thought he'd pretty much convinced people here that he didn't like to be bothered, so whoever was out there should consider this another clue. But then he looked back at the list of materials he'd just put together, wondering if it could be Stanley or Steve Fisher out there.

The knock came again. Even louder this time. Like he was deaf or something.

"Take a hint already," he muttered as King barked some more. Damn it, wasn't anybody scared of big, yapping dogs anymore?

After yet another round of beating on the door, Rob lay down his pencil, deciding if it *was* someone he was doing work for, the least he could do was answer. He was antisocial, but not completely unprofessional.

That's when a female voice called, "Hellooo? Are you home?"

Huh. A woman. Who thought he was deaf.

Hell. Letting out a sigh, he pushed to his feet. Then looked down at himself. He wore only jeans—hadn't put on a shirt yet—but that was too bad. His visitor would just have to deal. If he was lucky, maybe it would scare her away. Then maybe she'd tell the rest of the townsfolk how uncouth he was, answering the door like that, and it would ward off future unwanted company.

He strode to the door and pulled it open—to find the chick from last night. The drunk, pretty one with the freakishly huge suitcase. A big fur collar hugged her neck and she wore something sort of sexy in her warm brown hair, along with sunglasses that prevented him from seeing her eyes. He just blinked, then gave her a wary look. He did *not* need this.

The sunglasses flitted from his chest to his face before she cast a smile. "Good morning."

His vague effort at an answer came out sounding more like a growl, but he couldn't have cared less. With any luck, she'd go away soon.

He could tell his response caught her off guard—she swallowed visibly and shifted her weight from one foot to the other before raising the dark glasses back from his torso to his eyes. Why the hell did it bug him that *he* couldn't see *hers*?

"I didn't get a chance to say thank you last night," she said, "so . . . thank you."

"You're welcome," he replied brusquely, then stepped back to close the door.

It surprised the hell out of him when she pressed one hand against it to stop him. "There's more."

More. Great. "What?"

"Well, my name is Lindsey Brooks and I understand you knew my Great-Aunt Millie."

Aw, hell. No way. Couldn't be. After all this time? He *really* didn't need this. "So *you're* Lindsey Brooks, huh?" He crossed his arms over his chest.

She nodded, looking far too chipper. "Do you know my column?"

"Your what?" He had no idea what she was talking about.

But at least she finally reached up to take off the damn sunglasses, revealing blue eyes he'd not noticed the color of last night. "My column. Love Letters? Syndicated in over a hundred newspapers and online? Have you read it?"

"Uh, 'fraid not." Then he flashed a pointed look. "All I know about *you* is that you broke Millie's heart."

Three

Standing across the threshold from him, Lindsey struggled to catch her breath—but the cold morning air invaded her lungs and made them feel on the verge of collapse. She'd broken Millie's heart? Really? Oh God.

"I didn't mean to," she heard herself whisper. "It was all very confusing." And maybe that part was sort of a lie—she hadn't exactly been confused about anything, yet the words came tumbling out as a natural defense. Rob Colter's eyes were so . . . mean. They'd been fairly grim in the first place, but now that she'd introduced herself, they'd turned much more menacing.

"Yeah, well, whatever," he said, not exactly warming to her, it appeared. "What the hell are you doing here?"

Given the ferocity of his eyes, Lindsey let her gaze drop back to his chest. A nicer place, under the circumstances. Well, a pretty darn nice place period. It looked just as good as she'd suspected from seeing it covered in waffle weave—all broad and strong and hard. Only now she also knew it had a nice dusting of hair that narrowed into a line that led south—*oh God, stop looking at where it leads*—and a small tattoo near his heart. A woman's name: Gina. She'd been getting her breath back, finally—yet something about *that* took it away again.

She'd come here ready to be all business, but the moment he'd opened the door shirtless, she'd gone all melty—enough to make her wonder if perhaps lust had contributed to her "wobbly leg syndrome" last night just as much as alcohol. And, of course, she was dying to know who Gina was. But she'd also just been called on the carpet by this jerk—hottie of the century or not—so she needed to focus here and start making a better impression.

"Well, I'm taking a break from writing my column right now," she answered sensibly, trying to pretend his eyes weren't shooting daggers at her and making her feel like the scum of the earth.

Only then that dark gaze began to narrow as if in recognition, which smoothed out his features a bit, turning him more sexy than scary again. "Oh. That's right. Millie said you wrote something for a living. What *kind* of column?"

Of course, he sounded so skeptical already that she didn't expect this to revise his opinion of her, but here went nothing. Although that was when she noticed the big black dog's face next to Rob's denim-covered thigh. The dog stayed completely quiet, his expression a lot like his master's—snarly—and she noticed Rob's fingertips rested in the dog's fur, curving around one pointed ear.

She looked back to the man before her. "It's an advice column. Widely heralded and very popular. People all over the country come to me with their problems." She didn't mean to brag—she just wanted him to respect her.

But when he lowered his chin, grimacing slightly, she knew that wasn't happening. "What—like Dear Abby or something?"

"Sort of. But it's strictly advice on love and relationships.

And sex," she added for some unknown reason, nodding nervously, *also* for some unknown reason.

"Uh-*huh*," he said. As if she'd just spouted something ridiculous. Swell. Things with this guy just got better and better.

And the fact was, she was starting to get a little pissed off. So he'd kept her from sleeping in the parking lot. That didn't get him a free pass forever and she was about to make that clear.

So she stood up a little straighter, looked him squarely in the eye, and spoke with authority. "I'm here, Mr. Colter, because I greatly regret turning down my aunt's kind offer and I'd very much like to get to know her better." It wasn't a lie—just since arriving, she really did yearn to find out more about Aunt Millie.

"Uh, isn't it a little late for that?"

She tried not to let the question cow her. "Yes. Of course. But I meant that I'd like to know more *about* her. I'd like to spend some time around the places she loved—her business and home. I'd like to see her things, which I'm told were left with you. And . . . I'd like to buy the canoe livery from you."

She kept her gaze planted firmly on his. So he'd know she meant business. So he'd feel how serious she was.

At first he looked angry. *Typical.*

But then something lit his eyes that she hadn't seen before. It was almost like . . . humor. Although his laugh was a lot more sardonic than amused. "Are you fucking kidding me? No way in hell."

Okay. So, clearly, she'd moved too soon on the I-want-to-buy-the-business issue. But it was too late now—she had to barrel forward. "Listen, I understand your initial impression of me, but I'm here to rectify things, to fix what I messed up. Now that some time has passed, I realize that keeping Aunt Millie's canoe rental in the family is important to me. I could have had the place for free, but now I'm offering to buy it, and

I'll give you a good profit on your investment. In fact, I could even pay you to run the place for me after I leave town."

Uh-oh. He lowered his chin again, and was casting one of those you've-got-a-lot-of-nerve looks. Another mistake, darn it. "Oh, so you want me to work for you—is that it, Abby? Think you can just waltz into town with a purse full of money and get whatever you want? Well, I've got news for you, honey. Nobody pushes me around. Least of all somebody like you."

Somebody like *her*? What did *that* mean? She was just about to ask, but he kept going.

"So I suggest you just get back in your fancy car and head back to wherever it is you came from and let Millie rest in peace."

"That's why I'm here," she said quietly. "To carry out her wishes. So she *can* rest in peace."

"Hate to break it to ya, but her wishes changed after you turned her down. She sold the place to *me*. And it's not for sale. Got it?"

And then the dog growled, and she stepped instinctively back, and it gave Rob Colter the chance to slam the door in her face.

Whoa. Her heart beat way too fast and her stomach churned.

She'd never dreamed, never even imagined, that the guy would be so mad about her offer. Turning her down was one thing, but this was something else. She stood on the long, covered porch of the two-story log cabin trying to get hold of herself and stop feeling so freaked out. What a jerk.

Or maybe *she* was the jerk. She'd broken Aunt Millie's heart?

He'd said it, and he'd known her great-aunt, so it must be true.

All this time, she'd thought—hoped—that maybe her refusal had been only . . . *mildly disappointing* for Millie. But to hear him say she'd broken Aunt Millie's heart just made her want to cry.

Which she feared she was about to do.

The first tear slipped out, rolling down her cheek before she could turn away from the door. But then turn she did, rushing down the front steps—as much as one can rush in high-heeled peek-toe pumps. She walked briskly down the stone walkway toward the road that rimmed Spirit Lake, wiping away tears as she went.

Maybe this was a mistake. All of it. Coming here. Trying to fix something she'd messed up so royally. Marching down to Rob Colter's house thinking she could actually get a guy like *him* to be reasonable.

Walking along the quiet roadway, she took one last mournful look over her shoulder at the big cabin before it disappeared from view.

And then she saw it. The lone oak tree in the yard, set to one side of the house. It had been much smaller then, and a little wooden swing had hung from a thick branch at just the right height. She'd swung on it when she was five. Aunt Millie had pushed her. Aunt Millie had told her she'd put up the swing when she'd found out Lindsey was coming. She could see the woman's face—it had seemed elderly to her even then, nearly thirty years ago. But it had also been kind, soulful, loving.

And with the memory, now *her* heart broke, too. No wonder Rob Colter thought she was horrible. She was.

Rob went about the rest of his morning—cleaning up breakfast dishes, putting fresh water and Gravy Train in King's bowls, taking a shower and getting dressed for the drive to the lumber store an hour away.

But he was in a lousy mood now.

Because of *her*.

He couldn't believe the woman from last night was Millie's great-niece. Millie had told him all about the letter she'd sent, and he'd watched her wait anxiously all summer to hear that her niece was going to accept her gift of the boathouse—until Rob had gone to the livery one day to find Millie uncharacteristically down. Then she'd shown him the letter the niece had sent back—saying she wasn't interested.

Now, as he opened the front door and whistled for King to follow him out, he couldn't believe this girl had come all the way here from—where had Millie said she lived? Chicago? And hadn't Millie said she was engaged to what had sounded to Rob like some hotshot lawyer type?

And then, as he pulled the log house's door shut behind him, Rob found himself weirdly—and very suddenly—envisioning Millie's niece naked, having sex with the lawyer guy. And he had no freaking idea why.

But it was much more about her being *naked* than about the lawyer guy. It was about her body, in shadow, and then the shadows fading so that she was on full display, curvy and slender and ripe.

He supposed she just looked like a woman who might be fun between the sheets. And for some reason the vision in his head came complete with whatever sexy little animal-print thing she'd had in her hair today, too. Shit. What was *that* about?

That's what you get for not having sex in so long—that's *what it's about. First hot chick to cross your path and you're undressing her in your mind.*

But then he cut himself a break. It was only natural, after all. He was a red-blooded guy.

And hell, he *missed* sex. He missed touching a woman, the soft feel of female skin, the slick slide into her body.

His gut clenched as he crossed the lawn, heading for his pickup in the driveway.

If he were the sort of guy who wasn't opposed to paying for female company, now would probably be the time to head into some big city and do just that. God knew he could justify the act, given the weird circumstances of his life. But that didn't do it for him. It just wouldn't turn him on to be with a woman who hadn't chosen to be with *him*.

Of course, he could just as easily head down to Whitefish or Kalispell looking to get lucky for a night. This summer quaint Whitefish would be crawling with tourists. Yet something about that felt just as orchestrated, false. Going out *looking* for sex made him feel like some kind of overaged frat boy, like less of a man than he wanted to be at thirty-five.

So no matter how he sliced it, his past meant he simply couldn't ever again engage in that human connection, that seductive push/pull of the whole man-and-woman thing. *Not even if it's just meaningless sex*, he thought as he opened the passenger-side door and motioned for King to hop up inside. Because women, and sex—meaningless or not—always led to trouble for him. Big, life-altering trouble. He could still see the horror in the eyes of the various women he'd known over the past seven years. Deena in Boise. Melissa in Portland. Carrie in Tacoma.

He'd thought big cities were the right place for him, but when that had failed repeatedly, he'd started retreating, deeper and deeper into the wilderness, each time he moved on, until the road had finally led him to sweet old Millie, who'd been like the mother he'd never had. And to Moose Falls, the place he wanted to stay, in peace and quiet, for the rest of his life.

Those women, and others, too—none of them had been heartbreaking relationships on their own. Sure, he'd honestly cared about a number of them, but mostly they'd been fun, companionship, sex. But it had been the *reason* they ended, the looks in all their eyes, time after time, that had driven Rob to where he was now.

And it was a pretty damn good place—a better life for himself than he could realistically have hoped. But it came without people, without relationships of any kind—other than business, and only because that was necessary. It had to be that way if he intended to stay here.

He just hoped Millie's great-niece had gotten the message and took his advice about leaving.

Lindsey pushed open the window in her room, letting in the springtime air. As the day stretched on, it had grown warmer, more pleasant out. And still so amazingly quiet, too. Having lived in the city so long, she supposed she'd forgotten some places *were* actually quiet. Hearing the light twitter of a bird somewhere helped her feel a little more peaceful after her conversation with Rob Colter. Big, mean lug. Okay, big, mean, *hot* lug. But big and mean were overshadowing hot right now.

She didn't even want to have sex with him anymore.

Of course, she would probably rethink that if he suddenly turned nice, but she didn't see that happening.

Songbirds and a peaceful view aside, though, her stomach still churned when she thought of Aunt Millie. Of finding out how much she'd let her great-aunt down.

She needed a distraction, and she wasn't sure Moose Falls provided too many of those, so she turned to the only place she could think of—her laptop. Hauling it from her suitcase, she opened it on the table next to the window and thanked God for providing the Grizzly Inn with high-speed Internet access. Eleanor's decorations might be a bit heavy on bears and fish, but between the Internet access and her love of George Clooney, Lindsey was really starting to like her.

Lindsey surfed around, visiting a few of her favorite webpages—*People*, *Us* magazine, *Cosmo* online—glad to catch up on celebrity gossip and news, and also glad to see her naked apron shot hadn't made it to *those* sites yet.

And then she keyed in the URL for her blog.

She didn't know why—it would probably only depress her to see it sitting there unused for weeks now, all the comments old and outdated. But she also thought of it sort of like a friend in a weird way—it was something that belonged to her in this place where nothing else did.

The cheerful graphic heading—*Love Letters*—almost made her smile. Until she remembered it was sort of defunct now—like a house no one lived in anymore, gathering dust and cobwebs. She found herself reading her own post, the last one she'd made, on the very day her life had disintegrated.

Good morning, lovers.

Brrr. They say it's spring, but someone forgot to tell the Windy City. The good news, though, is that being cooped up inside has given me the time to read through many of the letters you've all sent me this past week. And you know I wish I could answer each and every one of you—but here's a dilemma I'm betting many of you will be able to relate to.

Dear Lindsey,

I'm thirty-five and I've been with the same guy for the past four years. We're happy together, we have a great time, and I want to make a life with him. Plus my biological clock is ticking pretty fast. I've hinted about marriage, but even though I know he loves me, he just doesn't seem to be taking the bait. What should I do?

Still Single in Savannah

Still Single, my friend, you have every right to want to take your relationship to the next level. And if your guy isn't making that move on his own, why not shake up his world a little and simply propose to him? *Who says the guy has to be the one to do that, after all? I know we girls like to romanticize certain things and it can be hard to give up such ideas, but we're living in a modern world where sometimes old traditions just don't hold up. So make your own* new *tradition and blow him away with a marriage proposal he won't be able to refuse.*

Of course, you're putting it on the line when you do this. But maybe you're ready to take that risk. If a proposal sends him running in the other direction, he's obviously not the guy who's gonna give you what you need in this life.

Some guys are pretty thick-headed, and some are cowards—and I'm not saying your guy is either, but I am *saying that, who knows, maybe there's a reason he hasn't asked you, and maybe if* you *ask* him, *he'll be head over heels in love with the idea, and with you, too. And if he's not, then he doesn't deserve you, right?*

Be bold, Still Single. And let me know what happens. I'm rooting for you!

And to the rest of you, check back tomorrow when—well, you know what day it is: Wedding Wednesday! I'll give you an update on my upcoming June nuptials, and just wait until you see the picture of the gorgeous white shoes I'll be strolling up the aisle in. They're dyeable, girls, so after the wedding, they might just become a lovely shade of coral. Or a pale buttery yellow for next summer. I'm still debating. But you won't want to miss this "treat for the feet."

Until then, wishing you all much luck in love. And if you need help in that area, you know where to send your love letters.

Oh boy. This had been a lousy idea. Reading her own advice only made her feel all the more like a sham. What did *she* know about having a happy love life? Or how to make a man want to marry you? When she'd written it, she'd thought she was qualified to speak on the subject, but turned out that wasn't the case.

Still staring at the screen, she hoped poor Still Single hadn't taken her advice—if she had, she was probably as miserable as Lindsey right now.

Then her gaze dropped to the little spot stating the number of comments readers had added to the post. She blinked, then looked again. She was pretty sure the last time she'd checked it—about an hour before she'd shed her clothes for a certain pink apron—there had been around a hundred and fifty. Now there were over seven hundred!

Her stomach sank.

For some reason, she'd not even thought about this—that her blog gave people free access to her. Usually, she monitored it closely and could delete anything inappropriate or unpleasant before anyone really saw it. And she'd never had much of a problem with that anyway—since her readers loved her.

Until now.

Since she knew what all those new comments surely held.

Accusations. Which were probably true.

Ridicule. Which was probably apt.

And insults. Which she probably deserved.

She didn't want to look—but she had to, of course. So she took a deep breath, her heart beating a mile a minute, then clicked on the comments link to see what horrifying things people had been saying about her since the apron incident and her subsequent disappearance from the scene.

She scrolled quickly past the first chunk—the hundred and more she'd already read the same day of her post, where she and her readers had been engaging in a lively discussion about Still Single's dilemma. Then she cautiously used her mouse to move farther down the scroll bar and read what came next.

From LisaK6222

Lindsey, I'm so sorry some idiot with a camera invaded your privacy at a bad time. Don't let it get you down.

From SweetReneeinOhio

Sending good thoughts your way at this upsetting time!

From RockinRobin1965

Don't worry, Lindsey. This too shall pass.

Hmm. People were actually being *nice*? But then, those had been early days. The earliest—right after it had happened. Maybe then her readers had held out hope it would turn out to be a cruel hoax or something.

Surely bad things were to come.

She paged down still farther, to more recent comments.

From juliejuliejuliedoyaloveme

Please come back, Lindsey. Your fans love you and miss you! We don't care about some stupid picture. We just miss your cheerful attitude and fun way of looking at life.

From WilliamTell1

I miss your advice. I've taken much of it to heart and feel like something is missing in my daily routine without your blog posts. I hope you'll come back when the dust has settled.

From JoniLovesHollywood

Dear Lindsey, what can we say to bring back Love Letters? You must be going through a terrible time right now, but let your fans help you through it. All of us "lovers" miss our daily Lindsey fix.

Lindsey simply sat there breathless and stunned. Every comment, every single one, was one of sympathy, hope, commiseration, or a request for her return.

She simply couldn't believe it. What wonderful, sweet, forgiving readers she had! How was it even possible in this day and age, when people seemed so eager to point fingers and condemn, that *these* people could be so very supportive?

Lindsey backed up, to the beginning of the new comments, then carefully read each and every one, all five hundred plus, so touched by their words that her heart felt near to bursting.

When she was done, she quietly shut down the computer, feeling more loved than she'd thought she ever would again. Of course, these people didn't really know her, not personally. And yet, in a way, *didn't* they? She put so much of her real self into her work that she truly felt a connection with her fans, even if she never saw their faces.

Just then, the sweet, fragrant scent of hyacinth wafted in through the window on a pleasant afternoon breeze. She glanced out to see a precisely set row of pink and blue blooming bundles along the walkway outside and let it remind her of living at home in her family's old house in the Chicago suburbs. She didn't get a lot of spring flower scents in her high-rise, and her parents had long ago moved to an urban condo. And somehow, the simple scent restored her sense of why she'd come here. For simpler things. For family ties.

Her cell phone still didn't work, even right in the heart of town, so she used the phone by the bed to call her mom and fill her in on her quest so far. Of course, she left out the part about getting drunk. And about wanting to get back on the sex horse with Rob Colter. And about him being a jerk who refused to sell her the canoe rental. Which meant she just let her mom know she'd arrived okay, and yes, the place was as pretty and peaceful as she remembered, and yes, she'd found out who owned the business and was working on buying it from him. Enough said.

Still in a refreshed, cheered-up mood after hanging up, Lindsey ventured back out into the bright afternoon sunshine. After pausing a moment to peer at the placid lake, she stepped into the Grizzly Inn's office to compliment Eleanor on her flowers, then made her way to the Lazy Elk. Spotting her car still in the parking lot, she reminded herself she needed to move it to the inn, then climbed the steps that didn't seem nearly as steep today as they had last night.

It was late afternoon and the place was empty but for two old guys playing checkers in a corner booth. Carla stood behind the bar, wiping down glasses and singing along to KT Tunstall's "Suddenly I See" coming from the jukebox.

She smiled when she saw Lindsey. "Hey, how's it going?"

Lindsey took her same stool from last night. "The answer to that, my friend, is complicated."

Carla looked delighted. "I'm all ears. Start talking." Then she held up a martini glass. "Cosmo?"

Lindsey cringed lightly. "They were delish, but . . . think I'll stick to something safer today. Give me a Coke."

Carla frowned, clearly disappointed. "A Coke? Seriously?"

"All right," she conceded with a light eye roll. "Make it a virgin Bloody Mary. How's that?"

Carla's smile returned. "Much better. Coming up. Now, what's the story?"

"Well," Lindsey began, "Rob Colter is a jerk and hates me. But my readers, it turns out, love me. More than I realized." Then she went on to tell Carla about her meeting with Rob, but also shared the news of all the encouraging messages on her blog.

Carla set a red concoction before her on a little square napkin.

"No celery stick?"

Carla tilted her head as if to scold. "This isn't—"

"Chicago, I know," Lindsey finished for her. "No celery. Fine, I'll live."

"So, does this mean you're going to start writing your column again? Since apparently people *do* still feel you're qualified to give advice?"

Lindsey took a sip of her drink, turning the question over in her head, then sighed thoughtfully. "No," she finally said. "Because *I* don't think I'm qualified anymore. I'd still feel like a sham."

"Then why are you in such a good mood? I mean, so far, nothing has changed from last night—except maybe things have gotten worse. Last night you'd given up your old job with the hopes of buying the canoe rental. Today you've given up your old job and Rob has told you he's not selling."

Lindsey nodded. "True enough. But what's different is—today, now, I suddenly believe in myself again. I don't believe I should be giving people advice on their love lives, but my faith is restored in *me*. The *me* in me, you know, the deep-down part. After reading all those comments, I believe that I can get what I want, that I can do whatever I set my mind to."

"Apart from sounding like you're giving the class valedictorian's speech, how does that translate to the situation at hand?"

"I'm not giving up, Carla. I'm going back to Rob's."

Though she'd expected Carla to give her a high five or something, instead her bartender buddy just flashed a look of disbelief. "Uh, this wouldn't have anything to do with getting back on the sex horse, would it?"

Lindsey rolled her eyes and said an emphatic, "No. After this morning, I wouldn't ride the sex horse with him if he were the last . . ." She held up her hands in a stopping motion, a big enough person to acknowledge her exaggeration. "Okay, maybe I would if he were the last man alive—but only if he were a *nicer* man."

"Fat chance of that."

"My point exactly."

"Then what's your plan?"

"I'll let you know after I come up with it."

"Oh. I thought you meant you were going back to his house, like, *now* or something."

"I am. As soon as I finish this tasty Bloody Mary."

Carla raised her eyebrows, obviously questioning the decision.

Lindsey explained. "I'm a fly-by-the-seat-of-my-pants kind of girl. It works for me. *Usually*," she tacked on, thinking her recent track record didn't really look too convincing. "I'll figure out a plan by the time I get there—and this time I'll just use a little more finesse, and before I know it, he'll be handing me the canoe rental on a silver platter."

Dear Gina,

Do you ever look at the stars? Take a blanket outside in the yard and lay on your back and look up at the universe?

I remember nights when I was younger when the sky was just overflowing with them—but I hardly looked, never even stopped to appreciate them. Now I can't see them from where I am and it makes me miss them. Kind of like I miss you.

On TV, I heard there were more stars in the sky than there are grains of sand on the earth's beaches—and I'm still trying to wrap my head around that, around a universe that huge. I try to think about that when I lay down to go to sleep at night, about how small we really are in comparison to everything else, because it makes my problems seem smaller, too.

Only then I wake up the next morning still wishing we were together. I guess some things can't be measured.

All my love,
Rob

Four

Lindsey grabbed a quick burger at the Lazy Elk, then drove to the Moose Mart up the street, where she filled up with gas and met the quickie mart's proprietor, Maynard, who also happened to be the old man she'd first greeted last night upon entering the bar. Maynard was missing a tooth or two and could stand to be a little more thorough with a razor, but he told her she had a mighty nice car and that her bright pink sweater sure did add some color to the place, so she decided she liked him.

After driving back to park in the single row of spaces in front of the inn, she crossed the street to the lake and sat on a bench not far from the boathouse. Again, she found herself unduly smitten by the view and understood why Aunt Millie had loved this place. The tiny little town was quirky but quaint, and the lake and pine-blanketed hills surrounding it were like a picture postcard come to life. There was something warm here, something peaceful and good. Despite being a city girl, she didn't yet miss the hustle and bustle of "action" all around her. That would come, she was sure. But it hadn't yet, and she found herself appreciating the serenity of Moose Falls more than she could have imagined.

She also used the time to work on a plan. She wanted to fly by the seat of her pants, but not totally without a net.

Peering out over Spirit Lake, she tried to channel Aunt Millie. Looking back, she recalled how wise and sweet all of Aunt Millie's old letters had been—and she only wished she'd not remembered it too late, wished she'd not been so very under Garrett's influence at the time of Aunt Millie's *last* letter. She'd been so into building their life together then, making joint decisions. What a huge mistake.

Time to stop making them, she told herself. *Time to do some things just for you. Time to get something you can always hold on to, something that will be yours and yours alone.*

As she'd eaten her lunch, Carla had confided that, despite her sometimes discouraging words, she knew where Lindsey was coming from, having moved to Moose Falls from Whitefish five years ago to buy the Lazy Elk. She'd not known anything about owning a business or running a bar, but she'd simply done it—because it was for sale and she was a single woman who'd wanted something of her own, just like Lindsey did now.

So with all that in mind, Lindsey followed the road around the lake the short distance to Rob's house again, ready to approach this from another angle. Nearing the log home this morning, she'd been cold, watching her feet as she walked to make sure she didn't stumble—because she'd been a little nervous. Now, though, it was late afternoon, the sun was shining bright, and she felt confident and ready to face Mr. Sexy Flannel Jerk, and instead of watching her feet this time, she studied the house as she got closer.

Two stories with a long covered porch stretching across the front, it exuded the warmth of her great-aunt's personality, and though she didn't want to like anything about Rob Colter, she couldn't help admiring the well-kept yard, the freshly painted mailbox, and the basket of red geraniums he'd gone to the trouble of hanging from the front awning.

Walking boldly up the stone path, she didn't hesitate to knock on the door.

From inside, she heard his dog bark, and wondered if she'd have to knock and knock and knock like earlier. *You can try to ignore me, Rob Colter, but I'm not going away.*

She was just about to knock again when the door flung open abruptly. This time he wore more clothes—a dark tee with another flannel shirt over it, open—and a scowl.

"Hello," she said, her voice crisp and clear and direct. She tried to look pleasant, but also like a woman who meant business.

"Why are you back?"

What a charmer. But she let his rudeness fuel her. "Because it seems that you knew my great-aunt fairly well. And whether or not you want to sell me the canoe rental—"

"I don't," he interrupted.

"—I'd still like to learn more about her."

"Why?"

She sighed, irritated. And wishing he weren't still so nice to look at even while he irritated her. *Stay focused, Lindsey.* She answered honestly. "Because I wish I'd taken the time to get to know her, come visit her."

"A little late for that."

Just have to keep twisting that knife, don't you? "So you keep reminding me." Taking a deep breath, Lindsey looked Rob Colter right in his big, gorgeous, dark brown eyes. "Look, I know you don't like me, but I'm not *asking* you to like me. I'm asking you to tell me more about my great-aunt. That simple."

"Like what? What is it you want to know?"

She tried to ignore his snappish tone, but found herself giving her head an annoyed little shake in reply. "Just . . . tell me something she loved to do."

To her surprise, instead of delivering another snotty retort, he actually appeared to be thinking it over. "Okay," he said a moment later. He didn't exactly sound friendly, but maybe as if he was willing to meet her halfway on this particular point. "She loved to take morning hikes up the Rocky Face Trail to Rainbow Lookout."

Lindsey smiled, feeling slightly victorious simply to get a real answer from him. "Excellent," she said. Then got an idea. "I want to do that, too. Hike up that trail to—what did you call it? Rainbow Lookout."

In reply, he crossed his arms, lowered his chin derisively, and went back to looking at her like she was ridiculous.

But she didn't let it cow her. She was serious about this. She wanted to . . . walk in Aunt Millie's shoes, as it were. "Will you take me?"

At this, Rob's eyes widened into his typical expression of disbelief. "Why should I?"

Man, this guy was hard to get along with. Lindsey just sighed, then shifted her weight from one pink pump to the other. She narrowed her gaze on him and made an observation. "You know, you were a lot more attuned to the damsel in distress thing last night at the Lazy Elk."

"You're not in distress anymore," he pointed out.

But she simply blinked. "Look again and you'll see that I am. Because I've come all this way and I refuse to leave without feeling I've gotten something for my trouble. If I can't buy the livery, I at least want some small piece of my aunt to take back with me. Like, say, a hike to a place she loved." She planted her hands on her hips and attempted to stand a little taller—since even in four-inch heels, he still seemed to tower over her. "And frankly, I'm betting if Aunt Millie were here right now, she'd *want* you to help me know her better." *Take that, buddy.*

Rob just tilted his head, flashing a look that said, *Low blow.* "Fine," he bit off. "You want to hike? We'll hike. Meet me here tomorrow morning at five, and don't be late or the deal's off."

Five, huh? But on her Chicago-set body clock, that was actually seven, and seven she could probably handle. "Great."

His gaze strayed down over her body—which gave her a little shiver—but then landed on her shoes. "And wear something sensible to hike in."

"Don't worry," she assured him.

He only rolled his eyes in response as he started to close the door.

"And thanks," she said. She hadn't actually meant to, but it came out—she was a naturally gracious person.

"You're welcome," he told her, just as gruff as usual, but even as the door shut in her face, she couldn't help thinking she'd made a little headway with him. Maybe. Sort of.

It truly *would* be wonderful to walk in Aunt Millie's shoes, to soak up a little more of what she loved about this place. Not that Lindsey had ever actually gone on a hike before, but how hard could it be? It was just . . . walking, right? To someplace pretty. It sounded nice.

Of course, she had a dual purpose, an ulterior motive: wearing Rob Colter down.

If he was forced to spend time with her, he'd realize she wasn't a bad person. He'd see that she truly cared—about this place she was coming to know and about Aunt Millie's last wishes. She'd convince him, slowly, to change his mind and sell her the canoe business, after all.

And in the meantime . . . well, in the meantime she was going on a hike with a hottie.

But she still wasn't interested in riding the sex horse with him.

No matter *how* it had felt when his eyes had passed over her breasts, and lower.

Nope, with a guy like him, she had to stay focused. Keep this all about her plan, about getting what she'd come here for.

And as for the sex horse, it would have to wait until another place and time, when she found a more suitable partner.

Now, she thought as she traversed the stone walkway toward the road, if only she could quit thinking about the way he'd looked in nothing but blue jeans this morning, she might actually believe herself.

William Bent turned his head slightly to one side and watched in the bathroom mirror as he dragged the razor up his jaw, smoothing away the shaving cream. Guster's "Barrel of a Gun" played in the background, the bouncy beat helping him wake up a little.

He had a good life according to most people. A good job as a computer programmer, a nice home in an affluent Portland suburb where he attended block parties and took part in community rummage sales and jogged three healthy miles every evening past tidy two-story homes with well-manicured lawns, all green and fresh with spring right now.

Only *he* knew how disheartened he felt to realize he'd turn thirty-six soon and still not have a wife, a family. Maybe that didn't sound so old to some people, but to him it did. He'd wanted something more by now. And he'd never even come *close* to getting it.

Sure, he'd had a few girlfriends, and the occasional one-night stand—he'd found some sex over the years. But no love. No one had loved him and he'd loved no one.

The shrink they'd made him see after high school had said he was developing intimacy issues, even then. So now he guessed they'd gotten a lot worse. Inside, he was a friendly guy—he liked people, he wanted to know them, he wanted to open up. But he never did.

Oh sure, he went to the happy hours, he chatted with the neighbors in the driveway after mowing the lawn or when dragging the trash can to the curb. But no one knew the *real* him; no one knew the thoughts in his head.

No one knew how much he still missed his brother. Or his mom and dad.

Still. After all these years.

He was just lonely. Life was passing him by.

Sometimes it felt almost as if he'd died along with them all, he thought as he slid the razor up his face a little too briskly, nicking his skin and causing a dot of blood.

Swallowing back that thought as he dabbed the bright red spot away, he finished shaving and rinsed his face clean with cool, clear water that woke him up still more. Then he looked back in the mirror, into his own eyes. Strange, sometimes even *he* thought they looked a bit vacant, empty. Sometimes he felt like he didn't even know *himself.*

Still wearing only the fresh underwear and white tee he'd put on after his shower, he walked into his home office and sat down at his PC. He keyed in the URL for the Love Letters blog just to check—but when it came up, he saw the same old post that had been sitting there for weeks. Still nothing new from Lindsey. Damn.

He wasn't sure why he felt such a connection to someone he'd never met, but he just missed her "voice," missed the smile he felt in her words. He'd not quite realized until she'd quit posting what an integral part of his day her advice had become. Not that he had much of a love life to worry about, but God knew he thought women were a mystery, so he soaked up her suggestions and advice in case he ever needed it—he saw it like . . . training, lessons, something he'd take out in the world and put to use someday. Hopefully soon. And he didn't even mind when Lindsey went off on tangents about her wedding, or fashion. In fact, he thought it was cute.

Maybe he just liked knowing there was a beautiful, sophisticated woman out there somewhere whom he felt he could relate to.

Oh sure, in real life, she probably wouldn't look twice at him. But he didn't know that for *certain.*

And it was nice to think that maybe, just maybe, if they

ever met, she would like him. Not just sexually, either. He liked sex as much as the next guy, of course, but he was about more than that. And maybe she'd see that. And if not, well, it would be enough if she simply thought he was a nice guy, if she enjoyed his company.

Whoever took that awful picture of her should be beaten to a pulp. What an asshole! Just thinking of it sent a red-hot blast of fresh anger blazing through him.

Of course, just as bad were the places that had printed it or put it online. There was no sense of justice or privacy in this world anymore.

And what a jerk her ex-fiancé must be. Captions or articles that appeared with the picture in various places had reported that they were no longer engaged, which pleased him. He had no idea why she'd thrown a dessert at the guy, but knew the idiot must have done something awful.

And God—just to think of a woman opening a door to *him* wearing only that little apron and those high-heeled shoes. He got a little hard now, just imagining that: Lindsey, welcoming him home after a long day's work—like that. He'd treat her right, that was for sure.

Now he thought of her out there somewhere feeling bad about all this, embarrassed, alone. The alone part he could relate to. He only wished there was some way to let her know she didn't need to be embarrassed. Because the truth was, everybody wanted certain things—love, passion, sex. She'd got caught offering those things to her boyfriend—no crime in that. The crime was that the guy clearly hadn't appreciated her the way she deserved.

Maybe he'd leave another comment on the blog—just in case she decided to check it. He clicked to access the comment box, signing in with the screen name he'd used online for years now—WilliamTell1—then typed his message.

Lindsey, whatever Garrett did to cause your breakup, he's a fool. We all miss you. Come back to us.

He looked at his words. They didn't say even half of what he felt. But he wasn't sure what words *would* or even *could* truly express his empathy. So he clicked on Submit and hoped the simple sentiment would somehow be enough to let her know he really cared.

Then he put on his suit and tie, ready to fake his way through one more corporate day, where he would smile and act normal when he got coffee from the break room and where maybe he'd even go out to lunch with someone if they asked, all while he felt like nothing inside.

Rob hadn't slept well. He'd had vague dreams of her. Or of a woman in some sort of animal-print teddy who he at least thought *might've* been her. And dreams could be so damn real sometimes. He could still almost feel her bare breast in his hand, firm but soft, pliable.

Shit, this was bad.

On the other hand, though, it was better than nightmares, so maybe he shouldn't complain. Although they hadn't been a problem since he'd come to Moose Falls, he'd had more than his fair share of nightmares in his life.

As long as he kept the fooling around with Dear Abby strictly in his dreams he supposed it wouldn't be the end of the world.

And the truth was, he'd been disappointed when his alarm had gone off before the dream had ended. Before the *sex* had ended. Before they'd really even *gotten* to the sex, in fact—his impression had been of vague writhing around, touching, moving together. But no more. Nope, just enough to get him horny.

Now he sat on the sofa in the early morning stillness staring out the back picture window as dawn began filtering the air with pale light. His gaze dropped to King, curled up and sleeping on his rug by the back door. He gave his head a small, incredulous shake as reality came back to him. What the hell was he doing hiking with her?

It wasn't that he minded getting up early—when it got warmer out, he'd start working about this time every day. But at the moment it seemed strange to be up before dawn, to have been creeping around in the dark trying not to wake the dog, all because Millie's great-niece had suddenly somehow invaded his life.

He glanced down at his crotch. She was due any minute and he had a hard-on the size of Montana. Well, maybe not Montana, but it showed through his jeans pretty prominently. Great, just what he needed—to let Abby know he had the hots for her.

Pushing to his feet, he walked quietly to the bathroom, where he bent over the sink without turning on the light, reached for the faucet, and splashed some cold water on his face.

Whew, brisk.

But not brisk enough to kill his erection.

Just as Rob reentered the living room, her damn knock came on the door. It sounded ten times louder in the quiet of daybreak and the dog flinched, then leapt up and started barking like a maniac. Shit, he'd somehow forgotten she'd be knocking or he'd have waited on the front porch—although, after yesterday, he wasn't sure *how* he'd forgotten her particularly grating way of pounding on a door.

He looked to King and spoke in a soothing tone. "Go back to sleep, buddy."

The dog gave him an are-you-sure-because-this-is-out-of-the-ordinary look, but when Rob softly added, "Come on now, lie back down," King obeyed and curled back into sleeping position.

Rob rushed to grab up his down-filled winter vest and put it on—he needed it for the cold, but also hoped it would camouflage what was going on behind his zipper. Then he opened the door before she started beating on it again.

She stood before him in that little black coat with the thick fur collar she'd worn yesterday, along with dressy-looking jeans and fancy high-heeled black boots with pointed toes. She looked gorgeous. And also ridiculous. "You think this is *sensible*?" he asked, eyes stuck on her feet.

"Good morning to you, too. And they're boots, so yes, of course they're sensible."

"You can't hike five miles in them."

"How would *you* know?"

He blinked, confident about his argument. "Have you ever before?"

"Well, I've walked the Magnificent Mile in them—numerous times on the same day. So there." She punctuated the statement with a nod, seeming to think she'd proven him wrong.

"I don't think the Magnificent Mile is strenuous, hilly terrain."

She answered with a little huffing noise, then said, "Do you want to argue all day, or do you want to hike?"

"I don't especially want to do either, but given the choices, I'll take the second."

She rolled her eyes, and he stepped outside, gently closing the door.

And then he smelled her. The scent of something light and fresh and just a little flowery. Her shampoo, probably. But it was nice, and apparently his penis liked it, too, since it didn't seem to be deflating any.

As they set off toward the trail—him trudging along the quiet roadway, her following a few paces behind—he was still irritated that he'd agreed to do this. But she'd been right saying Millie would have wanted it and she'd seemed to know that would get to him. The truth was, he'd have done anything for Millie. He'd known her for less than a year, but she'd . . . well, she'd become the best friend he'd ever had.

He didn't let himself feel softly toward people, but he had toward Millie—almost from the start. It was something in her eyes, her voice. A gentle wisdom, the charitable way she looked at life.

Which really did mean she would want him to take her niece on this hike, which was exactly why he was doing it.

And as they walked along the road rimming the lake, the sun beginning to rise and throw a little light onto the water, he soaked up more of the peace he'd discovered here last summer and felt thankful he'd found Millie and let her turn his life around.

Of course, the morning walk would be more peaceful if he were alone and not having to deal with the city girl behind him and the clickety-click of her boots as she struggled to keep up. Damn, this was going to be a long hike.

Lindsey had no idea if Rob was walking fast on purpose, trying to prove her boots were the wrong thing to wear, but she wasn't going to let it get the best of her. And the fact was, she was extremely skilled at walking in heels. It wasn't that her feet didn't get sore and tired, but the joy she took in her footwear overrode any discomfort she might experience.

When they reached the trailhead—complete with a cute little wooden sign—near a bend in the road, she was relieved, deciding that walking on the dirt path would probably be easier than stomping along on the hard asphalt. Rob stepped off the road and under the cover of dense trees that shaded the start of the trail and she followed.

Almost immediately she found herself on a rapidly ascending hill, the trail pockmarked with rocks and bumps and the occasional tree root stretching across the path. And walking there wasn't any easier. In fact, it was pretty darn challenging, and she was beginning to see Rob's point about her boots. Not that she'd admit it in a million years.

"Who owns this land?" she called toward the back of his head. Weren't most trails like this usually in parks?

"*I* do," Rob said, surprising her. "It was Millie's and came as part of the deal."

"Oh." She hadn't known there was land involved, too. Not that it would have made any difference in her original decision, but still, it was odd to think that if she'd accepted Millie's offer, all of this—all these huge, towering trees and the ground beneath them—would be hers. Now the path they followed leveled out, twisting through flatter, moss-covered terrain that made her feel as if she'd stepped into another world. She couldn't help looking around with a bit of wonder—the unexpected sight took her mind off her aching arches and the smoother ground made it so she didn't have to be so careful choosing where to place each step.

"She kept it natural like this other than posting a few trail markers," he added, shocking Lindsey by actually volunteering information. And not sounding so angry for a change. "And she blazed this and a few other trails herself over the years."

"Truly?" Now this took Lindsey aback. Aunt Millie—trailblazer. As difficult as she found the trail to walk now—and oh God, they were going up again, around a twisting, rocky bend—she couldn't imagine what it would be like to *make* the trail. To figure out the best way—or *any* way, for that matter. To actually make it *lead* somewhere. "That's . . . pretty impressive."

"She was an impressive woman," he said, still marching along ahead of her as if the current steep terrain they traveled was nothing. "She always let the weekenders use the trails, too. She named them all herself, and she made trail maps to give out."

Amazing as all that seemed, as Lindsey reached another more level part of the path, she moved on to what she *really* wanted to find out. "How did you get to know my aunt so well before she died?"

In front of her, he shrugged. "I moved here last spring and needed work. She hired me to help with the canoes and do some maintenance around her house. Then she recommended me to other people who needed construction jobs done."

Lindsey took it all in, feeling instinctively as if more lay beneath the surface of his words. "Sounds as if she took a liking to you."

Another shrug. Then a "Watch your head" as he ducked under a low-hanging branch. She did, dipping beneath it behind him while minding her footing and hoping like hell she didn't twist an ankle before this was through.

"You must have been nicer to her than you are to everyone else," she mused.

At this, Rob stopped and turned to give her a look. And she knew it was supposed to be a *mean* look—but at the moment, she saw more of a *steamy, smoldering* look. Maybe her brain was better off when he was being an asshole if this was what two minutes of civil conversation wrought.

Trying to ignore the tingling sensation that rippled down her spine, she found her voice. "Just telling it like it is. You seem like a tell-it-like-it-is kinda guy, so I figured you could appreciate that."

She couldn't quite read his expression for a change—but maybe that was because she'd just gotten kind of lost in those big brown eyes of his. Although from time to time Lindsey and Rob emerged from the thick canopy of greenery covering much of the trail, at the moment they stood reimmersed in it, which made things shadowy despite the sun rising higher overhead, and which made her feel sort of . . . cocooned with him here. Kind of . . . private. Like they'd been in her room a couple of nights ago when she'd wanted him so much. She was afraid she was wanting him *again.*

And a rocky, dusty trail didn't seem like the *best* place in the world to have sex, but she figured she could do it if that's where events led.

"I suppose I can," he finally said.

Have sex? she thought, stunned. But then, no—they were talking about telling it like it was, and about him appreciating that.

"She and I just hit it off," he added.

Him and Aunt Millie, he meant. Because that's what they

were talking about. Not sex on the trail. Not lust in the dust. Too bad she wanted to kiss him so bad right now.

And then she thought of a way to nip that in the bud—something that would surely squelch any further thoughts of the sex horse today. Which was important to do, because she really *couldn't* have sex with a guy who'd treated her so shabbily, even if he *was* walking testosterone. "Tell me more about . . . how disappointed in me Aunt Millie was."

"That's a hell of a weird thing to ask for."

"You're right." *But I don't want to start liking you and I'm sure you'll say horrible enough things now to stop me. And* . . . "But I think I need to hear it. I think I need to . . . better understand what was in her heart. Maybe it'll . . . make me a better person in the long run, you know?"

As soon as she spewed all that truth, she realized this completely contradicted her make-him-like-me-and-he'll-sell-me-the-livery plan—but she meant it all. She needed to deal with what she'd done to Aunt Millie or it would be like a dark cloud hanging over her that she could never get rid of.

Rob turned around and started walking again, up a particularly steep part of the trail. She followed, chugging along, and just when she'd decided he wasn't going to respond to her request, he started talking.

"She told me about you for the first time last June, just after the start of canoe season. She was fond of you, and proud of everything you'd achieved—that's when she told me about your newspaper writing, I guess. She was concerned about having somebody to leave her place to, and she thought you were the perfect person. She thought it would give you a home away from home, a place for you and your husband to get away from the city."

"I'm not married," she said quickly. "Or engaged anymore, either." She couldn't help spewing it out.

"Oh," he said in a hushed tone, pausing his steps. Then he

turned to glance at her. "I thought you were. Engaged, I mean."

She shook her head vigorously. "Nope, that's over, and good riddance."

Their eyes met, and she thought he might ask what had happened—but thankfully, he turned back around and continued walking. And talking. "Anyway, she wrote to you completely expecting you to accept the gift. Because it *was* a gift, after all—and most people don't turn down gifts. Especially ones that come from the heart."

Oh. God.

Lindsey's heart crumpled and it was almost hard to keep walking.

That's what she'd done—turned down a gift. It was as if Aunt Millie had held it out to her and Lindsey had stuck her nose up in the air, or spat upon it or something. "I . . . didn't want to take something dear to her and then just sell it."

He glanced over his shoulder briefly again. "I didn't ask for an explanation. Do you want to hear this or not?"

She pursed her lips and gave a light nod, then watched as Rob pressed ahead on the winding path.

"All right then," he said as he walked. "She spent the weeks after that waiting to hear how happy you were to accept. She was hoping you'd come visit in the fall and she could show you around. But then your letter came, turning her down. She didn't expect that at all. I'd never seen her as quiet and withdrawn as she was that day, so I asked what was wrong. And I think it . . . almost embarrassed her to tell me. She never even really got the words out—just shoved your letter into my hand and I read it myself."

Lindsey kept walking, putting one boot in front of the other on the uneven terrain—because what else could she do? Break down and cry? No way, not in front of Rob Colter. She'd asked for this, after all. It was just a cruel twist of fate that the person with the crushing answers she sought was also the person she most wanted to stay strong in front of—so she watched her feet as he spoke, trying not to feel his words too profoundly. Only they cut into her anyway, slicing deep.

"So," she finally managed to say, "I guess she thought I was an awful niece and that her faith in me had been misplaced."

"No." He shook his head. "Millie wasn't like that. She didn't judge people. She was just . . . hurt. She thought you were too busy for an old woman. She thought maybe it meant Moose Falls and the canoe rental wasn't as special as she'd always thought. It kind of . . . made her feel like everything she loved was unimportant. Like *she* was unimportant."

Okay—now Lindsey felt light-headed. Weak. Miserable. Like someone who didn't deserve to live. As if Rob Colter had every right to treat her like a terrible person—because she *was* terrible, and his coldness was the *least* she deserved.

She stopped walking, not by design, but because her feet stopped moving. She'd been winded and sweating in her coat before Rob had even started answering her question—and now she felt too nauseous to go on. They traveled along a hillside that sloped down on one side of the path and sharply upward on the other, and she found herself reaching out to press her hand against a large boulder protruding from the side of the earthen wall. Then she leaned back against it to keep from collapsing right on the trail. And felt like an idiot. For wearing heels today. For trying to buy what she hadn't even wanted for free a year ago. For coming here at all.

"Are you okay?"

For a brief moment, she'd actually forgotten Rob was there. But now she looked up from her shame to find that he'd stopped, too, and had taken a few steps back toward her. Suddenly, his eyes looked almost kind. Kind and . . . impossibly sexy. Although it was hard, at this moment, to fully feel the sexy part—even though that would have been welcome compared to what she *did* feel.

"Maybe I shouldn't have told you," he said, "but I thought you could take it."

She raised her gaze once more, only briefly, before dropping it back to the ground. "So did I."

That's when something warm touched her fingers and she glanced to see that it was Rob's hand, softly squeezing hers.

Despite her current distress, frissons of electricity skittered up her arm, down into her breasts, lower. She bit her lip and didn't meet his gaze, just studied their hands, joined. His skin was slightly darker than hers, his large fingers rougher. His nails were short and well kept. She couldn't believe this man—*this man*—was offering her comfort.

"Look, Abby," he said, his voice surprisingly gentle, "it worked out the way it should have. Millie sold me the place because she knew I loved it and would care for it. And that's all she really wanted, somebody who felt that way about her home and her business, somebody who would keep the things she'd built thriving."

Lindsey's heart beat too fast. He stood close to her now—she could smell the scent of a masculine soap mixing with the sweet fragrance of perspiration. She peered up into his eyes and her chest felt like it was stretching, expanding, with need. She was feeling the sexy part again. But something more than that, too. A strange desperation to make him understand. "Despite what you have every reason to believe, I'm not a bad person," she told him.

He met her gaze under the shade of the pine boughs. "Listen, it's not for me to judge—thinking about Millie reminded me of that. And besides, it doesn't matter what I think anyway. It's between you and Millie."

She swallowed, emotion rising to her throat, threatening to get the best of her and burst out of her in tears. "But Millie's not here anymore. And it's important to me for you to believe me. I'm not an awful person."

He shook his head softly. "Why? What do you care what *I* think?"

Excellent question. One she didn't have an answer to. "I don't know. But you're the closest thing I have to her right now, and I just don't want you to hate me, okay?" It was more important to her than she could understand, and she wasn't sure her explanation even made sense—she only knew a burning need for him to like her, simply like her.

He looked a little dumbfounded, but after a long pause said, "Okay. I don't hate you."

"And you don't think I'm terrible?" she prodded feebly yet hopefully.

He hesitated, which made her want to slug him.

"*Well?*"

Finally, he sighed. "I don't know you very well, but okay, I don't think you're terrible."

"I have reasons for what I did last summer," she insisted.

"Which are?"

Hard to explain. "I was brainwashed."

"Some sort of fashion cult?"

She rolled her eyes in response. "It's a long story. And not one I particularly care to share, but let's just say I wasn't thinking clearly then. Only I am now. And I'm so sorry I hurt Aunt Millie so carelessly."

Gazes still joined, he said, "Okay," this time more softly, and almost sounding sincere.

Which was when he abruptly dropped her hand—the way he might if he looked down and realized he held a snake. He'd been holding it all this time, and she immediately missed the warmth it had provided in the chilly morning air. And inside her, too.

"Let's walk," he said, any signs of tenderness leaving him. "We're almost there."

Thank God. She wasn't sure how much more her feet could take. Or her emotions. "I'm ready," she said, sounding stronger than she truly felt. "Lead on."

A few minutes and one big turn in the trail later, Lindsey and Rob surfaced again from beneath the cover of trees and Lindsey saw that the trail abruptly ended at a wooden railing which—*oh my God*—overlooked Spirit Lake from a stunning bird's-eye view.

She knew they'd headed mostly upward on the grueling hike, but she'd had no idea they'd climbed this high. The lake was larger than she'd realized, and with the morning sun shining across it, it had become an almost Mediterranean shade of blue. She'd known Moose Falls was quaint and the lake scenic, but from up here . . . she couldn't help thinking this was how God must see it.

The boathouse was barely visible in the distance, the Grizzly Inn and Lazy Elk situated behind it. Up here, the town looked so small compared to the lake itself, the sweeping hillsides of majestic pines seeming to cradle it all.

"You didn't warn me," she said.

She felt Rob's gaze, but was unable to tear her eyes from the view. "About?"

"How breathtaking it is."

"Mmm," he murmured. "I guess I . . . didn't know if a girl like you would notice."

He didn't even sound snotty, just as if that was how he saw it—but she snapped her eyes to him anyway, crossing her arms. "Maybe there's more to *a girl like me* than you think."

He cast her only a sideways glance, but relented. "Maybe." And something in his tone—as if perhaps he actually *wanted* to find out what there was to her—threatened to turn her knees to jelly. Especially since the strenuous hike and staggering emotions she'd suffered on the way up already had her legs pretty weak as it was.

Looking down to where her hand now rested on the rail that kept hikers from tumbling off the edge of a cliff, she couldn't help wondering . . . "How on earth did this get here? I mean, someone had to haul the materials from all the way down *there*." She motioned toward the familiar road edging the lake.

"Millie originally built it," he explained as if it were nothing.

Lindsey felt her jaw drop as she pulled her eyes from the view to flash a look of disbelief.

He only shrugged, saying, "She was something, that's for sure." Then glanced down at the wooden railing himself, giving it a slight shake with one hand as if to test its sturdiness. "I put this one in last year, though, since the old one had rotted. She didn't want hikers leaning on it and breaking through."

And now Lindsey wasn't sure whether to be more amazed at the things Aunt Millie had done for Moose Falls or the things Rob Colter had done for Aunt Millie.

"Why is it called Rainbow Lookout?" she asked, peering back over the lake and surrounding hillsides. The sky grew bluer overhead as the morning deepened, promising another gorgeous day like yesterday.

"The first time she made it to this point," Rob explained, "it had been raining. But right when she got here, the sun came out and a big, beautiful rainbow stretched all the way from one side of the lake to the other."

Lindsey tried to envision it. "Wow, a full one? I've never actually *seen* a full one. Only the ones that go halfway and then fade."

"You're kidding," he replied, not with malice for a change, but raised eyebrows.

With a slightly self-deprecating smile, she admitted, "This may surprise you, but . . . I haven't spent an enormous amount of time outdoors."

He kept a completely straight face. "Yeah, I'm stunned."

Still admiring the view, Lindsey turned to the left, where the lake stretched out like a long finger, its other end too far away to see. "Wow, an island," she said, spotting a small mound of land sprouting the tall spires of narrow pines.

"Misty Isle," he said. "It gets covered with fog and mist most nights."

"The whole lake was like that when I got here."

He gave a short nod. "The fog spreads pretty far some nights. But the island gets like that *every* night."

"How do people know that?" she asked. "I mean, you can't see it from town."

"There are a few houses hidden on that opposite hill," he said, pointing to what looked like uninterrupted forest from here. "And sometimes—especially around Halloween, Millie told me—people boat out there to roast marshmallows and tell ghost stories because the mist makes it spooky."

"Speaking of ghost stories, I was wondering—do you know why the lake is called *Spirit* Lake?"

"Came from a local Indian legend. One of the tribes around here used to believe they saw their ancestors and departed loved ones in the swirling mist at night. They thought it meant the ancestors watched over them and kept them from harm while they were there."

Lindsey couldn't help being enthralled with the concept. She hadn't heard any "legends" about Chicago lately. "That's so freaking *cool*," she said.

And to her surprise, Rob actually laughed. "Yeah, I guess."

Their eyes met once more and Lindsey couldn't help herself. "At the risk of making this a habit—thank you. For bringing me up here."

He just shrugged, his hands in the pockets on his vest.

And though she'd warmed up on the ascent, now that they'd stood here a few minutes, she was getting chilly again, too, and shoved her own hands in the front pockets of her jeans. "This really *does* make me feel closer to Aunt Millie," she told him softly.

His answer came just as quiet. "Good." And then he spoke up more. "But I'm still not selling you the livery."

Despite herself, she only smiled. "Message received, loud and clear."

And she still wanted the canoe business—she wanted it more now with each passing hour, with each new bit of beauty or charm she saw in this place—but for today, just connecting to her aunt through Rainbow Lookout truly was enough.

"Ready to start back?" Rob asked.

Lindsey took another look—panning the view all the way from Misty Isle to the tiny buildings of Moose Falls at the lake's opposite end. "Yeah," she said, although it was hard to leave behind the serenity she felt here, the true sense of understanding Aunt Millie better than she ever had before.

Of course, five minutes later, it was her aching feet that took center stage in her brain. Well, those and Rob's ass. His vest was short enough that she could see his butt, the slightly faded denim of his jeans making it look damn fine. Given Lindsey's usual propensity for men in suits—she was generally more attracted by Armani than Levi's—the fact that she liked Rob's butt in blue jeans so much was just one more thing to make her feel thrown off her game in Montana.

And while logic had told her that going *down* the hill would be easier than coming *up* had been, nature was playing a cruel joke on her. Turned out that hiking down actually put much more stress on her thighs and the steep parts were downright challenging to descend. Rob never said a word, but each time he had to stop and wait for her to catch up, he cast a derisive glance toward her heels. Which were indeed an even bigger problem now, making her feel like she was going to go tumbling forward with every step she took on the downward grade.

Not that she'd *ever* admit it. Never, never, never. High fashion was her friend. That was her story and she was sticking *to it.*

God, what a morning. The worse her arches hurt and the more her toes got crammed forward in her boots, the less she could feel Aunt Millie's presence, and the more she found herself focusing on less savory things: her guilt over her aunt, her lust for her guide. The good news was, her feet hurt so bad that she could barely process either.

It was then that she came barreling around a twist in the trail to see Rob resting on a rock, staring at the ground—and not noticing the humongous bear that had just wandered onto the trail ahead of them. *Whoa.* And this one wasn't a wooden statue, either.

Nope, this was the largest animal she'd ever seen, with front paws big enough to crush her head. After it mauled her to death. Holy crap.

"B-bear," she managed, her heart pounding wildly against her ribs.

Rob looked up, toward where she pointed.

And the bear looked up, too—at them. Then began to amble in their direction. Lindsey's pulse pounded in her ears.

"Calmly back away, up the trail," Rob said in an even tone. But his eyes told her he was freaked out, too, as he pushed slowly to his feet.

Lindsey *tried* to back up like he'd said—but instead she just stumbled in her heels and went plopping down hard onto the packed earthen slope behind her with a heavy "Oomph."

And, oh boy—the bear was even more gigantic from down on the ground. She felt paralyzed, helpless to scramble to her feet or even move at all. She feared she might throw up.

That's when Rob, who was also trying to back gingerly away, tripped over her sprawled legs and fell next to her, muttering, "Shit," as he went down.

The bear's big, dark eyes seemed to connect squarely with Lindsey's as it continued lumbering toward them at a pace that in one sense seemed slow—except that it brought him too close for comfort in only a few short seconds. As the bear grew closer, closer, her chest threatened to explode, and she found herself regretting lots of things—but mainly wasted time. She regretted all the time she'd squandered with Garrett, she regretted not getting to know Aunt Millie, and she regretted not putting the moves on Rob Colter—jerk or not—when she'd had the chance.

Watching the bear approach, she reached down and latched on to Rob's wrist. "What is he doing? What is he thinking?"

Rob still managed to sound incredulous, even under stress. "Do I look like a fucking bear psychologist?"

"No," she said. "But you're all I have right now."

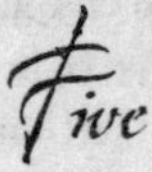

This was the first time Rob had encountered a bear in the woods, even though Millie had told him there were plenty in the area. He'd immediately remembered her instructions—don't turn around, just back calmly away.

Which he'd tried to do, but Abby and her fancy boots had screwed that part up.

And shit, that was a damn big bear—still moving slowly but purposefully toward them. Rob didn't want to rise back up now, afraid the move might seem adversarial. What else had Millie told him to do?

"Give me your purse," he said.

"My what?"

"Your purse, damn it, your purse." Rather than waiting for Abby to hand it over, he snatched it away. It was red.

He held it out before him, showing the grizzly as he softly said, "Look at this, buddy."

Then he tossed it gently into the brush and woods below the trail.

Next to him, she gasped—but they both watched as the

bear halted in place, his eyes turning toward where the purse had landed. Rob could still see the bright red leather from where he sat in the dirt, Abby nearly crushing his wrist.

He held his breath as the bear slowly began to ease its massive body down off the trail, traveling the ten yards or so necessary to sniff the purse, then paw at it once.

After which he appeared to lose interest—and started meandering down through the trees, the brush rustling around him until he was out of sight and the only remaining sound was that of a lone twittering bird.

"Okay, he's gone," Rob finally said. "Think you can release your death grip now? You're cutting off my circulation."

"*Oh*," she said on another small gasp, letting go of his wrist. He wouldn't have thought she'd be so strong. His skin started to tingle without her touch—but he decided it was only because the blood was actually making it to his hand again.

Next to him, Miss Fashion Plate shook her head in wonder. "I can't believe that just happened."

"I know," he murmured. "That was one huge bear."

"No, I mean I can't believe you just threw my purse away." She peered up at him, genuine emotion shining in her blue eyes. "It was a Fendi."

He blinked in disbelief. "Well, it might have just saved your life. If you back away from a bear and it keeps coming, you're supposed to throw a brightly colored object to distract its attention. And looks like it works."

When she didn't answer, he could tell she was still mourning the purse—and for some reason, he decided to take mercy on her.

"Don't worry, Abby—we can get it back."

And with that, he started to push to his feet, ready to walk down off the trail and retrieve her little red life-saving handbag. So he was pretty damn surprised when her fingers closed back around his wrist, not so tight this time. Just warm. And kind of urgent.

He looked down at her, met her gaze, and saw true concern there.

"Are you sure he's gone? Sure it's safe for you to go down there?"

Hell, why was his groin tightening? Just from looking into her eyes? He tried to play it off light. "Relax—if he comes back and makes breakfast of me, you can make a run for it."

But she didn't appear even remotely amused. "Shut up—that's not funny."

"Aw, come on—I'm surprised you're not teaming up with the bear. After all, get rid of me and you've got yourself a canoe livery."

Her expression still didn't change. "That's not what I want," she said earnestly. "I mean, it *is*. But . . . I don't want anything to happen to you."

Her eyes remained glassy with fear and emotion—and Rob's dick started to stiffen. Why didn't she hate him by now? Why did she suddenly seem so sweet, so honestly concerned for his safety? How was it possible that a girl who placed so much importance on purses and boots could also make his heart feel like it was stretching in his chest?

Yet then he pulled his hand away. "No worries, Abby," he said matter-of-factly, "I'll be fine." And as he stepped carefully down off the trail, he decided this was all about what had just happened—a life-and-death situation. His heart still beat like mad and she was probably still recovering from the stark fear, too.

He located the purse, nestled on a bed of bright green moss, and returned to the trail to find his companion still on the ground, her back resting against a large tree root arcing across the path. He passed the purse down to her. "Here you go."

"There's a scratch, a claw mark," she observed. She didn't seem angry, just kind of freaked out.

"Consider it a war wound."

She nodded, still studying the bag, her voice still sounding distant. "This will make quite the conversation piece when I go home to Chicago."

"Are you okay?" he asked.

She nodded—but didn't look okay.

So he reached out a hand to help her up.

She peered at it, then held out her own, taking it. Warm, small. *Shit.*

All this damn hand-holding with her on the trail today—it was the first real, human touch he'd felt in a long while and it sent waves of heat echoing through his body.

He pulled, ready to tug her to her feet—but halfway up, her boots slipped out from under her and she managed to take them both down again. This time he landed half on top of her, so he quickly rolled to his side on the ground.

"Sorry," she said, looking up at him.

Aw, hell. Her eyes were so close to his now. Her mouth, too. " 'S okay," he mumbled, but couldn't seem to look away from her face. Her cheeks shone pink—from cold or fear, he couldn't say. Her lips were only a few shades darker, and looked so soft that he wanted to run his fingertips over the full, lower one.

"Listen," she said softly, so near that he could feel her cool breath, "thank you."

He tilted his head, again tried for a smirk that didn't quite get there. "Again? I thought you weren't gonna make a habit of that."

Her eyes had dropped to *his* mouth, too, lingering there for a moment and making him harder. "I wouldn't have come on this hike if you hadn't agreed to bring me. And what we just experienced," she said, her voice so gentle it was barely audible, "was . . . amazing. Wasn't it?" she added, as if maybe she needed reassurance that she wasn't alone in that.

And he couldn't deny it now that she'd put it out there. "Yeah," he said quietly, "it was."

"I mean, it scared me—but to see what we just saw, in the wild, to make eye contact with such a big, beautiful animal . . ." She stopped, shook her head. "I'm blown away."

He only nodded. And got even harder. He was blown away, as well—but by more than just the bear encounter. There *was* more to Lindsey Brooks than he'd thought.

Their faces remained close and he wanted to kiss her so bad he could barely breathe. It had been so long, and her lips would feel so pliable and warm beneath his. She wasn't engaged. And she looked . . . well, the expression in her eyes made him think she wouldn't push him away. He hovered now, so tempted he was starting to sweat despite the morning chill. Or—maybe it was just a leftover reaction from the scare. *Yeah, you keep telling yourself that, buddy.*

His gaze drifted to her mouth again—ready, waiting for him.

But hell. He couldn't. He just fucking couldn't. It was like a diet, or smoking. One slip-up and he'd only want more.

And since he hadn't responded to her in a while, had just lain there staring at her—she started looking unexpectedly . . . nervous, and then she began to babble. "I mean, wow—did you know bears were so huge? I had no idea. And did you see how big his feet were? I mean, just his feet? They must have been about a men's size twenty or something, don't you think? Not that a bear is going to wear a man's shoe, of course, but you know what I mean."

Rob sighed and ran a hand back through his hair. "Are you done?" he asked when she finally shut up.

"I suppose." She swallowed visibly.

He guessed so much silence and nearness had made her uncomfortable, but it was the first time he'd seen Millie's niece act that way—and it pretty much killed the moment.

Which was good.

So he pushed abruptly to his feet, hoping he hadn't appeared rushed about it but knowing it was definitely time to go. "Come on, Abby," he said. Only he didn't reach down a hand to help her this time. He might end up on top of her again and he was in no state of mind to risk that.

Lindsey planted her hand on the root next to her and managed to get up without falling. Dear God. She'd thought he was going to kiss her. And she'd wanted him to—bad. Nothing to get your mind off a humongous, ferocious bear like a little gut-wrenching passion. Apparently, she was able to process lust again, sore arches or not. Heart-rattling fear or not.

But something had held Rob back—he'd just stared at her so intensely that she'd suddenly started talking about crazy things like a bear's shoe size, for God's sake. And now he walked on ahead of her, clearly ready to finish this hike.

"Hey, wait up," she called. "Safety in numbers. There are bears out here, you know."

Within mere moments, Lindsey's feet were at it again—more than aching now; instead, sharp darts of pain shot up her calves. And what had felt dangerously like a tender moment with Rob soon seemed as if it had never even happened, considering that she was practically having to race down the hill to keep up with him. And that it was an effort not to yelp with each and every step.

"What's slowing you down back there?" he turned to ask at one point.

"I'm not used to hiking."

He only arched one accusing eyebrow as he dropped his gaze to her feet.

But damn it, she was not going to admit she'd made a bad choice in footwear this morning—even if it killed her, and she was starting to think it might.

She stayed shaken as she trudged after him—shaken from nearly being eaten by a bear and equally as shaken from nearly being kissed by Rob Colter. His quick about face—or hop to his feet, as it were—left her to conclude he really *must* think she was a bad person for what she'd done to Aunt Millie.

But maybe she could change his mind. Not just because she wanted him to kiss her, though, but because what she'd told him on the way up the trail was true—she honestly wanted him to like her. Maybe because she felt so judged and scrutinized by the whole world right now. Or maybe because she was beginning to realize that, for some reason, Aunt Millie had held Rob in high regard. Whatever the reason, she yearned for his respect. It felt like the closest she could come to earning Aunt Millie's.

By the time they arrived back at the trailhead and exited the woods onto the lakeside road, Lindsey was pretty sure her feet would never recover. And even back on flat ground, she had serious doubts about making it the rest of the way. It felt like there was fire in her boots. And she was lagging behind.

Finally, Rob stopped and turned around, crossing his arms. "What's the problem, Abby?"

"No problem," she claimed, trying not to cringe. "Just . . . enjoying the scenery. Are we in a hurry or something?"

"Uh, yeah, actually. I have work to do today."

"Oh. Well, sorry. Tell you what, though. You go on ahead. I can get back okay from here—just follow the road into town, right?"

"Right," he said—but he didn't go anywhere. He just stood there looking all brusque and woodsy in his flannel shirt and puffy vest like he could be the next Brawny Man, waiting for her to catch up. Which made walking even harder, because now she had to keep from scrunching her face in pain, an act that had somehow made each step a little more bearable—up to now.

"Well?" she said. "Go on. Go. I'm fine. Thanks for the hike and see ya later." She made a shooing motion with her hand.

But instead, the big hot hunk of man just stood there, watching her, and finally said, "No. I'll wait."

"Why?"

"Don't want you to become bear food."

"Frankly, that surprises me."

He shrugged, straight-faced, but to her surprise, she saw a slight twinkle in his eye. "Besides, it's fun to watch you pretend your feet aren't killing you."

She flinched at hearing the truth and held her head a little higher, prepared to deny it. But instead she heard herself say, "It's not so bad." Which was really just as big a lie.

"You're dying," he accused.

And all her resolve went right out the window as sheer physical and emotional exhaustion officially got the best of her. "Okay, fine, so I can barely stand to put one foot in front of the other at this point—what of it?"

And—finally—Rob Colter smiled. "Nothing of it—I just wanted you to be honest about it and stop the charade."

Talk about stopping the charade, buddy—you wanted to kiss me so bad you could taste it. And then you had the nerve to act like it didn't happen. So what about that, *huh?*

She didn't say that, though. Too much pain. What she *did* do was stop walking, coming to a dead halt on the edge of the asphalt. Because there was no other choice. She simply could not . . . go . . . any . . . farther. "So it's stopped," she said, "and so am I."

Rob just looked at her for a minute, and she tried to figure out what to do. It was too cold to shed her boots—she only wore thin socks underneath. But maybe it was her only choice. And just as she was about to bend down, raise one leg of her jeans, and start unzipping—a miracle occurred.

Rob walked back to where she stood, turned around to face away from her, and stooped down. "Climb on," he said.

She was glad he couldn't see the astonishment surely written all over her face. "Piggyback?"

"You have a better idea?" he asked over his shoulder.

She smiled down at him and then placed her hands on his shoulders, ready to attempt the awkward task of spreading her legs across his back, and not quite able to believe her morning hike had resulted in getting closer to Rob Colter in so many different ways. She wasn't exactly climbing back on the sex horse yet, but she was climbing onto Rob, which was better than nothing. And a step in the right direction—both the sex horse direction and the getting-Rob-to-sell-her-the-livery direction.

Rob considered carrying the woman on his back all the way to the Grizzly Inn, just to get her out of his hair, but decided that would be letting her off too easy. So when they reached the walkway that led up to the log house, he turned right.

"Oh, we're stopping here?" she said over his left shoulder. Her arms looped across his chest and her breasts pressed into his back, even through her coat. Another good reason to end the piggyback ride, he decided. She was too warm, too curvy, too . . . everything, given the unwitting physical attraction he'd somehow developed for her. Given that she'd even started seeming a little bit likable over the course of their hike and that it had been all he could do not to kiss her when they'd been lying on the ground together. Yep, it was high time to end this physical connection.

"You're heavy," he lied, and a moment later deposited her into the porch swing.

"Ow," she said, hitting the swing with a *plop*.

"Quit complaining," he groused softly, turning to face her. "You're lucky I was nice enough to carry you."

Only maybe facing her wasn't a great idea. He'd managed to spend much of their walk not looking at her, and now he was reminded exactly why he'd wanted to kiss her. Like it or not, she was pretty. And sexy. Her jeans showed off long, slender legs that seemed to stretch a mile. And though her fitted coat only hinted at what was underneath, he could still almost feel the plumpness of her breasts pressing against him a minute earlier, along with the way her thighs had stretched across his hips to hug him from behind. He'd held on to those thighs while they walked—it had been impossible not to—and despite exhaustion from the hike combined with carrying his hiking partner for the last quarter mile, he was back to being hard again.

That's when he realized he was studying her body, pretty damn obviously, and jerked his gaze upward to her eyes.

Hell. The soft sultriness there told him she'd noticed. So he was thankful when she let her expression shift to something more bright and cheerful to ask, "So, what's next?"

She'd said it like they'd agreed to spend the day together or something, which he definitely hadn't done. She was lucky she'd gotten the hike. "What's next is you leave and I go to work."

"Carla at the Lazy Elk told me you do construction. What are you building?"

Grudgingly, Rob found himself telling her about his plans for the day, working at Steve Fisher's. She had a way of pretty much forcing a guy to talk whether or not he wanted to.

"Although," she said when he was done, "when I asked what was next, I didn't really mean *right now*. I meant what can we do next to help me walk in Aunt Millie's shoes some more?"

Rob could only sigh. "You're not serious?"

She blinked, looking dumbfounded by his reaction. "Completely."

He lowered his chin and crossed his arms and got completely honest with her. "You wanted to hike, so we hiked. I thought I'd be off the hook now."

But Abby appeared completely unfazed by his bluntness. "The hike was great," she said. "But there has to be more. Aunt Millie had a whole life here—a life you seem to have . . . sort of taken over in a way. So if I want to keep learning more about her—and I do—you're my go-to guy."

"Lucky me," he said dryly. And he knew he could refuse her, just like he'd refused her ridiculous offer to buy the canoe livery. But what she'd said was true: he *had* taken over

Millie's life in a way. She'd entrusted it to him. And just like Abby had also pointed out, Millie would want him to do what Abby was asking of him. To turn her down flat would feel like dishonoring Millie's memory. And he could be a pretty cold guy, but dishonoring Millie in any way—well, that was something he'd never do.

"So then," Abby said, crossing one leg over the other and loosely threading her fingers together over her knee, "what's next on our agenda?"

Rob thought through the options at hand and came up with what actually seemed like a good idea. Since maybe it would make Abby decide she'd had enough of Millie's shoes. "You can help me open the boathouse for the season. Which means work, hard labor. Think you can handle that?"

To his surprise, a pretty smile spread across her face. "Absolutely. I'm ready for anything."

Anything, huh? Despite himself, her eager words tightened his hard-on. He ignored that—as much as a guy could ignore a raging erection—and tried to refocus on the matter at hand. Sure, she sounded gung ho right now, but they'd see how she felt after he put her to some serious work. "Come to the livery tomorrow after lunch—around one," he instructed. "And wear gym shoes this time—if you even own any."

To his surprise, she finally looked a little sheepish about her shoe situation. "I do, but I didn't pack them."

Rob just blinked in disbelief. "You came to Montana to buy a canoe business, but you didn't bring any practical shoes."

Abby's brow knit. "I fail to see the correlation. I was just going to *buy* the canoe business, not actually *work* at it."

He simply shook his head, at a loss, then informed her, "Stop in at the general store—not far past the Moose Mart. They have a little bit of everything, so I'm sure they'll have some shoes for you."

She looked perplexed and he knew that Miss Fashion Plate was cringing inside at the idea of buying no-name shoes from a general store, but to her credit, she kept quiet—except to glance at her pointy boots and say, "A shame it's so far away."

"Don't worry," he said, deciding to take pity on her one last time today. "Wait here."

Heading inside the house, he gave King a scratch behind the ear, then returned a minute later with a pair of old red Converse basketball shoes from the back of his closet, which he dropped on the porch next to her feet. "You can wear these."

"Thanks," she said softly, but in his opinion, she didn't look very thankful. Horrified was more like it.

Still, she quietly unzipped her boots and slid her feet out of them as he watched. She wore thin nylon socks underneath that made him think, *No wonder her feet hurt so damn bad.* And also made him think she had *cute* little feet, especially when she stopped for a minute to massage each one. He kind of had the urge to take over, to sit down beside her in the swing and shift her feet onto his thigh and mold them between his fingers. And—

Stop this. You're acting like a horny sixteen-year-old kid.

So he stopped watching, instead shifting his gaze out onto the lake, knowing it was a much safer place for his eyes.

A minute later, he sensed her standing up beside him. "How do I look?" she asked.

Swinging his gaze in her direction, he let it move down her body—until he reached the big red shoes protruding from beneath her stylish jeans. "Ridiculous," he said.

"That's how I *feel,* too," she admitted. "Like I'm wearing clown shoes or something."

"See you tomorrow, Abby. And don't forget to bring my shoes back."

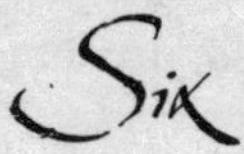

The Moose Falls General Store looked like a calm, quiet establishment on the outside—a wooden storefront painted brown, pots of yellow pansies hanging between the awning posts, and three old guys drinking old-fashioned bottles of Coca-Cola near the front stoop. But inside—dear God!—it looked like a Wal-Mart super center had exploded, and into a much smaller space than a Wal-Mart super center. Everywhere Lindsey looked, she saw something new: canned goods mingled with sleeping bags, fishing rods with cleaning products, and small TVs were stacked to the ceiling—alongside mattresses and baby beds. Rob had been right—the general store had a little bit of everything, or in some cases, a *lot* of everything.

"Ya look perplexed, darlin'. What can I help ya find?"

She turned to see a small, elderly man stooped over a cane who looked like he might be a nursing home escapee and probably needed his meds. He should have retired twenty years ago at least.

"Um, I was wondering if you have any ladies' tennis or athletic shoes."

"Tennis shoes? Course we do. Follow me," he said, then took off like a rocket, even with the cane. He started down an aisle housing cereal and lawn chairs, and Lindsey could barely keep up.

Finally, the old guy took a wild right turn, veering off into an entirely new room of the store, making her realize it was bigger than it looked from outside. They passed ladies' clothes and some sporting goods just before he announced, "Here ya go. We got mostly Keds. Will Keds work for ya? 'Cause if you need another kind, we can order 'em in."

"Um . . ." The truth was, she owned some gym shoes but hadn't used them in so long that she wasn't exactly sure about it. "Let me give the Keds a try."

"Sure thing. Name's Bernard if ya need help or want me to order in somethin' fancier. I'll be up front stockin' shelves."

With that, Bernard departed, going just as fast as he'd come, and Lindsey watched in awe. Stocking shelves, huh? They didn't make old people like this in Chicago.

The shoe selection was slim at best, but she chose a simple pair of white leather Keds. It was on the way back past the women's clothing that she caught sight of some fairly cute cotton skorts and given that she hadn't exactly brought a lot of "work clothes," they caught her eye. After all, the shorts underneath made them practical, but with a skirt on top, they were way cuter and more *her.*

Just then, she saw Bernard streak past the end of an aisle and called his name.

A moment later, he was back. "Find ya some shoes, darlin'?"

Lindsey smiled and nodded, then held up the skorts she'd selected. "Don't suppose you have any dressing rooms?"

Bernard looked at her like she was crazy. "Course we got dressin' rooms. Follow me." And as she raced along behind him, he tossed over his shoulder, "I reckon you must be Millie's great-niece."

At first it took her aback, but then she remembered once more what a small town this was, and that since it wasn't quite yet tourist season, a stranger was surely fodder for talk. "That's me. Lindsey Brooks. Nice to meet you."

"Eleanor told me you're stayin' at her place. Boy, we sure do miss our Millie."

"Did she shop here a lot?"

Bernard stopped outside a thin, paint-worn door and knocked. No one knocked back, so he opened it for Lindsey, then said with great pride, "You can't live in Moose Falls and not shop here. Moose Mart's good for quick stops, but my general store is the lifeblood of this community. So yes, ma'am, Millie shopped here all the time."

Ten minutes later, Lindsey had decided to get the skorts in white, black, and khaki, and as she checked out at the register up front, Bernard said, "Take a gander at the sign over the door on your way out. Millie stenciled and painted that herself a few years back. Good with a stencil, that woman. And she was right easy on the eyes, too, if ya know what I mean." He gave a wink that made Lindsey laugh as she exited back out into the sun.

Sure enough, the sign fronting the Moose Falls General Store looked crisp and bright with yellow lettering shadowed by dark red, and the thought of Aunt Millie working on it gave her another reason to feel happy.

She really *was* walking in Aunt Millie's shoes, feeling her great-aunt's presence around her more with each passing hour. But she knew she'd be lying to herself if she didn't also admit that her general giddiness had to do with knowing she would see Rob again tomorrow.

Of course, part of her wasn't exactly sure why that should make her giddy. He'd hardly turned into Mr. Sunshine or anything and still regarded her presence grudgingly at best. But that piggyback ride had been *nice*—and not just because it saved her aching feet. She'd gotten to feel that big, broad, warm, muscular back beneath her body, gotten to wrap her arms around his shoulders from behind. There had been something unerringly intimate about spreading her legs across his lower back, too. She'd felt it at her very center, tingling madly.

Of course, she'd then had to walk away from him in his big clown shoes. And she'd had to walk *slowly*, too, to keep from tripping and going down face first. But since she was already having to work to repair his image of her, she was trying not to feel too hideously embarrassed. Tomorrow she would show him she was tougher than he thought.

After a quick lunch at the Lakeside Café, where she got to tell Mary Beth and Eleanor, along with a nice older woman named Mrs. Bixby, all about the bear encounter—including showing off her bear-clawed purse—Lindsey retreated back to her room to rest up from what had, so far, been a pretty wild day.

She quickly realized, however, that she was too keyed up to rest. So she called her mother and told her about the hike and the bear and admitted that it was going to require some finesse to get Rob Colter to sell her the livery. Then she found herself back at her desk, opening up the same window as before, letting the scent of the hyacinths bathe the room in fragrance as she sat down at her laptop.

Which inevitably led back to her blog.

She found still a few more new, encouraging comments—more of her readers begging her to come back. Regulars WilliamTell1 and ChrisMarie both told her Garrett was a fool to have lost her, and somehow that was the final thing she needed . . . to give her the courage to compose a new post.

Dear Lovers,

Forgive me for being away so long, but sometimes life can throw you a curveball, and I'll be honest—when life threw one at me, I didn't duck fast enough. Long story short, in case you don't know, my engagement has come to an abrupt end. That's right, no fabulous dyeable shoes, no miniature tulip bouquet, no silk chocolate wedding cake.

She stopped then, and realized—she needed to step out of her usual, fun-loving Love Letters persona here and be *real*, deep-down real; it was the only way.

But please don't think I'm making light of the loss—certainly a broken engagement is about much more than shoes and cake. I have been put in the unfortunate position of discovering that the man I wanted to marry didn't really love me, which both broke my heart and made me feel like . . . well, a bit of a sham when it comes to giving advice. That's why I haven't been blogging lately and why you're seeing "reruns" of old columns in your local newspaper.

But yesterday I finally gathered the courage to get back online, and color me overwhelmed by all your stunning support. Your understanding is amazing and has warmed my heart more than I can say. So I'm dipping my toes back into the bloggy waters here, trying it back on for size. I'm not sure any of you want to take advice on your love life from me any longer, but just knowing I have so many friends out there is enough for now.

As for how I'm recovering from the curveball, well, I'm turning to family for support, and I'm remembering what's important in life—which, for me, so far, has something to do with where you come from, and taking a step back toward a simpler existence. You will all be surprised to hear that I'm cur-

rently in a small town in Montana and that this morning I actually went on a hike! That's right, Lindsey Brooks—in the wild!

I even met a big grizzly bear on the trail, but my hiking companion, being more educated about such matters than I, saved the day by tossing my favorite Fendi bag off the trail to divert said bear's attention. The bag now has a "scar" to show for its role in saving the day—our bear actually left a claw mark in it! So this proves that a simpler life can still hold plenty of excitement, right?

Tomorrow, I learn about the joys of canoeing, and I have even bought tennis shoes (that's right, kids, Lindsey Brooks now owns a pair of Keds) for the occasion. I'll let you know how it goes and am heartened by the fact that bears can't walk on water.

Oh, and Still Single in Savannah, if you read this, please let me know how things are going. I've been thinking about you, wondering how your relationship is faring, and hoping I didn't steer you wrong.

Until tomorrow, lovers, thank you again for understanding that nobody's perfect and that while love is a many-splendored thing, it can, as Pat Benatar once taught us, also be a battlefield. I'm nursing my wounds right now, but please know that I still believe wholeheartedly in love. It's out there somewhere, just waiting for all of us to find it.

The truth? That last part was a stretch—her breakup with Garrett was far too fresh for her to know how she really felt about love anymore, but for the sake of her readers, she'd felt she must end on such a note. Whether or not she honestly believed in the romance of "true love" anymore, she knew her readers *needed* her to believe, and so, for them, she would.

Taking a deep breath, Lindsey hit the Submit button and watched the post go live on her screen. For better or worse, the Love Letters blog was back in action.

The sun was out, shining bright, and according to the old-fashioned thermometer bolted to the outer wall of the boathouse, the temperature had climbed into the mid-sixties. Rob shed his flannel shirt, leaving the faded blue tee he wore underneath, but before he started working, he took a minute to stand on the edge of the dock and peer out over the placid waters of the lake. Part of him looked forward to summer weekends when the lake would be dotted with colorful canoes, people coming and going—he knew it would remind him of Millie and give him the pride of knowing he was keeping things running the way she'd wanted. But mostly, he liked the lake as it was right now—quiet, serene, and probably not much different than it had been a hundred years ago, or five hundred, for that matter.

He didn't know how long all the surrounding ponderosa pines had been here, but something about the forest always struck him as primeval, powerful in its vastness. He'd never felt so much *life* as he did when he was wending his way up one of Millie's trails, the trees on all sides of him. Not life like people or animals, but a life so peaceful and silent and thriving that he'd known soon after arriving here that it was the best place he'd ever find to live the kind of quiet existence he wanted.

He'd gotten a bid to Stanley Bobbins yesterday, and since then had put in an ample amount of work on Steve Fisher's room addition, so he didn't mind taking the rest of this Friday afternoon to start getting the boathouse ready. Mostly it would require cleaning, and checking to make sure the dock and all the canoes were still sturdy and safe.

Of course, he'd have help. Or a hindrance—that part remained to be seen.

But his bigger question was—how had this happened? How had this girl worked her way into his life? When he'd imagined spring coming, imagined preparing the canoe rental for business, he sure as hell hadn't imagined having a prissy woman who never wore sensible shoes as a "helper." A prissy woman who never wore sensible shoes and who made him stupidly horny on top of it.

Well, after today, that was it—no more Abby. She was too damn tempting. And sometimes annoying.

He sighed, crossing his arms. Okay, in truth, maybe she wasn't as bad as he'd first thought, but still . . . he couldn't give in to lust, and that would be a lot easier if he didn't have a sexy, pretty woman in his face.

Dropping his gaze to the canoe nearest him, turned bottom up on the dock, he bent to examine a scratch in the fiberglass hull. The canoes had been stacked inside the boathouse for the winter—he'd just hauled them out last week—but he still wanted to test their flotation to make sure none had sustained any damage or wear and tear he didn't know about. First, though, he needed to scrub them all down, inside and out, and that's where Abby came in.

He retreated into the boathouse to the closet where Millie had kept cleaning supplies and grabbed a couple of five-gallon buckets, along with sponges and a bottle of dishwashing liquid. And he'd just exited back out into the sun . . . when he spotted Abby headed his way.

Damn. She had on some kind of short skirt that gave him a perfect view of those long-as-sin legs, and a snug little T-shirt that hugged her breasts and instantly tightened his groin. And on her feet? A cute, casual pair of tennis shoes that, for some reason, made her look all the more adorable.

She'd just crossed the road from the Grizzly Inn and now rounded the edge of the lake, headed toward the dock. She lifted her hand in a wave and flashed a smile, and Rob numbly lifted his hand in return. This working-together thing was a very bad idea and he suddenly couldn't believe he'd come up with it himself.

He kept his eyes on her face as she approached, taking care not to let them stray south. Except *her* eyes were kind of sparkling in the sunlight and he could see her face better than ever before because she'd pulled her long brown hair back in a ponytail. His chest tightened just watching her walk toward him and he wondered if she could see his reaction on his face.

"Did you bring my shoes?" he asked when she reached the dock.

She held out a plastic sack bearing the general store's logo. "Sure did. Why? Does clown school start today?"

He almost smiled at that. *Almost.* But instead he just took the bag and replied, "They only look like clown shoes on *you*. On *me*, they're perfectly normal."

She shrugged. "If you consider red shoes on a guy normal."

This time he *did* smile, despite himself. "After some of the things I've seen *you* wearing, I don't think you have much room to talk."

She planted her hands on her hips. "I'll have you know that in Chicago I'm the height of fashion. Speaking of which"—she glanced down at herself—"is this okay for what we're doing?"

Rob's chest went hollow—since, of course, his eyes followed hers. Down over her tight little tee and her tiny skirt. "The shoes are good," he began. "But, um, the skirt might be a little short. Not that I mind a short skirt," he added, then wanted to slap himself. He did *not* flirt with Abby. He didn't flirt with *anyone*. In fact, he was surprised to find he even knew *how* to flirt anymore.

"No worries," she assured him. Then she shocked the hell out of him by turning around and flipping up the back of her skirt—to reveal shorts underneath. But seeing the shorts didn't allay his worries—it mainly just gave him yet *another* freaking hard-on, for God's sake. Because for a split second he'd thought she was going to flash him, and even when that had turned out not to be the case, those shorts still hugged her ass way too nicely and made him think about her body way too much.

"See?" she went on. "Shorts underneath. Am I practical or what?"

"Or what," he replied—but when she turned back toward him, playfully rolling her eyes, he accidentally let another grin sneak out, damn it.

So he was relieved when she seemed more interested in the livery than in him. She looked around her at the place. "So this is the famous boathouse," she said, sounding happy but also a bit wistful.

He decided not to acknowledge the wistfulness—they'd been over that before; his job now was to let her feel a little more connected to Millie, then work her to death so she'd decide she'd had enough. "Come on inside," he told her and led the way through the old wooden door he'd put a fresh coat of red paint on last fall at Millie's request.

Inside, the décor was sparse—a desk and some built-in cabinetry, a stool near the window where customers paid. Opening another door, they entered a covered dock area housing a motorized fishing boat hoisted above the single bay and an open storage space that currently held only a couple of canoes in need of repair. "Wow," she said, peering up at the old exposed wooden beams. "Rustic. Cool."

He supposed they didn't have places like this in Chicago and found himself pointing out a bird's nest in one corner. "See that? We had a little house wren and her babies in here last summer. Millie was a nervous wreck, afraid vibrations were going to knock the nest free."

Abby looked up at him. "But all the birds survived?"

He nodded, and thought, *Since when do I start conversations and volunteer information with this person I'm trying to get rid of?* Then worked really hard to take his eyes off her, because she was so easy to look at, especially in the shadowy lighting of the boathouse's interior.

"Was that Millie's?" She pointed to the small motorboat.

"No," Rob answered. "It belongs to the local authorities, for cases of emergency on the lake. Otherwise, no motorized boats are allowed."

She tipped her head back in understanding, then asked, "Are there lots of those? Emergencies?"

He shook his head. "Millie told me a teenager fell out of a canoe about fifteen years ago and had to be rescued, but the police boat is mostly a precaution."

Next, Abby turned to the old wooden desk pushed against the building's outer wall. "So this is where Millie ran the operation, huh?"

He nodded. And for some damn reason couldn't stop himself from offering still more information as he pointed to a plastic brochure container on one corner of the desk that said *Take One*. "Those are the trail maps I told you about."

She plucked one out and opened it up, studying the copy of Millie's ink drawing and the typed guide below. Then her eyes dropped back to the desk and caught on something—until she reached forward to pick up one of two snapshots resting there. In them, Rob and Millie stood on the dock, taking a break from work—one was a full-body shot, the other closer up, and Abby had chosen the close-up.

"Forgot we left those down here last year," he murmured. He'd meant to take them to the house, put them someplace where they wouldn't get lost. But maybe this was a good enough spot for them now that he thought about it, since he'd be spending a lot of time here this summer.

"I hadn't seen her in a long time, even in pictures," Abby said, her voice soft, kind of sad, as she touched the tip of one slender finger to Millie's face. In the photo Millie wore her blue fishing hat, along with a pair of khakis and a summery blouse. "I'd . . . forgotten how old she was."

"Only seventy-three," Rob reminded her. "But she had an old soul. Eleanor took these one day last summer with her new digital camera and made prints for us. Well," he added, correcting himself, "for Millie. But they're mine now."

The air between them grew silent and Rob felt too sentimental—the last thing he needed was to share emotions like that with Abby. So he gently took the picture back out of her hand, careful not to let their fingers touch, and returned it to the desk, propping it against the wall. "Time to get to work," he announced.

"Aye aye, Skipper," she said, standing up straighter and saluting him.

He rolled his eyes and walked outside, muttering, "Come on, Gilligan," over his shoulder.

From there, Rob educated his helper on how to properly wash a canoe, then used the outdoor faucet to fill the buckets he'd brought out earlier. He set Abby to scrubbing down the outer hulls, and when she was done with each, he flipped it over and scoured the inside.

It wasn't the most grueling work a person could do, but it wasn't easy, either, especially considering the number of canoes—around twenty-five. He kept waiting for her to complain, but just like when they'd hiked together yesterday, she never did. And to his surprise, she was better at cleaning canoes than at hiking. He mostly focused on his own work, but every now and then glanced over to watch her. Little wisps of hair snuck from her ponytail to fall in loose curls around her face, but she just blew them out of her eyes or pushed them behind her ears. Water sometimes splashed onto her little skirty shorts and he noticed some dirt smudges on one shapely calf, but still she never grumbled or whined or looked unhappy—even if she did appear a little tired from time to time.

Damn. She was actually impressing him a little. He didn't like admitting that to himself, but it was true.

"Wow, it's a beautiful day," she offered up without warning as she knelt on the dock dipping her yellow sponge back into the bucket, then squeezing it out. "The mornings could be warmer, and so could the nights—but the afternoons here are perfect."

"Don't worry—the mornings and nights'll get warmer soon." Of course, as quickly as the words left him, he realized that it sounded like he thought she'd be around for that. Which he hoped wasn't true. "But I guess you'll head back to Chicago any day now."

She stopped working and looked up, her expression pleasant but inquisitive. "Is there some reason you're trying to get rid of me, Rob Colter?"

Yes, because I want to rip your clothes off more every time I see you. A reckless part of him suddenly wanted to just say that, just put it out there, see how she'd respond.

But he was stronger than that. He could resist her. He'd done well enough the last year, yet this was his first real test at the celibacy thing, so he had to pass it.

He tried for a small smile. "I'm just not . . . the most social guy. I like being alone."

"So I've heard."

He blinked, caught off guard. "You've heard?"

"When I first got to town and was asking who owned this place."

He just nodded. He hadn't quite realized he'd earned a reputation for being a hermit, but he didn't mind. He didn't necessarily like people talking about him, but he supposed in a place like Moose Falls it was inevitable.

"So—sorry I'm cramping your style," she added, but she was still smiling and he didn't get the idea she was really very sorry. And hell, maybe—at this moment—he wasn't really very sorry, either, if he was honest with himself. Shit.

"Anyway," she went on, sloshing soapy water on the back of a bright yellow canoe, "I haven't done work like this since I was a kid."

"What kind of work did you do *then*?" he heard himself ask.

"Oh, you know, just washing cars in the driveway, that sort of thing." She looked upward toward the sun. "But I'm remembering that work like this isn't so bad if you've got gorgeous weather to do it in. Right?"

And again, despite himself, he smiled, and even replied, "Right." She couldn't know how much he echoed that sentiment. Rob pretty much lived and breathed to be outside.

It hadn't been that way growing up—he'd spent a lot of time outside *then* because it hadn't been pleasant to be *inside*, or at home, period. But now it was different. A person didn't know how much he missed the outdoors, fresh air, sunshine, until he didn't have it—and now he *craved* it. Even in winter, he went out a lot. Just to feel the cold air on his face. Just to see the sky. And despite himself, he liked Abby a little better somehow just knowing she could appreciate a pretty day.

Rob looked back to his work, toiling over a stubborn spot in the bow of a green canoe and wishing he'd brought a CD player to drown out all this talk and fill the quiet space that sounded *so* quiet when the talk ended. Usually, he didn't mind quiet—silence was another thing he'd learned to appreciate because it had been so absent for much of his life. But for the first time in a long while, it felt a little awkward to him—or maybe it just meant he missed her voice, actually *liked* talking to her.

Well, if that's the problem, buddy, you'd better snap out of it.

Just then, a scraping noise made him look up to see that Abby had taken it upon herself to turn over the canoe she'd just finished—a job he'd handled up to this point. It was too heavy for her and she'd lost control and was about to drop the boat in the water, face down.

He pushed to his feet and rushed to help her, stepping up behind her to grab the end of the canoe still teetering in her grasp. The move brought them close, close enough for him to feel her body against his—just a brush of his jeans against her ass and then his arm against hers—but the heat it sent skittering through him made it difficult to concentrate on the canoe.

They stood frozen in place for a few seconds, Rob thinking of nothing but the way his chest was contracting, his body wanting. It sizzled through him in a slow burn. Aw, hell.

Until—finally—he managed to haul the boat back onto the dock and disentangle himself from Abby. Thank God.

"Heavier than I thought," she said softly then.

And for a split second, he wondered if she was talking about the canoe or something more—like the vibes passing between them, since he was pretty sure he wasn't the only one feeling them. And that made them all the more dangerous.

And when their eyes met again, their faces still a little too close for comfort, and when his gaze dropped to her lips, which looked *too* damn kissable—she broke into another babbling streak, just like yesterday on the trail. "I mean, who would have thought a canoe would be that heavy? They float, after all. But then again, so do ships, right? How the heck does *that* work? I mean, how do they make something that big *float*, for heaven's sake? Boggles the mind, doesn't it?"

Rob just sighed. "Finished?" he asked after she quieted.

"Pretty much." But she still sounded nervous. "Sorry. About almost dropping the canoe." Her eyes traveled downward to it.

"No worries," he said, keeping his eyes on the boat, too. "Just let me do the flipping from now on."

"How did Millie do it?" she asked, and he could tell the question had just hit her. "How did she handle the canoes all those years before you came along to help her?"

The fact that she started babbling every time he had the urge to kiss her definitely helped keep him from it, yet it also seemed to silently highlight the moment in an awkward way, too. But since Millie always seemed the safest topic to pass between them, Rob cautiously let his eyes rise to meet hers again. "She hired high school kids to help her the last ten years or so, but before that, she did it on her own. She was a strong woman—she stayed physically fit."

"All that hiking," Abby said.

He nodded. "And she took care of her yard and even did all the maintenance on this place. If a board needed to be replaced on the dock, she did it herself."

"You know so much about her," Abby said, that wistful quality coming back into her voice.

Which made him realize he was talking too much again. So now he only shrugged.

"You really got close to her, didn't you?" Abby asked then, head tilted inquisitively, and Rob felt the question in his gut, because it was true. True in a way that had changed him and given him back at least a *little* bit of faith in life, and the world.

"Yeah," he said, more quietly than intended. "We were close."

"How did that happen? I mean, she spent all these years in this town with people who clearly loved and respected her. So why, at the end of her life, were you the person she was closest to, even though you'd only known her a short time?"

Rob hardly knew how to explain since he barely understood it himself. "Millie and I just clicked. She . . . saw something in me that most people don't, and we . . . shared a lot of stuff in those months. And when she got sick, I took care of her. I was with her when she died."

He'd gotten too serious, and the stark silence of the sunny afternoon only seemed to highlight the emotions gushing through him. He hadn't meant to tell her the part about Millie's death—but it had just come out.

Glancing up, he saw Abby swallow as her eyes went grim and a little glassy. "What was that like?" Her voice came out hollow.

"Hard," was all Rob could say, wishing like hell he hadn't brought this up.

"I . . . I'm ashamed to admit this, but I didn't even know she was sick before she died. We were only told that she passed away."

"It was cancer," he said. "But don't let it get around. Millie didn't want people to know—didn't want anyone feeling sorry for her."

Abby just blinked, looking stunned. "My God."

Now that Millie was gone, and given that Abby was family, he supposed it was okay to tell her. "She was diagnosed a few weeks after I met her. It had already spread from her liver into a lot of other places. She didn't want treatment—said she'd lived a good life and would rather keep living it that way as long as she could rather than go through chemo, and the odds were pretty bad anyway. So she lived out what was left of her life until she got sick—about a month before she died."

"And you were there with her. You took care of her." Her voice remained soft, and it somehow transported Rob back to the winter. In some ways it seemed a long time ago, but in others it was like yesterday.

He nodded. "It was the least I could do."

He watched as Abby pulled in a deep breath, then let it *whoosh* back out. Her eyes suddenly looked tired, sad. "This means she knew she was dying when she wrote to me, when she offered me this place."

He only nodded.

Then saw her begin to look unsteady—until she murmured, "I need to sit down," and plopped back onto one of the upturned canoes she'd just washed, despite it not being dry yet. She let out a discouraged-sounding sigh and bent to rest her forehead in one palm.

And whereas a couple of days ago Rob would have been completely unsympathetic, now . . . well, now he cared. "Listen," he said, "it's like I told you. Things worked out the way they were supposed to. By the time she died, she knew the place had ended up in the right hands—mine. She had no doubts or regrets about that."

Abby looked up—her eyes still weak. "But I refused the last request of a dying woman. I mean, until now I thought she'd just been planning ahead for some undetermined time when she would pass away. If I'd known she was sick . . ."

Rob couldn't help asking, "What? What would you have done? Would you have taken the place?"

"Truthfully, I'm not sure." She shook her head. "But I would have done *something* differently. At least come up here for a visit. Said goodbye. Helped her in some way."

"But that's exactly what she didn't want. Pity. She wanted things to go on like normal without cancer being a part of it."

Abby bit her lip and looked so sad and pretty that he almost, *almost* stooped down in front of her, took her hand.

But instead he steeled himself against her emotions. He held his ground and returned to work, reaching for the sponge he'd dropped in his bucket a few minutes ago.

"Did she hate me?" she asked.

He allowed himself to look up only briefly. "No—and we've been over this already. She said you were young and had a busy life a world away from here. She was disappointed, and hurt, but she didn't hate you."

"I'm so jealous," she said suddenly.

"Of?" He looked back to the canoe he was currently scrubbing, focusing on some grime on one of the seats.

"How well you knew her."

At this, he only shrugged. Feeling sorry for Abby was dangerous, so he officially stopped it. "Could have if you'd wanted to."

She let out another big sigh, then asked, "Do you believe in forgiveness?" Again, the question came in the soft, gentle voice that made his stomach twist a little.

But he blocked that part out and felt an old darkness move

into him as a lone cloud drifted past overhead, covering the sun and throwing a chill into the air. "I believe people *talk* about forgiving a lot more than they actually do it."

She said nothing and he was sure his answer didn't make much sense to her in the context of the conversation, but he didn't care. He believed people *could* forgive; he just didn't believe they really did it very often. And if she was asking him if *he* could forgive *her* for hurting Millie, well . . . he didn't know the answer, and he didn't intend to dwell on it.

What he *intended* was to get the "Millie show and tell" over with as soon as possible and get this girl out of his life along with all the strange, conflicting emotions she built in him. Other than feelings for Millie, and maybe his dog, he'd done a pretty damn good job of cutting emotions out of his life, right along with relationships, and this was no time to backslide.

Without looking up, he saw from his peripheral vision that Abby was finally getting back to work, kneeling next to another canoe, sloshing soapy water across the hull. Good. And about time.

"Spend some time on that stern. A lot of grunge around the edges."

She looked up, blinked. "Stern?"

He just pointed to the end of the boat, then turned back to his work.

Twenty minutes later, Rob was on the verge of feeling at peace for the first time since his "helper" had shown up today. First there'd been the lust, then the emotional stuff about Millie's death—but now he'd shut most of that out of his brain. All was quiet but for a songbird twittering up in the pines somewhere, the sun was back out, and he was hard at work—he could feel the labor stretching the muscles in his shoulders and back, the sensations of physical exertion always making him feel alive, vital in some way.

And then Abby said, "Will you show me some of her things? Picture albums, maybe? Books? Old records?"

Rob could only sigh, and he didn't try to hide his dismay.

"I know, I know," she said. "You're all Mr. I-Vant-to-Be-Alone and I'm all please-keep-showing-me-Aunt-Millie's-life. But I've come so far and I just need more. So maybe I could come to your house tonight and you could show me some of her stuff. And from all I've heard about Millie, I bet she has *great* picture albums. So, how about it? Cut a girl a break?"

"I'm pretty sure I've cut you a few already," he muttered.

"Just one more, Rob. And then I'll leave you alone. I promise. Okay?"

Rob moved his jaw from side to side, weighing her words. One more and then she'd leave him alone. She promised.

Finally, he let out a grudging, "Fine."

Two canoes over from him, Abby looked downright bubbly. "Excellent," she said, then tilted her head. "Is it possible to get pizza around here?"

"Why?"

"I thought we could do it over pizza. My treat. For all your help."

He couldn't deny it sounded like a decent idea. Any added distraction would be welcome, and pizza qualified. "Bob's Pizza is down the road from the general store. I like pepperoni and sausage."

Abby looked perplexed. "*Bob's* Pizza?"

"Yeah. Why?"

"Well, that's just not a very original name for a pizza place."

Rob shrugged. "It is when you're the only pizza place in Moose Falls."

Dear Gina,

It's summer and I took my dog out to the park today. I try to spend time outside <u>*most*</u> *days, but today was different—the blazing hot sun and deep blue sky came with a nice breeze and for some reason it made me wonder what you're doing on a summer Saturday. Could be a million things, I guess, but I imagined you having a picnic, maybe throwing a Frisbee or flying a kite. Are you with friends? Or maybe a guy? That thought bothers me, but it's okay—I want your life to be good.*

I don't know much about having a good life—I've never had one yet and probably never will. So in that way, it's best we're apart. I know I can't give you what you need—I'm not a guy you could ever be proud of. I know you're happier without me. Or I hope like hell you are anyway. I'm not much of a praying man, but I pray for that—for you to be happy, always. I figure prayers are the only thing I can give you now.

All my love,
Rob

Seven

For the last hour, Lindsey had been sitting at a little round table at the Lakeside Café having iced tea with Carla—before picking up the pizza and heading to Rob's. She'd spent most of their get-together so far proudly telling Carla about her canoe-scrubbing venture today—which had been hard for someone not used to physical labor, but also invigorating in a way, and satisfying on a gut level, too, when she thought about Millie doing the very same work.

As soon as Carla came out of the bathroom, they planned to walk over to Moose Falls so Lindsey could see the town's namesake. Apparently, it was a short walk, and she'd learned that she'd even driven right past them before, but since they weren't visible from the road, she hadn't seen them yet.

What a day it had been already, though.

This morning, she'd started out as happy as could be, checking her blog to find all sorts of wonderful, positive comments from her readers heralding her return to the Internet. Reconnecting with her fans had lifted her spirits more than she'd even anticipated. And given that her confidence hadn't exactly been at an all-time high lately . . . well, it helped to know there were still people out there who thought she was fabulous. She still had no intention of giving relationship advice, but she'd simply enjoyed chatting with her old online buddies and responding to their comments.

Of course, after that, there'd been Rob. And canoes. But mainly Rob.

God, that man did something to her. Just seeing him hollowed out her stomach and made her feel like putty in his hands. Not that she'd been in his hands, but if she *had* been, she'd have been putty, pure and simple.

And then there'd been the news about Aunt Millie dying of cancer. Which made her guilt infinitely worse. She'd hated letting Rob see her in such a raw state of emotion, but it had been impossible to hide. The news also made her want to know Aunt Millie even *more*—such a strong woman who'd dealt with her impending death so . . . bravely, gracefully.

It was hard to imagine a guy as brusque as Rob Colter nursing Aunt Millie through a difficult passing, but the picture it put in her head . . . well, clearly there was a softer side to him if he'd been willing to help an elderly woman die with dignity.

"Ready?" Carla said, shaking Lindsey from her reverie.

Lindsey lifted her gaze to her friend, picked up her favorite beaded Prada bag, and pushed to her feet. "Yep." Then she zipped up her black coat and followed Carla outside. It wasn't yet dark, but the sun had dipped behind the pine-covered hills to the west to usher in a chilly version of dusk.

Carla led her across the road where it curved away from the lake, leading toward the Moose Mart and the general store. Although Lindsey had traveled this way by car before, it was her first time on foot, bringing her close enough to see the creek emptying into the lake. "This is pretty," she said, watching the water cascade over smooth, rounded rocks and the occasional fallen branch.

"Moose Creek," Carla informed her.

"How much farther to the falls?" It was pretty, but her feet were starting to hurt a little since she'd slipped into a pair of high-heeled black boots for the evening and she hadn't yet completely recovered from the previous day's hike.

"Not far." Carla glanced down at the boots and shook her head. "Some people never learn, though."

Lindsey had told Carla over tea about the whole Rob/shoe situation. "I can wear tennies to work in," she explained, "but not for an evening out."

Carla stopped and looked around—toward the general store on one side and the rushing creek and tree-dark woods on the other. "Do you see something here I don't? I hate to break this to you, but we don't have *evenings out* in Moose Falls."

"Well, going to Rob's is about as close as I'm going to get, and I want to look nice." Just then, the falls came into view, thankfully taking her thoughts off her aching arches—as well as the *other* parts of her that started to ache when Rob crossed her mind. "Oh, we're here."

They stepped off the path lining the edge of the road to a short stretch of planked fencing clearly intended to keep people from plummeting headlong into the creek below while they looked at Moose Falls. The falls weren't tall or wide or breathtaking or dramatic—they were more like an uneven staircase that sent the creek's flow tumbling a story or two lower than where it started. But they were as pleasant and welcoming as the town named after them.

"Do moose come to drink water here or something?" she asked Carla.

"Eleanor saw one just across the creek one morning in 1992, I'm told. Other than that, though, no sightings directly at the falls—just a story that the town's founders back around the turn of the century had seen lots of moose in the area. But Eleanor got a snapshot of *her* moose. You should ask her to see it."

Lindsey smiled and leaned forward to rest her arms on the railing. "I'll do that. And by the way, I was wondering, whatever happened to Wallace, Eleanor's ex-husband? I mean, he made the bear and mounted Millie's fish, so where is he?"

"Ran off with a waitress from Cedarville and the last Eleanor heard from him, they were living in a commune in Arizona."

Lindsey gasped. "That's awful!"

But Carla just shook her head. "Nah. He was Eleanor's third husband and he drove her crazy—they bickered all the time. She was actually glad to see him go and told me three husbands were more than enough for a woman to have in a lifetime. And speaking of Eleanor, she came in the Lazy Elk last night and ordered a cosmo."

Lindsey let her eyes go wide in delight. "Did she like it?"

Carla nodded. "A lot. She told me you recommended it. Thanks."

Lindsey only shrugged. "Merely spreading the love, my friend."

Just then, Carla glanced down and motioned to the fence. "Millie made that, by the way."

For a split second, Lindsey was surprised—but then she wasn't. *Of course* Millie had made it. Eleanor was right—little bits of Millie were still *everywhere* in Moose Falls.

"According to Bernard," Carla went on, "she petitioned the town council for it around twenty years ago. They approved it, but no one got around to building it for a while, so she finally did it herself." Then Carla appeared to study the railings more critically. "Of course, I don't know who'll maintain it now that she's gone."

"Rob'll do it," Lindsey assured her.

Carla lowered her chin doubtfully. "Mr. Sunshine? I doubt it."

Lindsey peered back over the falls. "Oh, you'd be surprised what he'll do in the name of Millie. He's very driven to keep everything she built thriving."

"And speaking of Rob," Carla said, eyebrows raised, "exactly how are things going with him?" The café had been crowded—by Moose Falls standards—so they hadn't gotten down to the nitty-gritty over tea. And frankly, Lindsey couldn't believe it had taken Carla this long to ask.

"Well, as you know, he's consented to show me some of Millie's personal things tonight, and within the walls of his very own house, no less. But he won't even *talk* about selling the livery, and as much as I really want it now, I'm pretty sure bringing it up again—at least at the moment—would be a bad idea."

"Oh, I knew *that*. I was talking about the sex horse."

Just then, a cool breeze lifted Lindsey's hair and gave her a chill, but it was welcome since she'd just gotten a little hot thinking of Rob and sex. "I wouldn't mind riding it with him, that's for sure. And sometimes he seems attracted to me, but other times he acts like I have the plague. And sometimes these reactions come in rapid succession—like one minute I'm feeling this very strong vibe of mutual want, but then I blink and he's Mr. Surly again."

"Sounds very fourth-grade-crush," Carla remarked.

But Lindsey didn't think that quite captured what was going on here. "It's not that he's shy. I mean—sometimes he looks at me like he's going to devour me and there's nothing *timid* about it, believe me. But the dude's definitely got some deep-seated problems that I probably don't want to be a part of." Lindsey paused, thought, then flipped her hair over her shoulder. "On the other hand, though—he's *so* hot, and it would only be an affair, right? A fun, wild little fling."

"Right. It's about getting back on the sex horse—that's where we got the term sex horse, remember? We didn't say *relationship* horse—just sex horse."

"Oh yeah." Made sense. "So it would only be sex."

"Again—correct. Which means if you get the chance, you should go for it."

"Of course I should. And I will. I'm not sure I could resist."

And like she and Carla both kept saying, it *would* only be sex.

So why did it feel like it might not only be sex? Now that she'd gotten to know him a little. They'd actually shared a few jokes now. And they'd encountered a wild bear together. And he'd given her a piggyback ride. And now she had this poignant image in her head of him caring for her dying aunt. That last one made her let out a sigh.

Well, if she got a shot at Rob, she'd have to *make* it only sex. Because he was a complicated, troubled guy and she had enough complications and troubles in her life already.

"So what does Rob like on his pizza?" Carla asked.

"Pepp and sausage."

Carla nodded knowingly. "Carnivore. I'm not surprised."

"Which reminds me," Lindsey said, peering up the road beside the falls, "how much farther to Bob's?"

"Past that next bend," Carla explained, pointing. "Quarter mile or so."

Lindsey was aghast. "*Quarter mile?*"

"Relax, princess," Carla said, "and give me your car keys. I'll walk back to the Grizzly Inn and pick you up. You can drop me off at the Elk on your way back past."

Lindsey felt like a total wimp, but somehow, with Carla, that was okay. And it was nice to have a friend with whom she could so quickly be herself, weaknesses and all. "You're a good friend," she said, pressing the keys into Carla's palm.

"I'm only doing this because I don't want you to be in too much pain to enjoy yourself if you get lucky tonight."

Hmm. Lucky. Tonight. As she watched Carla stride away from her in the falling darkness, she realized that as much as Rob turned her inside out with a glance, and even as much as she wanted to look attractive when she saw him, she'd sort of quit thinking this was going to lead to sex. Rob just didn't seem into it.

Oh sure, there were those occasional torrid glances and the way his gaze would linger over her breasts, and there had been those couple of moments when she'd been sure he was going to kiss her, but . . . he hadn't done it. All he'd done was make her start babbling like a crazy woman.

And she just didn't think tonight was going to be any different.

Her most realistic hope was that, with any luck, maybe she could at least keep the babble to a minimum.

Lindsey stood at Rob's door, holding the pizza, peering down at the same big dog who'd stood protectively by his side the *last* time she'd been in this spot. She raised her eyes back to her host, though, who looked as good as usual—tonight wearing a simple blue button-down shirt, untucked, over jeans. "Hi," she said.

"Hey." As usual, no smile, but she was getting used to that.

Her eyes dropped back to the German shepherd. "Um, what's your dog's name?"

"King."

"Will he bite me?"

"Only if I tell him to."

Her gaze darted up to his again.

"Relax, Abby. You're not *that* much of a nuisance." With that, he stood back and let her inside, instructing the dog to go lie down, which he did, on a braided rug near the back door, across the large living room.

Stepping into Rob's log cabin home felt . . . almost surreal. Everything about it was masculine, from the dark wood-plank walls and exposed log beams in the vaulted ceiling to the dark colors and the prints of bears and moose on the walls. The décor fit better here than at the Grizzly

Inn. The surreal part, though, was that even as much as the place felt like Rob's, she could also feel Aunt Millie here, too—still.

She had the vague sensation that when she'd visited as a child the home had been done in the country blues and pinks of the day, that there'd been feminine touches of lace edgings and curtains with bows on them. But somehow her great-aunt's vibrant aura still existed here—even if this was the first time she'd ever really thought about someone's aura.

She spotted a chandelier constructed of antlers dangling high above, much bigger and more dramatic than the one in her motel room, and a pair of old snowshoes mounted on the wall above the stone fireplace. A blanket with a red and green southwestern print draped the back of a brown leather sofa, two matching chairs situated around it. She simply held on to her peace-offering pizza, looking around, taking it all in.

"You all right?" Rob asked.

She turned to see him casting a skeptical glance in her direction.

"Yes, fine." Stepping out of her zombie-like study of the place, she held out the pizza box bearing Bob's logo on the top. "Just sort of . . . trying to remember what's the same about the house from when I was little, and what's different."

He took the pizza and padded to a large wooden kitchen table in gray-sock-covered feet. She liked that—him in socks. Made him somehow seem a little less gruff and a little more snuggly. Not that she thought she'd be snuggling with Rob Colter anytime soon, but the idea was nice and helped warm her up after the chilly walk from his driveway across the big yard.

Alternative music played softly from somewhere—currently "Got You (Where I Want You)" by the Flys—and it pleased her to realize they shared the same taste in music. She spoke loud enough to be heard above it. "Was most of this stuff

Millie's?" She motioned to the living room furniture. "Or stuff you bought to make the place your own?"

"Little of both," he said without looking at her. He opened an overhead kitchen cabinet to pull out plates and glasses. "These were hers," he said, holding up a simple but stylish ceramic plate of forest green. "Most of the furniture was hers." Just then, Lindsey noticed an antique rolltop desk in one corner. "Those snowshoes were hers—she really used them, for winter hikes."

"Wow," Lindsey breathed, imagining her great-aunt out in the snow, probably enjoying the season as much as if it were summertime.

"But I've brought in things of my own—some of the stuff on the walls, that blanket on the couch, the television."

Lindsey spotted a big-screen TV in one corner, tucked tidily into a large, rustic-looking set of shelves. "Nice entertainment center," she remarked.

"I made it," he said, but he spoke lowly, as if maybe he didn't want to brag.

And for some reason, Lindsey felt that in her chest. His sudden modesty, and the work and time he must have spent on it. The edges were intricately carved. "It's beautiful," she told him, but her voice came out unintentionally soft, too.

That's when she noticed a plethora of reading material on some of the shelving. "The books?" she asked, fully expecting him to say they were all Aunt Millie's.

"Mostly mine, but a few were hers."

She couldn't help being surprised. There was *still* more to Rob Colter than met the eye. Trying not to appear too nosy—since she found it perfectly acceptable to be nosy about her great-aunt but not about him—she moved across the hardwood floor to the books and let her eyes sweep across the spines. *Red Badge of Courage. Count of Monte Cristo. The Adventures of Huckleberry Finn.* Dear God—he read classics! Guy-centric classics, but still classics.

"Come eat," he said, again without looking her way, and

she saw that he'd already taken a seat at the table. Rather than ask what she wanted to drink, he'd put ice in her glass and set out three different varieties of two-liter soft drink bottles and currently filled his own glass with Coke.

As she sat down and reached for the Sprite, she thought it surprising that he'd seated her next to him on the same side of the long table, but then she realized why. He'd set out a stack of photo albums and must have figured it would be easier to look at them together if they were beside each other. Which she liked—the idea that he planned to look at them *together.*

So after taking a slice of Bob's Pizza, which turned out to be surprisingly thick and yummy, she pointed to the albums. "Millie's?"

His mouth was full, but he nodded. "Help yourself," he said after swallowing.

The first one she picked up was more of a scrapbook than just a plain photo album, and the first thing Lindsey set eyes on was a clipping from the *Moose Falls Gazette* for the 1988 Fish Festival, featuring a picture of Millie and her prizewinning fish. "Oh, Eleanor told me about this!" she said excitedly as she skimmed the article and studied the accompanying snapshots of Millie, the fish, Millie *with* the fish, Millie with a then-younger Eleanor, and Eleanor with the fish.

The next page contained photos of Millie at the canoe livery and handwritten notes about the summer season of 1988. She'd bought three new canoes to add to the "fleet" and it had been unseasonably warm that year. One picture featured Millie on the dock with a tall glass of iced tea in one hand as she mopped her brow with the other. Later came a copy of Millie's trail map, along with shots from a few of her favorite trails. And a few pages deeper Lindsey found a small watercolor of the lake and livery, with the note: *Trying my hand with a paintbrush! Much to learn!*

The next book Lindsey opened was an old-fashioned

album, the pictures secured by glued-in photo corners, and held Polaroids of Millie and John when they were young. Although Lindsey knew the two had met when Millie's family visited the area, she was surprised to learn from Millie's printed notes that the boathouse had originally belonged to John's parents. Which meant the canoe rental was a bigger part of Millie's history than Lindsey had even realized.

Another scrapbook displayed more clippings from the *Gazette*—tiny, wonderful snippets about the bear going into the roundabout, a new owner at the Lazy Elk, and Mary Beth opening the Lakeside Café. Only gradually did she realize the clips weren't printed on regular newspaper but simple white copy paper. Still, each cut-out came with photos, and often Millie would draw in tiny illustrations of butterflies or ladybugs to dress up the pages and make them more completely and undeniably Millie. Just as with every new thing she saw or did that related to her great-aunt, Lindsey's heart filled with still more love and admiration for the woman.

"These are so wonderful," she said, breathless over what a full and happy life her aunt had led here. Then she touched her finger to one of the clippings. This one in particular told of the new sign at the general store and featured a black and white picture. "I didn't realize Moose Falls had a newspaper."

"It doesn't. Anymore," Rob said, still munching on pizza. Lindsey had nearly forgotten hers, even as good as it had tasted. "Millie ran it—and made copies to put in the Grizzly Inn lobby, the Moose Mart, and the general store. It was only a few pages about community stuff, but she kept it up until she got sick."

Lindsey sighed. God, that made her sad. To think of it dying with Millie. Then she gave Rob a bittersweet smile. "I'm surprised *you* didn't keep it going."

"Not my kind of thing, Abby." He *didn't* smile.

But it was the first real time she'd looked directly at him

since sitting down beside him and his face was so close, and he didn't look away, either. And her skin tingled and her heart beat faster and it was another one of those moments when she knew, just knew, that he felt it, too—whatever this thing was passing between them—and just like before, she wondered if he would kiss her.

Instead he said, "If you're done eating, let's look at the rest of these someplace else. Get them away from the pizza and drinks."

"Good point," she heard herself say. Since it was. But her heart kind of plummeted because she was *so* ready to be kissed by him, surly or not.

Both of them stood up and as Lindsey carried the remaining albums to the coffee table in front of Rob's couch, he cleared the dishes and put the remaining pizza in the fridge. She thought maybe he'd ask if she wanted more to drink, but then she remembered who she was dealing with. She was probably lucky he'd given her a plate to use and supplied the soda.

While she waited, she made her way back to the bookshelves. "Which books are Millie's?" she called toward the kitchen as Death Cab for Cutie sang "I Will Follow You Into the Dark" on Rob's radio. The song was about death and love and a life well lived, and it made Lindsey sad even as she felt glad Millie had led such a wonderful existence.

"The top shelf," Rob called back.

She lifted her gaze and found copies of the *Living Bible*, *Under the Tuscan Sun*, *A Tree Grows in Brooklyn*, and *Jane Eyre* along with pretty books about flower gardens and nature. She ran her fingertip absently down the spine of the Bible and wondered if Millie could be looking down on them somehow, and if she could maybe forgive Lindsey from up in heaven.

When Rob came back, they sat on the floor in front of the coffee table, on a large area rug, ignoring the couch—and like before, his face was close. She could see him in her peripheral vision, and even as she studied dried cuttings of plants and leaves that Millie had collected from the Western View Trail, she also silently made note of the dark stubble on his chin, the arc of his jaw, and the relaxed way he sat, with one knee bent, his arm resting on it, the other leg stretched out alongside the end of the table. She could smell the rich, musky, guy scent of him—like before, wood shavings, and something cool and earthy that reminded her of the lake.

Together, they looked through years of Millie's life, a study in nature and a love of Moose Falls, and Lindsey soaked up every bit. Until finally Lindsey reached the last album, a weathered one, light blue and darker around the edges from handling. This one was a traditional photo album with sticky pages covered in cellophane.

And it was from the summer she and her mother had come to Montana.

She gasped when she saw the picture of herself with Aunt Millie on the first page—she wore a little white sundress with Mary Janes and a small blue barrette held back one side of her then-pale-brown hair. "Oh my God, Rob. This is me. With her. From the time I visited here as a little girl."

"Yeah," he said quietly, "I figured that when I saw them."

She couldn't stop herself from giving him a smile.

He didn't quite smile back, but he didn't look quite as mean and grim as usual, either.

And she was tempted to hold his gaze a bit longer, once again try to draw a kiss from him—but she wanted too badly to look at the album and figured the kiss was a lost cause anyway.

So she thumbed delightedly through the pages that captured memories of a picnic by the lake, a cookout in the backyard, and a lazy ride in a canoe that she didn't remember. Lisa had been off to 4-H camp—that had been part of the reason for the trip, Lindsey recalled. Lindsey had been jealous of her big sister and wanted to go to camp, too. Instead, she'd gone to Montana, which had been a good substitute. The pictures brought back more snippets of memory—things she'd completely forgotten up to now: a yellow cat named Whiskers that Aunt Millie had had owned at the time, and a pretty pink sleeping bag Aunt Millie had bought to make Lindsey's bed-on-the-couch seem special.

Another turn of the page and she gasped at seeing her five-year-old self holding up a chocolate Hostess cupcake, the kind with the white filling inside and the layer of dark icing on top. "Oh my God, I'd forgotten."

"About what?" Rob asked.

She bit her lip, sinking into a long-lost memory, so long-lost that she'd never shared it with anyone. "See this cupcake?" She pointed to the fading photo.

He nodded.

"Aunt Millie bought box after box of them while I was here and when my mother wasn't around, she let me eat the icing off the top and throw the rest away."

Finally, a full-blown smile spread across Rob Colter's face. And from where Lindsey sat, it lit up the room. His dark eyes sparkled, his teeth shone straight and white, and up-to-now-unseen dimples punctuated his cheeks. "You're kidding."

She shook her head. "No. I'd forgotten all about it, but now it's clear as day. She offered me one when we first got here, and I ate the icing off the top and then just nibbled around the edges since I didn't really want the rest. She caught on and we started our little secret of her letting me eat just the icing. I remember thinking how utterly cool she was to let me get away with that."

He gave a slow, sure nod, still smiling slightly. "Millie was definitely cool."

Looking back down, Lindsey turned the page again, and this time she found the swing—the very one she remembered hanging from the big tree in the side yard. "See this?" she said to Rob. "She put that up just for me, just for my visit. I remember asking if there were other little kids around since I wondered whose swing it was, and she told me that it was mine and that . . ." She stopped then, as the recollection shook her.

"That what?"

She pursed her lips in regret. "That it would always be here for me, for whenever I came back." She looked up at him. "I'm so sorry that never happened."

"Water under the bridge, Abby," he said next to her.

She tilted her head. "You think so? You think I shouldn't feel guilty?"

He shrugged. "You were five. You weren't responsible for getting yourself back here."

"True," she agreed.

"Now later, that's another story. But why even go there?" He motioned back to the album. "Just look at your pictures."

Lindsey did as he suggested, trying to forget her regrets and just bask in the joyful memories.

"You can have that one," Rob said. "That album. To keep."

She looked up, pleased and touched. "Really?"

"Only makes sense," he said, then let his eyes drop to the pictures—in particular, he honed in on one of her on the swing, the angle revealing the white panties under the little yellow minidress she wore. He quirked a grin in her direction. "Wearing short skirts even then, huh, Abby? If you're gonna wear those, you need to keep 'em pulled down."

She lifted her gaze to his with a smile that felt . . . more playful than any she'd offered him before. More *sexy.* "I thought you *liked* short skirts."

"I do," he said, voice deep, his eyes still on hers. "On grown-up girls."

"*I'm* a grown-up girl," she heard herself remind him in a deeper, saucier tone than she'd ever quite heard leave her throat before. And then she decided to push the issue, push the flirtation, push this invisible something between them, once and for all. Her voice came out just as warm. "Did you like *mine*?"

Those dark eyes of his stayed on her a long, scintillating moment more—before they dropped briefly to the floor. So she was surprised when he lifted them back up to slowly answer her. "Yeah." Their gazes stayed locked. "Too much."

Lindsey felt short of breath. "Too much for what?"

"My peace of mind."

His eyes were so brown, everything about him so masculine. She'd forgotten all about the pictures. "What does that mean?"

"Nothing. It means nothing." He gave his head a light shake and started to lower his chin, pull his gaze away—but this time she didn't let him.

Working on pure instinct, Lindsey lifted her hand to his stubbled cheek and kissed him. His mouth was soft and warm under hers—still at first, and maybe a little tense, but then she experienced that delicious pleasure of having her kiss returned.

He moved against her, opening his mouth, opening as if to capture more of her, and she met the hot pressure, letting that first uncertain kiss turn into another, and another, each becoming less tentative and more firm, intense.

His tongue pushed past her lips and she met it with her own, feeling the response between her thighs.

And then his hand was in her hair at the nape of her neck, gently massaging, sending tendrils of tingling heat outward over her scalp, back, shoulders, breasts, and—without planning it—she kissed him harder.

She'd not come to Montana thinking of sex, of wanting another man so soon. In fact, she'd been thinking just the opposite—that she didn't *need* a man, that there was *more* to life, other riches and pleasures to be found. But right now, oh boy—she needed this man. She needed him bad. She needed him inside her, and she needed him in a way she didn't remember ever needing a man before.

Rob's hand moved down her back and into the curve of her waist, his fingers squeezing, kneading, in rhythm with his kiss. She leaned closer, wanting more, more of *all* of him. The way he smelled, the way he looked, the way he tasted.

When his palm eased tenderly up onto her breast, she sucked in her breath at the hard jolt of longing that rocketed through her. She felt the touch everywhere, especially as he continued to knead and mold her in his large hand. She found herself pressing her chest toward him, wanting to somehow offer herself, let him know how much she desired him. His thumb raked across her nipple through her top and bra, making her sigh as the juncture of her thighs spasmed. So good. So good.

Finally, they stopped kissing, both breathless—and Lindsey thought they'd move onto the couch, or maybe just decide to screw the couch and start taking each other's clothes off right here on the floor.

But when their eyes met, his changed. She saw it. She saw his expression shift from the deepest passion to . . . to putting that same stubborn distance between them that he did every time their attraction became apparent. Only this time it was much worse because they'd just been making out, finally acknowledging what they both wanted. She hadn't messed it up by babbling. His hand still curved over her breast.

Until he pulled it away. Released her. Sat up straighter. "You need to go now."

Her jaw dropped in disbelief and she gave her head a sharp little shake. "What?" she whispered.

Now Rob even drew his *eyes* away, looking straight ahead, across the room, ignoring her distress. "You need to go, Abby. You need to leave. Now."

"But . . ." She didn't know what she wanted to say, yet

surely he owed her more than tossing her out of his house into the cold night.

"Just go, okay?" he said.

Then he pushed to his feet. And walked away.

To the staircase. Which he went up. Leaving her alone. His dog, who'd stayed quietly in place asleep up to now, even got up to follow him.

She continued to sit there on the rug for a minute, stunned and frozen in place.

She'd known Rob Colter was a jerk, but she'd also thought that underneath his icy surface there was something more and that she'd been seeing little bits of it.

But this . . . this was unthinkable.

"Asshole," she murmured.

And despite herself, the moment carried her back to *another* moment, a few weeks ago, when *another* man had made her feel like an undesirable idiot.

Well, undesirable she knew she was not. But an idiot—maybe.

For ever wanting anything more from him than what she'd come here for, the canoe livery.

Lesson learned, she thought, pushing unsteadily to her feet and heading numbly toward the door.

He didn't want her? Well, he wouldn't have her. She wouldn't darken his doorway again—ever.

She *didn't* need a man, and she *certainly* didn't need a man who made her feel like a fool.

This is the last time you make me feel bad, Rob Colter.

From the upstairs window, Rob watched her go, absently scratching behind King's ear. From the glow of the porch light, he saw her rush down the front steps and make her way across the soft spring lawn toward her car. His heart beat too hard.

What the hell was his problem? What had he just done?

He'd had a beautiful woman in his arms, wanting the same thing he'd wanted, and he'd just gotten up and walked away. Abandoned her in his own house.

He'd heard what she'd called him. She was right. "I *am* an asshole," he said softly to no one in the dark. Then he looked down to King, the dog's eyes shining darkly on his master in the shadowy loft. "And an idiot."

King simply let out one of those big dog sighs, which at the moment sounded suspiciously like agreement.

"It's gotta be this way, though. Getting involved with a woman is always a mistake for me. And I can't risk screwing up. Can't risk having to leave here. I can't. I won't."

King let out a tiny, muffled *woof* and Rob found himself wishing to hell he knew dog language. That's what he got, he supposed, for making "man's best friend" his true best and only friend.

"But then again, *she'll* leave here. She won't stay. Why *would* she? She has nothing here but memories of someone she barely knew."

And as long as she was leaving, then maybe, just maybe . . . sleeping with her wouldn't be the same mistake it had been with other women.

There would be nothing permanent or even semipermanent implied. No relationship. There'd be no reason for her to ever find out his secrets. And therefore no reason he'd ever have to leave Moose Falls.

He watched the red glow of her taillights as her expensive car backed from the crunchy gravel driveway onto the road, then listened as she sped away, too fast. After which he let out a sigh of his own and walked back downstairs.

Music still played. Photo albums still lay scattered across the coffee table.

But the space felt emptier than it ever had to him before.

That's when he noticed her coat, tossed across the back of a leather chair. She'd forgotten it in her anger.

He found himself hoping she wouldn't be too cold getting into her room without it.

Lindsey still couldn't believe it. He'd pushed her away. He'd kissed her like there was no tomorrow, he'd even fondled her breast—and then he'd actually pushed her away!

After screeching into her parking spot at the inn, she considered stomping over to the Lazy Elk for a drink, but decided she wasn't yet prepared to share her humiliation with Carla. Given how close it came on the heels of her humiliation with Garrett, well . . . it really *was* starting to be pretty damn humiliating.

So instead she stomped to her room, jammed the key card in the lock, then stomped inside. She took off her boots and threw them on the floor, then angrily wrestled her way into a lime-green cami and brightly striped cotton pajama pants.

She thought about watching a little TV to try to relax her, but felt too frustrated—both mentally and physically. And she thought about powering up her laptop to check in on the blog since that might cheer her up, but given that she'd been talking about Moose Falls and—even if in an indirect way—about Rob, she decided that was a bad idea.

When a loud knock came on her door, she was in no mood for company. She glared in the door's direction, but then figured it was probably Carla. She'd probably seen Lindsey's car go racing past the Lazy Elk—going the wrong way on the roundabout, no less—and sensed trouble. So . . . she might not be *ready* to tell Carla what had happened, but apparently she would have to anyway.

She yanked open the door—to find Rob standing on the other side.

Oh God.

And if that wasn't bad enough, he still looked all rugged and broad and sexy—good enough to eat.

Well, no more Mrs. Nice Guy. "What do *you* want?"

He held up her coat. "You forgot this."

Oh boy. It was a bad day for Lindsey when she walked off and left her favorite coat behind. Still, she only snatched it from his hand and tossed it behind her on the bed. "Anything else?" she snapped.

That's when she noticed his eyes had dropped to her chest.

Which was barely covered. The cami was thin and she knew her nipples were jutting prominently through, especially now that the door was open and cold air rushed in.

Rob looked lost somewhere between lustful and perplexed, and his voice came low. "Aren't you cold in that?"

Oh no. Having his eyes on her, dressed like this, produced a tremor between her thighs. And she didn't want to care. Or react. She was so damn mad at him. Because she knew that hot gaze would only lead to the same big fat nowhere everything had led so far.

But as usual, when he looked at her this way, and when he just *kept on* looking, it turned her inside out, dissolved her anger into that strange, edgy nervousness he always made her feel—and sent her into yet another spasm of jabbering. "Actually, no—despite the fact that I probably always seem cold, I get hot at night, so I can't sleep with much on. I know it sounds crazy, I'm only thirty-four, but I'm starting to think I'm perimenopausal or something. And—"

"What the hell does *that* mean?"

She blinked. "Well, it's when the female body begins to—"

Rob held up his hands in front of him and said, "Wait. Stop. Shut up."

"Huh?"

Then he stepped inside, forcing her to take a big step back, slammed the door shut, and started kissing her again.

Eight

His hands cupped her face and his tongue stroked into her mouth. Part of her wanted to stop this, given what had just happened at his house, but most of her simply couldn't. He was all raw heat now, in a different way than before, and she felt consumed by him already.

Slowly, kissing every step of the way, he backed her across the room until her shoulders bumped into the wall.

Even so, she closed her hands around his wrists and pushed him back just long enough to murmur, "You aren't gonna stop again, are you?"

"No way," he rasped, eyes glassy on her, voice heavy with desire.

She responded by thrusting her hands into his thick hair and lifting her mouth back to his. Now his arms wrapped around her in a full embrace, pressing their bodies together until she felt him, hard and ready, against her abdomen. A moan escaped her through their slow but feverish kisses and she needed more.

Since the moment they'd met, Rob had possessed the ability to make her feel more sexually aggressive than ever in her life, and now that came out as she reached between them, seeking the button on his jeans. It was hidden by his shirttail, but she snaked her fingers underneath, curling them into his waistband, feeling the warmth of his flesh against hers. And something about that—feeling his flesh—made her want to go for his shirt first. She'd seen him without it, but now she wanted to *feel* him without it.

She ran her palms up the flat of his stomach as he closed his hands over her ass and lifted her against him until that hardest part of him rested between her thighs. His breath grew thready, labored, his eyes falling half shut—but he still managed to devour her with them. She let out a hot whimper at the intimate contact, unable not to, because she felt it *everywhere.*

Extracting her hands, she worked at his buttons as he kissed her some more—hot, slaking kisses that made her feel wholly owned by him. She soon yanked his shirt open, pushing it past muscular shoulders to reveal the strong chest underneath.

Of course, her eyes fell on that damn tattoo on his chest—*Gina.* Yet she tried not to look, tried not to think about it, since—after all—whoever Gina was, she was long gone. Maybe she'd ruined him for all other women, but maybe that was also *changing*—since here he was, with *her,* no one else, just *her.*

For good measure, she skimmed her fingertips down over his skin, and the tattoo—some small way of proving to herself that it was just another spot on his body, another piece of gorgeous flesh.

And when her hands ended up back at his waistband, she didn't turn shy. His erection pushed up directly behind the button, yet she didn't hesitate to let her fingers go there and deftly pop it free. Then slide down his zipper. Then press the flat of her palm to the hard ridge encased in cotton and listen to a groan that sounded as if it had risen from someplace deep inside him. She felt it deep, too—drawing something so primal from him seemed to tug on her very soul.

His hands worked, as well—pulling at the drawstring ribbon on her pants until they dropped to the floor to leave her in her cami and a pair of white lace panties. She sucked in her breath and Rob looked down to let out a short "Unh." The mere sound made the small of her back contract and every part of her ached with longing.

With one arm still anchored around her—and thank God or she'd have probably collapsed from the passion—he hooked the fingers of his free hand around the white lace band at her hips and pulled downward in one brisk motion until it fell away, too. They peered into each other's eyes now—acknowledging the full measure of desire passing between them, and the fact that it was happening, they were really doing this, really having sex—as Lindsey pushed his jeans open wider and used both hands to lift his underwear over his erection.

Of course, her hands then found the erection itself—and they both shuddered.

As she wrapped one fist slowly but firmly around him, it was tempting to look away, to hold back some remaining shred of intimacy with this guy she didn't know very well and who had mostly not been very nice to her. But she worked to keep her eyes on him because she wanted this. *All* the intimacy. *All* the fire. *Everything.*

This will heal you. Those words drifted strangely through her head and she realized they might be true. If a man could want her the way Rob's eyes currently said he did, she *was* desirable. She wasn't *anything* Garrett had made her feel on that ugly night a few weeks ago.

And so she peered into Rob's eyes even as her lips trembled with the intensity of what they shared. Even as she squeezed and caressed his hard-on and listened to his labored breath. Even as the hand on her rear snaked inward, to her very center, to stroke her from behind.

Her head fell back as he drew his fingertips gently through her moisture, a small cry of shock and pleasure escaping her. He took the opportunity to kiss her neck, which she arched for him, and his unoccupied hand came up to firmly mold her breast. "God," she heard herself whisper—so much sensation, everywhere, threatening to bury her.

But she didn't have to suffer it much longer because that's when he hoisted her higher, lifting one bared thigh in his strong grasp, balancing her against the wall—and pushed his way inside her.

"*Oh!*" she cried at the entry. He was huge. Or at least he felt that way. She'd never had sex standing up before and having her full weight supported by his erection was . . . overwhelming, all she could feel.

Their bodies pressed together from torso to chest and their eyes still locked onto one another glassily. She wrapped her arms around his neck and hooked her leg over his hip.

He thrust, and she whimpered—the instinct made her meet his body with her own, every slow, deep, deliberate stroke filling her, making her forget anything but him, and her, and flesh, and pleasure. His slow, rhythmic plunges up into her body against the wall made her feel truly *taken* by a man for the first time in her life. He still kneaded her breasts through her cami and she heard herself sob, "Kiss me," before his mouth recaptured hers. They moved together that way in the most raw, intense sex Lindsey had ever experienced—she didn't know how long, since time ceased to exist. Along with thought or decision or anything but sensation.

As soon as he picked her up, both her legs instinctively twining around his waist, she realized everything inside her was moving the right way—good, so good—and in that moment nothing else mattered. "Don't stop. Like this," she breathed in his ear, her voice feather-light but her body raging inside.

She clutched at his shoulders as his fingers dug into her

ass. She moved against him with abandon, seeking, seeking that torrid ending she'd been needing from him for days now.

She heard her own thready breath and wasn't embarrassed, didn't care. He felt it all, too—she sensed that. He felt the wild woman inside her coming out, he sensed her nearing orgasm, and he needed to make it happen as much as she needed to feel it.

He thrust deeper, lifted her higher. She brushed her breasts against his chest, an urge to make him feel their hardened peaks. She gave herself . . . over . . . to him . . . completely.

Until a cry left her throat as she plummeted over the edge of bliss and fell deep, deep, arching against him, letting it all rush through her with a wild freedom she hadn't known for . . . maybe ever. Oh God.

Next, she was collapsing against him, eyes shut, holding on tight. That's what she did after an orgasm, she collapsed, her body giving in, giving up—yet she sensed him easing them away from the wall, and the world went topsy-turvy for a minute until her back hit the bed.

And she thought he would come back inside her then, but he didn't.

Instead, he hovered above her—she somehow felt him there and opened her eyes to find him studying her. And oh—she liked that, him just looking at her, at her face, her lips, her eyes. She liked looking at him, too, because he was such a ruggedly beautiful man.

Without meaning to, she lifted her fingertips to rake across the stubble on his jaw. He shifted just slightly to capture them in his mouth. She surged with moisture in response, a sexy ache shooting through the small of her back as their eyes stayed locked, just like before.

But then he and his dark, smoldering eyes headed south and she couldn't exactly complain about that, either. His gaze lingered on her chest until he slipped his thumbs beneath her thin shoulder straps and drew them down, slowly, slowly, until her breasts were revealed, the pink nipples beaded tightly.

He drew in his breath at the mere sight. And then, slowly, gently, he leaned down to bestow a tiny kiss on the left peak.

"Ah . . ." she sighed, the sensation expanding exponentially through her body.

The hint of a masculine smile curved his mouth.

And then he came back again, this time to her right breast, where he dragged his tongue up the lower curve, then raked across the pink bud at the center—just before drawing it into his mouth. "Oh," she whimpered, high and soft, after which he suckled her, seeming to drink of her, and her hands threaded into his messy hair to caress his scalp, then his neck and shoulders. Finally, he moved back to the other breast, kissing, licking, and making Lindsey's body feel totally worshipped in a way no man ever had.

Soon, Rob kissed his way down her stomach, still moving in an unhurried pace that made her feel . . . like a meal, but in a good way. Like a really *wonderful, gourmet* meal that he was lingering over and couldn't quite get enough of.

When he lowered another kiss just above the mound of her sex, she trembled and didn't worry about hiding the response. Did other women usually try to hide things like that during sex—or only her? She'd always wanted to appear in control of her body, of what was happening to it. But with Rob, she let all that go and simply let herself *feel.*

As he placed his hand on her thighs to slowly part her legs, she shuddered again—but relished the intimacy. She'd started getting used to that now—the stark nearness, the sharing of every bared part of herself.

He studied her there, then raised his gaze to her eyes as he lowered the first kiss to her inner flesh. Another whimper left her, the pleasure seeming to tingle through her very bones. She bit her lip and found herself parting her thighs wider—an instinctive invitation for more.

He took it, licking her, kissing her, pleasuring her in every way a man's mouth could pleasure a woman. And as much as she liked watching him, she eventually shut her eyes and felt herself digging her fingers into the comforter at both sides of her as she lifted to meet his ministrations.

She'd never been this . . . lost in sex. Maybe she'd never felt she *could* be, at least not with Garrett. He was so . . . uptight in ways, and while she'd always thought him an adequate lover, she'd never really felt him *needing* it the way she'd felt *Rob* needing it from the moment he'd come into her room. And that had only made her need it just as bad, give herself up to it just as completely.

Another orgasm rose inside her, getting closer and closer to the surface, until finally bursting through and—oh God—jerking jaggedly through her in almost violent spasms that drew rough cries from her throat. It rocked her body from the inside out, like some sort of electrical shock—but a wildly *pleasurable* shock. She cried out as the climax shook her very foundations and a tattered whimper left her toward the end, her muscles seeming to shudder within her skin.

Dear God. She'd never come *that* way before. She hadn't known an orgasm could even be like that.

Opening her eyes, she felt she needed to say something, to explain her uncontrolled writhings. "Intense," she whispered.

"Good," he said, eyes half shut, mouth slack, his focus on her face. She couldn't help thinking he didn't seem surprised. Maybe he'd given *lots* of women orgasms like that. Or maybe he'd given lots of orgasms like that to Gina.

Strange jealousy rolled through her then, unstoppable even as she told herself not to feel it, that it was silly and crazy. She barely knew him. This was nothing but release. It was getting back on the sex horse.

And still, she needed more—she needed to feel his body against her. "Please kiss me," she said, wishing she didn't sound so damn needy. "Hard," she added, and at first she had no idea why, but then she understood.

As Rob slid his muscular body back up over hers, then brought his mouth down onto her lips, *hard*, just like she'd requested, she *felt* him. All of him. Just like before. And she needed that—to make her stop thinking. His slow, lingering kisses and licks had been scintillating, and perfect—but *now* perfect meant having no room for thought or emotion. Now perfect meant only hot, quenching, physical sensation. "Make me feel you," she heard herself breathe without planning it. "Make me feel you."

Rob's hard-on went stiffer at Lindsey's commands. He liked a woman who wasn't shy in bed, who let him know what she wanted. He liked the pure need he felt rolling off of her and onto him. He liked it because he felt it, too—rumbling through him like an avalanche, gaining more strength and velocity with each passing moment.

Ah, damn, this was good. Too good. He felt like a starving man getting to eat again for the first time in a year. And she tasted . . . fucking incredible. He shouldn't be here, delivering these hot, punishing kisses to her soft lips—he knew that. But the mistake was made now, there was no going back—there was only wallowing in the pleasure while it lasted.

Rising off her slightly, he was ready to do what she wanted, make her feel him, and as her legs parted of their own volition, he braced his hands on the curves of her hips and pushed back inside her warm, tight body. The groan that left him rose from his gut, the heat stretching all through him as he drove deep into her moisture, as deep as he could go, and then, heart pounding like a drum, just rested there and met her gaze. *I'm inside you.* He didn't have to say it. He knew that's what they were both thinking, feeling, sharing.

"More," she said, and it fueled him, and he pulled out just enough to thrust deeply back in and make them both moan.

And then he surrendered to what his body craved and began to move in her, pound into her, make her feel him, more, more, more.

Oh God, it had been so long since he'd felt a woman's body beneath his. And it was so damn good. To feel her soft flesh. To touch her breasts. To kiss her most intimate spot. He'd truly never expected to do any of those things again and the shocking pleasure of it had taken over his senses. Every second with her had been . . . escalated, the tension knob turned higher than with any other woman, ever. And still it went on as he plunged into her, pushing toward his own release, letting his urges take him, watching the heated joy paint itself all over his lover's face. He should be regretting this, sorry he'd come, sorry he'd given in to his lust—but he wasn't, damn it, he just wasn't.

He was on the brink of exploding inside her, of finally, finally reaching that pinnacle he hadn't reached with a woman in so long now—when she said, "Stop."

He went still inside her, stunned. "What?"

"I don't want you to come yet. I just want to feel you inside me some more. Just a little while longer."

Rob swallowed as a strange combination of frustration and power assailed him. Slowing down, now, was like trying to stop a freight train from crashing, but if she wanted more . . . hell, he'd give her more.

So he forced himself to stay very still as he peered down into her eyes. He knew he should quit doing that, looking at her so damn much, but he couldn't help it. She was so pretty, and when she was aroused, God—she was beautiful. How was he supposed to take his eyes off her?

"I'm sorry," she whispered then. "Did I . . . did I ruin it for you?'

"God. No," he told her, voice low. "You couldn't."

She looked truly relieved. "Good. I . . . I want to make you feel good."

A strangled sort of laugh left him. "Mission accomplished."

And then he kissed her, partly to stop the talking, because he didn't want to make this feel any more personal than it already did, and partly because her lips looked so moist and her mouth rested half open in passion, even after their short conversation.

And then, gradually, he began to move in her again.

He kept it slow, feeling more controlled now, and found himself simply enjoying being on top of her, feeling the smooth slide of his cock into her slick warmth, the way her body accepted it, the way it filled her with each stroke, making her sigh or moan. The gentle curves beneath his hands, the soft female skin, it was all amazing. More amazing than he'd ever expected anything to feel again in his lifetime. How the hell did priests do it? Then again, he'd never claimed to be anything remotely close to a priest. He was just him. Doing the best he could. And he'd thought he was stronger than this—stronger than any push-pull of the man-woman thing—but he'd been wrong. No, he was *wallowing* in that push-pull, soaking it up. He felt like a kid licking the bowl after finishing the ice cream—he wanted every last drop of this, all he could get.

But he couldn't go slow like that for long.

It had been a year, after all. Hell—he was lucky he'd lasted more than a few minutes, all things considered.

She met his strokes as they increased, getting harder, faster, and the heat grew inside him again, that powerful pressure building, building, the pleasure gathering into a tight ball, ready to explode.

And then it did, the climax rough and deep, almost blinding as he shut his eyes and let it echo through him, absorbing every last pulse, every last sensation it delivered.

God. Oh God. He'd really done this. Really indulged his desire for Millie's niece. Lindsey. He couldn't believe he'd just given in.

Part of him wanted to just stay there, inside her, not even move. It was so warm there. Warm and good.

But instead Rob rolled off her, onto his back, and let sleep steal over him almost immediately, the last fleeting thought to pass through his mind that this was the first time he'd ever referred to her, even just in his thoughts, as Lindsey.

When Lindsey opened her eyes, the first thing she saw were the antlers overhead. After a split second of fearing she'd happened into the path of a big, many-horned animal, she remembered where she was. More importantly, she remembered what had just happened. Oh my.

He had been . . . aggressive. Hot. Hard. Attentive. *Amazing.*

He'd given her two staggering orgasms.

Of course, then she'd refused to let him have his own.

She mentally kicked herself in the head for that. *Pleasure hog.* God, if he hadn't thought she was self-centered before, he surely did now. She hadn't meant to be so bossy or selfish, but she'd never had sex that good, and she hadn't wanted it to end.

She couldn't help remembering that moment when she'd apologized, afraid she'd ruined it for him. *You couldn't,* he'd said, voice so soft and deep she'd wanted to melt in it. At moments during their sex, she'd felt almost . . . tender toward him. When she wasn't busy begging, demanding, or pleading for something. The memory astounded her—Rob Colter was the last person she'd have ever expected to feel tenderly toward. And then there'd been the stark jealousy over Gina—whoever she was. Insane.

So as she peered into the twisting antlers as if they were suddenly going to spell out the answers to all the mysteries of Rob Colter, she resolved to brush aside all the strangely intense emotions she'd suffered a little while ago. Crazily good sex was just making her brain work overtime. Because this was exactly what it was *supposed* to be: getting back on the sex horse. It had been mind-blowing. And a fabulous way to forget Garrett's horrible humiliation of her—and Garrett altogether.

She hadn't been thinking about her ex *much*, but she'd still been hurting from the horrible way things had ended, from the misplacement of her trust for so long—and now, well, this was a big step toward getting her confidence back and not having to worry about things like: *When will I date again? When will I sleep with someone again?* That aspect of her many worries was over now, and that was all that mattered here.

Wasn't it?

Next to her, Rob stirred, his arm brushing hers.

She bit her lip and glanced surreptitiously down at it without moving her head. Even though it was only spring, he was already tan from working in the sun. And those muscles had felt so strong when he'd wrapped his arms around her and picked her up and come inside her. She swallowed at the memory, her body going tense all over again.

Stop this. You can't keep remembering now. Because now you have to talk, and God only knows how a guy like him will be after sex. You can relive it all in your mind later. And she had a pesky feeling she definitely would. Over and over and over.

She turned casually on her side to face him. At some point, she'd readjusted her cami, and his jeans still remained around his thighs after all that—but otherwise, they remained undressed. She tried her darnedest not to let her gaze drop between his legs.

Which brought a question to mind. About protection. Which they hadn't used. Sheesh.

Almost as if he'd read her thoughts, he lifted his hips just enough to pull up his pants, even if he didn't bother zipping them. Not that she minded. He looked sexy as hell lying there like that.

"Hey," she said. She kind of wished she could reach her *own* pants, but they were too far away.

Yet when he returned her "Hey," glancing only slightly in her direction, she decided she needn't worry about feeling sheepish. He'd apparently grown bored with her again that quickly.

"Um, not to bring up an unpleasant subject, but . . . should I be worried that we didn't use a . . . you know?"

She watched his eyes fall shut as he scrubbed a hand back through his hair. "*Shit.*" Finally, he looked briefly over at her, regret in his eyes. "I didn't have one. I didn't even *think* . . ."

Though she knew it was just as much her responsibility as his, she said, "I thought all guys carried one in their wallets. I thought it was like . . . a guy law or something."

"I'm . . . out of practice on this," he replied, and the admission caught her off guard.

She simply nodded, again wondering why. Because of Gina? "Well, I'm still on the pill, so we've got that much going for us."

"Good." That earned her another glance from him—before he looked back away. "As for the other issues, no worries on my end."

"You're positive?" He'd been so quick to speak up, sounded so oddly definite.

"Yep. What about you?"

Lindsey sighed, thinking back over her personal history. "Well, I've been with the same guy for four years until a couple of weeks ago. And . . . I've never really had casual sex." The words forced her gaze downward, at them, their half-naked bodies. "Until now, I mean."

Another brief nod from him seemed to confirm that neither of them was going to give the other a disease, then he peered back up at the same antler chandelier that had held her attention a few moments earlier. "Don't be mad if I'm not here in the morning. I'm not a staying-over kind of guy."

"No worries," she said, completely unsurprised, but her voice had come out softer than planned. She made sure to sound more stalwart when she added, "I wouldn't expect you to be."

He didn't answer and she thought maybe he was going back to sleep now, so she took the opportunity to study him with his eyes shut. He was still just as beautiful as she'd ever thought him, but he looked different now—more at peace, and she couldn't help wondering what his life had been like, what had turned him into Mr. Surly, as she'd referred to him earlier with Carla.

Just then, he turned onto his side and looked her in the eye. She was just about to suffer the got-caught-staring embarrassment when Rob lifted a hand to her cheek, leaned in to kiss her, and said—without smiling, "That was the nicest thing that's happened to me in a while, Abby."

Oh wow. She replied honestly. "Me, too."

"And . . ." His eyes went a little squinty, and she could tell whatever he was about to say didn't come easy. "I'm sorry. About before—back at my place. Thanks for . . . not holding that against me."

She propped on one elbow and flashed her best I-am-woman-hear-me-roar look. "Who says I don't hold it against you?"

He raised his eyebrows confidently. "Well, you just had sex with me."

"That doesn't mean I can't still be pissed off."

"Fair enough." He gave a barely-there nod, then slowly rolled onto his back again.

"Care to explain what happened back there?" she asked, now bold enough to peer down at him even if he didn't return her look. His gaze was in the antlers again.

"Nope. I told you before—I'm just not a people person."

"Even when you get sex out of it?"

A quick laugh erupted from his throat and she liked the way the corners of his eyes crinkled when he smiled. "Even then. Usually, anyway."

"So what happened?" she had to ask. "What ruined your grand plan?"

She expected some toss-off answer, but instead he let his gaze fall on her again. "You," he said, looking sort of sad. "You're too pretty. Too sexy. Too hot. Too sweet."

It was the last one that blew her away the most. "Really? You think I'm *sweet*? How did I go from being the spawn of the devil to *sweet* in just a few short days?"

"Good question," he said. "But don't let it go to your head, okay?"

She smiled slightly, more than a little satisfied with his reply. It sounded almost as if Mr. Colter liked her. Maybe Carla had been right—maybe it was like an elementary school crush—pick on the girl you want to flirt with.

"Okay," she said, rolling over onto her back, too—then took the liberty of reaching for the bedside lamp, clicking the button that bathed the room in darkness. After which she listened to Rob breathing, the only thing she could hear in quiet Moose Falls, Montana, until she fell asleep herself.

It wasn't surprising when she woke up the next morning to find herself alone in bed. But she still felt tingly inside because she could literally smell him on her sheets and she stayed caught up in the intensity of what they'd shared.

Yet looking at the rumpled pillow beside her made her sigh, too. Because it was over now. The best sex of her life—over and done, and who knew when she'd find a man to make her feel like *that* again. She could only hope it wouldn't take another thirty-four years.

And when Lindsey thought ahead to her day, well . . . she wasn't sure what it was going to hold.

Up until now, she'd been on missions. Her first had been to get the canoe rental back. When that hadn't seemed to be working out, her focus had shifted to learning more about Aunt Millie, and she'd accomplished that—but she'd promised Rob that last night would be her final such intrusion into his life.

So maybe that meant . . . she'd done what she was meant to do here and it was time to go home. Maybe astounding sex with Rob was supposed to be the trip's big climax—in more ways than one—and now she was supposed to get in her car and head back to Chicago. After all, she'd climbed—with great gusto—back onto the sex horse now, so maybe the next task was to go home and figure out what she wanted to do with the rest of her life, since apparently she wasn't going to be running a canoe livery.

And yet . . . the very thought of leaving Moose Falls made her stomach churn. She liked it here and felt she was just starting to get to know people, and maybe even fit in—a little. She had Keds now, after all.

Stepping into the shower, she felt . . . confused and adrift.

Which, darn it, seemed a little too close to the way she'd felt upon *arriving* here.

So maybe *that* meant she *wasn't* ready to leave yet. She might not have the canoe business, and she might have learned as much about Aunt Millie as she could—but being here had truly relaxed her. The view of the lake out her window still made her feel at peace inside. The glimpse of Aunt Millie's old log home through the trees still made her feel inexplicably warm and safe. The tree-blanketed hillsides still made her feel protected somehow, tucked away from the prying eyes of Chicago.

So after dressing in a cropped one-button cardigan of powder blue over a white cami with dark-wash jeans, she put on her caramel-colored boots and set out for breakfast at the café. There she ran into Maynard from the Moose Mart, who was stopping in for coffee. A chat revealed that—much to her surprise, given his generally grizzled appearance—he'd been on the Moose Falls Beautification Committee since 1979. Which led to discussions about Millie's fence at the falls and the bear in the roundabout, and Lindsey gave him props for supporting each decision.

After Maynard's departure, Mary Beth served up the best blueberry pancakes Lindsey had ever tasted, and which she'd ordered on recommendation from Carla. She'd taken a table next to the big picture window, specifically so she could look out at the lake—completely free of mist this morning—while eating.

As she finished her meal and placed her napkin on the table, old Mrs. Bixby came in, and she stopped to invite Lindsey to the café's book club, same as Mary Beth had previously. "We're doing *Bridget Jones's Diary* this time. Have you heard of it?" she asked, clasping Lindsey's hand in her cool, wrinkled one.

"A time or two," Lindsey replied, hiding her smile as the older woman made her way to the counter seeking jelly-filled donuts.

"I'm trying to rustle myself up a date with Bernard and he's partial to jelly-filled," she informed Lindsey. "You know Bernard, over at the general store. Told me he sold you a fine pair of Keds."

"Indeed he did," Lindsey replied with a nod, adding, "Good luck. You'd make a nice couple."

"I think so, too," Mrs. Bixby said with a wink, then stepped up to the counter to place her order.

"So where are you off to after this?" Mary Beth asked a few minutes later, turning Lindsey's check face down on the table. "I saw you working on the canoes yesterday. Your great-aunt would've been pleased to see you there getting the place ready, that's for sure." Then Mary Beth's eyes slid down Lindsey's body. "But you don't look dressed for canoe work, so you must have other plans today."

"Well," she began uncertainly, "I'm off to Rob's for a photo album he promised to give me. One of Millie's." It had occurred to her in the shower that she'd forgotten it last night, and apparently so had he or it would have been delivered with the coat and the sex. But she hadn't quite realized she was going to go to his house to get it until the words left her mouth.

The truth was, she realized, she had nothing else to do. It was either go get the photo album from Rob or go get sloshed at the Lazy Elk, and it was far too early in the day for the latter.

The morning was sunny and bright, and a little warmer, just as Rob had promised would start happening soon, so she hadn't worn her coat. Her feet felt recovered enough from various recent abuses that she decided to walk the short distance to his place. She'd get her album, head back, and maybe sit on the bench by the lake to look at the photos again, more carefully this time. Perhaps she'd remember even more details about the long-ago visit. Maybe she'd even do some journaling about it. Not on her blog or anyplace public, but maybe she'd record some thoughts and memories the old-fashioned way, on paper, like she had as a little girl when she'd first taken an interest in writing.

When she knocked on the door, she heard King barking inside—and as a few moments passed, she wondered if Rob was even going to answer. She glanced over to see his pickup in the driveway, but for all she knew, he'd headed off on a hike or was working inside the boathouse where she hadn't seen him when passing by.

Still, she had a strange sense that he *was* home, so she knocked again—just before the door opened. The man who'd taken her to heaven last night stood before her in a fresh T-shirt and jeans, but his hair remained typically rumpled. As usual, King stood at his side and Rob's fingers rested in the dog's thick fur.

Just seeing him made her go tense with fresh desire, but she tried her darnedest not to let it show. "Hi."

He appeared . . . surprised and maybe a little bewildered to see her.

And—oh God—it was only in that moment that she realized how it must look for her to show up on his doorstep so soon—mere hours—after what they'd done. She suddenly felt unbearably clingy and needed to make her *current* mission perfectly clear. "Don't worry, I'm here for the photo album you promised me—not to stalk you. I forgot it when I was busy being thrown out last night."

He pursed his lips and, if she wasn't mistaken, maybe even looked a little guilty. "Didn't I apologize for that?"

She gave a succinct nod. "Yep, but I'm explaining myself thoroughly since I don't want you to get the wrong idea. I just came for the album."

He nodded back and said, "Come on in," then turned to pad across the hardwood in bare feet as she stepped inside and shut the door.

It felt strange to be back here already—she couldn't help remembering their kisses last night and where they'd ultimately led.

Still, she followed him to the coffee table where the album had been left open—to that picture of her on the swing that had taken them to flirting and kissing, and then to breast-fondling. Her breasts started tingling *now,* just remembering what a shocking and pleasurable occurrence it had been. Or maybe it was just from seeing him again so soon after the way they'd writhed and moaned together.

"Thanks again," she said, bending to carefully shut the old album, then pick it up. "For the pictures, I mean." *Please don't let him think I'm thanking him for sex.* "It really means a lot to me to have this."

When she rose back to her full height, Rob just nodded—but she saw his Adam's apple bob as he swallowed, and his eyes on her looked . . . different than before. Strange and unsettled.

Dear God, what *now*? "What's wrong?"

"Nothing," he said softly. But he was acting weird again, and though that didn't exactly *surprise* her, it still *annoyed* her. And he kept right on looking at her in that troubled way—until she realized it wasn't her face he was focused on so much as her shoulder.

So she dropped her gaze there, too, not particularly embarrassed to see her bra strap showing, which happened to be leopard-print—her sweater had slid askew when she'd bent over.

Yet for some reason, his expression—even as disturbed as he appeared—made her breasts begin to swell within the cups of her bra even as she reached to pull her sweater back into place.

And that's when it hit her that his look wasn't just troubled—it was filled with sex. Which got her even hotter inside. And as usual when dealing with him and his looks—*oh crap, why do I keep doing this?*—she heard herself beginning to babble nervously. "Normally, I would never wear animal-print under white, but I'm out of clean bras and I knew it wouldn't show through the sweater. Does Moose Falls have a laundromat? Or maybe the Grizzly Inn has a laundry room—I'll need to ask Elean—"

"Stop talking," he said, moving a step closer—which brought him near enough that she could smell the scent of him again. No wood shavings this time—just some sort of masculine soap and a natural musk that made the muscles in her stomach contract.

She peered up to see him looking almost angry now, when she thought if *anyone* should be getting angry it was *her*. "Why?"

He hesitated—and then his voice came out strained. "Because I want you again, damn it."

"Oh." Okay, that was enough to shut her up. And make her whole body hum.

"So you should go," he said.

She should? She blinked, perplexed as always with him. "Because sex with me is so awful?"

"Just the opposite, and you know it."

She sighed, both gratified and bewildered. "Then why . . ."

"Go, Lindsey," he commanded gruffly.

And—God, he'd actually called her by her name, for the very first time. Even as he was tossing her out again. What *was* it with this guy? She couldn't decide whether she liked him or hated him in any given moment.

Her lips trembled as she turned to walk away, the move

forced and mechanical and confusing since, in a flash, that hot passion had flared between them again, but Mr. I-Vant-to-Be-Alone was against good sex for some reason. Her heart beat a thousand miles an hour as she walked toward the door, her heels clicking with each step.

But then she stopped.

Because . . . well, *because*, she decided in a fit of irritation, she wasn't going *anywhere*.

Because she simply couldn't.

Every cell in her body was telling her it was wrong to go, that it made no sense. A woman couldn't have a man like Rob say he wanted her and actually *leave*—it was a physical impossibility.

So instead she set the photo album on the antique desk, along with her brown Gucci bag. And reached up to undo the single blue button between her breasts.

Turning, she began to move back toward him as she let the sweater fall from her shoulders and onto the floor.

He narrowed his eyes, lowered his chin. "What the hell are you doing?"

She answered only by coming closer, until they were face to face, standing next to the leather sofa.

"Damn it, Lindsey," he growled. "Are you trying to piss me off?" But his eyes said something else entirely, and so did the bulge behind his zipper.

"No," she said softly. "I just don't understand why you're fighting this so hard. We're attracted to each other. There's nothing wrong with that."

"You don't have to *understand* it," he said. "Just *respect* it."

"Sorry—that ship sailed last night. And FYI, you were definitely the captain."

She eased nearer still, driven now in a way she'd never been before—to truly go after what she wanted with a guy, to throw caution to the wind. She wasn't sure why—maybe she was tired of him being so gruff and mean and thinking he called all the shots here. Or maybe it was about getting back some kind—*any* kind—of control in her life. Or maybe, maybe, it was just about *yearning*, plain and simple.

With Garrett and the Great Apron Debacle, she'd felt no worry, but it had turned out to be the riskiest, most harmful move she'd ever made. Now, with Rob, she *knew* her aggression was risky—she knew he could turn her down and send her away feeling almost as humiliated and emotionally pummeled as her ex-fiancé had. But she found herself willing to take the gamble. Because the reward was that great.

Lifting both hands to her shoulders, she boldly hooked her thumbs into the thin white straps of her cami and lowered her top, revealing the leopard-print demi-bra underneath.

As Rob's gaze dropped to her breasts, he let out a hot little breath, then whispered, "Damn."

Right before he reached for her.

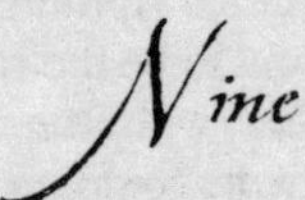

Nine

Hell—why had she had to wear *that, today*? It was bad enough that he'd indulged his lust last night. And it was rotten enough luck that she'd come back for Millie's album before he'd managed to mentally recover from giving in. But she'd had to wear leopard-print, too? A leopard-print *bra*?

Just like when she'd worn that animal-print thing in her hair—*that* it got to him. He didn't know why. He couldn't explain it to himself. But something about her and animal-print turned him on—and the moment he'd spotted that bra strap . . . damn it, he'd been a goner.

Now the curves of her sweet breasts pushed upward from the bra, seeming to beckon him, and how the hell could he resist when she was being so freaking aggressive? He couldn't. That simple. He was only a man, for God's sake.

So his hands found the soft flesh of her waist and his mouth came down on her lips, and his hard-on pressed blessedly against the tender flesh between her legs. Of course, there were two pairs of jeans between them, but there wouldn't be for long—he started working at her button and zipper even as they traded passionate tongue kisses, the heat soaring all through him like a bottle rocket gone wild.

He wanted to think clearly, wanted to stop this somehow—once was a mistake, twice was more like a habit—but he couldn't. He had to have her. And—aw, damn—a glance down revealed that she wore leopard panties, too. "Hell," he murmured on a hot sigh, even as he pushed the jeans to her thighs.

She glanced down to where his eyes rested at the moment. "You like?"

"Too damn much."

He never should have opened the sex door again—because now he couldn't seem to shut it. But no, it was worse than that. He never should have looked into her pretty blue eyes so much last night—*that* was the problem. He shouldn't have let things feel so . . . *whatever* they had felt. Like they were *sharing* something. More than just pleasure. He didn't even know what—but *something*. And they were sharing it again now because he was back to looking in her eyes—not wanting to miss one expression of passion, and he was studying her body, too, wanting to memorize every curve.

He plopped back onto the couch behind him and pushed her jeans all the way to her ankles, so she could step free, taking off the boots at the same time.

Then his hands were on her hips, her ass, pulling her nearer so he could kiss her stomach, the spot next to her belly button, then higher—but he couldn't quite reach her breasts until he drew her down with him, until she was straddling him and his face was buried between the cups of her bra, kissing her there, just feeling the very femaleness of her.

Their heavy breathing filled the room as she undid his pants, too, pushing them open, and his erection popped free. They kissed like maniacs as his hands found their way into her leopard-print to massage and tweak and tease, as *her* hands stroked him below, making him moan into her mouth.

Soon she had pushed his T-shirt up and he helped her get it off before he started tugging at her panties, telling her silently that those needed to go, too. She rose up and together they shoved the panties to her thighs—after which she rolled off him long enough to let him rid her of the underwear completely. Rob dashed them toward the coffee table, relieved when she was lifting one leg across his lap again. Even more relieved when she balanced atop his hard-on and began to slide down.

His chest felt like it was caving in as she sheathed him, slow, steady, tight. He didn't want to groan, didn't want her to know how deeply he felt this, but it was a lost cause.

God, she was hot and beautiful, moving on him so rhythmically, not hiding anything she felt. That in itself was beautiful and amazing—Lindsey riding him to heaven, her face etched with passion. And God knew he didn't want to think she was amazing—but he did.

He pulled down the straps of her bra enough to let her breasts tumble free, enough that he could lean in and suckle her, pulling deep, feeling it in his chest, listening to her moan.

His eyes fell shut for a while, but he opened them again, needing to see. He took in the natural slope of her breasts, a dimple in her hip. He saw the color of her eyes up close—more than one shade of blue, shards of dark and light blending to create a kaleidoscope of beauty. Her lips were the color of berries—pouty as she moved on him; sexy when she licked them, her head tossed back in passion; and pliable when he kissed them again.

"Come for me," he heard himself rasp. He hadn't exactly planned on that, but he needed to take her there.

The command made her moan, made her gaze drop to his. She kissed him hard, almost biting his lip. Then she thrust her breasts against his chest, her beautifully hardened nipples leaving little trails of fire on his flesh. Still moving on him in her hot little dance, she reached for his hands, leading them to her breasts. They both sighed heatedly as he squeezed and kneaded in rhythm with her movements, just watching her, helping her.

"Oh God," she whimpered, and her body jolted, just once, and he watched the waves of pleasure roll through her, listening to her orgasmic cries.

"Aw, damn," he muttered, because that was all it took to push him over the edge, too. He no longer held back, though—plunging deep up into her waiting body, again, again, emptying himself, losing himself, letting those hot, high waves consume him.

And then he came down from the high—and realized what he'd done, again.

Hell.

But . . . maybe she was right. They were attracted to each other. And she wouldn't be here forever—she'd go back to Chicago soon. Even if a little work at the livery *hadn't* sent her running, she just wasn't the kind of girl to last out here in the near-wilderness for long. So maybe, maybe, this would be okay. For now.

Maybe.

His arms looped her waist and her forehead rested on his shoulder. He studied the sexy bra strap still stretched tight across her upper arm, noticed how damn silky her skin was.

"Just so you know," she whispered in his ear, her breath tickling his neck, "I'm not usually like this."

He almost didn't want to ask. Because he didn't want to give her the idea he was into post-sex small talk or getting to know her. Still, he heard himself murmur, "Like what?"

She raised up, facing him, their mouths, eyes, only a few inches apart. "Um, I don't usually start taking my clothes off and forcing guys to let me have my way with them."

For some reason, it made him smile a little. He never judged people, least of all women, about sex—he'd never been into the double-standard thing. Yet something about her sheepish explanation was cute. "So what's the occasion?"

"Well . . . I wouldn't have if you hadn't gone all 'I want you again.' Once that's out there, though . . . it just seemed a shame to waste it, you know?"

Despite himself, a small laugh escaped his throat. But he also used the opportunity to lift her body off him, because they were still connected, and he was still *feeling* that, and it seemed high time to start winding things down here. He lay her across the couch and she pointed to the tissue box on the coffee table. "Could you, uh . . . ?"

He reached for a handful and neither talked about the fact that they hadn't used a condom this time, either. Bad form, he knew—but he believed her about being safe, and the same was true of him. She was the only woman he'd ever *not* used protection with.

A glance down at her mostly naked body reminded him all over again why this had happened. Her sexy bra still framed her exposed breasts.

She saw him looking and started to raise the cups back up.

"Wait," he said, perhaps a little too urgently.

"What?" she whispered.

The truth was, he didn't know if he'd ever see her breasts again. He'd just told himself maybe this was okay, having sex with her, but he sure as hell didn't know if he'd feel that way tomorrow. At the moment, he didn't feel like he knew much of *anything*. So he wanted to see them for just another minute right now. They were too pretty.

So he lay down next to her and bestowed a small kiss on the pink tip of one breast, using his hand to gently caress the other. After which he found her eyes on him, and he knew he'd gone way too tender all of a sudden. He wasn't sure what to do but make the move to pull her bra back into place *for* her, gently lifting first one cup, then the other, until her nipples were covered, after which he slid the straps back to her shoulders. "That's all," he said quietly, not meeting her gaze. "Just wanted to kiss them again."

They lay that way for a few more minutes, and Rob wondered where King was, surprised the dog hadn't gone crazy wondering what all the groaning was about. He peered out the wide back windows into the green of the grass and the pines. He listened to the nearly inaudible tick of a clock on the mantel.

"Why me?" she asked, voice soft but inquisitive.

He had no idea what she was talking about as he shifted his gaze to her. "Huh?"

"I've heard *lots* of women around here have the hots for you and you want nothing to do with them. So . . . why me?"

Good question. He tried to make light of it. "Would you believe me if I said it was the animal-print?"

A pretty trill of laughter erupted from her throat. "No." Then she got more serious again. "It's not so much that I want to know why me, but why no one else?"

Aw, shit. *Please don't start asking those kinds of questions, Abby.* Yet with her, he figured it was inevitable. "I told you, I'm just not a—"

"And I'm not buying," she cut him off. "That's lame. Guys love sex. All guys. So try again."

He sighed, looked her in those pretty blue eyes, and hoped she'd take some mercy on him as he said quietly, "It's a long story, Abby."

Her answer came just as softly, like an invitation. "I've got some time."

Mercy had been too much to hope for, so Rob briskly sat up. "I don't," he announced. "Work to do." And he reached to the table, where her hot little panties had landed, and gently pushed them into her fist.

"Construction work or canoe work?" She sat up, too, enough to slip her feet into the underwear and start sliding them up those slender legs.

Rob was afraid if he watched her get dressed, he might get worked up all over again and start taking it all back off her, so he stood up and zipped his jeans with his back to her. "Boathouse today."

"Want help?"

He turned to see her in her bra, little white top, and panties, sitting on the couch, peering cheerfully up at him. Oh hell.

To say no would make him look like, well, like a bigger ass than usual. Which generally wouldn't matter to him, but maybe he didn't want her to hate him anymore. He wasn't sure if they'd keep doing what they'd just done, but . . . despite himself, he liked her and couldn't be a *total* jerk to her now. He simply let out a sigh and replied, "I guess you can help if you want, but . . ."

"But?"

He kept his gaze on her, needing to make this clear. "Just . . . don't start thinking this is *something*, because it's not."

To his surprise, a small, cat-like smile spread across her face. "You assume I want it to *be* something when, in fact, I just got out of a long-term relationship and I want it to be nothing just as much as you do."

Well, that was a relief.

Even if it made his stomach pinch in a weird way.

"What happened?" he heard himself ask as he rounded the couch to pick up his T-shirt from the floor. "With the fiancé."

She hesitated a second, long enough for him to pull the shirt over his head.

"He changed his mind," she finally said, and his stomach pinched again, for her. She could be a pushy pain in the ass sometimes, but he could tell from the strain in her voice that she'd been hurt and he didn't particularly like it.

"Why?" he asked, wanting to know more. He walked back around the couch where he could see her, but she'd bent over to get her jeans and he couldn't make out her expression.

"Just turned out we . . . wanted different things," she said, but he knew, that quickly, there was more to the story.

Still, it would probably be best—for both of them—if he let it drop. So he turned his thoughts to the day ahead and was surprised to realize he wasn't really going to mind her company at the dock. So long as she remembered what he'd said—that this was nothing.

"All right then," he told her. "Head back to the inn and put on your tennis shoes, Abby. We've got some boats to float."

"What can I get you?" Carla asked that evening when Lindsey climbed up on a barstool at the Lazy Elk.

It was Saturday night and the place was hopping. Music played, people chatted and drank, she could hear Jimmy frying up food in the back, and she was feeling all-around festive. "How about a frozen margarita?" she asked with hopefully raised eyebrows.

"*Hola, señorita*—coming right up," Carla said with a grin. As she sought an appropriate glass, she added, "So, how was your day?"

"Busy."

"Care to elaborate?" Carla found something that looked more like a brandy snifter to Lindsey than a margarita glass, but who cared?

"Well," she said, thinking back, "I just had a long talk on the phone with my mom, which was nice. She tells me a lot of the hoopla about the whole apron-cheesecake fiasco seems to be dying down at home, mainly because an illustrious local politician was photographed with a hooker—thank heavens for small miracles. The only bummer is that it takes the spotlight off Garrett, too, and I'd have liked for him to suffer a while longer."

Carla looked up from her drink-making. "Does that mean you'll be leaving us soon?"

She liked to think Carla sounded a little sad at the prospect, which was nice—it was good to have a girlfriend again. Somehow, she'd given up most of her friendships when Garrett had come along—mainly because her friends hadn't liked him much and she hadn't wanted to hear that. So it was nice to just dish the dirt with another chick.

"No date in mind just yet," she replied. "I like it here. My mother thinks the fresh air is good for me—she thinks I sound chipper." Of course, when her mother had commented about her sounding chipper, it had actually been *Lindsey* who'd suggested fresh air and nice scenery as the reason why. As opposed to the real reason: mind-numbing sex with a near-stranger.

"What about the rest of your day?" Carla asked, adding triple sec and lime juice to the tequila concoction.

"Well, I worked at the boathouse some more with Rob. Today we made sure all the canoes were lakeworthy. Then I helped him repair a couple of scratches in one of the canoes—and by help I mean hand him stuff and watch. And then I helped him replace a couple of rotting boards on the dock—and by help I mean hand him stuff and listen to him cuss when he hit his thumb with a hammer. We also placed an order for snack crackers and chips at the counter, and called the vending machine people to get the soft drink machine filled later this week."

A coquettish smile grew on Carla's face as she poured the drink mix into the blender with some ice, then looked over her shoulder at Lindsey. "Well now, doesn't *that* sound cozy?"

"You think canoe repairs and snack orders sound cozy?"

She shrugged, her back toward the bar as she started the blender. "For Rob Colter, yeah." A second later, she uncapped the blender and turned back around to pour the margarita into the brandy snifter.

"It was really much more cozy," Lindsey said matter-of-factly, "the two times we've had wild sex in the last twenty-four hours."

Carla's jaw dropped—as she completely let the margarita overflow the glass.

Lindsey pointed. "Um, bartender, you're making a mess there."

"Crap," Carla muttered, then managed to scoop some of the overflow into a regular drink glass, announcing, "I'll drink the leftover—I think I'm gonna need it. Start talking, girlfriend."

"Well, I'm not usually one to kiss and tell," she said with a teasing grin as Carla wiped off her snifter and passed the margarita her way. "No lime?" she said, then, "Wait, I forgot where I was."

"Back to the kissing and telling," Carla prodded.

Lindsey took a sip of her drink. "Good," she said, pointing to the glass, then, "Okay, kissing and telling." She kept it short, briefly explaining her evening at Rob's, the kissing, the leaving, the showing up at her room, the leaving, the going to his house today, and the sex. The truth was, she still couldn't quite believe it all herself, and she especially couldn't believe how she'd behaved the second time.

"You're leaving stuff out, I can tell," Carla said, taking a big sip of her drink, eyes still enormous with shock. "I mean . . . how did it happen? How did the sex actually, you know . . . start?"

"Well, the first time, I was talking about being perimenopausal and he just started kissing me and after that, it was inevitable. The second time . . . well, the second time, I was talking about laundry and he told me he wanted me again so that I should leave. And since that didn't make any sense, I kind of . . . seduced him."

"How?"

"I kind of . . . took my top off."

Carla gasped.

And Lindsey held out her hands as if helpless. "I know. Not normally my thing, but he drove me to it. A guy like him can drive you crazy if you don't occasionally take charge of a situation."

Carla simply stood behind the bar shaking her head, mouth still hanging open. "I'm just . . . amazed."

"Join the club. Nobody could be more amazed about this than me."

"What was he like? I mean, did he talk much? Did he say nice things?"

Lindsey gave her head a slight shake. "Can't say he was much more jovial in bed than any other time. Although I occasionally got a smile—and a lot of moans, so I knew things were going okay. Oh, and he asked me what happened with my fiancé, but I didn't tell him." She'd actually been shocked that Rob would ask her *anything.* And she knew Garrett was an idiot, yet she still had no intention of telling Rob what had happened. She tended to be pretty open, but with this guy, and this topic—nope, he didn't need to know. It would only make her look like the fluffy, froufrou girl he'd thought her from the start. And possibly a loser, too.

Carla bit her lip and leaned conspiratorially forward. "So, was the sex good?"

Lindsey blinked, thinking a mere glance at Rob made the answer obvious. "Uh, do fish swim? Are margaritas tasty? Is there a bear in the roundabout?"

"Yes, yes, and yes."

"That pretty much sums it up."

"Hence your being so chipper."

She smiled, lifted her snifter, and she and Carla clinked glasses. "To getting back on the sex horse," Lindsey said.

"Ride 'em, cowgirl."

They both laughed, and someone yelled, "Yo, Carla, I need a beer down here," so Carla set down her glass and left Lindsey alone for a few minutes with her thoughts.

She'd been fairly stunned when Rob had agreed so easily to let her work with him today, and even more astonished by how accustomed she was getting to being with him. It was starting not to bother her that he didn't talk as much as she did—and she'd truly enjoyed helping him today. The weather had been the warmest yet and she'd even gotten some sun on her cheeks and arms from two days of working outdoors. Although canoe season hadn't officially started yet, she continued to fall more in love with the boathouse, and she only wished she'd been open-minded enough to come up and check it out when she'd gotten Aunt Millie's letter last summer.

The question remained, though: Would she have been insightful enough to see the beauty of the place *then*, when she'd thought her life in Chicago was perfect and wonderful? Or would she still have been so deeply under Garrett's influence that it wouldn't have made any difference anyway?

When Carla returned to Lindsey's end of the bar, she was still smiling. "So, you and Rob Colter. Miracles *do* happen. You must be more charming than I gave you credit for."

"He even thinks I'm sweet," Lindsey proclaimed with a solitary nod.

"I thought you said he didn't say stuff like that."

"Well, not most of the time, and he didn't even sound happy about it—but he said it."

"Hmm . . ."

Lindsey could see the wheels turning in Carla's brain. "Hmm what?"

Carla tilted her head. "Keep this up and you might wheedle the livery out of him yet."

Lindsey blinked her surprise. She hadn't been thinking much about getting her hands on the livery the last couple of days—she'd been too busy getting her hands on Rob. And though she certainly wasn't sleeping with him to try to wear him down on it, it was an . . . intriguing notion. "I thought you said he'd never sell," she reminded her friend.

"I also thought he'd never have sex with you, remember?"

* * *

Dear Lovers,

Wherever you happen to be on this lovely May day, I hope the sun is shining. Here in the mountains of Moose Falls—that's the little town I told you about in my last post—the weather is gorgeous and I'm in a magnificent mood.

Why am I in such a fabulous state of mind, you ask? Well, it could *be the fresh air and gorgeous scenery. (Or at least that's what I told my mom, who never reads my blog. ;)) Or it could be the lovely people I've met here. Or it could be the sense of reconnection I feel to my great-aunt, who lived and died in this town and truly made it her own in countless, wonderful ways.*

Or . . . it could be the steamy affair I'm having with the town's least eligible bachelor!

That's right, girls—I'm back in the saddle again.

So soon? I hear you asking. Yes, I know, I've always preached the merits of getting to know a guy before you hop in the sack. And to be honest—he's not the kind of guy I would normally get involved with: he mostly keeps to himself, he's not into the relationship thing, and from what I can tell, his wardrobe contains an inordinate amount of flannel. But I guess extraordinary times call for extraordinary measures. And let me tell you—this little walk on the steamy side is just what the doctor ordered because I can't remember the last time I felt this good.

And maybe it's, um, indiscreet *for me to share something so personal here, but again—extraordinary times and all that. I guess, given what I've been through lately, I just wanted to let you all know that it is indeed possible to come out on the other side okay, that a breakup isn't the end of the world. I'm not saying I'm completely over the whole thing, mind you—but let's just say it's good to get my mind off it all, and between Moose Falls and my shiny new affair…well, together they're doing a good job of helping me look to the future and get a fresh perspective.*

In addition to my new man—who would have a heart attack if he knew I was calling him "my new man," but it's all in good fun, right?—I have just joined the committee for the upcoming Moose Falls Fish Festival and Fry! That's right, people, I'm getting involved, becoming a part of something bigger than myself. Only a fish fry, you say? Maybe so, but to the folks of Moose Falls, this is a time-honored tradition and I'm excited to see what it's all about.

So, lovers, tell me, what do you *do when love goes wrong and you need a new perspective? Getting a new guy or girl is certainly one fun way to rebound, but when big life changes occur, don't we also need to look deeper at ourselves, at our lives? Don't we need to travel new paths? That's what I'm doing here in Montana, in more ways than one, and I want to hear how* you *have responded to breakups or tough times yourselves.*

Meanwhile, Still Single in Savannah, are you out there? I'm still hoping to hear from you!

Until next time, lovers…

Lindsey clicked on Submit and watched the new blog entry post. She knew it was *totally* indiscreet—maybe even shocking—to tell the world she had a new lover, but what she'd said was true. It was important to her to share it with her readers because it proved that life went on. And maybe that was a message they needed to hear. Maybe poor Still Single in Savannah needed to hear it right now if she'd actually taken Lindsey's stupid advice and ended up alone because of it.

And sure, Lindsey's life remained far from perfect. But so much had changed in less than a week—and definitely for the better. Sex with Rob was really just the cherry on top of the sundae. Albeit an admittedly huge and succulent cherry.

Of course, she'd made it sound to her readers as if this really *were* an affair—the ongoing kind—when she had no idea where she stood with Rob. She knew from being with him yesterday at the livery that he was spending the next few days putting in long hours on Steve Fisher's room addition. Which meant she probably wouldn't see him. And he hadn't suggested she come by in the evening or anything. In fact, when they'd finished working at the boathouse yesterday afternoon, his parting words had been the ever vague, "See ya."

Hence her joining the Fish Festival and Fry committee when Carla had suggested it last night. Lindsey had also been on her second huge snifter of margarita, so it was possible she hadn't been thinking entirely clearly. But she had no regrets. She knew from Aunt Millie's scrapbooks that she herself had always served on this particular committee, heading it up for many years, so this seemed like another good way to walk in her great-aunt's shoes a little more.

So now that she'd posted her blog, it was off to the Lazy Elk for the committee's Sunday afternoon meeting. She hoped she'd get some really good assignments like maybe emceeing the event or giving out the prizes and awards, or maybe, since she was Millie's niece, they'd make her honorary grand marshal or something. Whatever the case, it was a good distraction from thoughts of Rob.

Which had invaded her brain almost constantly the last couple of days.

And that had made sense when she'd been seeing him a lot, and talking to him about Aunt Millie, and going to bed with him—or to couch with him, as it were. But she wasn't so sure it was making good sense *now*.

After all, he was . . . sex. He was her leg back up onto the sex horse. And she'd gotten there, and ridden it—right to the finish line. Race won, ride over.

So it made no sense that she kept seeing his face in her mind, hearing his voice, remembering those rare moments when he'd grace her with a smile or maybe even a hint of flirtation. It made no sense at all.

Unless she really liked him or something.

Which seemed almost impossible given his personality. Not to mention that, as she'd told him, she *had* just come out of a relationship and certainly hadn't headed to Moose Falls looking for love. And God knew *he* certainly wasn't looking for love—no man she'd ever met had worked so hard to make that clear.

Yet here he was—on her mind.

Peering out her window over the ever-serene Spirit Lake, she let out a sigh. She was beginning to be afraid she'd just misled her readers. She'd been all I-have-a-new-lover-and-I'm-on-top-of-the-world, but she'd neglected to mention that she was beginning to miss him when he wasn't around, that when he smiled it made her tingle inside, and that maybe, just maybe, impossible as it seemed—she could be starting to fall for Rob Colter.

Ten

William sat at his computer, reading Lindsey's latest blog post. She was still in Montana. He liked that—since he was in Oregon. Oh sure, it was still a long way from Portland, but she was also a heck of a lot closer to him than she'd been in Chicago.

Outside, riding mowers chugged along and lawn sprinklers irrigated yards in a pulsating beat. As usual, he felt disconnected from it all and jealous of his neighbors. Glancing outside, he saw the handsome guy who ran past every evening with his black Lab on a red leash and he knew the guy's life was better than his. He probably had a great wife. Maybe a nice kid or two. He'd be willing to bet they left the kids with relatives and drove down to wine country every summer for a long weekend of wine-tasting and drunken sex in some quaint B&B.

Sighing, he tore his gaze from the window and back to the computer screen, where he read some more. And found out—

God. *Oh God.* Lindsey had a lover.

His stomach plummeted as equal parts jealousy and elation tore through him. It was good to hear her sounding so happy—Lindsey was such a bright light in the world, she *deserved* happiness. But it was also a little crushing to hear about this new guy of hers. He didn't sound worthy of Lindsey, and William only hoped the guy was treating her right.

The guy probably didn't know what he had in her, though. After all, to make love to Lindsey and not want to have a relationship with her—no, this guy wasn't right for her.

William clicked on the comments link, thinking maybe he would tell her so—maybe he would just gently point out that she deserved much more than a guy like that could give her.

But then he started reading all the comments already posted. Mostly from women, as usual, they were all ridiculously thrilled by Lindsey's news. He let his eyes slide down over them, not stopping to notice who sent them.

You go, girl! Way to show us how it's done!

Lindsey, I'm so happy for you, but you have to tell us more about your new guy. Even if he's the quiet type, he sounds dreamy. And flannel can be very snuggly!

I knew that ugly situation with stupid Garrett wouldn't keep you down for long!

Lindsey, I've always respected your views on men and sex, and I'm a believer in getting to know a person first, too—but if you've decided to make the leap into bed with this guy, it must be the right thing to do. You sound happy and that's what counts.

Tell us more! What's he look like? What's his name? And does he have a few hundred brothers for the rest of us? ;) I, for one, LOVE a guy in flannel.

William just sighed. He was in no position to tell Lindsey what he really thought—he'd get cyber-booed off the blog. And as for these women cheering her on and failing to see the guy's shortcomings, they were morons who probably let guys walk all over them and had no self-respect.

He wished there was some way he could e-mail Lindsey privately, but her e-mail address wasn't displayed anywhere, which meant all communications with her had to be public.

So, with a heavy heart, he typed in a comment:

You sound happy, Lindsey, and I'm glad. Just be sure you take care of yourself; take care of your heart. I care about you and wouldn't want you to get hurt again.

Maybe it was too bold to say he cared about her, but he hoped he'd tucked it between words that masked the meaning a little, while at the same time letting it out. He just wanted her to know that her welfare truly mattered to him. So he hit the Submit button and watched the comment appear. Maybe she'd read it and somehow *feel* what he really meant. He believed in that kind of thing when a connection between two people was strong. As kids, he and his brother had sometimes shared a sort of ESP. But since Tom had died . . . well, William couldn't remember the last time he'd felt that kind of link with someone. His heart had died with his brother—he knew that. But he also knew that if he ever found a girl as vibrant and alive as Lindsey, she'd be able to bring him back to life inside.

Rob put down the truck's windows to let the air blow in. It was just past seven on Monday and he'd gotten a hell of a lot of work done on Steve Fisher's new room today. It was slow going, given that he was only one guy, but he always made sure people understood that when they hired him—and hell, with a few more days like today under his belt, he'd have the room under roof and be ready to start subcontracting out the drywall and electric work. Which was good, since he'd gotten a call from Stanley Bobbins last night—he'd liked Rob's bid and wanted him to build his new supply shed.

As his truck wended its way around the tiny mountain road leading from Fisher's place, thick pines lining both sides in the dusky air, Marty Casey & Lovehammers sang "Trees" on the satellite radio—Rob's one splurge in life because he didn't think he could live without music again and Moose Falls didn't get any radio stations, so he'd invested in satellite in both the truck and the cabin. The lyrics were so sure, confident—the guy in the song knew he wanted this girl in his life, knew they'd find the answers together, intended to make it happen. Rob had never felt that way—and due to circumstances beyond his control, knew he never would.

Of course, any other day and he wouldn't be thinking like this—he wouldn't be listening to the words, picking the music apart for the meaning—but today was different and he knew why. He'd fucked up big time. With her.

And now she was on his mind. And he was suffering pangs of regret because he'd never know what the guy in the song knew; he'd never have that with a woman. The hell of it was that he'd been fine with that a few days ago, but now Lindsey had reminded him how good sex was, how nice it was to have a little companionship—hell, it had been nicer than he could have imagined just to eat a meal with somebody. He'd first noticed that when they'd shared pizza the other night, and he'd been aware of it again yesterday when she'd taken a break at the boathouse, walked over to the café, and brought back lunch. They'd sat on the dock, eating ham sandwiches and drinking cans of Coke, and the simple act had made him feel so . . . strangely human. Normal.

But he *wasn't* normal, so he couldn't start thinking he was or letting himself want the things other guys wanted. Damn her for screwing with his mind this way. Even if he couldn't exactly blame it on her. She didn't know his history—thank God.

Still, though, no more Abby. Or . . . at least not tonight. He was determined to make tonight perfectly normal—normal for *him* anyway.

Maybe he'd grill up a few burgers on the back deck—two for him, one for King. He'd sit out and enjoy the night until it started getting cold. Then he'd watch a little TV, maybe do some laundry before he ran out of the T-shirts he worked in. The most important part of it all, though, was that he'd be doing it *alone.*

In fact, even if he was thinking about her, a certain sense of peace pervaded as he pulled into the driveway, the gravel crunching beneath the big tires, just seeing the cabin sitting quietly and knowing it would stay that way tonight. He slammed the door and strode to the house, singling out the right key on his chain. King sat inside, peering out the window, releasing one excited bark that seemed to say, *You're home!*

"Hey, bud," he said, pushing through the door a few seconds later, watching the big dog's tail slash back and forth through the air as he barked another hello and leapt around a little. "You're a good boy, aren't you?" he said in a voice he planned never to let another human being hear in this lifetime. "Yes you are."

Once the evening greetings ended, he tossed his keys on the small table by the door, went outside to get the grill going, then came back in, ready to grab a quick shower before he made the burgers. When the phone rang, he thought about letting the machine get it—but he was expecting to hear from Stanley Bobbins with some final specs on the shed.

"Hello."

"Um, hey—it's Lindsey."

He let out a breath and his chest tightened. He didn't know why. But wait—yes he did. It was about sex. That was all—nothing more. That was the only reason her voice sounded so good. "What's up, Abby?"

"Well, I'm sure you know the big Fish Festival and Fry is next Sunday."

"Yep."

"And historically, I'm told, the boathouse is kind of the headquarters for it. You know, where they set up refreshments and give out prizes. And there's a big canoe race that takes place. Did you know all that?"

"Yep. I was here for last year's." Although he'd kept to himself and had only come because Millie had just hired him and had pretty much insisted. And even that early in their relationship, he hadn't wanted to let her down.

"Well, I joined the festival committee and—"

"You're kidding." He couldn't help interrupting—only Abby would come to town for a brief visit and get herself on a committee.

"No," she said, ignoring his tone, "and I've been elected to ask you if it's okay for us to use the dock the same way as usual."

The question caught him a little off guard. "Well, yeah. I figured they were planning on it—I didn't expect anybody to ask me." It was a town tradition, after all.

"Well, actually, I think everyone on the committee was . . . afraid to."

"Oh." He wasn't sure how to feel about that. True, he didn't like being bothered, but he also didn't want people thinking he was an ogre. He had businesses to run, after all, and he couldn't have the whole town hating him.

"I told them you're not as mean as you seem," she added.

Hmm. So she was taking up for him, telling people he was a decent guy. Which bordered on incredible given that he wasn't altogether sure he'd treated *her* very decently so far. So he just said, "Don't let that get around, Abby," and realized too late that he'd made a joke and even sounded a little flirty.

"It'll be a big relief to everyone that we can use the dock," she said. "Otherwise, there'd be no place to crown Little Miss Fish."

"Little Miss Fish?" he asked skeptically.

"Hey, I didn't name it—I just work here."

He laughed softly—then promptly regretted that, too. Damn her—she had a way of making him smile.

"So," she went on, " there's a pre-event party at the Lazy Elk on Friday night, if you want to come. Apparently it's a big thing—free burgers, desserts from the café, that sort of thing."

Rob's stomach hollowed. Because for some odd reason, he almost wanted to go. A little. But . . . "You know I don't like being with people."

"Yes, I know. But it will be the first year without Millie and since the boathouse is the center of the event, I think it would be nice if you made an appearance so people will feel welcome on Sunday. Plus . . ."

"Plus?" he asked when she trailed off.

"*I'll* be there. And I thought you might, um . . . want to see me. Or something."

He hesitated, then said, "Or something," but knew a smile leaked out through his voice.

"So you'll come by on Friday night?"

Jesus, he felt suspiciously like he'd just been asked on a date. He needed to make it clear that wasn't the case. "Maybe for a little while. But I'm not staying long. And don't expect me to be very social."

"It's better that you don't. Because if you did, people would start having heart attacks and the whole party would be ruined. See you then."

She hung up, so Rob did, too.

After which he stood there for a minute, thinking, *Wait a minute. What just happened here? Why did I just agree to go to a party?* And the bigger question: *Why am I kind of glad?*

When Rob walked into the Lazy Elk a few nights later, he was . . . pretty damn horrified. The place was packed. He'd never seen it this way before, and he thought about turning around and marching right back out—until he heard someone call, "Hey, Rob, glad you made it!"

He looked up to see Carla, the bartender who'd served him a beer once or twice. Lindsey had mentioned being friendly with her. She stood across the room behind the bar, so he got by with only lifting a hand in her direction.

"Burger?" someone asked then. He looked to his left to see Jimmy, a young guy who he knew to be Carla's cook, carrying a tray that brimmed with them.

"Uh, thanks, but no," he muttered.

"More comin' out soon if you change your mind," the blond-headed kid said, then disappeared into the crowd with his hamburgers.

"Well, hello there, Mr. Colter. I hear you're hostin' our fine little event on Sunday."

Rob felt his eyebrows shoot up as he looked down to see the spry old guy who ran the general store. "Hosting? No, not me."

The little old man—what was his name? Bernard or something—just laughed good-naturedly. "Didn't mean to scare ya there, friend—just meant we're usin' the boathouse."

Rob tipped his head back, relieved. "Oh—yeah. Sure. It's no problem."

"Hi there, Rob." He shifted his gaze to the sugary sweet voice to his right and remembered why he so seldom came in here. This same woman with big hair had tried to pick him up his first time in last spring, too.

He probably knew her name but had forgotten it. "Hi," he said.

"If you're looking for a place to sit, there's room at *my* table. I'd love to buy you a drink."

Rob was seriously considering killing Lindsey—but where the hell was she? For the first time since landing in Moose Falls, he wanted a woman on his arm. At least Lindsey he was used to. At least Lindsey he actually liked. Most of the time now anyway. And the truth was, he'd sort of waited for her to show up somewhere in his life this week—but she hadn't. Just that phone call on Monday. And . . . well, if he was honest with himself, he wasn't going to mind seeing her. "Uh . . . I'm meeting somebody. Sorry."

He caught Bernard winking up at him as the woman walked away. "She's a saucy one, huh? Cuts hair over in Cedarville. My new squeeze, Ann Bixby, goes over there when she needs her hair set."

Rob could only nod. He grunted a little, too, mainly because actual words wouldn't come out. Until he thought of some worthwhile ones. "Have you seen Lindsey? Millie's niece?"

"Oh, now *she's* a cutie. Don't blame ya for lookin' for that one—no sirree. Try over by the bar. I hear she's always makin' Carla mix her up fancy cocktails."

"Thanks," Rob said, then wove his way through the crowd, thankful when no one else stopped him.

That's when he saw Lindsey talking to some guy in his twenties who women probably thought was good-looking. His chest tightened slightly. Not that he cared who Lindsey talked to.

Still, he tried to listen in over the music and conversations going on around him. And felt a little perturbed that she hadn't even noticed he was standing three feet away from her in the crowd.

Then a weird thought hit him. He hadn't heard from her for days—and now here she was talking with this goofy guy. Could she be sleeping with him? Nah, no way. And what if she was? What did *he* care? Even if the very thought made him feel a little crazed inside.

"I've read your column in the paper," the dude was saying to her. "Good stuff." He held a glass with some girly drink in it—it was nearly pink.

"Thanks, but I'm not writing it anymore." *Her* drink looked like some kind of martini.

"How come?" the guy asked.

Her smile never wavered, but Rob had spent enough time with her to notice the way her eyes dulled—just a little. "I recently broke up with my fiancé, so I needed a change. And I decided maybe I didn't really know enough about love to be advising people on it."

Her companion looked doubtful. "Aw, come on—from what I've read, you seem to know a *lot* about love. And *sex*." The way he let his voice linger over the last word grated on Rob's nerves.

Lindsey's gaze dropped—to the big cake on the table she and the guy stood next to. "Great cake, huh? Mary Beth over at the café made it." Rob couldn't see the whole cake from where he stood, but could tell Mary Beth had created a rainbow trout with gray icing. And that it was smiling.

"Sure," the guy next to Lindsey said. "But about that column of yours, I bet you'd still do a good job with it. Especially the sex parts."

"And you're basing that on . . . ?"

The guy shrugged, took a sip of his pink drink, then let his eyes slide up and down her body. "You just look like you'd be good in the sack."

Christ. Rob had experienced a similar thought upon first meeting her, but he never would have *said* it, for God's sake. And even as he kind of wanted to pound the guy into the ground, he couldn't help feeling relieved to figure out this was obviously their first conversation.

"Well, thanks," Lindsey said, still cool as a cucumber in a way Rob couldn't help admiring, "but I gotta go. See ya later." With that, she turned away, ready to drift off into the crowd—but the damn guy grabbed her arm.

Rob's spine stiffened and he started to take a step toward them—as Abby looked pointedly over her shoulder at the guy.

"Why don't you show me?" the guy said.

"Huh?"

"How good in the sack you are."

She flashed a cutting look. "You're *not* serious."

"I don't think she's interested, dude," Rob heard himself say, low and gruff. Not that he didn't think she could take care of herself. But maybe he just didn't like her *having* to.

"Says who?" the guy asked, looking up at Rob with all the dumb masculine bravado of youth.

"Says *me*."

"And who the hell are *you*?"

"Her date."

"Oh."

"Yeah."

"I didn't, uh . . ."

"Yeah, I know you didn't."

At that point, the goofy guy slunk away with his girly drink, which forced Rob to look down at Lindsey. "Just to make it clear, I'm not really—"

"My date, I know," she said, smiling. "It would be tragic if anyone here thought you had a date."

"Just thought it looked like you could use a hand."

She peered up at him, her blue eyes sparkling beneath the bar lights as she reached out to lace her fingers with his. "I'll gladly take that hand, thanks. Despite the caveman-like qualities of the discussion."

He raised his eyebrows. "Caveman?"

She spoke in a low, brusque cartoon voice, making fun of him. "*Says who? Says me.*"

He just shrugged. And liked holding her hand too much. Something about it made him feel all of fourteen. So he just looked down at the cake and said, "Nice fish." The cake said *Happy Fish Festival* in green icing. "But he wouldn't be smiling so big if he knew about the 'fry' part."

She laughed and even squeezed his hand a little, but then let it abruptly go. "Oh, I'd better be careful or someone will think we're on a date."

On impulse, though, Rob grabbed her hand right back up. It was warm. "On second thought, maybe that's okay." He'd just spotted the saucy hairdresser from the corner of his eye, headed his way. "That woman with the big hair wants to buy me a drink."

He watched Lindsey glance over, then slowly bring her eyes back up to his. Damn, she looked pretty tonight—she wore a sparkly tank top under a denim jacket and her long, straight hair fell over her shoulders like silk. And she kept smiling. "Rob," she said, sounding like he was being dense, "at the risk of giving you a big head . . . they *all* want to buy you a drink."

"Huh?"

"Look around," she said softly.

So he did. Subtly. And . . . shit. Maybe he *was* dense. At a glance, he found at least five different women watching him, giving him . . . that look. And he guessed he knew from the past that women generally seemed to find him attractive, but this was a little overwhelming.

He tried to ignore that as he peered down at Lindsey—the one set of eyes in this room he was comfortable looking into—and let the tiniest hint of a smile leak out as he spoke. "Guess that makes you . . . a lucky girl."

A wide grin spread across her face. "Yes," she said, "it's a true thrill to be on a pretend date with the guy every other girl in the room wants." Then she turned to start dragging him through the crowd. "Let's get you a drink. And I think I need to freshen mine."

"What is it?" he asked, glancing toward the greenish liquid in the bottom of her glass.

"It *was* an appletini."

"Ah." Then, as they finagled themselves onto two just-vacated barstools, facing each other so that their jean-clad knees touched, he heard himself say, "Hey, Abby."

"What?" She still held his hand.

He spoke softly, despite the loudness of the place. "About that date. It . . . isn't just pretend."

He wasn't sure why he'd said it, but he could tell it threw her. "No?"

He tried to shrug it off. "You asked me to come tonight. I came."

"So that makes it a date?"

"If you want it to be."

Their eyes met and he tried to read hers, but couldn't. He thought maybe he saw something serious in those blue depths, something that should have scared him but didn't.

Finally, she grinned and said, "Okay, yeah, let's call it a date. It sounds better to say I'm actually dating the guy I've been sleeping with."

They both shared a laugh and, still holding hands with one of her knees locked between his now, he was starting to feel it again—the need to be with her, to have her.

Oh hell—the truth was that he'd never *stopped* feeling it, not since the *last* time they'd been together. But now that she was back with him and touching him, now that he could see her eyes and smell her perfume and sense the softness of the flesh in that shadowy place between her breasts, he was feeling it a lot *more*. As for all this talk about dates—shit, he didn't know what he was doing, where his words were coming from. But right now he could only go with it. And at the moment, it felt . . . more than fine.

"Hey, you two," Carla said, stepping up to them behind the bar. "Linds, you look like you need another appletini. What can I get *you*, Rob?"

"Uh, beer."

But Lindsey shook her head at him. "No beer."

"No beer?" What the hell did *that* mean?

Carla only laughed. "Lindsey is making everyone order real drinks tonight. For me. Because I like making them. And because she's a good friend."

He glanced around and realized that the twenty-something dipwad who'd propositioned Lindsey wasn't the only one drinking a girly drink—the room was filled with colorful concoctions. "Uh, then—rum and Coke."

But Lindsey shook her head again. "We have a three-ingredient minimum. Try again."

He just looked at her, thinking she had the ability to be annoying as hell. But that it also somehow equaled *cute*.

He could barely remember the last time he'd had a mixed drink, so he thought for a minute and finally said, "How about a gin and tonic?"

Lindsey's palm came down gently on his knee as she reminded him, "That's only two ingredients."

"Doesn't it come with a lime wedge or something?"

"No lime," she said, making the same motion as when an umpire called a runner out.

"No lime?"

"Not at the Lazy Elk. No fruit wedges at all."

"But it *is* supposed to have one," Carla pointed out. "In all fairness."

"Thanks, Carla," he said, seeing sense prevail. "'Cause I'm getting thirsty here."

As Carla went about making the drinks, Lindsey told him all about the plans for the Fish Festival and Fry, seeming utterly ecstatic that she got to crown Little Miss Fish. "Odds-on favorite is little Shelby Jones because she takes ballet lessons and her mother made her a fancy dress. But I've seen pictures of the entrants and I think Morgan Wright looks like a dark horse who could come from behind and take the whole thing."

"I guess that explains why I haven't seen you for a while. You've been working on Fish Festival plans."

"Fish festivals don't throw themselves," she pointed out. "And you'd better be careful, Mr. Colter, or I'll start thinking you missed me or something."

Rob ignored that, but found himself telling her a little about his work the past few days and about his new job for Stanley Bobbins. Turned out Lindsey had met Stanley's wife and little boy at the Moose Mart last night and thought they were "lovely people."

"Oh, and guess what," she went on. "Eleanor told me she has some reservations for next weekend! And you know what that means. Canoe season! So don't plan anything. Or . . . if you have something you need to do, I could work there *for* you. Or . . . we could do it together. If you want."

At the moment, that was sounding far too good to Rob. But next weekend was a damn long time away in terms of him and her, so he just set down his drink and took her hands in his. "Let's just see how it works out, Lindsey, okay?"

She smiled and he could see she was getting tipsy. "You just called me Lindsey. Not Abby."

Shit—he hadn't realized. "Well, don't get used to it—I can't promise it'll stick."

"About the livery," she said, "I don't mean to be pushy. I mean, I know it's not *my* thing—it's *your* thing. Yours and Millie's, I get that. But . . ."

"But?"

"I bought all these cute little skorts, and my Keds, of course, and . . . I just like it there."

Her face was so earnest, and she was so pretty—and maybe he was getting a little drunk, too—because despite how far away next weekend felt, he heard himself say, "You can work with me at the boathouse whenever you want, okay?"

She smiled and extracted one hand from his to sip her drink. "Thanks." Then her eyes drifted to some point behind him and she said, "And if I were you, I might kiss me right now, because there's a stacked blonde giving you the eye so hard that I don't think just holding my hand is scaring her away."

Two weeks ago, Rob wouldn't even have considered kissing anyone, let alone doing it in a public place, surrounded by nearly every person in a town that loved to talk. But at the moment, it was a pretty easy suggestion to take. "Okay," he said, then leaned forward to gently press his mouth to hers. And damn—she tasted good, kind of like apple and kind of like alcohol, but mostly like Abby. So he automatically slanted his mouth the other way over hers and this time lingered there, drinking her in, feeling how close he was to her, and how much closer he wanted to get. He found himself squeezing his knees around hers, his groin tightening, his heart beating harder against his ribs.

"Did that scare her off?" he breathed, his mouth as near to hers as it could be without touching.

She only glanced briefly away before bringing her eyes back. "I think the coast is clear."

"Good," he said, but he didn't mean it, since he wouldn't have minded another reason to kiss her again.

Just then, Eleanor stepped up through the crowd to greet them. "Well, look who's here. Rob, it sure is nice to see you out and about."

He gave a short nod. "Thanks, Eleanor."

Then her gaze dropped to where their hands and knees touched. "Well, you might not have known her when she got here, but looks like ya do now," she said, adding a wink—yet then changed the subject so easily that Rob didn't even feel weird about what she'd just said. "Did you see my Mary Beth's cake? Is that a masterpiece or what?"

"Rob likes the way the fish is smiling," Lindsey told her, and he couldn't help chuckling silently inside.

"Mary Beth'll be glad to hear that. She was trying to capture the friendly spirit of Moose Falls. I've already taken pictures, so I think it's time I track her down and get her to start cutting it. Have you seen her?"

"She was over in the corner with some of her book club ladies when I got here," Lindsey said.

And then they were alone again, as alone as you could be in a crowded room anyway, and Rob said, "Why don't we get out of here, Abby?"

"You don't want a piece of fish cake?"

"No."

"Then what do you want?"

He lowered his voice just slightly. "A piece of *you.* You taste better."

"*Oh,*" she said, their eyes meeting and hers filling with a sensuality that made him hard behind his zipper. "Well then, yeah, let's go," she said, still sounding a little intoxicated. "Who needs fish cake anyway?"

Eleven

A cool breeze blew off the lake as Lindsey and Rob walked hand in hand up the road toward his house—and she couldn't believe Rob was actually *holding* her hand. Sure, she'd started it at the bar, but he'd kept it going. She barely knew what to think—who *was* this masked man? This man who'd actually declared this a *date*.

But she felt too giddy to care, and too *ready*, as well—the crux of her thighs ached a little more with each step she took toward the cabin. Of course, she was in heels—between-the-toe leopard-print slip-ons to be exact—so the walk was slow. Yet she didn't mind that, either. She liked soaking up every moment with him. Despite the breeze, it wasn't as cold as past evenings, and a half-moon shone overhead, casting a ribbon of light across the water.

"Nice night," she said.

He squeezed her hand and she felt it in her panties. "About to get nicer," he said deeply.

Oh my. She felt *that* hot little promise even *more* intensely. She didn't know Rob *did* seductive. But she liked it.

At first, she'd been disappointed when the Fish Festival committee had only wanted her to call Rob, but then again, it had given her a good reason to call Rob. Of course, the days between then and now had been fairly grueling—she'd finally gotten jobs like helping with banners and concocting kids' games, but she'd also spent the whole time lusting for him and worrying that wherever he was, he'd taken his fill of her and forgotten she existed. Now, though, he'd even let this be a *date*, so given that she'd also finally finagled her way into getting to crown Little Miss Fish, this committee stuff was working out all right. And so was this date stuff. Rob had actually invited her back to his place. As opposed to fighting his urges like usual. Premeditated sex. This was good.

Something about approaching Rob's place late at night, the sound of crickets in the trees, made her want him all the more. She felt like he was leading her into a dark haven of seduction, like it was a much different place than when she'd come here before. Maybe it was just a testament to how much she wanted this man. In a way that went deeper than in the beginning. This was about more than his body now. This was becoming about his soul.

Oh God, she thought as they climbed the steps and he stopped to find his keys. *His soul? Please let that be appletini-induced crazy talk in my head. You can't be thinking about Rob Colter's soul! If he knew you even thought about him* having *a soul, he'd be running like a madman in the other direction—so stop it. Enjoy this. Enjoy your rebound sex. And remember, like it or not, that's all this is.*

When Rob pushed open the big wooden door and flipped on a dim light, King barked, just a little, clearly not expecting a visitor at this hour. "Hey, bud," Rob said to the dog, "settle down. It's only Lindsey."

And as her whole body warmed—not just from stepping in from the cool night—she was forced to realize how much she liked when he called her by name, and how much his simple words to King had sounded as if . . . as if she were truly welcome, like she . . . belonged here now.

"Hi, King," she said softly, deciding she needed to make friends with him. Rob had never said a word about the dog, but it was clear he treasured him. So when King looked up at her from those big black doggie eyes, she even reached down to stroke her fingers over his furry head, scratching a little behind his ear. She hadn't had a dog since childhood, but the natural way to show affection to one came back to her, especially when King stood still to let her pet him. "Nice doggie," she heard herself whisper down to him.

"Want something to drink?" Rob asked.

Truthfully, her head still swam from the appletinis. "Um . . . I think I've had enough. I'm a little tipsy."

"Yeah, I know," he said, hanging his jacket on a peg board by the door. Then he grinned, arching one brow. "The easier for me to have my way with you."

Her whole body warmed further as Rob took her hand and drew her toward the stairs that led to the bedroom loft. Given how hard Rob had been fighting their attraction just a few short days ago, it aroused her to her very core to hear him talking sexy—even if teasingly.

The first thing her eyes fell on upstairs was the big, woodsy bed made of knotty pine, covered with a pretty country quilt of pink and white and blue. "Millie made the quilt," he volunteered, still holding her hand—a new habit she liked. "I thought about changing it, but it fits the room, and it's . . . Millie."

Lindsey nodded, understanding. Somehow taking the quilt out of this room would have ruined the space, made it less alive, less inviting. "Yeah, it's good here," she said, bending slightly to run her hand across it, to feel the stitches Millie had sown across the calico fabrics.

Then her eyes drifted to a daybed situated next to the front window.

"Millie kept a teddy bear collection there," he said, "but

before she died, she donated them to the hospital down in Whitefish for the children's ward. So now sometimes I sleep here when it's raining. Even if it's cold, I keep the window open. I like the smell of rain. Like to listen to it."

Again, Lindsey quietly nodded. To her, rain had always been bad—it messed up traffic and turned her hair frizzy and sometimes damaged her shoes. But here . . . none of that mattered. Not at all. And it was enlightening to have Rob suddenly make her think of rain in a different way. "Since it's nice out," she suggested, "can we open the window even though it's not raining?"

"Sure," he said, then leaned across the daybed to push the window open. Night sounds and sweet-smelling spring air rushed in.

The first two times they'd had sex, it had been heated, urgent, and that had been wildly exciting. But tonight, after long days apart, she wanted to *know* him, really *know* him. *Explore* him. *Pleasure* him. She suffered the overwhelming urge to simply *give* of herself to him. She'd come to Montana trying to *take* something from him, and Carla kept innocently encouraging it, and even Lindsey herself continued flirting with the idea—but in this moment, she knew . . . she no longer wanted to take this place or the canoe rental away from Rob. She just wanted to be close to him.

As he turned back from the window, she blocked his way, met his gaze in the dim light from a Tiffany lamp he'd flipped on across the room, and heard herself say, "Here." Then she let her jacket fall to the floor behind her.

"Wherever you want," Rob said, his voice dropping, too, to something quiet and raspy as his big hands closed over her hips, molding to her curves, the mere touch making her surge with moisture.

Lowering himself to the edge of the daybed, he drew her between his parted legs, then leaned in to place a kiss on her stomach, through her top. Which made her not want the top there anymore. "Take it off me," she heard herself whisper.

She'd become so sexually confident with Rob in such a short time—she could barely believe she'd issued the command, especially after the Great Apron Debacle.

But—at least when it came to sex—Rob never made her feel any less than wholly desired. And that feeling only grew as he peeled her tank up over her head, then let his gaze fall on the pink bra underneath, bearing black polka dots and a tiny black bow between her breasts. Her flesh swelled from the underwire cups, making her feel sexy as sin.

"Did you find the laundry room at the inn?" he asked, the corners of his mouth quirking slightly upward.

She nodded, his breath warming her skin and making it difficult to talk. "Mmm-hmm."

"This is pretty," he said, then used his fingertip to trace a path down the inner curve of one cup. His words had come out ragged, hot, and it was all she could do not to tremble.

"I have on matching panties," she managed.

"Show me."

"Help me," she countered.

And Rob reached for the button on her jeans.

A moment later, she assisted him in pushing the denim over her hips, after which the jeans dropped to her ankles, and she stepped out of them and her leopard-print shoes at the same time.

"So pretty, honey," he murmured, eyes lingering on her panties and making every cell of her body lust for him—then his gaze dropped to the floor. "Killer shoes." He raised his eyes back to her. "You could leave those on if you want."

She giggled softly as her arms fell easily around his neck. "Your animal-print fetish is showing again, Mr. Colter."

"I never had one until . . ."

"Until what?"

He hesitated, eased his arms slowly around her waist, and let his eyes slide up her body to her face. "Until you."

She barely heard the words, he'd said them so softly. But

they echoed down deep inside her, moving her to climb onto the daybed with him, straddling his hips.

He took the opportunity to shift them both, laying her back against a pile of throw pillows as he leaned over to lower one scintillating kiss to the ridge of her breast. She felt it everywhere, and when a *whoosh* of cool air blew in the window, lifting the curtains and even her hair, it heightened every sensation in her body—every want, every need.

"Sure you aren't gonna get cold, Abby?" he asked, clearly misreading her lustful trembling for a chilled shiver.

She didn't like that she was shaking—in fact, she wanted to appear more in control than she actually felt at the moment, which made her a little nervous. "I'm sure. I tend to get hot during sex. I really *do* think I'm perimenopausual and—"

His interruption came softly. "Abby. Shhh. Kiss me."

His handsome face was only a few short inches from hers and the very nearness took her breath away. "Okay," was all she said. Whispered, actually.

His mouth was tender but firm on hers, and as always when Rob kissed her, she felt consumed by his maleness. When his capable hand slid onto her breast, she let out a hot sigh and he kissed her harder. Her whole body tingled as he kneaded her through her bra, gently stroking her hardened nipple with his thumbs. Her breath grew thready, the small of her back aching with desire.

She tugged at his shirt—a simple beige button-down—to let him know she needed him out of it. He lay on top of her now, so their bodies separated just enough for him to rip it off and toss it aside.

She caught just a glimpse of that perfect, muscular chest and torso before it descended back over her and they were flesh to flesh, eye to eye, until he raised up to lower one bra strap.

He peeled down the cup and wasted no time closing his warm, wet mouth over her, the sensation intense enough to make her gasp. Her back arched involuntarily, and he shifted until—*oh my*—his erection settled squarely between her thighs. "Unh," she heard herself moan as her legs curved around his hips, pulling him tight, moving instinctively against him. And then he suckled her as she ran her fingers through his thick hair, as the night breeze wafted over them, as the crickets sang and the world seemed like a much better place to Lindsey than it had a couple of weeks ago.

When finally he released her breast, the cool air from the window made it tingle so intensely that she sucked in her breath and flashed her lover an enraptured smile. And she almost whispered, *More.* Because she wanted him to kiss her breasts some more, wanted to feel how hard he was against her most sensitive spot some more, wanted to feel *everything* he gave her when they were having sex some more.

But she held her tongue because she didn't want to get completely lost in this like usual. Well, she did—but she wanted something else, too. She wanted to pleasure him. More than she ever had. She wanted to make him feel as, as . . . *worshipped* as *he* made *her* feel when they were intimate.

Hearing her own labored breath, louder than the crickets now, she pressed her palms to Rob's chest and pushed him up, over, until he lay on his back, reversing their positions. She slanted her mouth over his, feeling the scratch of his stubbled chin against her skin as his tongue entered her mouth. His breath came heavy now, too—and she intended to make it come a lot harder still.

She could have traded tongue kisses with him all night, but she retreated, trailing kisses over his jaw, down onto his neck—which he arched for her, sighing his pleasure—then onto his broad chest.

She kissed, licked, nibbled her way slowly down his body, taking the time to touch and caress, to study with her eyes—to learn him. She found a small scar under his ribs and what looked like a tiny birthmark near his navel. She tried her damnedest to ignore the tattoo on his chest, even if it made her stomach tighten to kiss her way across the scripted letters.

She listened to his breath—yes, heated now, like her own, as she studied the thin line of hair that led to his zipper. She let the flat of her hand rest on the column of his erection—sensing the power of it even as it lay hidden behind his jeans—just for a few seconds before finally undoing his pants, then lifting his underwear over his hard-on. She pushed his jeans wide and let the sight hollow out her stomach even as it stole her breath.

She lifted her gaze and their eyes met, his look wild, feral—strangely even almost frightened, like an animal who wasn't sure what would happen next. She'd never seen him this way before, not even close.

And then she remembered. He hadn't been with a woman before her since coming to Moose Falls. At least a year. And who knew how long before that? How long had it been since a woman had given him this particular gift?

The question made her want to go slow for him, make it perfect. She knew guys were hardly picky about this sort of thing, but she wanted it to be the best he'd ever had.

Wrapping her hand around his length, she massaged lightly, then lowered a kiss to the very tip. His guttural moan filled the air, permeating her senses, making her feel . . . oh God, even more connected to him somehow. She didn't know what he'd suffered, but it dawned on her now that whatever it was, it had to have been a hell of a lot worse than what Garrett had done to her, and that had made her feel *awful*, so how did *Rob* feel? What made him close himself off from people, women? And maybe the bigger question was: What had made him open himself back up, at least a little, to her?

But she was already feeling too much for him, falling for him too hard, so she didn't let her mind explore that question. Instead, she turned back to concentrating on the task at hand. And making it perfect for him.

She lowered her mouth full over him, sinking down.

She felt his groan in her gut.

She listened to his hot sighs of pleasure as she moved on him, the power of his erection and the rugged beauty of his body assailing her senses more with every second. She wanted to take him to heaven, and she thought maybe she was on the way to doing that when she realized *he* was trembling now. His hands in her hair were trembling. When she looked up, his lips quivered. His eyes shone on her glassy and hot. She wanted to make him climax this way, her own pleasure be damned. No, her own pleasure would come from his.

But then he lifted her head, pushed her away. "Getting too close," he growled, his body still shaking.

She ran her hand down his bared thigh, kissed his hip. "I want to make you come."

"Not that way."

"Why not?"

"Too fast," he breathed. "I'm not even close to being done here yet."

Oh. Well, she couldn't exactly argue with that. "Okay," she whispered, then kissed her way back up his body—still trying to ignore the Gina tattoo, but not doing very well, so she focused instead on what they'd just shared. "You . . . liked that a lot," she said upon arriving at his chest, resting her chin there. She just wanted to hear him confirm it.

"Yeah," he agreed warmly, and she felt the simple answer at her core.

But then heard herself ask, "Why?" More with each passing hour now, she yearned to know what had happened to make him such a loner.

"*Why?*" he asked, incredulous. Which made sense, she supposed. "How could I not? Plus it's been a while. And you're good at it."

Not exactly the detailed explanation she'd been fishing for, but she took the flattery for what it was worth. When she smiled at him, her mouth felt pleasantly stretched, swollen, from the affections.

"Did you like it, too?" he asked.

She nodded, stomach fluttering. There had been times in her life when she'd done that particular thing but not liked it so much. With Rob, she loved it.

"Tell me why."

"Because . . ." She stopped, swallowed, hoped he didn't see that she was nervous about her reply. "I want to make you feel good. And I . . . want to be closer to you."

She waited for him to freak out, mentally kicking herself for going that far and being that honest—but he didn't. He just met her gaze. Gave her a chance to study his eyes. So brown, deep. Full of secrets, but at this moment not running, not hiding—just being. Just letting *her* be a part of his world, at least for the night.

He reached to kiss her, softly, slowly, then whispered, "You're a sweet girl sometimes, Abby."

She smiled lightly, peering close into his eyes now. "You said something like that once before. Does it surprise you?"

He tilted his head against the throw pillows. "Just not what I expected when I met you."

"Well . . . we all have different sides to us, right?"

He hesitated, then nodded. "I suppose."

"And right now," she said, "I'm not feeling very sweet."

She felt his body tense slightly against hers, saw fresh heat reinvade his gaze, and knew he understood what she meant. "What are you feeling?"

"Like I need you inside me. Deep."

A slow, lustful expression took over his face. "I like that feeling."

"Show me how much," she whispered.

He answered with a kiss, his tongue pressing sensually between her lips as he shifted them to lay side by side on the brass daybed. And she met his tongue with hers, definitely back to caring about her own pleasure again. Rob's hands traveled her body with a slow thoroughness that always managed to make her feel more special than he probably intended, and she couldn't help soaking up the heady sensation. Especially when his touches drifted downward, over her ass, and then around to the front of her panties.

She hissed in her breath when his fingers sank to the silk between her thighs, petting, stroking. She parted them, whispering his name.

Don't do that. He'll hate that. But she did it again anyway, couldn't help it. "Rob. Oh God, Rob."

When his fingers eased inside her underwear, she tensed, then cried out softly as they sank home. A hot groan left him as he felt how wet she was for him. And then he rubbed, caressed, dragged his fingers through her folds, and made her crazy, the pleasure in her rising higher, quickly, hard.

More words she couldn't hold inside. "Oh, Rob. Yes. Please. Like that."

Their kisses were almost like hot little bites now at each other's mouths and she moved against his hand and sensed how much he liked it. She reached out and found his hard-on, still solid and commanding, and stroked him, too.

"Jesus," he breathed.

Her eyes fell shut at some point as orgasm neared—oh God, he knew exactly how to touch her, exactly where. No man had ever been so in tune with her needs, the rhythm of her pleasure. She thrust herself against his fingers and drank in the sweet air and *now* she was lost to it, lost to him. Now nothing else mattered but heat and mindless pleasure. Oh God, when Rob gave in to his desires, he made this—sex—so easy, so good.

She knew it would happen soon, so soon—and for the first time in her life, she wanted to come for a guy as much as she wanted it for her own pleasure. She knew it mattered to him to make her feel good. The same way *she'd* needed to pleasure *him* before.

As if reading her thoughts, he whispered, "Let go of me, honey. This is all about you right now."

He still didn't want to come yet and now she was glad. *Save it. Make it last.*

So she released him from her fist and kissed him as she moved against his hand, pressed herself closer to him so her chest rubbed his, so everything worked together in that perfect, blissful way . . . until she dropped over the edge of ecstasy.

The pleasure pulsed through her like sweet hot rays of sunlight warming her skin, lifting her closer to the sky—*yes, yes*—before finally lowering her back to the bed next to him. Ah, God, yes.

It hadn't been the most intense orgasm she'd ever had, or the hardest, or the longest—but she thought it might have been the sweetest.

When the vibrations had passed completely, she bit her lip, smiling up at him.

"Good?" he asked.

She liked knowing he needed that confirmation, too. "Mmm," she assured him, not quite able to summon words yet.

He leaned in to kiss the curve of her breast. "You felt *so* nice, honey," he told her, and for a short second, she thought those mere words, coming from Rob, could almost take her there again.

"Still need you inside me, though," she whispered, weak from the climax but also ready for more.

Rob met her gaze as he rose onto his knees and slowly pulled her pink panties down and off. Then he shed his jeans completely before leaning down to finally remove her bra.

She parted her legs, welcoming him. "Please," she said, desperate now to finally connect their bodies in that oh-so-primal way.

He didn't hesitate, easing tight and deep into her. They both released long, low moans as their bodies slowly interlocked.

"Oh God," she said on a sigh.

"You're so tight," he whispered in her ear.

She smiled a naughty smile he couldn't see. "That's because you're so big."

He drew back to look at her. "Am I?"

She nodded. "You know you are." He wasn't uncomfortably big, just *perfectly* big—a tight, warm fit that filled her with intense pleasure and utter fullness.

His eyes told her it wasn't the first time he'd heard this—he was just seeking confirmation again, the same way she did.

He moved in her, slower than ever before—sliding deep and then pulling gradually back out before sinking in again. It was the closest thing she'd ever felt to making love. The soft night air wafted through the window, cooling their skin as she wrapped her legs around his back to pull him tighter into her. Oh God, this was nice. Nicer than . . . anything she could ever really remember. Nicer than anything with Garrett. Nicer than anything in Chicago. Just nice.

They moved that way together for . . . she didn't know how long. It didn't matter. It wasn't rushed—it was just good. She felt him basking in the slow, deep, unhurried pleasure the same way she was.

Sometimes they kissed, other times not. Occasionally, he drew back to mold her breasts in his hands or drag his tongue across one turgid pink nipple. At moments, she whispered his name, told him how good he felt. He whispered back, called her honey in that sexy way of his, told her again how tight and warm she was, told her he wanted to do it all night long.

It *didn't* last all night, but longer than Lindsey had ever had sex before. And when finally Rob came, thrusting deep, groaning his pleasure, making her feel those last hard, pounding strokes at her very center, she knew that when he pulled out of her, she was going to feel like she'd lost part of herself. Their bodies had been connected for that long.

So when he started to go, she lifted her hands to his hips and whispered, "Stay like this. For just a minute more. Okay?"

He didn't even question it. Just said, "Okay."

When she came back from the bathroom, she wondered if he would expect her to leave now. Which was, of course, the last thing she wanted to do. She wanted to cuddle in Rob's strong arms all night long. Even if it meant sleeping with her cheek on the name Gina.

So as she padded naked across the hardwood, her heart warmed to see that he'd crawled beneath the blue comforter on the daybed and now held the covers open for her to slip in beside him.

Mmm, God, he was warm and cozy.

Which meant maybe she *should* go. To save her sanity. She was getting way too attached to Rob and sleeping naked with him wasn't going to help.

But just then his arm curved comfortably around her and she sank a little deeper into the bed with him and knew she didn't have a prayer of making herself leave.

"This turned out a lot better than the *first* night I met you at the Lazy Elk," she mused.

She felt his sexy grin more than saw it, since she'd flipped off the lamp before climbing into bed. Now only a slash of moonlight arcing through the window lit the room. "I'd almost forgotten about that," he said, sounding sleepy.

"I wanted you even then," she heard herself admit. Damn—she'd thought sex had sobered her, but she still wasn't completely in control of herself or she'd have kept that inside.

To her surprise, he laughed. "You would have passed out on me."

"True," she agreed, pleased he wasn't shocked by her confession. Maybe he'd wanted her then, too? Just a little? "Actually, I did pass out as soon as you left. But just so you know, I'm not usually like that. I hadn't eaten since lunchtime and I was so tired from driving, and when I woke up the next morning I was totally embarrassed."

She turned to find him looking at her in the dark. "Why are you telling me all this now?"

She let out a sigh—and got honest. Because despite how things had changed between them since they'd met, she still couldn't help worrying that . . . "I just don't want you to think . . ."

"What?"

"That I'm a bad person." She hadn't realized she was still concerned about that, but apparently she was. Apparently it had taken some long, slow, intimate lovemaking to bring it to the surface. "First I let down Aunt Millie. Then I looked like a lush the first time I met you. And *now* . . . well, now I keep having casual sex with you, which isn't really normal for me." And of course, it wasn't really *casual* for her anymore, either, but a girl had to draw the line on honesty *somewhere.*

"I thought we'd been over this," he said, "but I don't think you're a bad person."

"Promise?"

"Yes."

"Do you forgive me? About Aunt Millie?"

"What?"

She sighed. "Remember, I asked you once if you believed in forgiveness. And I . . . want your forgiveness, Rob." She swallowed, feeling guilty again, about the whole Millie thing. Another issue she'd thought she'd started putting behind her, but maybe she hadn't. "I can't get *her* forgiveness. So I at least want yours."

Rob lifted a hand, gently brushed his fingertips through the hair near her face. "Don't worry, honey—yes, I forgive you."

God, she liked when he called her honey—it made her

pool with moisture, even now, after marathon sex. And she had no idea why she'd spewed all that out except that she'd grown emotional from being so close to him. "Thank you," she whispered in the dark, then curled toward him in bed, bringing her head to rest on his chest.

And then, of course, there it was—right next to her cheek: *Gina.* And as much as she'd been trying to ignore it, not think about it, not feel it . . . well, there was just something troubling about having sex with a guy whose chest bore the name of another girl. It was sort of like having another person in the room with them.

So since she was feeling bold and he was being sweet, she said, "Can I ask you a question?"

He peered down at her in the shadows, his answer slow, eyes wary. "Maybe."

Here goes nothing. "Is Gina the reason you don't, um, indulge in women very often?"

She couldn't have been more stunned when a low laugh escaped his throat. "Uh, no."

She bit her lip, lifting her head to peek up at him. "Who is she?"

"Nobody I want to talk about."

"Then why is her name on your chest?"

Above her, he sighed. "All right, new rule. No liquor for you."

"I'm not drunk anymore," she assured him. "Just nosy."

"Well, stop it. Go to sleep."

She hesitated, but then decided it was pointless to go on. She'd pretty much known he wouldn't tell her—even if he did sometimes surprise her. This just wasn't one of those times. "Rob," she whispered instead.

"Hmm?"

"Tonight was nice."

"Yeah," he agreed simply, quietly.

And as she turned in bed, seeking a comfortable position to fall asleep in, he wrapped around her from behind, his hand sliding easily up to cup her breast. And at first she wondered how she was ever going to get to sleep that way, but then she quit caring because it felt too good.

During the night, Lindsey eased from the warmth of Rob's arms for a trip to the bathroom. Coming back, she stopped at the sight of the moonlight drifting through the window to fall across his slumbering form and studied his rumpled hair, his mouth half open in sleep, the sexy stubble on his chin. Even asleep, he was totally hot, and she began to tremble a little inside. She still couldn't quite believe she was here, sleeping in his bed.

As she started back toward him, her movements created a breeze that sent a small sheet of paper fluttering to the floor from a desk in the corner. She stooped to pick it up—and couldn't help seeing the words scrawled at the top of the page. *Dear Gina.*

Oh God—her heart nearly stopped. And her eyes quickly traveled the page.

Dear Gina,

Would it surprise you to know how many letters I've written you? Would it surprise you to see your name next to my heart? Maybe it's crazy, after all this time, that I still sit down and write letters you'll never see. But somehow it makes me feel close to you, like maybe you're right down the street. Like maybe you're somewhere thinking about me, too. I know that's impossible, but it's a nice idea and a hard one for me to let go of—one of those little things that keep me feeling alive.

I told Millie about you the other day. I asked her if it was crazy to love someone who was so far away, someone who wasn't really in your life. I asked her if it made any sense, if it was really even love if the person was so far gone from your world that they exist mostly in your thoughts now.

She said yes, because she still loved John, all these years after his death.

I'm not sure that's the same thing—you're living somewhere, existing, breathing—but her answer still made me feel better.

All my love,
Rob

Oh boy.

Clearly, this letter had been sitting here a long while, at least since the winter, before Millie died—maybe from when he was taking care of her. It answered a few questions for Lindsey, but created so many more.

Why hadn't he sent it, or the others he referred to? Apparently, he didn't know where Gina was. And just how many letters *had* he written to this woman?

Lindsey let out a rough sigh, then looked up to make sure he was still asleep.

God. A tattoo was bad enough—a tattoo could mean a bad decision he couldn't take back. But to know he'd written her letters and pined for her for years—that stung deep.

Looking down at the piece of paper still in her hand, she set it back where it had come from and noticed that, sure enough, the desk was covered with a sheen of dust—clearly, Rob hadn't thought about this letter in months.

So that was a good sign, right? He might have written her a lot of unsent letters, but he wasn't writing them all the time, every week, every day. And maybe he hadn't thought about Gina at all since meeting Lindsey—or at least since having sex with her.

Which would account for all of a week or so.

Still, that was something.

You have to forget about this letter.

But how could she? It meant Gina wasn't some long-forgotten woman in his life; she wasn't someone whose name had gone onto his chest as a mistake, something he'd done too soon, too fast. It meant she mattered to him. Still.

But she's not the one in his bed tonight, is she?

As Lindsey eased back into his strong arms, she hung her emotions on that. *You're the one he's holding, the one he wants—at least right now.*

And this was just a casual back-on-the-sex-horse affair anyway, right?

Yeah, sure, right. Oh God, he was warm.

When the sun blasted through the window the next morning, the first thing Lindsey felt was the chill in the air as a breeze struck her face. The second was the warmth from being tucked under a comforter with Rob and soaking up all his sexy body heat. The third was a nip of fear—because she'd spent the night and wondered if morning would change things, make things awkward, if Rob would regret having her here. Especially now that she knew Gina wasn't just a distant memory.

Lindsey rolled to face him. His eyes remained shut peacefully, his hair messy and pointed in all directions, the dark stubble on his jaw heavier than even during the night when she'd studied him by moonlight. He was beautiful and her heart beat faster just looking at him.

At that moment, his eyes slowly opened. "Hey," he said quietly.

"Hey," she returned.

When he hesitated slightly, she thought, *This is it. This is where he remembers he's still in love with somebody else.*

This is where things get weird and I have to throw my clothes on and slink out of here like a one-night stand.

Instead, he said, "You like eggs?"

"Eggs? Um, yeah."

"We could make some. If you want."

Breakfast. He wanted to have breakfast with her. She gazed up into his eyes and tried not to let her happiness show too much. "That would be nice."

Hello, lovers! Ah, what a glorious Moose Falls Day. I woke up in my *lover's bed to the sun on my face and a view of the most gorgeous blue lake you can imagine. And to my lover, of course. I wish you could see Rob, ladies (sorry, guys—gotta have a chick moment here). He is* so *hot,* so *big and virile and lumberjack-like that sometimes I want to melt just looking at him. And when I'm in his arms, then I* definitely *melt.*

We made breakfast together—just eggs and toast, but it was perfect—then sat on his back deck to eat. It was brisk out, I admit, but I liked it anyway. I wore this big flannel jacket-like thing of his to keep warm, and a pair of his sweats. I probably looked ridiculous, but hey (and I never thought I'd say this), I feel too good to care. I mean, for once in my life, it was just about being with this guy, sharing a moment with him, rather than what I looked like. Shocking, lovers, but true.

He had to work today, even on a Saturday, because he runs more than one business and duty called. But that's okay because I had plenty to do myself.

Once I shed my flannel, I went to the Lazy Elk—the local watering hole—and helped my friend Carla and some other ladies finish painting the big banner for the Fish Festival. I tried to paint a fish but was soon relegated to lettering done with stencils. Probably best, or people might have thought we were having a big whale festival instead.

After that, I drove down to Kalispell with Carla and we bought prizes for the kids' games and picked up some trophies and crowns that had been ordered. The festival is tomorrow and I think it's going to be très *fun! Did I tell you I'm crowning Little Miss Fish?*

That's all the news for now, lovers. But I want to thank you for all the wonderful comments and tremendous support you've shown since I've gotten back online. I'm sorry I've not had the time to answer each one of you personally, but I read every word and love you guys for it.

And I see that a few of you have even started asking me questions again about your love lives. I appreciate your faith in me, but forgive me if... well, if I just don't feel comfortable addressing them. As you all know, I'm still trying to sort out my own *love life, so why would you trust me with yours? If I ever get the love thing straightened out in my head, well, maybe* then *I'll consider myself a worthy giver of advice.*

Until next time, I hope your Saturday is going as "swimmingly" (that's Fish Festival humor) as mine!

After hitting the Submit button, Lindsey leaned back in her desk chair and peered out her window to the lake, still and serene on this Saturday afternoon. Of course, when she leaned to the right for a different view, she could see Carla and a few other townsfolk up on ladders, trying to erect that last banner they'd finished this morning—Bernard stood below pointing this way and that, giving instructions. After stashing the prizes in the boathouse for overnight storage, Lindsey had offered to help with the setup, but Carla had told her she'd already done enough—mostly by softening Rob up so much that no one was worried about him putting a damper on the event. So she'd retreated here to send out a happy blog.

It only made her all the *more* happy to see new comments from her readers pouring in on a regular basis, and even if she still had no intention of answering their questions about love and sex and dating, she found it gratifying that they were still asking.

Just before getting up to walk away, she clicked on the Refresh button to check for any early comments to her new post—and lo and behold, she saw Still Single in Savannah had checked in!

> *Lindsey, I'm so sorry for what you've gone through, but please don't stop giving out advice to those of us who need it! I can't thank you enough for what you've done for me. The reason I haven't been online lately is because I've been on my honeymoon! That's right—I asked Carl to marry me and he said yes. When he realized marriage and children were important to me, he whisked me off to Jamaica, where we got married on the beach and spent the next week lounging in the sun and . . . spending a lot of time in our room, too. (Wink, wink.) Lindsey, you've changed my life by giving me the courage to go for what I wanted. Now I have it, thanks to you!*

Holy crap. She couldn't believe it! Still Single in Savannah was no longer single! Because of her advice! And she sounded happy as a clam!

Lindsey couldn't remember the last time she'd felt so fulfilled. Maybe this meant she wasn't such a loser in the love-advice department, after all.

Not that she felt qualified to suddenly go back to giving it right now or anything, but . . . maybe someday. Maybe someday soon.

Of course, one lucky break for Still Single and one sleep-over with Rob hardly meant she was the sage of romance, but still, it all felt like a step in the right direction. And, glancing to the little shopping bag she'd tossed on the bed after getting back from Kalispell, she started feeling like she should celebrate.

By giving Rob a little surprise.

Of course, maybe it was too soon after last night.

But she wanted to see him again. And things had definitely started changing between them for the better. Maybe she wanted to . . . get some sort of foothold in his life, prove to herself he wanted more of her, and not more of Gina. Pushing to her feet, she walked over, reached in the shiny pink bag, and plucked out the sexy leopard-print negligee she'd bought at the Kalispell Center Mall—which wasn't exactly the Magnificent Mile, but it had done the trick. Since her man definitely had a thing for animal-print.

She'd confided that to Carla when she'd spotted the lingerie in a store window.

"You know his weakness now," Carla had pointed out. "You can use this and others like it to get your livery back."

"You make him sound like Darth Vader or something." Now that she'd gotten to know Rob and was feeling all gaga about him, she was also beginning to feel guilty for viewing him as the enemy when all this had started. "He's really not so bad."

"Oh, I know," Carla had said. "But I'd like to see you get what you came here for. I'd like to see you . . . stay. And I'm not sure you'll do that if you don't have a business to run. Like you've said before, Rob has another business—you don't."

Stay. Hmm. She'd never really thought that far ahead, and she'd certainly not come here *planning* to stay.

But the thought of leaving still sounded pretty weird, too.

Even so, she'd decided not to think about the future. Thinking ahead to the future with Garrett had only turned out to be a huge disappointment in the end. And since coming to Moose Falls, she'd kind of been living in the moment, taking one day at a time. She decided she should look at the whole Gina thing the same way—Rob was now, she was now, Gina was yesterday. One day at a time. One sexual encounter at a time.

And as for the sexy, silky leopard-print chemise in her hand—which came with a matching G-string—she had no intention of using it as a weapon. Nope, she'd had enough battles with Rob—and tonight was going to be all about the spoils of victory.

Rob measured the two-by-four he was about to saw in half, then measured it again. His father hadn't given him much, but the measure-twice-cut-once rule had always been one he lived by. Actually, when it came to work, he supposed his father had given him a *lot* of useful instruction—it just hadn't felt that way during high school summers when he'd wanted to run around with his friends and chase girls instead of help his father do handyman work all day. But now he supposed he should be thankful—his father had taught him a useful vocation and a work ethic. As it had turned out, Rob took great satisfaction in creating things, leaving *something* where *nothing* had been before. It proved he was here. Made him feel like he mattered in some small way. It was just a shame his father had been such a shitty parent in most *other* respects.

Hammering the wood into place a minute later, he found his mind drifting. Back to those summers. The hot, hardworking days. The cooler, better nights with girls and friends and the beer his best friend Billy had always stolen from his grandpa's fridge in the garage. It had been so good to be out of his family's crappy little house. Good to be with people who liked him. And then there'd been the discovery of sex, those first times with that first girl, when it was so unbelievable and new.

How many times had they done it that summer after graduation when he'd thought he had a whole, normal life stretching before him? Maybe only a handful. At least twice in his old Monte Carlo. Once in Billy's grandpa's basement when the grandparents weren't home and everybody else was upstairs. Once at her house when her family was at church.

Hell—he guessed he'd been a pretty bad kid in ways. But he'd been a product of his upbringing. He'd just been trying to get by, grow up, have a little fun. As for the sex, back then it had seemed like more than just a few times—it had seemed like *everything.*

Too damn bad you had to go bragging about it. Too damn bad about a lot of things.

Rob just shook his head, banishing the thought, and concentrated on the task at hand, driving another nail. He didn't let his head go there anymore—just didn't, couldn't.

And if he wanted to think about sex, it made a lot more sense to think about it in the present tense, with Lindsey.

Part of him was downright miserable for letting this start—because he didn't know where it was leading and Rob was a man who needed to have a handle on his life, needed to have full control. Let that go and he had nothing.

But at the same time, part of him was having . . . hell, too much fun to try to stop it. And not just fun. He could lie to himself and call it that, but there was more to it and he knew that.

For him, sex had always been about hooking up, feeling good, mutual needs, a good time with a woman he liked. But somehow, sex with Lindsey had gone beyond that—damn fast. At moments it was *exactly* that—hooking up, fun—but at other moments everything he felt ran too deep.

You should be scared shitless, buddy.

After all, there was a reason he didn't let himself get close to people.

But he made himself feel better by reminding himself she was just a visitor here. Soon she'd get her fill of him and Moose Falls and Millie and she'd go back to her life in Chicago and everything would be fine. And maybe he'd be kind of lonely at first—he'd quickly gotten used to her companionship, in bed and out—but he'd also gotten used to being alone before, so he'd get used to it again.

As for now, he couldn't believe he was actually looking forward to the damn Fish Festival tomorrow. He couldn't deny it—he wanted to see the light in Lindsey's eyes when she crowned the fish queen or whatever it was called. He wanted to hold her hand and walk by the lake and not care, for a change, if anyone was watching. He just wanted to spend the day with her and be a normal guy.

Strange what a woman could do to you.

An hour later, Rob had knocked off for the day and headed home. Stepping inside, he gave King his customary scratch behind the ears and told him what a good boy he was, then looked up when the phone rang. Man, never a dull moment lately.

But unlike usual, he didn't even consider not answering. "Hello."

"Hey, it's Lindsey."

Just hearing her voice made his chest contract. "Hey."

"Are you busy tonight? If you are, just say so. But if you're not . . . I have a surprise for you."

Say you're busy, dude. It's the smart thing. And she's turned out to be a reasonable woman—she'll understand. She even gave you an out.

But Lindsey was offering him a surprise. And Lindsey had given him the best blow job of his life last night. And Lindsey just plain made him feel good, like it or not.

"I'm not busy," he said.

Twelve

For the first time Rob could remember, hearing that knock on the door made him happy. He'd taken a shower, put on fresh jeans and a white button-down, and had been sitting on the couch waiting for her like a kid ready for a first date. Ridiculous. But he was glad she was here.

He opened the door with King at his side, as usual, but the dog seemed more relaxed around her now, especially when she reached down to pet him. She looked as gorgeous as usual—tonight in faded jeans and a clingy, gauzy top that flowed around her hips and tied behind her back. She also carried a big Bob's Pizza box.

"Here," she said, holding it out to him.

"My surprise is pizza?" he asked, taking it from her. He hadn't realized he was so intrigued by the surprise portion of the visit—until he found himself hoping like hell the pizza wasn't it.

"No," she said, stepping inside and closing the door. "But I haven't eaten and thought maybe you hadn't, either."

"I haven't," he said. "I was gonna see if you wanted to

drive over to the steakhouse in Cedarville—I've heard it's good. But pizza is great."

She snapped her fingers in mock disappointment. "Sounds like I blew it. Like we were gonna have another official date."

Lowering the pizza to the kitchen table, he turned to face her. "Nobody says it's not a date just because you stay in." Damn, she looked pretty—the top was a springtime shade of pink and a quick glance down revealed her toenails were painted to match. On her feet she wore little white flip-flops encrusted with clear, sparkly stones. Leave it to Lindsey to turn flip-flops into high fashion. "So, what's my surprise?"

He really didn't mean to act like a little kid here, but . . . maybe it had been a long time since anyone had done anything special for him. Maybe he . . . couldn't exactly *remember* the last time.

And then Lindsey lowered her chin, bit her lip, and cast him the sexiest look he'd ever seen as she reached down to slowly lift her pink top up over her stomach . . . to reveal animal-print underneath.

He went hard in a heartbeat. "Aw, *honey,*" he practically growled, stepping toward her. "Come here."

She smiled into his eyes and for a split second he found himself wondering what he'd done to deserve this—this woman who'd come pushing her way into his life out of nowhere, this woman who kept giving him the kind of pleasure he'd thought he'd never experience again.

But then he quit wondering because his arms were sliding around her waist and he was pulling her close, feeling her soft curves pressing against his harder body, feeling her pliable mouth under his as he kissed her. In between kisses, he rasped, "Let's get straight to the surprise."

Her slender arms locked around his neck as she whispered, "The pizza will get cold."

"That's why God made microwaves," he murmured, "and you just made me hungry for something else."

She didn't fight him, thank God.

She just let him kiss her—again.

She just let him pick her up and set her on the big kitchen table, where he could stand between her parted legs.

She just let him untie that pretty top and peel it up over her head to reveal the sexy little leopard-print thing underneath, her round breasts swelling from the top, her nipples jutting prettily through.

She let him run his hands over her, feel her through the lingerie; she let him make her sigh and gasp and pant.

Soon she was unbuttoning his shirt, pushing it open, grazing her hands over his chest, making him crazy. And then she was undoing his jeans, reaching inside, giving him more of that impossible pleasure he'd thought he'd never know again.

He undid her jeans, too. Told her to lift up so he could pull them down. Got to feast his eyes on the leopard-print nightie that flowed down to flirt with the tops of her pretty, bare thighs. And then he got to see the barely-there panties underneath, just enough fabric to cover her.

And he couldn't go slow anymore. Not that they'd been going particularly slow—not like last night. But now he needed more, fast. "I need these off you, baby," he growled, tugging at the little panties.

She only whimpered and sighed and helped him get rid of them.

And then her legs were wrapping around his hips, still clad in blue jeans, and he was leaning over, curling his fingers into her perfect ass, and driving himself deep inside her.

They both cried out at the impact. And he thought for a strange second about science and nature, about two atoms colliding so hard that they become one. This was like *that*, and now they were moving together, hard, fast, meeting each other's thrusts, colliding, again, again. He was conscious of wanting to pull her into him somehow, of wanting to move deeper, deeper, into her. You couldn't get closer to a woman than he was in this moment, but somehow he still wanted more.

Soon he heard her breath come harder, a little slower—and he'd been with her enough to know it meant she would climax soon. So he slowed, too, letting her set the pace. God, he loved making her come, loved watching that most extreme pleasure wash over her face, feeling it vibrate through her body. He loved making her lose control to him, just for a few minutes.

"Come for me," he heard himself whisper, and their eyes met, hers glassy with passion, and her hot, ragged breathing filled the air. She didn't look away, kept their gazes locked, and he said it again, urging her, willing her body to go there. "Come, honey. Come hard, baby."

A ragged moan erupted from her throat and she moved against him, gentle, rhythmic, then hard, hard, hard, sobbing her pleasure as she convulsed around him.

And before Rob knew it, he couldn't hold back. He was driving deep into her moisture, still following that impossible urge to connect their bodies tighter somehow, then laying her back on the table as he exploded inside her. Like that morning they'd had sex on the couch, seeing her come had made it happen for him, too—she was too beautiful that way for him to hold on to his own sanity in that moment. The pleasure roared through him, thick and consuming as he plunged hard, felt her legs wrap around his back, and thanked God for bringing him this woman.

But it's only temporary—remember that. Only temporary.

That's what he *needed* it to be, after all. Nothing else would work in his life and knowing this was temporary was the one and only thing that made it okay.

It was just going to be hard as hell now, he was afraid, when she left.

They lounged on the couch eating pizza, listening to music, and talking about the fact that King had watched them have sex and it embarrassed Lindsey. They decided maybe King needed a little more of a social life and Lindsey announced that Carla had a female Collie named Butterscotch.

"Maybe we can get you a date, too, buddy," Rob said to the dog, holding a bite of sausage plucked from the pizza down to King's mouth, and Lindsey laughed, and Rob realized he wasn't even uneasy about her knowing he'd been celibate for a while until she'd come along.

And sure, she'd asked about Gina last night, but when he hadn't answered, she hadn't pressed too hard. He knew she wanted to know things about him, but she seemed to respect his boundaries. And the truth was, it was . . . nice to have someone give a shit, nice to have someone care enough to ask him questions about himself. He couldn't tell her—or anyone else—the answers, but it was nice to have her care.

He'd told Millie, of course—he'd told her everything. He'd instinctively known she was different than other people, that she wouldn't judge him, that she'd truly understand. And she had. She'd kept his secrets, taken them to her death, and she'd handed her life to him in the bargain.

After pizza, they got dressed and took a walk by the lake in the dark. Lindsey hadn't worn a coat, so he pulled one of his big hooded sweatshirts over her head and put on a denim jacket himself. At times, they talked, about everything and nothing. From Fish Festival rituals to wondering if Millie was somewhere watching them right now. Rob wasn't usually the sort of guy comfortable with that kind of talk, stuff about the afterlife—he wasn't even sure what he believed—but somehow, with Lindsey, it was easy.

When the stroll was through, he wondered if she expected him to walk her back to the Grizzly Inn, if it was time to end the "date." But the hell of it was—he just plain didn't want to.

"Wanna come back inside?" he asked, voice low, as they neared the house. It was either turn right up the walk or go on to the inn.

"Sure," she said, her voice soft.

And he thought, *You're just asking for it, buddy, just asking for trouble.* But he couldn't help it. *This is why you can't have a woman in your life. You're bound to get attached, and then what?* Every other time he'd started getting even *remotely* attached in the past, it had ended with the truth—*his* truth—and disaster.

Yet still, here he was inviting her back to the cabin, back into his life, deeper, deeper—just like when he was moving in her, he kept wanting to go deeper. And also like when he was inside her, he couldn't seem to stop himself.

They lay naked in Rob's bed, under Millie's quilt. No lights, but again they'd opened the windows, letting in the air and night sounds. They'd had sex twice more since coming back in, and Rob felt simultaneously exhausted and more alive than he had in . . . hell, was it possible he'd *never* felt more alive?

No. That summer when he'd just turned eighteen—he'd been alive *then.* Alive and feeling everything there was to feel when you're that age. For a little while anyway.

But he wasn't sure life had felt this . . . complete.

"What brought you here?" she asked in the shadows. "To Moose Falls?" She lay on her side next to him, caressing his chest. He rested on his back, liking how close she was, the way her leg crossed over his beneath the covers, the way her breasts pressed into his arm. From downstairs, "Chasing Cars" by Snow Patrol echoed upward, low and potent, and he could have sworn they were singing about Lindsey's perfect eyes.

"Nothing in particular," he told her. "Everybody's gotta be somewhere—this is just where I happened to land."

"But . . . why? I mean, where are you from?"

"Oregon," he said. The truth. Just not much of it.

"Why did you leave?"

"I grew up in a small town, but . . . I didn't like it there. So I went to Portland—and some other cities. And then I found my way here." Another non-answer—all he could give her.

She quieted then, and he thought that maybe, blessedly, the conversation was over. Until she said, "How on earth does someone find their way to Moose Falls if they're not looking for it? I mean, I had a *map* and I barely found it."

Someone finds their way to Moose Falls when they want to hide.

But he couldn't say that. He didn't know *what* to say. He was fucking tired. Tired of lying. And just . . . tired. From today's work and the sex. So he couldn't come up with a good answer. "I . . . can't tell you," he heard himself reply. Shit.

Her voice came hushed. "Why?"

He sighed. "Just can't. It's private."

"Something bad happened to you, didn't it?"

Damn it, don't do this to me, honey. "Abby, I don't want to talk anymore. I'm beat. Let's go to sleep."

"Did Millie know? Why you came here? Why you don't like people?"

He guessed she was done respecting his boundaries. And maybe he couldn't blame her. When he was inside her, he knew, understood, he owed her more of himself. And now . . . now he was beginning to feel worn down. "Yeah," he admitted, his voice going as shadowy as hers, little more than a whisper.

"That's why you two were close," Lindsey said.

"Kind of, yeah."

"If you told *her*, why can't you tell *me*?"

He was still out of good answers and heard the honesty creeping into his responses. "Because I don't want you to know."

"Why?"

"Because you'd hate me," he heard himself say. "Just like every other person I ever told. Except for Millie."

She stayed quiet next to him, and he cursed himself for being such an idiot. *You used to be a better liar.* But lying wore him out, and the truth was, he didn't *like* lying, especially not to someone he cared for. And he cared for Lindsey. And this was where he always got into trouble. This was where he always lost *everything*.

"I can't imagine anything you could tell me, Rob," she began, soft, sure, "that would make me hate you."

He turned on the pillow to look at her. It was dark, but he could make out her eyes, the shape of her face. "You might be surprised, Abby."

And then he lifted a hand to her cheek and he kissed her, hard, desperate. He had no idea why. Or maybe he did. He needed to feel her mouth under his—in case this turned out to be the last time. In case, by not telling her, he drove her away.

She kissed him back, just as hard, then whispered to him, "Please, Rob. Trust me."

He didn't answer. Just looked at her. Just wanted to be someone else. Someone without a past, without secrets.

"Please," she said again.

He was honest. "I can't tell you because if you told anyone, *ever*, it would ruin my life. And that's too much weight to put on your shoulders."

"You trusted Aunt Millie," she reminded him. "Why can't you trust *me*?"

"She was dying," he said frankly. "She didn't have to keep the secret long. And she was . . . like some kind of angel, Lindsey, different than anyone I ever met." Telling Millie had been hard at first, but by the end of the story he'd known it was okay—he'd been able to see in her eyes that it would stay just between them.

Lindsey's hand closed gently over his shoulder and her voice came low, sweet. "I'm no angel, Rob, but I care about you. I know you're a good person. So whatever it is—"

Rob sighed, feeling tied in knots, confused, weary, and he looked again at Lindsey next to him in the dark. "Why do you want to know so bad?"

"Honest?"

"Yeah."

She hesitated, even leaned her forehead over on his shoulder. Then lifted it up again. "I know I told you I didn't want this—you and me—to be anything, because I just got out of an engagement, but maybe I was wrong. And if that sends you running in the other direction, well then, my loss. But there it is, the truth. And I can tell something hurt you really bad, Rob, and I hate that. And I just want to know—in case, maybe, there's something I can do to make it better."

Rob took in her words. They *should* send him running in the other direction. God knew a week ago they would have. But a lot had changed in that week.

He still couldn't tell her, though. He *couldn't.* It was fucking suicide. She wouldn't understand. She would be afraid of him. She would tell other people. And then word would spread and he'd have to leave Moose Falls, just like all the places he'd left before. Only this time it would be worse because he'd be leaving Millie's legacy behind, and somewhere along the way it had become *his* legacy, truly *his*, the place he was going to take care of and the way he was going to spend his life.

So it made no sense, no damn sense at all, when he heard himself beginning to tell her, his voice quiet as death. "One night, when I was eighteen, I was out drinking with a couple of buddies."

She rubbed his arm, just a little, silently saying it was okay, urging him to go on. *Please let it be okay.* Because the shocking truth he realized in that moment was—he wanted to tell her. He *needed* to. He needed to purge his soul. He needed to have someone on this earth who knew *everything* and still cared for him anyway.

"Billy was my best friend, same age as me. Tommy was his little brother. We lived in a shithole town about an hour outside of Portland where there wasn't much to do but drink and get in trouble. And I'd do pretty much anything to get out of the house at night—my parents hated each other and mostly took it out on me." It came back to him then, that saggy little house, his tiny room with the fan in the window, the yelling and screaming, the holes punched in walls. He used to lock the door to his room at night to sleep—for no other reason than it made him feel a little farther away from them.

"So I was dating this girl, Karen," he went on.

"Did you love her?"

The question caught him off guard. "I don't know," he said, then honesty made him add, "I guess not." He didn't think he'd *ever* been in love or really knew what that even was—but Lindsey didn't need to know that. "We were having a pretty hot and heavy thing, though, having sex.

"And so, on this night, me and Billy and Tommy were hanging out at the bottom of this old water tower outside town that wasn't in use anymore. We were drinking beer Billy got from his Grandpa's fridge. They lived with their grandparents because their mom and dad had been killed in a car wreck about a year earlier."

"God, that's tough."

"Yeah," he said, feeling a little numb to that part of it now, but remembering, "it was."

The last time he'd let himself think through this next part was when he'd told Millie, and he'd hoped never to go there again. God knew he'd replayed it in his head enough times in the first ten years afterward—he'd simply stopped after that. But now here he was, going back there one more time, to a memory that seemed surreal, more a story he knew than something he could completely recall.

"We ran out of beer and Billy left in his car to go get more. And Tommy—Tommy was drunker than me. Only sixteen, and none of us should have been drinking, but we were kids—and drinking, in my house, was pretty normal. I was . . . the rough kid Billy and Tommy hung out with, the bad influence."

"Really?"

He liked how genuinely surprised she sounded—and the way her breath teased his ear. "Yeah," he said. "And so while Billy was gone, I got into an argument with Tommy—over Karen. I didn't know it, but he'd had a bad crush on her the whole time I was with her. He started saying that I was treating her like shit and didn't care about her, and I didn't have any idea where it was coming from. I was like, 'What are you talking about, man?' and I eventually figured out that he was crazy about her."

He stopped then, paused, remembering the strangeness of the next part, how freaked out he'd been, how impossible it had seemed, and how scared it had made him. His voice dropped lower. "Turns out she'd told him she was pregnant—and that she was afraid to tell me. That's why he was so mad. He knew I wasn't really in love with her. And I guess he thought I wouldn't do the right thing by her. So he's telling me all this and I'm trying to wrap my head around it, around the idea that she's really pregnant and that the rubber must not have worked and that my whole fucking world was about to come crashing down.

"So I'm trying to get him to tell me more—he's babbling, angry, throwing punches and shit at me, and I'm trying to get answers from him, asking him exactly what she said, trying to make sure this is real—and he starts to walk away from me. I was pissed at him by then, and upset, so I started after him. And for some reason . . . some reason I'll never know . . . he started climbing up the ladder, up the side of the water tower."

"Oh God," Lindsey whispered, and he was glad, because it meant she sensed what was coming, mostly, and that he could go through this part quick.

"So I followed him. Stupid, I know. But it's what I did. I followed him and he kept climbing and I kept going, too. I was still just so damn mad and confused, and nothing seemed more important than making him tell me again what she'd said, finding out for sure if she was really pregnant."

As Rob spoke, he could feel the dark Oregon night closing in on him, could feel that massive space all around him as he rose higher and higher up that rickety old tower. "I just . . . wasn't thinking clearly," he said, shaking his head a little on the pillow. He'd long ago quit questioning his actions of that night, quit considering the ifs and whys, quit wishing things had been different.

"Long story short," he said, a little breathless now, "when we got to the top, we were still yelling and screaming at each other. And a farmer who came out of his house a field away heard us and testified that he was 'pretty sure' he'd seen me push Tommy in the moonlight." He could still remember how Tommy had been there one minute and gone the next, just gone, and how long it had taken Rob to understand that he had fallen. And how he'd known instantly that you couldn't fall that far without dying. And how he'd stood frozen, paralyzed by the fear and the reality, and how his arms and legs had felt numb as he'd tried to climb back down, and how long it had taken and how scared he'd been and how there'd been tears rolling down his cheeks by the time he finally reached the ground. And how seconds later the blue lights and sirens had come and his life had pretty much ended.

"I went to prison, Lindsey," he whispered.

Her body had gone tense next to his—he could tell. And he couldn't blame her. He'd even expected it. Now he just had to get the rest out and be done with this.

"I went to prison for ten years, from the time I was eighteen until I was twenty-eight. I'm an ex-con—that's who I am, that's my secret, that's why I keep to myself. Because I know what people think of ex-cons. I know because anytime I ever trusted anyone enough to tell them—particularly women I was seeing—my life would change. I would lose jobs, or stop getting work. People I thought were my friends weren't anymore. In Boise, people started vandalizing my house—their way of telling me to move on. And so I did.

Again and again. Until finally I figured out that I just couldn't tell anybody anymore. Especially when I came here, when I liked it here, when Millie helped me find a real life here. I realized I couldn't get close to anyone, because every damn time I did, I ended up trusting them, telling them, and then watching my life dissolve before my eyes—again."

He was looking at her now, wondering if she was getting what he was saying, the irony of the fact that he'd just done it one more time—just let himself care for someone enough to tell her his awful truth. And he was waiting for that look of horror to come over her face—even in the dark, he would know that look, would know he'd just become some kind of monster to her, someone she couldn't be with, someone who frightened her. He waited for that look, that look that always came after the stiffening of the body, the stark quietness while he told the story. He waited for that look . . . wondering where it was, why it wasn't coming.

"Lindsey," he said, "I understand if you don't want to be around me anymore, but all I ask is that you don't tell anybody. Not Carla, not Eleanor, not anybody. I just want to live here quietly, mind my own business—that's all. I'd never hurt anybody."

"Did you push him?" she asked quietly.

"No," he said. He'd almost, somewhere along the way, quit believing that even mattered. It hadn't mattered *then*; people had formed their own opinion—he'd been guilty by proximity and reputation. "The railing gave way—it was rusty. I was nowhere near him. I swear," he added, and he wasn't sure why except for that same reckless urge that had made him start telling her in the first place, that gut need to make someone believe in him. And not just someone—*her.* He needed her to have faith in him, to know he wasn't the kind of person who would do something like that.

"I believe you," she whispered. And it was in that moment when he realized the look he'd been waiting for, bracing for, dreading . . . really wasn't coming.

"You don't hate me," he said, more than a little amazed.

She shook her head against the pillow and he saw the shimmer of tears in her eyes. "Of course not."

"You believe me." He knew she'd just said that, but he needed to hear it again.

"Yes."

He sighed as the shock of relief flowed through him. "No one ever has. Not really. No one."

"Except Millie?" she reminded him.

"Except Millie," he confirmed. Then he ran his fingers through her hair, just needing to touch her, feel her. She was still here. Even knowing the truth about him, she was still here. And he was still suffering a numb sort of shock. "I'm starting to think you two had more in common than I thought."

They both laughed softly at that, and it made him realize he was crying a little, too, and he hoped she didn't see. Prison had made him tough, or at least taught him the value of appearing that way—it was ingrained not to let anyone ever think any different, even now.

"*Was* she pregnant?" Lindsey asked then. "Karen?"

His stomach tightened a little. "Yeah."

"And the baby?"

He shook his head. "I . . . don't know." And he realized telling her this part was almost as hard as the rest. "We . . . agreed I shouldn't be a part of the baby's life since I was going off to prison. And she'd met a nice guy who wanted to marry her and was willing to raise the baby as his. It seemed best."

"God," she breathed. "I'm sorry."

But he only shook his head against his pillow one more time. "It was better that way. I was in no position to be a dad. And I'd probably make a lousy one anyway."

"Why do you think that?"

He shrugged. "I'm an ex-convict. I'm not good with people. I let my dog watch me have sex. The list goes on."

She laughed again, which made him smile through the pain, and the next thing he knew, he was hugging her, tight, just holding her. And more importantly, she was hugging him back.

"Thank you," he whispered. "For believing in me. Not . . . many people have."

In response, she tightened her grip around his neck and kissed his cheek. "Thank you for trusting me enough to tell me."

"I . . . kind of can't believe I did."

"Well, I plied you with animal-print," she said, making him laugh again—at a moment when he really couldn't believe he was laughing so much.

Then she suggested, "We should probably get some sleep. We have a big day tomorrow—canoe races to run, fish to fry, a Little Miss Fish to crown. It's going to be exhausting."

Just like that. No more questions, no more talk. He'd just told her he was a hardened criminal, a convicted murderer who'd spent ten freaking years in prison—and she was ready to go to sleep next to him like nothing had happened.

He knew then that Millie *was* looking down on them tonight. He wasn't usually sure if he believed in that sort of thing—but tonight, he did.

Dear Gina,

I've been sleeping better lately. It was tough at first, but I guess I'm getting used to being here. Glen says it just takes time. Sometimes I can even remember my dreams now, dreams of better things, better places—not even places I've been or can remember, but places I guess I'd like to go.

Sometimes I dream I'm on a boat sailing through the sea with open water all around me. I'm sure that's about freedom. Other times I dream about a horse running across an open plain, and I think maybe that one's about escape. And sometimes I dream I'm just walking through a big, empty field and there's this lone tree I'm heading for in the distance, but I never quite get there. I walk and I walk, but the tree is still just as far away. Sometimes I wonder if that one's about you. But then I think that maybe I wonder too much in here. This place gives a man too much time to think.

Which is to say you've been in my thoughts again lately. I find myself trying to see your face in my mind, wondering if your hair is long or short now, trying to see your eyes. I wonder what you dream of at night, and I hope it's all good. I hope your whole life is like my dream of the sea—warm sun, cool breezes, no worries, just floating, floating along...

All my love,
Rob

Thirteen

Lindsey closed the door to her room behind her, then set out on foot to the Moose Falls Fish Festival and Fry. She could see the banners in the distance, hung above the road near Rob's house—which was closed to traffic today—and all the people milling about as the party got started on a bright and blessedly warm Sunday. She wore a flowered, summery skirt and a lace-edged cami of apple green, again having donned her white, jewel-encrusted flip-flops, which she'd decided were the perfect shoe compromise for life in Moose Falls—flat but fun and fashionable. She made a mental note to stop by the general store and see what Bernard had in sparkly flip-flops.

As she got closer, she singled out Rob in the crowd on the dock and surrounding area—he stood talking to the guy she remembered as Steve Fisher. Her lover wore a dark, striped cotton shirt open over a slightly faded maroon tee and he looked handsome and rugged and as perfect as ever.

And was she crazy? Crazy not to care what he'd told her last night? That he'd spent ten years—almost a third of his life—in prison? Prison!

And yet, as shocking as it was, she'd never even *thought* about abandoning him, or being afraid of him. She'd been stunned at first, but never scared. She'd felt no worry—only heartbreak over what he'd suffered. Rob was gruff sometimes, but also gentle, too. How could anyone who looked—*really* looked—not see that?

But then, maybe the people in his past hadn't really looked. Hadn't really *seen.* The way he loved King. The soft light in his eyes when he talked about the smell of rain. The way he felt obligated to help strange, intoxicated girls get to their rooms so nothing would happen to them.

And so, yes, she thought of him *differently* now that she knew he'd been through horrible things she'd never understand—but he'd *told* her, *trusted* her, and that was enough to bridge any gap.

So when he left Steve Fisher's side to walk toward her, she smiled up at him, same as always. "Hey." And her panties got damp, same as always.

He lifted his hands to the tops of her arms, giving a soft, affectionate squeeze, then leaned closer. "Are we still good?"

After last night, he meant. "Of course."

Maybe she was foolish to give him such blind faith, but she'd felt how desperately he'd needed it, and she simply didn't fear him. Millie had trusted and loved him, after all. So why shouldn't Lindsey trust him? Love him.

The masculine scent of him swept through her as he bent to press a slow, warm, utterly scintillating kiss to her lips. It only ended when she remembered they were standing in the middle of a festival. "Watch it, Romeo," she whispered, "or you're going to make my nipples show through my top."

He glanced down, his eyes filled with just a hint of masculine arrogance, then said, "Too late."

Letting her eyes drop to her chest as well, she gasped, then crossed her arms, trying to cover herself.

A small smile quirked the corners of his mouth as he kept

his voice low. "And here I thought the Fish Festival wouldn't be any fun."

"I'll have you know I have to go help Carla run the kids' games like this."

"Good luck," he said with a grin. "Maynard roped me into helping set up the grills and deep fryers for later, so I'd better get started."

With that, he delivered a quick but potent kiss goodbye, they exchanged another short smile, and as she turned to walk away into the crowd seeking Carla, she knew . . . she was in love with Rob Colter.

It was hours later when Rob stood behind Lindsey, trying to teach her how to cast a rod and reel. The fishing contest was on and she'd insisted on taking part, even though she'd never held a fishing pole in her life, and even though she wasn't "wild about killing innocent fish just for sport, but I'll try this because it's, you know, walking in Aunt Millie's shoes a little more."

"It's not just for sport," Rob had pointed out. "We're eating them later."

"Well, that would be swell if we were pioneers in the woods, but we're not. We all have plenty of other things to eat."

"Look, this was your idea, so do you want to argue or do you want to fish?"

And finally she'd stood still and let him show her how to operate the reel. Not that he was an expert fisherman, but he'd fished a little when he was young, and again with Millie a few times last summer.

Now he stood back watching her poised at the edge of the lake in her pretty skirt as she drew the pole back, released the reel, and flung the line into the water. She was a little unsteady on her feet, looking more like the rod was controlling her than the other way around, but it was her best cast so far.

And damn, she was beautiful—her long hair mussed from the breeze and shoved behind her ears now, her cheeks and shoulders turning pink from the sun, all her concentration squarely focused on her fishing pole. And she believed him.

He still couldn't get over it. He'd had so many occasions in the last seven years since his release to think he could trust someone, to finally confide, and then to watch it all fall apart. With Lindsey, of course, it had been less than a day, but somehow he knew, just felt, she wasn't going to flip on him. She was going to stand by him, keep believing him. It was—well, besides Millie—the best thing that had happened to him in seven long years.

Just because a man was let out of prison didn't mean he was free. He'd not realized that at first, but slowly it had become clear that once you were found guilty of a crime that bad, you were *always* guilty—it didn't go away just because the bars weren't there anymore. The bars just became invisible. Until someone found out. And then they were there again, trapping you again, or making you run to yet another new place where no one knew and maybe you could start a life.

Even as the words had left him last night, he'd been thinking, *What the fuck am I doing?* He'd been sure *this* life would be taken from him, too, sure he was foolishly throwing it all away by trusting in her.

But it wasn't gone. *She* wasn't gone. Amazing.

Now the kids' games had been played, and true to Lindsey's prediction, little Morgan Wright had beat out the competition to become Little Miss Fish. When Lindsey had bent down to crown her, she'd said to the little girl, "Congratulations—and those are fabulous shoes, by the way." God, she made him smile.

And as much as he wouldn't have believed it a week ago, he was having a hell of a nice time today. Just being out among people . . . well, it wasn't bad. Because today, suddenly, he didn't feel the need to hide so much, to keep to himself so much. He wasn't *good* at being with people—he hadn't had a lot of practice—but he didn't mind it today. He supposed having a girlfriend who *was* good at being with people helped.

And that's when it hit him—Lindsey was his girlfriend. And he didn't mind that, either. In fact, if he didn't watch it, he might almost start feeling normal here.

"Rob, we need you at the grills."

He turned to find Eleanor rushing toward him, her digital camera around her neck—she'd been snapping pictures all day. "What's wrong?" he asked.

"We've got a grill problem, and what Maynard knows about gas grills I could put in a fish's eye. Danged old man *acts* like he knows grills, but when there's a problem—nope, not an idea in the world how to fix it. Anyway, you seem like a guy who'd be able to figure it out. Come with me," she said, taking his arm and pulling him behind her to where three old men stood around a grill looking as puzzled as if they were trying to do quantum physics.

"Let me take a look," Rob said—and ten minutes later, the grill was heating up and he was a hero, everybody slapping him on the back and saying nice things and making him feel like . . . well, like he was a part of things here.

Just then, he looked up to catch Lindsey smiling at him in the distance—fishing rod still in her hand and line dipping into the lake—and realized she'd seen the whole thing. He smiled back, his chest constricting with some combination of lust and an emotion he didn't quite have a name for—but it was a damn *good* emotion that made him want to wrap his arms around her and just stay that way for a very long time.

Which was when she got a bite. He saw the line yank, saw the bobber disappear under the water, and called, "Honey, you've got one on the line." She flinched, blinked—then turned to pay attention.

She looked terrified and he realized she didn't know what

to do, so he gave her some instruction as he started jogging toward her. "Reel it in," he told her. "Slow, steady—not too fast or you'll lose him."

Next thing Rob knew, Lindsey was reeling when her line jerked again, harder this time, even bending her rod down. "Damn," he said. Then, "Reel, honey, reel."

As she started to try to draw the line in, a small crowd gathered—mainly other fisherman who'd been stretched out along the shore and had now abandoned their rods to come watch the mounting drama on Lindsey's.

"Reel that sucker in, little girl," one of the older fellows said, to which she responded, clearly frustrated, "I'm trying, but it's hard—I can't get the thing to turn."

Rob stepped up behind her. "Want me to help?"

"No," she snapped, resolute. "If I'm gonna catch this fish, then *I'm* gonna catch this fish."

She said it with such determination that they *all* took a step back from her and went quiet as she resumed her struggle. The fish below the water's surface still pulled hard, bending her rod further as it tried to break free, but she fought to hold on with one hand while she forced the reel around with the other.

Slowly, the other guys started giving her more directions, just quieter now, like people talked on a golf course. "Don't let loose of it and give him any headway."

"That's gotta be a big 'un."

"It's just you and him now. You gotta show him who's boss, reel him in one inch at a time."

As Rob stood watching, he hoped to hell, for her sake, that it didn't turn out to be some mud-covered tire that had been stuck in the lake for forty years.

"Reel, reel, reel," one of the old men cheered her on as she finally started gaining some momentum, pulling the line in closer and closer.

Until finally Lindsey hoisted an enormous rainbow trout out of Spirit Lake, the size of which made all the other fisherman gasp in awe. It had to be over two feet long—which Rob knew was a hell of a rainbow trout!

Then they applauded and Rob's chest swelled with pride for her as she looked around and smiled—until she stumbled forward and he had to rush to help her get the fish to shore before the weight of it pulled her into the lake.

Later that day, Eleanor—as chairperson of the Fish Festival and Fry committee—awarded Lindsey with a large trophy, practically making all the hard-core fishermen at the event weep. Turned out that her twenty-nine-inch, nine-pound eight-ounce rainbow trout was the largest pulled from Spirit Lake since Millie's award winner back in '88.

As dusk fell that evening, Lindsey lounged on Rob's couch in her skirt and flip-flops, recovering from the fun of the day. After getting her trophy, the frying and grilling of the fish had commenced—but not hers, her prizewinning trout was currently resting in a freezer at the Lazy Elk. So they'd all eaten fish and corn on the cob and baked potatoes, and then wrapped the day up with the annual canoe race. She'd talked Rob into being her partner and they'd lost badly—no small wonder since she'd never actually been in a canoe before—but it had still been fun to take part, and at least they hadn't come in last. That honor rested with Bernard and Mrs. Bixby, who it was rumored had stopped to make out on the far side of Misty Isle.

"What a day," she mused on a sigh as Rob came from the kitchen with an open bottle of wine and two stemmed glasses. The sight caught her off guard. "Why, Mr. Colter, I didn't know you were a wine connoisseur."

"I'm not," he said. "Eleanor gave it to me at Christmas to welcome me as a Moose Falls business owner. Seems like a good time to break it out, to celebrate your big win."

As he sat down next to her and poured the white wine, she said, "I wish Aunt Millie could have seen that fish."

"Me, too," he said, then lifted his glass. "To Millie."

Lindsey couldn't think of a more appropriate toast, so she clinked glasses with Rob, then took a sip. "This might sound silly," she confided, "but I think I feel more connected to her because of the fish."

"It's not silly," he said, leaning over to deliver a sweet kiss.

"I can't wait to see the pictures." Eleanor had, of course, taken lots of them—Lindsey with her fish, Lindsey and Rob with her fish, Lindsey with her trophy, the trophy and the fish by themselves on the dock. "You know, I was thinking—Aunt Millie's last scrapbook had some empty pages in the back. Do you think she'd mind if I added my fish pictures to it?"

Rob's smile warmed her and he even leaned in to kiss her again. "I think she'd love that, Abby."

"I know Millie's fish is at the Grizzly Inn—what do you think I should do with mine?"

"If you want, I'll have it mounted and hang it in the boathouse."

Lindsey couldn't have been more delighted by the idea. "That sounds perfect! Like the perfect homage to Millie! And then it will always be there for people to see." She laughed, feeling downright joyous from the day, then added, "I never imagined being so excited about mounting a fish."

Rob set down his wine glass and lowered his chin, flashing an ultra-sexy look. "I know something else you could mount that will excite you even more." Then he dropped his gaze to his crotch, where an arousing bulge pushed prominently against his jeans.

Mmm, his naughty talk melted through her like slow, sugary syrup—she felt it in every part of her body. The truth was, in between all the wholesome family fun and fish-catching excitement, she'd been wanting him all day, too—bad.

So she didn't hesitate to set aside her wine and move toward Rob on the leather sofa. She pushed up onto her knees, then used her body to press him back into the couch pillows.

Feeling supercharged with longing, she followed the urge to rub her breasts against his chest, to press the juncture of her thighs against the hard-on in his jeans, moving against him instinctively. Oh yes—this *was* more exciting than mounting a fish.

"Damn, I like when you're like this," he breathed between kisses, his arms closing around her.

"Like what?" she whispered.

"Aggressive."

"Really?" She wasn't sure why that surprised her, but . . . "You didn't like it at first. The first time I kissed you. You pushed me away."

"That wasn't because I didn't like it. And if you think back, you'll remember I showed up at your room five minutes later and fucked your brains out."

She hissed in her breath, surprisingly turned on by his off-color talk. Garrett had never talked like that. "True enough," she agreed. "I guess you couldn't resist me."

He chuckled deeply, his eyes still colored with want. "Of course, I like when *I'm* being the aggressive one, too," he said. "I guess, with you, I like it all."

Her breasts seemed to swell within the cups of her bra, her whole body aching for more, but . . . what he'd just said struck her, made her stop, made her say, "I want to ask you something."

He sighed, sounding tired. "If it's about the tattoo, forget it."

"No, not that," she said, smacking playfully at his chest, then got to the heart of the matter. Despite that letter, after the last day or two, Gina wasn't on her mind right now—this was just about him . . . and her. "If you were coming over to my place for dinner, and I answered the door wearing only an apron and a sexy pair of shoes ready to have my way with you, what would you think?"

He blinked, looking all the more aroused. "What would I think? That I'm one *hell* of a lucky guy."

And maybe Lindsey had already known what his answer would be. But hearing it, finding out for sure, made her fall a little bit more in love with him—something that was starting to feel a lot more wonderful and a lot less scary all the time. She couldn't help kissing him again in reply.

When the kiss ended, he said, "But that's a weird question—so, uh, why?"

Once upon a time, she'd resolved never to let Rob find out how her breakup with Garrett had happened, but everything had changed since then. And she considered trying to explain the whole thing—but it just seemed simpler to show him. Still lying on him, she said, "Do you have a computer with Internet access?"

Looking understandably bewildered, he slowly nodded. "I don't use it much—mostly for billing—but yeah."

"Where is it?"

He pointed to the antique rolltop desk by the door. "Why?"

Without replying, she got up and walked to the desk. Lifting the rolled-down cover, she found a laptop and opened it, hitting the power button. "Come here," she said.

"Um, weren't we busy over here? I was about to get you naked, we were gonna let the dog watch us have sex again—ring any bells?"

She gasped slightly, having totally forgotten King lay on his rug across the room—but then turned back to the computer, watching it boot up. "I'm sorry," she said, "but I need to show you something. It's . . . important to me."

As she started clicking her way into his Internet browser, she heard him getting up, muttering low beneath his breath. "Not sure why you have to show me *now*, but okay. I'll just tell my penis to take a few hours off, go get a beer or something."

She couldn't help smiling to herself at his dry sense of humor. But, of course, *her* humor faded as she efficiently Googled herself to choose from the many sites that had posted the dreaded apron picture. She was sure it graced no one's front page anymore, but it was still there, probably for eternity, for anyone to see. Rob stepped up behind her just as she clicked on one of the gossip sites and the picture appeared, filling much of the screen.

"What's this?" Rob asked, but then studied it a second and said, "Hell, that's *you*. And . . . is that Garrett?"

When he looked up for confirmation, she nodded and could see the empathy in his eyes before he peered back at the screen.

He pointed to a spot on Garrett's face. "And what's that? *Blood?*"

"Oh—gosh, no. But there were strawberries and glaze involved."

Rob silently studied the picture a minute more before finally turning back toward her. "What did he do to make you throw that on him?"

She swallowed. She hated this part of the story—it took her back there, felt too fresh. But she knew *her* story was nothing compared to the one Rob had told her last night, so she forced out the words. "He said I wasn't the kind of woman he wanted to marry. He said I was self-absorbed and high-maintenance and that I talk too much."

"Oh. Damn." His eyes changed then, looking sad for her. "Sorry, honey. This is how you broke up?"

She nodded, and he cringed on her behalf.

"I was trying to do this special, playful, wild thing for him," she explained, "and he humiliated me and hurt me. I haven't felt that belittled since . . . ever, I suppose. He made me feel like a classless loser." She went on to tell the whole story of the window washer and *Chi-Town Beat* and the demise of life as she knew it—and even though it measured nothing to how Rob's life had been taken from him once upon a time, she knew he would understand. "Garrett blamed me for everything from being too tacky to be on his arm to not noticing it was window-washing day," she concluded.

And she couldn't help being pleased when Rob's eyes darkened. "I ought to kick his ass."

The words drew a small, even if sort of sad grin to her face. "Inconvenient, given the distance," she said, "but thank you for that."

Then she slid her arms around his neck and kissed him again, pressed against him again, went back to wanting him again. "I wasn't going to tell you about that, because it was so humiliating," she explained between kisses, "but now . . . I just needed to, you know?"

He leaned forward, pressing his forehead to hers, and softly replied, "Yeah, I know."

"I hope your penis didn't go too far," she said then, peering up hopefully.

A small laugh escaped Rob's throat. "No, honey, I was just teasing about that. He wouldn't even *think* of leaving if he knows he has a chance of getting close to you."

"I *like* him," she said.

"Feeling's mutual." With that, Rob slid his hands to her ass and hoisted her into his grasp—her legs wrapping automatically around his hips. Kissing her, he carried her back to the couch and lay her down, clearly ready to get back to business.

But he paused for just a second, glancing back over his shoulder to the computer—then gazed down into her eyes. "Just so you know, Abby, you can do wild things for *me* anytime."

That night, they made love on the couch—that quickly, they'd forgotten about King's presence—and then moved upstairs to Rob's bed.

On Monday, he worked at Steve Fisher's place and Lindsey assisted in Fish Festival cleanup, answered blog comments, and posted a new entry about how wonderful the event had been—and, courtesy of Eleanor, she even had a shiny new digital photo of herself with her winning fish to include. All the pictures had turned out great, so she planned to work on adding her own experiences to Aunt Millie's scrapbook later this week.

She lunched with Carla and Eleanor at the Lakeside Café, then they all walked over to the Lazy Elk, where Carla made them three sex-on-the-beaches to drink, the very name of which put Eleanor into stitches. And when Lindsey told the other ladies Rob's plan for her fish, they sighed as if he'd bought her a dozen roses.

That night, she picked up some steaks at the general store—a full-service grocery in addition to everything else Bernard stocked—and she and Rob cooked them on the grill. After eating, they put on jackets and took King out in the backyard, where Rob threw an old yellow tennis ball for him to fetch over and over again. She discovered she liked watching them together, simply because Rob's affection for the dog warmed her heart despite the chilly, dusky air. Later, they snuggled up on the couch and caught an old movie on satellite.

And as the movie went off and the credits rolled, she found herself wondering: How did this happen? How had she ended up in such a cozy, comfy place with a man who couldn't stand the sight of her a couple of weeks earlier? She'd come here to buy a canoe livery, but she'd fallen in love instead.

Not that she planned to tell Rob that anytime soon. Sure, he'd opened up to her—*a lot*—but she could still envision the L-word freaking him out. So for now, she'd keep her giddy, happy, I'm-so-in-love feeling to herself and just bask in the pleasure it brought.

"I'm thinking of taking the afternoon off tomorrow," he told her, clicking off the TV.

"Oh?"

"Eleanor has quite a few guests coming this weekend now, so it really *will* be official canoe season as of Saturday. So I just thought, before that happens . . . maybe you and I might want to steal a canoe ride alone before the lake is full of people. Interested?"

Now *this* felt like a Rob version of a dozen roses. A romantic, private canoe ride. "Very," she said, her voice coming out all whispery.

Then they went upstairs and had slow, sweet sex that somewhere along the way transformed into hot, urgent sex—but either way, she liked it. She fell asleep in his arms.

Now it was Tuesday and she was getting ready for her canoe date. She was picking up a picnic basket from the café, but had driven to the general store first to do a few errands.

"Well, hello there, darlin'," Bernard said. "Don't you look pretty as spring itself."

She'd worn a pale yellow sundress sporting a row of appliquéd daises across the straight-cut bodice. A pair of yellow slip-on wedges with a silk flower between the toes finished the look. "Thanks, Bernard."

"You don't look like you're out grocery shoppin' today—what can I help you find?"

She smiled. "Do you have any flip-flops, particularly any with sparkles or embellishments on them?"

"Don't rightly know what an embellishment is, darlin', but what I *do* know is that you're gonna run me clean outta shoes," he said, then took off with his cane at a lightning pace, which she took as her cue to follow.

"A girl can never have too many, Bernard," she pointed out.

A minute later, they arrived in the shoe department and, a row over from the Keds, she spied several beaded flip-flops that might just fit the bill. Jimmy Choo they weren't, but that didn't matter so much in Moose Falls. "Oooh, these look promising. I'll just try them on."

"You know," Bernard said, "if you're gonna stick around, maybe I oughta stock up on shoes."

If she was gonna stick around. Hmm. It wasn't the first time someone had brought up the question.

She certainly hadn't come here *planning* to stick around, that was for sure—she'd seen this only as a temporary hideaway. But now she'd made friends. She'd helped with the festival. She'd worked at the boathouse. And she had a lover. More than a lover. A man she loved.

She wasn't sure where any of it would lead, but feeling like she didn't care if she ever saw Chicago again, she said, "Maybe you should." Then, as Bernard started to walk away, she added, "One more thing—do you have picture frames?"

"Well, of course." He pointed. "Right over there by the lamps."

"Do you have any that would hold two pictures, one on top of the other?" To illustrate, she reached into her matching yellow straw bag and pulled out the two photos she'd subtly lifted from the boathouse the other day when Rob was busy helping people fry fish and keep grills going. She held them one above the other to show Bernard what she meant.

"Hmm," he said, and she knew it—she'd finally found something Bernard didn't have. "Don't know that we do," he admitted. Yet then he lifted a finger triumphantly in the air. "But we can order it, by golly!"

"Great. How long will it take?"

"Don't know. Never ordered 'em before."

But by the time she approached the front register with a new pair of black flip-flops embellished with multicolored beads, Bernard had a catalog out, showing her an array of suitable frames. She picked a simple one of natural wood that would go well in the boathouse or the cabin, thinking it would make a nice gift as Rob started his first official canoe season as owner of the Spirit Lake Boathouse.

After dropping her car, flip-flops, and stolen pictures back off at the Grizzly Inn, she grabbed her picnic basket from Mary Beth and walked over to the dock, where she found Rob readying a bright red canoe for their excursion.

"Hey," she said, smiling.

He smiled back, giving her a once-over. "Honey, you look like pure sunshine, but those shoes aren't gonna work in a canoe. Haven't you learned your lesson yet?"

Having become skilled at being adaptable to her new home-in-the-woods, Lindsey replied, "Not a problem," then took off first one shoe, then the other, tossing them both into the canoe.

Rob just grinned at her. She'd looked damn pretty before, but now, in her bare feet, the toenails still painted a soft, pearly shade of pink, she looked adorable. "Come on, Abby," he said. "Let's go for a ride."

He held the canoe steady against the dock as Lindsey stepped carefully in, easing her way down on the seat, then he joined her and pushed away into the water, passing her an oar.

As they started to paddle, Rob looked around at the tree-laden hillsides that cradled the lake, drinking in the fresh air and sunshine. Last summer, that was what he'd found here—the beauty of nature, and a dear woman who was willing to help him rebuild his life. Now he had *another* woman—a very *different* woman, for whom he felt very different emotions. He couldn't have seen it coming if he'd tried, but she sat in front of him now, chocolate brown hair spilling down her back, yellow dress spread out around her, dipping her oar serenely into the water—and he couldn't find a reason in the world to tell her she wasn't doing it right and that he was the only one actually propelling the boat forward.

"I like this," she said over her shoulder. "That it's just us. So quiet."

"Me, too." He'd discovered late last fall that it made him feel at peace to bring a canoe out onto the lake by himself—floating along the glassy surface at dusk was the closest he'd ever really come to feeling God.

But he hadn't found the time to come out alone this

spring—until now. And he'd chosen to bring Lindsey with him. It wasn't the same as being alone, but he was beginning to think being alone was overrated; it was nice to share this with her.

He paddled the canoe to Misty Isle, landing at a sandy spot that wouldn't hurt the bottom of the boat and made it easy to exit onto the shore. He liked that Lindsey didn't even balk, just stepped out into the cool, wet sand in her bare feet and walked up onto the packed ground where the trees and greenery started. He followed with the picnic basket, spreading the checked tablecloth inside on the ground like a blanket.

As they ate chicken salad sandwiches and potato salad and grapes, they talked about . . . everything.

She told him more about her breakup with Garrett and how she'd started to feel like he'd had some strange hold on her for a while, and how it had influenced her response to Millie's offer. She told him she was starting to miss her work, advising people on their love lives. "I still don't know that I'm an authority on the topic anymore, but . . . I think people liked what I had to say." She told him she was considering driving down to Kalispell again to shop for some shorts for the summer, and maybe even some hiking shoes. "In case you want to take me on some more of Millie's trails," she added, clearly hinting.

"I think that can be arranged," he replied.

He told her a little more about his life growing up. Not the ugly details, just the general way things were. He admitted that until he'd found Millie, life had just been something you struggled through—he'd never really known much happiness until getting here. "And maybe it sounds weird to say I was happy being alone in the cabin, doing my work and nothing else, but I was. I mean, I am," he added, correcting himself. "Although . . . I don't mind having some company lately."

They talked about music and books, and he explained that

when a guy spent as much time by himself as he did, stuff like that became important, became the way he related to the world. "I started reading in prison," he said, the words sounding strange to his own ears. He wasn't yet used to having her know that about him. But it was nice to have one person, just one person, he could be honest with now. "I couldn't keep the books," he explained, "but I made a list of what I read that I liked and bought my own copies later."

"I can't imagine . . ." she began, her voice soft, sad, wondering. "I can't imagine what it was like there."

They lay stretched across the tablecloth now, the wicker basket between them, and he rolled on his back to look up at the sky. He wanted to talk, to tell her things, but despite himself, it remained difficult—there was still such a stigma of shame attached, even if she believed he was innocent.

"It was . . . cold," he said. "Not in temperature, but cold as in . . . stark. Hard. Gray. I appreciate being outside more than I ever did before. I notice things—the trees, the clouds, the way the seasons change. I see it in a way I never did before—I never want to miss a thing, a single day, because I missed so many."

"Was it . . . scary—in there?"

He closed his eyes. He didn't really want to go back there, but for Lindsey, just for a minute, he would. "Yeah," he finally said. "I mean, I went in at eighteen. The only thing that saved me was my cellmate, Glen. He was older, in his forties—he'd been in a long time, but he was a good man, a good friend. He taught me how to survive, how to be a badass."

"That doesn't seem like you. Even when I met you and you weren't very nice."

He quirked a slight grin. He had honestly disliked her at first, for hurting Millie—but that was different than the persona he'd been forced to wear in prison. "I . . . had to learn to be a scary dude. You kind of either . . . scare or *be* scared, you know?"

She nodded, even though he knew she couldn't *really* know.

"It cost me some time. I was denied parole due to bad behavior. But what that parole board couldn't possibly understand was that I had to be that way to get by, to keep from getting hurt—I had to put on an act. It kept me safe."

He saw her swallow next to him and felt the fear welling in her. Had she not wondered before? He could tell she wondered now. "So then, you were never . . . um . . . ?"

"Raped?" He bit his lip, shook his head. "No. That's where being a badass comes in." He'd known guys that had happened to. Even now it was too ugly to contemplate. He turned to face her on the blanket. "Bad shit goes on in prison, Abby, but I came out okay—that's all you need to know. Although I wouldn't mind not talking about it anymore, if that's okay with you."

She nodded briskly and said, "I'm sorry. I didn't mean to make you think about it."

And he leaned over and kissed her. "It's okay. It's my life. I have to deal with it."

"Are you still friends with Glen?"

He sighed. Glen. The one thing he actually missed about that godforsaken place. "He was serving a long sentence, so unless a miracle happened, he's still in. When I was getting out, I said I'd write to him, but he told me not to. Said it would just make him think too much about what it was like to be out here. So I didn't write."

"What did you do when you got out? Why did you move around so much—why didn't you go home?"

Home. That was a strange concept to him. Moose Falls was *starting* to feel like home—finally. In a better way than anyplace else ever had. "Nothing to go back there for," he finally said.

"Your parents?" she asked with raised eyebrows. "Family?"

He didn't like telling her this because he knew her family loved her, so this probably wouldn't make any sense. "My mom and dad only came to see me once in prison, when I first went in. And even then I could tell it was only obligation. I never heard from them again." The memory brought back that feeling of . . . final abandonment. Knowing he was really alone in the world.

He saw how sad she looked, and he hoped it wasn't pity. "God. What about other family?"

He just shook his head. "I was an only kid. And I never met my grandparents—all the relatives lived somewhere in California."

"You never told me . . . about Billy. Did he believe you? That you didn't do it?"

He just looked at her. For a city girl, sometimes she was pretty naïve. "His brother was dead. I was on the water tower with him. What do *you* think?"

"Sorry," she said, voice low.

"In fact, Billy pretty much cracked. He'd just lost his parents a year before, so when Tommy died, he kind of turned into a lunatic. His last words to me were that I'd better hope I died in prison, because if I didn't, he'd come looking for me when I got out."

At this, she gasped—and he supposed he forgot sometimes just how damn horrifying parts of his life had been. "Was he serious?"

He shrugged. "*Seemed* serious. It was another reason not to go back."

"But you've never heard from him?"

He shook his head. "I wonder sometimes what became of him—but I don't really want to know. That all seems . . . like it happened in another life, to somebody else. Or that's how I try to think of it, anyway."

She gritted her teeth lightly. "And I keep making you talk about it."

"It's okay, honey," he whispered. And he meant it. He *hated* talking about it, but he also knew that once you told somebody something like that, you had to answer their questions. He didn't want to give her any reason to start doubting him *now.*

She nodded, then reached out, past the picnic basket, to hold his hand. And he let her. It was too easy. He liked her touch too much.

"Tell me about Aunt Millie," she said.

And he laughed. "Haven't we been through this a few thousand times?"

But she shook her head. "Tell me about when you met."

Ah, that he could do. "I showed up here, just driving, looking for someplace quiet, off the beaten path. I'd just left Butte—I'd been working construction there, but as usual, I messed up and told a woman I was dating about my past, and she worked in the construction office, and the next thing I know, I don't have a job, or her, or the few friends I'd started making there. So I told myself it was the last damn time I would let that happen, and I put King in the truck and set out for someplace where I could just make my own way, live alone, be alone, as much as possible.

"I stayed at the Grizzly Inn—Eleanor was nice enough to let King in—and when I asked about work, she told me Millie could probably use some help at the livery. It was a little over a year ago—almost Fish Festival time and the start of canoe season. She hired me, and also had me doing yard work and repairs around the house. We spent time together, and she got to know me and could tell, I guess, that I'd been through some hard times. I'll never forget how she got me to tell her about prison."

"How?"

"She said, 'I'll tell you my secret if you tell me yours.' I thought, *What kind of secret could this sweet old lady have that would matter at all?* And then she said, 'I'm dying, and nobody knows. Except you now. Don't tell, or it'll ruin everything, okay?' And I . . . understood that she really, truly had confided in me, and I knew I could trust her, and I told her. Just like I told you." He shook his head. "For a guy who doesn't like people and doesn't like to talk, I can't seem to shut up, can I?"

Lying next to him, she smiled. "You like people. And you like to talk. You've just been . . . afraid to."

God. She was right. And it was so obvious, but up to now he'd been so angry that he'd just wanted to close himself off from everything. He just nodded and swallowed back his surprise, and said, "Some people. Like you." And squeezed her fingers.

Then added, "There's something I think I should tell you." And when she sat up, looking a little anxious, he sat up, too, and took her hands in his. "It's about Millie." He sighed then—because he was telling her another secret. And he knew he didn't have to, but he *needed* to. Needed to be *completely* honest with her now.

"She didn't actually sell me the livery or her house, Lindsey. She left them to me in her will. She wanted me to have them—so I wouldn't have to worry about money, so that my construction and the canoe business would be enough to earn a healthy living. I argued with her about it, but she insisted. She wanted to make my life easier." When he finished, he felt a little breathless, almost like when he'd finished telling her about prison the other night.

"Why," she asked, "do you seem upset about this?"

He sighed. "Because it felt like . . . taking something from your family. Something that should have come to you. Not so much the business or the house themselves, but the money they're worth."

Yet Lindsey just shook her head. "Rob, it's okay. We . . . never even thought about the money. We don't need it. We're . . . fairly well off."

He'd known that, but . . . "I've let people think she sold it to me because that's what she wanted. So it's another secret I've been keeping, and I just wanted to tell you. Lindsey, she trusted me with everything she had, and that's . . . why I can never give it up. Not even to you. I hope you understand that."

Across from him, she nodded. "Rob, I've known for a while now that I can't take the canoe livery from you. I understand what it means to you. So don't worry—I won't ever try. I wouldn't do that to you."

Ever since Rob had told Lindsey about his past, he'd felt . . . nearly overwhelmed with emotion for her. And just knowing she understood, not only about what he'd been through but about what Millie's enormous gifts had meant to him, would *always* mean to him . . . it all rushed through him like a river. "I need to kiss you," he said, the words sounding a little feverish.

Looking as impassioned as he felt, she met him halfway, their mouths colliding in a hard kiss that quickly turned slower, deeper, melting warmly through his body and turning him hard for her in an instant.

Pushing the picnic basket aside, Rob lay her back on the blanket, watching the way the sun sifted down through the trees to cast speckled rays of light across her body. He bent to kiss her neck, her chest; he let his hands graze upward over her breasts, lingering there, let his thumbs brush lightly across her beautifully hardened nipples through her dress.

She thrust her hands up under his T-shirt—and damn, he liked how she always wanted his clothes off as bad as he wanted to get to her, too. He obliged by yanking the shirt up over his head and tossing it onto a nearby clump of moss.

Her fingers splayed across his chest, kneading, and he felt it between his legs, pulsing, growing.

"You know," she said then, breathless, breasts heaving, "there's one thing you still haven't told me about."

Aw, shit. Here it came.

"Gina. Who is she?"

Sometimes he had to curse himself for that damn tattoo. He moved against her, hard at the apex of her thighs, and his voice came just as thready. "Nobody you need to know about."

"She's out of your life?"

"Completely."

"Did she hurt you?"

Hell. "Not intentionally. It wasn't her fault."

"What happened?"

Damn it, if he was *ever* gonna tell her about Gina, it wouldn't be *now*, for God's sake, when he wanted under her skirt. "Nothing. It's a dumb tattoo."

"Then why did you get it?"

"It was a prison thing, something to pass the time."

He saw her pull in her breath as she ran her fingers across the name on his chest. "It was a *prison tattoo*?"

"Yes, Abby, it was a prison tattoo. Happy now?"

Her voice went softer. "She must have been special."

Christ. "Drop it, Abby."

"But . . ."

"Look, do you want to talk or do you want me to give you an orgasm you'll never forget?"

She bit her lip as renewed passion sparked in her eyes, but said, "That's a tough choice—because I'm really curious about Gina."

Okay, enough of this. "Here," he said, "I'll make the decision *for* you." Then he flipped up her dress, bent over, and gently bit at the silky cotton covering her mound.

When she gasped, he smiled—because he knew he'd finally made her forget about the tattoo.

Fourteen

Rob's kisses covered her panties, making her crazier with each passing second. Reaching down, she ran her fingers through his hair, the only way she could touch him right now, and she *needed* to touch him. Her heart hurt for all he had gone through, and all he was forced to keep inside him. Well, except for when he was with her.

He's falling in love with me.

He had to be. Otherwise, she knew a guy like him—gruff, mean Rob Colter—would never have opened up to her. Not like this. Not telling her his deepest secrets, his hardest memories. And oh *God*, they were hard. Hard to even hear, let alone to imagine living through, surviving.

"Please," she heard herself breathe.

His hands cupped her ass as he nibbled through the fabric covering her. He murmured a reply. "Please what, honey?"

"Take off my panties. Kiss me there."

Their eyes met and the heat and love passing between them was palpable. And—oh, his eyes were beautiful. Even more so now that she knew the dark truths that hid behind them.

"Lift up," he whispered.

She did, and he pulled her panties slowly down until the breeze hit her newly revealed flesh, making her shiver—and making her spread her legs for him.

He moaned in response, then gave her what she'd asked for.

Her low moans mingled with the songs of birds singing in the distance, the sound of wind in the pines overhead. She lifted against Rob's mouth, uninhibited, unafraid—of anything. She didn't fear the strength of what she felt for him; she didn't fear he would ever hurt her or use her or embarrass her. What should have perhaps felt hedonistic and forbidden and wild . . . simply did not. In fact, nothing she'd ever done with a man had ever felt so right.

His ministrations were skilled, giving, perfect. Her fingers curled into the cloth of the blanket on both sides of her as *Rob's* fingers pushed their way inside her, heightening every sensation. Her moans turned to passionate sobs, but she made no effort to stifle or control them. With Rob, sex was so easy. It didn't matter if she was hot and seductive or more demure and submissive. With him, she could be whatever she felt like being in any given moment, and he *took* that, almost seemed to cherish that. He made her feel beautiful no matter what she became with him.

So she let out her cries of pleasure, and she moved against his mouth, and she let the heat rise inside her, climbing higher, higher, toward that ultimate peak—until finally she tumbled down the other side, crashing into ecstasy. Her shrieks of orgasm filled the air and she didn't care, just let them come, let them be one more part of nature here. She let every ounce of sensation vibrate through her before finally going still and quiet.

Rob's gaze met hers, his eyes glistening with passion.

"Oh my God," she murmured, breathless. "That was *so* good."

Her words made a wicked smile unfurl across his handsome face.

And she asked him again for exactly what she wanted, no

holding back. "Please come inside me, Rob. I need to feel you there."

His eyes darkened at the request as he growled, "Aw, *baby*," then rose up onto his knees to undo his jeans. She watched with rapt anticipation, her chest expanding in pleasure when his erection burst free.

"I need you in me," she whispered, their gazes locked. "Nothing feels better."

He arched one brow, looking slightly skeptical. "Not even when you come like that?"

She didn't hesitate. "Not even when I come like that."

And his expression changed, turned more serious, and she knew he understood what she was saying—that what they shared was about far more than orgasms now. He said nothing—but dragged his gaze down over her body, his hands following, his breath growing heavier until he gripped her hips and pushed his way inside.

They both groaned, and she let her eyes fall shut, because her words had been *so* true—nothing felt better. They moved together, his strokes slow, deep—then turning harder, faster, until finally he said, "I'm coming in you, honey, coming in you."

She met his deep plunges, taking in as much of him as she could, and when they lay quietly in each other's arms a minute later, she said, "Remember what you told me about the Indians, how they felt safe here on the island?"

He nodded, his face close to hers.

"I feel safe, too."

"Good," he said.

"It's not far from town and yet it feels . . . like a private little world."

"That's why I brought you here," he whispered.

"Then you feel that way here, too?"

He gave a slight nod. "Remember, honey, you're not the only one looking for something safe in this world."

* * *

Dear Lovers,

I come to you on this Wednesday dizzy with joy. I probably shouldn't tell you this, but . . . my guy and I made love on an island yesterday. Out in the middle of the lake. Nothing but us and the trees and the canoe we paddled there in. It was possibly the most romantic sex I've ever had, and given some of the sex I've had with him, that's saying a lot. He just makes me sigh, lovers.

So . . . add that to winning the Big Fish trophy at the festival a few days ago and I'm happier than I could have imagined. Not bad for a girl who was too heartbroken to even post a blog a couple of weeks ago.

Back then, I thought I was a prime example of failed love, misplaced trust, and everything else we're all trying to avoid on the rocky road of relationships. And it's true, I was *those things.*

But now I feel I'm an even better *example of bouncing back, of finding passion and joy where you least expect it. God knows I didn't come to Moose Falls looking for a new relationship, lovers—but maybe that's the real joy of life, the real gift. That sometimes you get these wonderful things when you most need them and least anticipate them.*

So onward and upward, lovers. If you're down on love right now, I hope you'll walk out the door today with a hopeful heart, and with the full knowledge that the perfect guy (or girl) can literally be right around the corner at any time. And if you're in a happy place—celebrate! That's exactly what I intend

> *to do today. With a big piece of lemon meringue pie at the Lakeside Café. And then I'm going to borrow Carla's copy of* Bridget Jones's Diary *so I can bone up on my favorite parts and be ready to join the café's book club next week!*

As soon as Lindsey clicked on Submit, she wondered again if she'd gotten too personal—since it was one thing to say she had a lover she was crazy about and another to give actual details about her sex life.

On the other hand, sex made the world go around and the Internet had turned so many personal things public these days that surely sharing something like that was no big deal. It was just how she connected with her readers. If Britney Spears could flash her vagina to the world on the Internet, surely it was no great crime for Lindsey to mention making love to Rob.

And it really *had* been making love. God, she *loved* him! She thought about him every second. When she was away from him, she burned to see him. And when she was with him, she felt . . . completely satiated in every way. Carla had informed her she was officially getting "sappy" about him, and Eleanor had started rolling her eyes every time Lindsey said Rob's name—which she guessed meant she'd been saying it a lot lately.

After taking a shower and getting dressed—in capri pants and a tank that would coordinate with her new black flip-flops *and* her leopard-print clutch—Lindsey returned to the computer to check for new comments. As usual, they were flooding in. Some were saying how happy they were for her and her new guy, and others continued to comment on the Fish Festival and what a versatile chick she'd turned out to be—God knew the Lindsey Brooks of a few weeks ago wouldn't have been caught dead fishing. Still more were starting to shoot questions at her about *their* love lives.

And the truth was, she wanted to answer them. Now that she had her head back on straight after the Garrett fiasco, and now that she had her confidence back, too, she felt she knew the answers these people needed.

And so . . . she cautiously took the first step back onto the advice-giving tightrope, hoping she wouldn't fall.

In the comments section, she selected only two or three advice-seekers to address. She kept it short, she kept it simple—she wanted to tread carefully here.

JackieBlue, your man is right—you work too hard. Surely you know what they say about too much work and not enough play? I know it's hard when you're a workaholic, but trust me, you'll be a happier, more well-balanced person if you find more time for your guy.

MollieInTheMiddle, you need to make a decision. I agree, they both sound like great guys, but the longer you keep them hanging on a string, the better chance both of them will give up and let go. Men are more sensitive than they seem, and they have big egos. Imagine your life without each guy in it, one at a time. Who's the one you can't live without? Who's the one who makes you laugh? Who's the one you can be totally yourself with? That's the man for you.

And NYGal, any guy who cheats isn't worth it. I'm not saying guys can't change, I'm just saying most of them don't. If he can't treat you right, you don't need him in your life. It's a road to ruin, girlfriend, and you don't want to be on it.

Of course, by the time she'd written all that, more comments had come in, mostly from her regular cheerleaders: SweetReneeInOhio thought her island sex sounded dreamy and wonderful, and WilliamTell1 said he'd never seen a prettier fisherman—but one comment in particular caught her eye. MargaritaMary had fallen for a guy who seemed crazy about her, yet she feared he was hung up on a girl in his past. Mary said he refused to talk about it, which worried her. *Should I be scared of this mystery woman, Lindsey?*

Lindsey's stomach churned a little as she typed an honest reply. Maybe it was *too* honest, but at least it would remind people that she really didn't have *all* the answers.

> *MM, I know where you're coming from. Despite everything so wonderful about my new beau, he has a mystery woman in his past, too. All I really know about her is her name—Gina. And maybe I wouldn't be so worried if it weren't tattooed on his chest. That's right, ladies, my man's got another woman's name engraved on his skin and he won't tell me anything about her. So why am I putting up with that? Well, because he's opened up to me about a lot of things so far—just not that one. Men can be so good at simply shutting down when they don't want to talk about something—and it can take a great deal of patience to learn everything we want to about our guys. So, Mary, all I can advise on this one is to take a wait-and-see attitude. Remember, girls, I always have strong opinions, but at the same time, I'm just feeling my way through this love thing, same as you. I hope you find your answer soon, though. And I hope I find mine, as well.*

Sadly, after she sent the reply, she almost regretted it. Because she knew how it would look—like she was a fool. She was making love to a man with a girl's name on his chest—who wouldn't tell her anything about that girl. If someone wrote to her with that exact problem, she'd probably tell them to dump him flat.

Just then, her computer chimed to let her know new e-mail had arrived, so she clicked to see a message from her editor. Whom she'd not heard from since she'd announced she was going on hiatus for a while.

Oh boy. Maybe this was it. Maybe she was being fired. Maybe it wasn't even her decision anymore whether she kept her advice column going.

With her stomach churning, she opened the message.

Lindsey,

Here at the paper, we've all been reading your blog with great interest and all I can say is: brilliant! Your carefully constructed reemergence onto the Internet has you connecting with readers on a personal level like never before. Don't know if you've checked your stats, but hits on the blog are through the roof. Clearly, you've thought your way through what happened and figured out how to make it work for you—kudos, kudos, kudos! We're waiting with bated breath to hear you're ready to resume the column, and the letters are still pouring in.

Best,
Corinne

P.S. Congrats on the guy, too. You're making us all want our very own lumberjack.

"Well, I'll be damned," she murmured, staring at the screen. Her boss thought her blog posts were all some elaborate, well-thought-out plan. And her hits were through the roof. Clearly, it *was* time for a slice of Mary Beth's lemon meringue pie.

That night it rained and they made love on the daybed with the window open. Lindsey listened to the drizzle and let the scent fill her senses, until finally she told Rob, "You're right. Rain's not always so bad."

"Nothing is, not really. Nothing in nature, I mean. Anything outside is better than four walls."

She got the idea he was getting more accustomed to talking about his past. Now that it was becoming a common topic between them, it no longer shocked her when it came up—and she thought he was starting to look less pained when he spoke of those times. She never said so, but she had a feeling it was probably *good* for him to talk about it sometimes, that it was purging his soul of all those bad memories.

I love you.

Watching his eyes drift shut, the moonlight casting a shadow across his unshaven face, the words wafted through her mind. That happened often these days, and she wished she could tell him. But with Rob, she still thought it was better to take her time. He'd given her so much of himself already.

Of course, he still hadn't told her about Gina, and maybe that was another good reason to keep her *I love you*s to herself. As good as things had gotten between them, she supposed she still harbored the fear that she'd suddenly find out he was still in love with Gina and maybe always *would* be.

She watched him sleep for a few minutes, then realized she wasn't yet sleepy herself. It was early for her to go to bed, only around ten—which was eight in Chicago—and Rob put in hard physical labor every day, so he had a lot more reason to be tired than she did. After a few minutes, she decided to get up for a while, maybe drink some hot tea, maybe look through some more of Aunt Millie's things. Rob had mentioned there were still boxes of Millie's on the high shelves in his bedroom closet that he hadn't gone through—old letters and keepsakes from when she was young. To get a window into Millie's life back then sounded appealing, like a whole new Millie left to discover.

Stepping into Rob's walk-in closet, she pulled the chain

that turned on an overhead bulb, then quietly shut the door so the light wouldn't wake him.

His clothes hung neat and straight on either side of her; his shoes and work boots stood in a tidy row on the floor. Right now she wore one of his T-shirts, an easy thing to throw on after sex, and she loved having the feel and smell of him so close to her body—so a whole *closet* of his clothes made her feel weirdly warm inside.

Peering upward, she spied old hat boxes and shoe boxes and keepsake boxes tied with ribbon and string. So many of them—and Lindsey thought of the hours she would spend sifting through them all. But she could barely reach the lowest shelf, so for now she selected the box easiest to grab on to—a simple brown shoe box with the word *Letters* written in felt-tip pen on the side.

Sitting down cross-legged on the closet floor, she set the box before her and took off the lid. It was almost full: folded letters written on all different sorts and sizes of paper, no envelopes.

She plucked out the first, written on plain white stationery in black ink, the script jagged and masculine-looking. And then she saw the salutation: *Dear Gina.*

Oh God. These weren't Millie's. These were Rob's. The ones he'd mentioned in the letter on his desk—which had disappeared since she'd first seen it, probably into this box.

Up to now, she'd thought maybe the other letters he'd written no longer existed—that maybe he'd thrown them away or something. But no—here they were, right in front of her. A whole shoe box full.

She should put them back right now, she knew that.

But how could she? How *could* she?

Maybe it made her less of a good person than she wanted to be, but she couldn't help reading the first line . . . then the second.

And then . . . she was drawn in. Drawn in by his simple

words—a strange, soft beauty to the thoughts he put on paper, to the images in his mind.

And so, she kept reading. And reading. First one letter, then the next.

And she soon realized that she still wasn't learning much about Gina—there wasn't one detail about her, not one memory of a time they'd spent together, not one reference to what they'd shared, nothing.

The only thing they told her about Gina was that her worries were well founded. Whoever Gina was, he'd *really, really* loved her. Just like the first letter she'd read—which she did indeed find among these now—she could feel it in every sad, thoughtful word. The letters weren't dated, but there were so many of them—and more than she'd have hoped appeared recent, the paper crisp and fairly new.

Lindsey had begun to think that maybe Rob loved her, too. Even after the earlier letter she'd read. But this changed things. So many letters. So damn many. Clearly, he loved Gina more. He had to. Because he'd loved her for *years*. Lindsey had known *that* from the first letter, too, but somehow it seemed more serious when she saw how brown some of the paper here had turned with age, even tearing at the creases. His love for Gina went back a very long, deep way.

Who *was* she?

Not the girl he'd known as a teenager—that was Karen. Was this someone else from those days, before prison? Had Gina broken his heart so badly that he couldn't even bear to talk about her?

Lindsey sighed, running her thumb over his signature on one of the letters. *All my love, Rob.* That's how he signed them all. Giving her *all* his love. *All* of it.

Maybe it was stupid to think so hard about this, but how could she not? Sure, she'd managed to shove it halfway from her mind after finding that first letter, but now she sat in the small space, her stomach churning, beginning to feel like a perfect fool for falling for him, for thinking this was really *something*, really *going* somewhere. She had a whole box of letters right in front of her that said the opposite.

And to think she'd told Bernard he should order more shoes in case she stayed. Because she'd really been considering that. The truth was, almost *planning* on it—because why on earth would she leave this little town she'd started to love, this *man* she'd started to love?

Obviously, that had been premature and too optimistic.

Lindsey refolded the letter in her hand and put it in the pile she'd already read. Then she reached for the next, even though reading was painful now, like torturing herself.

But it suddenly felt very necessary. Because maybe it would make her realize she had to back away from this, away from *him*. She needed to quit spending the night here, in his bed, in his arms. She needed to make this just sex again, just getting-back-on-the-sex-horse again.

Could she do that now? Was it even possible? She didn't know. But she wasn't up for being hurt again, not so soon.

How dumb that she'd let herself get emotionally involved with another guy so quickly after Garrett.

And she'd gotten over Garrett way faster than she'd ever thought possible, but with Rob . . . she just didn't think it would be that easy. Garrett had turned out to be a schmuck. But Rob . . . Rob was turning out to be a *beautiful, beautiful* man.

She took the next letter from the box, this one written on a small piece of yellow paper from a mini legal tablet, braced herself for all the love she'd feel in his words, and began to read.

And then, *then*, with that one lone letter, everything changed. From that one lone letter, she suddenly knew who Gina was.

Dear Gina,

Today is your birthday and I wonder if you're having a party. I see you surrounded by balloons of red, blue, yellow, and by stacks of presents with big, shiny ribbons streaming off them.

It's hard for me to believe you're already five. Where I am, time stands still—nothing changes, nothing moves. I like to think of you growing, playing, skipping, jumping . . . just living—it reminds me that there are much better places than this.

What color are your eyes? In the picture your mom sent when you were born, they were blue, but I read somewhere that the color can change. I like to imagine them being brown, like mine. Just so I can think of you carrying some little part of me with you, even if you never know it.

I made a little dollhouse in the woodshop today, and Glen painted it up real nice—put a red roof on it. It doesn't make much sense, I guess—I know you'll never see it. But I'm thinking about you, Gina, always thinking about you. Happy birthday.

All my love,
Rob

Fifteen

Oh God. *Oh God.*

Gina was his child.

The one he'd given up because it would be best for her.

And though he'd looked pained when he'd told Lindsey that part, she'd had no idea . . . He'd given her up and missed her and loved her and he'd been telling her so for years now in all these letters he'd never sent!

Lindsey did the math in her head: Rob was thirty-five and he'd gotten Karen pregnant at eighteen. So that made Gina . . . around sixteen. Oh God. He'd been missing her and wanting to be her father for sixteen long years.

Lindsey could barely breathe. Not so much from relief—that Gina wasn't a lover—but from sadness, for him. She'd never been a parent, so she could only imagine the feelings of loss he'd harbored all these years. As she sat rereading the letter about Gina's fifth birthday, tears began to roll slowly down her face.

She read more of the letters then, but through new eyes now that she understood. And even the letters that were vague made a fresh new sort of sense and the love poured through Rob's words even more.

Lindsey wasn't sure how long she sat there reading—an hour? Two? Only that she was near the bottom of the box—when the closet door opened and she peered up to see a rumpled-looking Rob staring down at her, his eyes narrowing on the stack of letters.

"What the hell are you doing?" he growled.

Oh no. She was an awful, prying person. She set the letter in her hand aside and rushed to her feet, still a little teary—still trying to get over what she'd learned. "Rob, I'm sorry, I really am. I couldn't sleep and I thought they were Aunt Millie's. But then when I saw who they were to . . . I'm sorry."

He just stared at her, mouth grim, and she could tell he was trying to appear angry—but other kinds of emotion came through his eyes, too.

She pressed her hands to his bare chest, caught a glimpse of her fingertips passing over the name there, and felt the gravity of the tattoo that much more. "I'm so sorry you didn't get to have her in your life, sorry you're not with her."

He just shook his head, clenched his fists—but his eyes shone glassy with regret. "It was best."

"Maybe not," she whispered. Then, "Why wouldn't you tell me who she was?"

He raised his eyebrows and spoke pointedly. "Maybe because I didn't want you to know?" After which he turned and stalked back to the daybed. The rain had stopped, but the air coming in the window stayed sweet with the scent, and crickets sang again.

"Why?" she asked. "I was going crazy thinking Gina was some woman you were deeply in love with. Why didn't you just tell me the truth instead of letting me wonder? Why keep that such a secret?"

He sat with his back against the pillows and brass

headboard, clearly sleepy and irritated. "Look, it's just something that started when I went to prison. I was lonely and scared—and when Karen sent me a baby picture with her name and birthday, it was . . . something to hang on to. So I hung on to it. She was . . . something to occupy my mind, that's all."

Lindsey shook her head. "That's *not* all, Rob. You're her father. You care about her. My God, you have her name tattooed over your heart."

He sighed, looking as if he'd been caught at something. His brow knit. "I guess I saw it as a way to always keep her with me, even though she's not here. A way to make sure I never forgot her."

Lindsey thought of the big box of letters she'd just read, spanning sixteen years. "I don't think you're in any danger of forgetting her, Rob. And I don't get why you seem . . . almost ashamed. Of loving your daughter."

"Because it's selfish, okay?" he snapped. "I gave her up because I knew she'd have a better life without me in it, and I'm about ninety-nine percent sure that's how it worked out. I met the guy who was going to be her dad and he was a good guy. Clean-cut, had just graduated from college and gotten some kind of suit-and-tie job. He loved Karen and was committed to the baby. It was perfect."

"For everyone but you."

"Right. But that's the selfish part."

"Have you ever . . . contacted Karen? Have you tried to be part of Gina's life?"

He looked at her like she was crazy. "Are you kidding? I gave up my rights. The last thing I would ever do is go nosing around in their lives. Can you imagine? Having the ex-con father suddenly show up? Can you imagine how *she* would feel—to find out her dad wasn't really Mr. Suit and Tie but a guy who'd been convicted of manslaughter? I feel selfish *enough*, weak enough, just . . . thinking about her at all. That's why I don't talk about it, and I don't think about it, and when I do, I put it in one of those letters and try to be done with it. But the last thing I'd ever do is mess up her life by coming back into it."

"I understand now," Lindsey said, "I get it." This was one more way Rob cut himself off from the rest of the world because he knew society didn't really accept people with a past like his. And she even understood why people were like that—she'd have probably felt that way, too, if she'd found out before she'd gotten to know him. And he was probably right—maybe bursting into a sixteen-year-old girl's life would be more hurtful than helpful. But none of that made her any less sad for him.

Quietly, she put the letters away and turned off the light in the closet and crawled back into the daybed with Rob—which, for them, had definitely turned out to be more of a night bed. "Thinking about her helped you get through prison, didn't it?" she asked. Although his letters never said so, she'd been aware many of them had been written from there.

His arm slid around her, pulling her close, so she guessed he wasn't mad at her. "Remember I told you I had to pretend to be a badass?"

She nodded.

"When you're not *really* a badass but you have to fake it every damn day, it's pretty stressful. I needed something good to focus on, and it was her. From the moment Karen sent me that picture, it was just . . . her. Thinking about her made me feel quiet inside. The only other times I felt relaxed were in the woodshop. I learned to carve things to pass the time. They had big, mounted saws—things you couldn't take apart and use as weapons—so when I wasn't in trouble, they'd let me go in there and make things."

"Like the heart-shaped box I read about."

He nodded. "Other things, too. I knew I could never give them to her, but it was something to do, and maybe . . . when I was actually making them, maybe I pretended I *could* give them to her, you know?"

She nodded against his chest and kissed him there. And then she took in the scent of him and looked up into his eyes. "You always smell like wood—wood shavings."

"I'm a carpenter, Abby."

Yet she shook her head. "This smell is different than when you've been working."

He looked at her as if she'd discovered yet one more little secret. "I still carve some stuff—I have a woodshop downstairs. It used to be Millie's sewing room. I haven't spent much time there lately, though—because I've been spending most of my free time with you."

"Sorry," she said.

And he quirked a half grin, for the first time since the closet. "Don't worry, honey—I'll take sex over woodwork any day."

"I never even realized there was a woodshop in the house."

"Behind the laundry room." He shrugged. "It didn't seem important. And we've been . . . kinda busy."

She smiled, then said, "Show me. The woodshop."

"Okay," he agreed. "Tomorrow."

"No—tonight."

"Honey, I'm tired."

And God knew the man had a *right* to be tired—besides working, she kept ousting so many secrets from him lately that he was probably *mentally* exhausted, as well—but . . . "I want to see the stuff you've made."

"It's not that special."

"Pretty please."

"What do *I* get out of it?"

"Sex."

A hint of masculine arrogance colored his speech. "I get that anyway."

"My undying affection," she added—teasingly, but she meant it.

"Fine," he said, but sounded more indulgent than annoyed

now, and together they went downstairs, turned on lights, and Rob led her through the kitchen and laundry room—to a door she'd always assumed was a closet.

Inside sat workbenches mounted with large saws, and other tools scattered the space. The place was covered with dust, and wood shavings littered the ground, but the smell was fresh and woodsy, just like Rob.

"I'm working on a bench right now," he said, showing her the partially constructed piece. "Thought I'd put it outside the boathouse, on the dock."

"Wow—it's gorgeous," she said, and it truly was. Much more intricate than anything from a store, it reminded her of the entertainment center he'd made for the living room.

"Then, over here," he said, picking up some finely carved slats of wood, "I've got pieces started for an Adirondack chair for the back deck."

She nodded, scanning the rest of the room—but her heart caught in her throat when she saw the items piled in a back corner. A rocking horse. Several dollhouses. And a small heart-shaped box.

Oh God, he'd been carrying this stuff around with him, wherever he went, since he got out of prison.

She was drawn immediately across the room to pick up the box. "This is what you wrote about. It's beautiful," she said, studying the decorative carving on the lid.

"You want it? You're welcome to it."

She looked up, met his gaze, spoke quietly and seriously. "No. This is Gina's."

"She'll never see it."

She tilted her head. "Then why do you keep all this stuff?"

He lowered his chin. "I don't know. It doesn't matter. But it would be smarter to use it for something. It just sits in here gathering dust and cobwebs."

It *was* dusty, and it would have looked great on the mantel or a dresser, but still she said, "I'll just leave it here. In case you ever get the chance to give it to her someday."

"Won't happen, Abby. But okay."

Setting the box back down, Lindsey crossed the small space back to him and looped her arms around his neck. "Thank you for showing me," she said, then lifted a kiss to his mouth which, as usual, moved all through her, slow and intoxicating.

"Thank *you*, honey. For caring," he whispered in her ear as if his words were yet another secret to keep.

The following days were filled with a mix of peaceful times and more exciting ones.

As promised, the weekend brought the first tourists of the season a week before Memorial Day, and the canoe livery was in business. Even a few of the locals came out to paddle the lake, perhaps inspired by seeing the canoes dotting the water. Although one person could have easily handled the work, Lindsey ran the pay window, along with selling snacks—in a skort and Keds, of course—and Rob got the patrons in the boats, gave them instructions, and helped them back out when they returned an hour later.

And though she kept her room at the inn, she hadn't slept there in . . . a while. All her nights were spent in Rob's arms now. They never talked about their relationship—where it was going, what it meant. But Lindsey was cool with that. She liked where they were. And she hoped it would last—but knowing Rob as she did, she wasn't inclined to push him into talking about that. She just held all the *I love you*s inside and cherished everything they shared, from the sex to the talking to walks by the lake or playing with King in the yard.

Now it was Monday evening, and though the weekend had been gloriously bright and sunny, a light rain had started falling this afternoon and hadn't stopped. Lindsey had spent most of the day in her room at the inn, working on her blog, catching up on phone calls home, and trading a few e-mails with her editor, promising she was thinking about resuming the column very soon. She'd also stared out her window into the drizzle, doing a lot of soul-searching, and realizing the lake was still pretty even on a rainy, cloud-covered day.

As night fell, she put on her stylish fuchsia raincoat and grabbed up her umbrella, then headed to Bob's to pick up a pizza, which she then took to Rob's, along with the small overnight bag she'd gotten accustomed to carrying there, too.

"Leave it to you, Abby," he said, holding open the door as she stepped up onto the porch, "to have a leopard-print umbrella."

She handed him the pizza, then swished her umbrella playfully back and forth before setting it on the covered porch to dry. "Don't tell me even my umbrella gets you hot, Colter," she teased.

"Well, I gotta admit, it's the sexiest umbrella I've ever seen."

"Try to control yourself until after pizza," she warned, shedding her coat, then leaned closer to him, smiling. "You smell good. Have you been in the woodshop?"

"Guilty as charged," he said, toting the pizza to the coffee table. "I've been here all afternoon—rain was too steady to work outside. I'm waiting for the drywaller to finish at Steve's place, so I'm starting Stanley Bobbins's shed this week, but didn't get very far today."

"I'm sorry you didn't get to work, but I like when you smell this way," she said, proving it with a kiss.

They settled on the couch together to eat, music playing in the background—Crowded House's "It's Only Natural"—and Lindsey said, "I did a lot of thinking today."

He cast her a look of mock worry. "Uh-oh."

She gave her head a defensive tilt as she reached for a second slice of pizza. "Thinking about *me*, not *you*," she clarified.

"Well, that's still scary, but okay—what have you been thinking?"

She took a deep breath. "Remember I told you that in

Chicago I had somehow started living Garrett's life, letting him reshape me into what he wanted me to be? Until he realized that even *that* wasn't good enough for him, that is."

Rob nodded and she went on. "I was talking to my mom about that today, and turns out my parents had seen this all along and were actually happy when we broke up. When I first decided to come here, they were awfully quick to help pack me up and send me on my way, and I thought it was just because Mom was interested in getting the livery back in the family—but today she admitted that they just felt I needed to find a simpler sort of life. They thought I needed to be someplace warm and inviting after the apron-picture scandal, and they knew the town would welcome me because of Millie. She also admitted that she got a letter from Aunt Millie just before she died, telling her about the cancer, and also saying she'd found someone—*you*—who she wanted to leave her home and business to. So they didn't dissuade me from trying to buy the livery if that got me out here, but they knew it probably wouldn't happen."

"Wow," he said, looking nearly as surprised as she had been.

But all of that wasn't even her point, so she moved on. "And what I realized today," she said, "is that maybe Mr. Quick-on-the-Draw-Window-Washer was the best thing that ever happened to me. Because without him, I'd never have found the *me* . . . that I've found *here*."

At the other end of the couch from her, Rob slowly smiled. "That's a hell of a revelation, Abby."

"And another thing," she said—and for this, she even set her pizza aside. "When I came here, I was bent on getting my way, no matter what it took—but when I look back on my plan to finagle the livery from you, that just seems so very . . . Garrett-like. And I know I've said this before, but . . . I would never take anything from you that you don't want to give me. And I would never try to take the boathouse from you now."

At this, Rob set his plate on the table, too, and shifted closer, to wrap his arms around her. "That's good," he said softly, lowering a kiss to her forehead. "Because I would never let you."

And for some reason, she laughed. At how Rob could temper his gruff underside with sweetness now. The harder parts of him still existed, but the Rob she'd first met wouldn't have bothered with the sweet part, so this was a much-improved version of the man she'd fallen for at first sight.

"You know," she said quietly, "as important as this place is to you, sometimes I'm surprised you told me. About your past. Because what if I *had* told people? What if I'd ruined everything?"

Hearing him take in a deep breath, she looked up to study his warm brown eyes. Finally, he met her gaze and said, "I guess deep down there was just a part of me that *wanted* to trust you, honey. That *needed* to."

His words dug into Lindsey's soul—it was as close to an admission of love as she'd ever gotten from him. And instead of answering, she leaned over to kiss him—discovering that even when they both tasted like pizza, he still made her wet.

"I have only one regret," she admitted.

"What's that?"

Rob had picked up his pizza and started eating again, but Lindsey had pretty much forgotten the food. Most of her soul-searching today had been good, confirming for her that she was on the right path. Yet there was one thing she couldn't resolve, and it had hit her hard. "No matter what I do," she said, shaking her head, "I can't go back in time and make things right with Aunt Millie. Somehow, I thought if I came here and tried to buy her business back that it would mend things. And then I thought if I learned about her life, if I walked in her shoes, that *that* would mend things. And all of that helped . . . *me*. But what it comes down to is—I can't fix this. She's gone and I hurt her, and as long as I live, there's no way to repair it, is there?"

At this, Rob set his pizza back down and turned to peer deep into her eyes, and she knew he'd felt the gravity in her words. "The truth?" he said softly. "No, there really isn't."

Lindsey let out a sad breath. She'd known that already, but it still stung to have it confirmed. "When I think through it all, I just can't make peace with that."

Rob spoke slowly, surely. "Then I guess now you know a little about how *I* feel."

"What do you mean?"

He sighed, shifted his gaze to the darkness beyond the picture windows across the room, then looked back at her. "I didn't push Tommy off that tower, but he still fell because of me. I can't change that. I can't fix it. It's with me for the rest of my life."

Oh God, she'd never thought of that aspect of his past. And part of her wanted to argue, say it wasn't his fault, try to make the truth go away. But denial hadn't fixed her dilemma with Aunt Millie, and she knew it wouldn't help Rob, either. So she simply shook her head, at a loss. "How do you *deal* with that?"

"You just have to . . . learn to live with the things you can't change and trust you did the best you could at the time. You have to try to forgive *yourself,* since the other person isn't here to do it."

She bit her lip, pondering the thought. "Do *you* forgive yourself? For Tommy?"

He shook his head shortly. "Not yet. Still working on it."

She had a feeling she'd be working on it for a while with Aunt Millie, too. Maybe a lifetime. And if that was the case, she'd learn to live with it, she supposed. Just like Rob did.

Deciding it was definitely time for a happier topic, she announced, "I'm thinking of starting my column again. My editor keeps asking me to."

When he cast a small smile, she was glad she'd changed the subject. "So you feel qualified again?"

"Sort of. But there's more to my decision that just that," she informed him. "When I found your letters to Gina—"

"Good God," he interrupted with raised eyebrows, "do we have to go *there* again?"

"Only momentarily," she assured him, then went on quickly before he could stop her, because she really wanted to tell him this. "When I found your letters to Gina, I realized in a whole new way how, when people reach out to one another, it's all in the hopes of simply getting something back, some sort of response, some validation that what they're going through really matters. And it hit me that Love Letters is actually *important* to people.

"First, I abandoned Aunt Millie, and then I abandoned my readers, too, who truly depend upon my advice. And I can't *un*abandon Aunt Millie, but I *can* be there for my readers again. So that's what I'm going to do."

It rained all day the next day, so Rob worked in the woodshop in the morning while Lindsey used his computer, then they drove down to Kalispell to buy her some hiking boots and a practical rain slicker. Her hot-pink raincoat was too fancy for most rainy Moose Falls days and it didn't even have a hood.

Sometimes those little, impractical things about her drove him nuts. But mostly, he didn't mind. Because he liked having a girlfriend.

More than a girlfriend.

A woman who slept in his bed every night. A woman he trusted with . . . hell, pretty much everything now. He'd told her all his secrets—and nothing bad had happened. Nothing.

He was forced to admit to himself that . . . life was better right now, today, than it had ever been before. And when Lindsey had first started becoming important to him, he hadn't been entirely comfortable with it, entirely sure he could trust the things that were happening. He wasn't used to things working out in his life in a good way. But he was finally beginning to get comfortable *now*, finally beginning to trust.

He even found himself wanting to ask her to move in with him. It seemed silly for her to spend money on a room where she spent only a few hours during the day while he was working. He had plenty of space, he was happier when she was around, and hell, even the dog got excited when she came over now and acted depressed when she left. And King was a pretty damn good judge of character.

Now it was late afternoon, the rain still fell, and they'd found their way into bed. The first few times they'd had sex, it had been amazing because he'd never expected to touch a woman that way again. Now it was just amazing because he was crazy about her.

Today it had started when she'd been standing at the stove in jeans and a tight little T-shirt, trying to make some sort of stir-fry thing for lunch that she'd kept promising him he would like. The rain and dark skies had seemed to sift in through the windows, cocooning the house the same way nighttime did. He'd started watching her, and wanting her, and he'd moved in behind her, wrapping around her from behind, letting her feel his hard-on against her ass.

They'd eaten the stir-fry, which he hadn't liked, but he also hadn't cared very much since the main thing on his mind had been his erection and the fact that her nipples were poking through her bra and that he wanted *them* in his mouth much more than what he was eating. When they were done, he'd simply said, "Want to go upstairs?"

She'd bitten her lip and said, "Race ya."

It had become a frantic, urgent coupling—he got like that when he had to wait for it. And hell, sometimes he just got like that anyway. He'd pounded into her welcoming flesh hard and fast, making her cry out with each stroke, until he'd erupted inside her—and now they rested beneath the quilt, watching the rain pelt the window across the room, because they hadn't taken the time to open it in their hurry to get naked. Music echoed up the stairs, the Indigo Girls singing "Closer to Fine," the lyrics echoing his feelings about his life the last few days.

"I have an idea," Lindsey announced.

"Oh boy," he replied dryly. He was crazy about her, but sometimes it was hard to adjust to having someone around who *thought* so much.

"Why don't we try out my new hiking boots?"

"Sure. When?"

"Now."

He blinked. Only Abby. "Honey, it's raining."

"I know, but I'm anxious to see what it's like to hike in actual hiking boots, where my feet aren't in pure agony—I think I might really like it."

"And maybe you didn't hear me. It's raining."

"People don't hike in the rain?"

"Not people who are already cozy and naked in bed in a nice, dry house."

"I thought you *liked* rain," she protested.

"I do—but right now I like your naked body more." He pulled her closer and delivered a kiss high on her breast in hopes of convincing her this was a better rainy day activity.

"Come on," she said anyway. "Let's hike to Rainbow Lookout. I can wear my new rain jacket. And who knows, maybe we'll get our own rainbow out of it."

"You can't predict a rainbow, Abby."

"I know, but . . . I just want to go. I kind of . . . need to."

He blinked again, trying to understand. "You *need* to try out your new hiking boots and slicker?"

"No. I need to walk in the rain. Experience life. Take it all in. The way Aunt Millie did. I've never willingly walked in the rain before, so I think you should indulge me."

"Oh." Well, that he couldn't argue with. "Fine then," he bit off. "Get dressed. And put on one of my sweatshirts under your slicker—it'll be cold up there."

The trail was slick, muddy in places, but Lindsey didn't let it deter her. And she sort of hated getting her shiny new lace-up hiking boots messy, but she kept her mouth shut about that. "They'll wipe off," Rob said anyway when he saw her glancing down at them. He knew her too well.

Once she got used to the mud and wetness, though, she embraced the experience, just as she'd intended. As she drank in the scent of rain in the trees, she thought of Aunt Millie taking in the same smell, and of the way Aunt Millie had found wonder in everything around her. She wasn't sure she'd ever be *that* much like her aunt, but she wanted to try. And she also discovered that, even in slippery mud, hiking was a thousand times easier with proper shoes. Damn Rob for being right about that.

Not that she really wanted to damn Rob for anything. Watching him walk ahead of her, she bit her lip, so much in love that she could barely fathom it. God knew the guy had faults and plenty of them, and God knew the scars he bore from his past probably ran much deeper than she could see—but after a picture-perfect guy like Garrett, who had turned out not to be so picture-perfect, a man like Rob felt so *real* to her, in her arms *and* in her heart.

"Watch your step," he said over his shoulder, and she looked down to see him crossing a tiny stream cutting its way across the trail as it ran down the mountain. She looked up the steep hillside to her left to see the tiny waterfall above, from which the stream flowed. And she thought about how she'd never know about that if she hadn't come out here in the rain. About how many millions of tiny waterfalls there must be in the world's wilderness and how nobody saw them. Except she was seeing this one, and she thought Aunt Millie would appreciate that.

"It's different on the trail in the rain," she said. "Like a whole different world than when it's dry." It sounded different, smelled different, turned the ground under her feet different. "I'm glad we came, because I wouldn't have known that otherwise."

She thought for a minute that Rob was just going to keep hiking on, not answer her, and she didn't mind much because he was Rob and sometimes that was just his way of moving through life—but then, without warning, he stopped, turned, lifted his hand to her cheek, and gave her a damp kiss.

It warmed her chest and made her smile up at him. And God, he even looked sexy in a big wet yellow hooded slicker. "What was that for?"

"Because I like you like this," he told her. "I like when you notice things. Things that are . . . bigger than us."

She just nodded because she understood. There was an inherent beauty in figuring out the world didn't revolve around you.

By the time they reached the lookout point, the rain had stopped. Together, they gazed out on the lake—something else that appeared different in this weather. Sure, the gray skies turned everything a little dreary, but a light fog had formed over Misty Isle, making Lindsey imagine the Indians there, seeing their ancestors in the mist.

"Thank you for bringing me," she said, peering up at Rob.

"As much as I hate to admit this," he said, "it wasn't a bad idea."

He leaned in for another kiss and she closed her eyes as the sensations dripped through her, then opened them again just as the sun came out. She smiled, then Rob's face went blank with shock as he murmured, "I'll be damned."

She blinked. "What?"

He pointed out over the lake, and Lindsey turned to see . . . a rainbow.

It wasn't the best or the brightest rainbow she'd ever

seen—it didn't arc all the way across the sky like Aunt Millie's had. But chills still ran down her spine as she gazed up at it, drank in the colors and curves, all looking so tangible she almost believed she could reach out and touch it. She'd never felt so in awe of any sight she'd ever beheld. Or . . . so deeply at peace inside.

"Guess I was wrong, Abby. Guess you *can* predict a rainbow."

Lindsey simply continued staring up at it, *feeling* it. "You're gonna think I'm crazy, but . . ."

"I already think you're crazy," he teased her softly. "But what?"

She shifted her gaze from the rainbow to his eyes. "I think maybe this is from Millie. That maybe this is Millie telling me it's okay—that she forgives me." She looked back at the rainbow again—they both did. "Do you think that's totally nuts?"

Rob spoke quietly. "Well, either way, honey, I think part of forgiving *yourself* is starting to believe the person who isn't around anymore forgives you, too."

She was talking about Aunt Millie but knew *he* was talking about Tommy.

"I think he forgives you, Rob," she said.

And he didn't answer, but she reached out and took his hand, squeezing it tight, and felt her chest contract as they watched the rainbow a few minutes more—until it faded slowly from the sky.

William's chest swelled with a sense of anticipation as he pulled up in front of the Lazy Elk Bar and Grill. Even in the falling dusk, he could see instantly why this place—the whole lakeside town—appealed to a woman rebounding from an ugly public humiliation. It felt isolated. Possibly more isolated than anyplace he'd ever been.

Of course, his heart hardened as he remembered why he was here, and it made the isolation feel like a gift from on high. Or it would have if he'd believed in such things. He had as a boy. He didn't anymore. He hadn't for a long time. He understood about faith, how it was supposed to be blind—but he thought most people who had faith had also received inklings, flashes of good fortune, had prayers answered, that made their faith more . . . well, more evidentiary than blind. And he had nothing to base any faith on.

If he did, maybe he wouldn't be here. But since he didn't, he didn't have much to worry about. Guilt—that came from doing something that felt wrong. This didn't feel wrong.

The air outside smelled sweet and fresh—he'd driven through rain earlier, so it must have rained here, too. He liked the smell, let it pervade his senses.

But then he took a deep breath and pushed through the corner door of the bar, ready to move forward. Lindsey could be in here. So could her damn boyfriend.

Instead, though, the place stood almost empty.

He was willing to bet the woman standing behind the bar, wiping it down, was Carla. She didn't look like the sort of woman Lindsey would be friends with—she dressed too simply; *everything* about her was simple, and she was slightly overweight. Yet at the same time, he found her attractive—when she looked up, she had pretty eyes, hazel, with little specks in them.

If he hadn't been here for a reason that would require all his focus, maybe he'd consider asking her out. Lindsey made it seem like people here were different, and for a fraction of a second he found himself wondering if maybe it was true, and if maybe coming here could heal him the same way it had healed her.

But stay focused, William, stay focused.

He'd come here to be healed in a different way. For once in his life, he would take action, make life happen—rather than just letting it all happen *to* him.

"Hi there," Carla said. It made him feel weirdly powerful just to know her name without her sharing it.

"Hi." He worked up a smile as he climbed onto a barstool. Had Lindsey ever sat on this particular stool?

"What can I get you?"

"Whiskey on the rocks." Hard liquor made him feel tough, like a man who could get the job done.

As Carla reached for a glass, she said, "Welcome to Moose Falls."

He cocked another grin, this one a little more sincere, because she was clearly a woman who paid attention to what was going on around her. "Guess you don't get too many strangers in here."

She offered a little smile before looking back to the drink. "Some, especially as summer sets in. But I know everybody in town, so when someone new comes in, I notice. What's your name?"

"William."

"I'm Carla."

It was hard not to say, *I know.*

"Here for a little hiking and fishing?" she asked.

"Yeah," he lied. "I've heard good things about the place."

"From who?" After trickling Jack Daniel's over the ice, she set his drink on a napkin in front of him. He thought her question sounded a little too pointed, and it made him like her a little less.

"Actually, I read about it on a friend's blog."

She tilted her head. "Is that so? Who's your friend, if you don't mind me asking?" She smiled, but he could see she wasn't liking him very much, either. He wasn't even surprised—it was the story of his life.

But he wasn't worried. Because this was going to be so easy, all of it—he could feel it in his bones. This was . . . serendipity, things coming together—finally. "Lindsey Brooks. You know her?"

Her eyes changed, darkened just a bit. "Yeah, I do. What did you say your name was again?"

"William," he said, taking a drink. The whiskey burned going down, but it made him strong.

"How do you know her?"

He kept it simple. "We go back a long way. She's given me a lot of advice the last couple of years." He neglected to mention that this, too, had been through her blog.

Carla only nodded and he felt her suspicion growing. Big fucking deal. He took another drink of the Jack and let it warm his chest. He was starting to feel stronger and stronger. Just knowing where he was, what he'd come here to do, that alone gave him power.

"So, you know this guy, Rob Colter, she's hanging out with? What's he like?"

"He's . . . big," Carla said. "And pretty mean."

This made him laugh inside. Carla was trying to scare him away.

But she'd also told him exactly what he needed to know, filled in the last little piece of the puzzle for him. Lindsey's Rob was indeed Rob Colter. The guy he'd been looking for unsuccessfully for years now. The guy who'd once been his best friend—in another life. The guy who'd murdered his little brother and taken the last shred of his happiness.

Sixteen

Rob watched her move on him, riding in rhythmic waves, looking like some kind of towering goddess with her silky shoulders and perfect breasts, the nipples tight and dark. His palms curved over her hips—he liked to *feel* her movements, the way she swayed within his loose grasp; he liked to watch her eyes, half shut in ecstasy.

Being inside her now was different than at first—he'd grown used to a woman's body again, used to that warmth and being able to give in to the arousal. Arousal was once again a friend, not something to fight. But it was still just as good as in the beginning. Or maybe even better. When they'd first started this, he'd been angry at himself about it, and even angry at her. He'd been worried. He'd felt as if his world could crumble because of it. But now all those negative thoughts were long gone—now he was able to fully enjoy her. Now it was like music—the rhythm of their sex, the rhythm of having her in his life, made him feel alive and took him away from his troubles.

After that unbelievable moment when they'd seen the

rainbow, they'd sloshed back down the trail through mud and puddles and the little streams still crossing the path, taken showers, then made lasagna together. Now it was dark and they were back in bed—the daybed, next to the open window, where the breeze was cool and the air sweet—and he realized as he pumped up into her that he'd spent the whole day with her. Yeah, he'd worked in his woodshop for an hour or so this morning while she'd kept up with the blog she'd told him about, but mostly they'd been together all damn day—and he didn't mind a bit.

Now they both panted their pleasure and he lifted his hands to tweak her nipples as she neared orgasm. He could tell now—he'd learned her patterns, the way her breathing came louder and her movements slower yet more pronounced—and he liked watching it happen and trying to make it even better. He knew that playing with the turgid peaks of her breasts would push her over the edge, so he rubbed them, pinched slightly, then whispered, "Come, honey," and she tumbled, her body pitching forward, then jerking back as the spasms shot through her.

Her hot moans cut through the night and made him feel somehow even harder, bigger, inside her. His chest tightened, his cock filled with more blood—and he tried to let her come down, recover, but he wanted to thrust so hard and deep right now that he wasn't sure he could resist.

And then the damn phone rang. "Shit," he muttered. But at least it helped him regain control.

The phone was downstairs—he got so few calls, he felt no need for an upstairs extension—so it went without saying that they weren't even going to *think* about answering.

When the machine picked up, they both went briefly still to listen, although it was difficult to hear up in the loft, especially since they'd left music playing in the living room, too. "Rob, this is Carla. Is Lindsey with you?"

Carla kept talking, but that was all he was able to make out before Lindsey said, still breathless, "I have a lunch date with her tomorrow. She must need to change plans or something. I'll call her back in the morning."

Rob wasn't arguing. He was inside her, after all. Where she was wet, warm.

He only responded by finally driving upward, nearly lifting her from the bed. She cried out, arching her back, and when their eyes met again in the dim light of the Tiffany lamp, hers were filled with a hungry heat that said orgasm hadn't even come close to killing her desire. "Do that again," she told him.

A hot growl escaped his throat as he gave her what she wanted, lifting them *both* off the bed this time—and it pushed him over the edge. "Shit, honey—now," he breathed, and thrust again, again, still hard, still deep, wrenching their bodies, making them groan together with the repeated impact as he spilled himself inside her.

A moment later, she collapsed on his chest, snuggling there, and his arms closed around her.

"Thank you, honey," he heard himself whisper unplanned.

Her sexy giggle teased his shoulder as she said, "I liked it, too."

"Not for the sex."

"What then?"

He hesitated only slightly. "It was a nice day."

He felt more than heard her sigh as she lay resting against him. "Yeah, it was."

As the first rays of light glanced through the window, Rob bent to touch her shoulder, kiss her cheek, where she lay sleeping in his bed. They'd moved from the daybed after that last round of sex, both thoroughly tired and wanting to stretch out and sleep. Even so, their limbs had tangled together in slumber and he'd woken half an hour ago to find himself spooning her from behind.

"Leaving," he whispered near her ear.

Her eyes fluttered open. "No rain this morning?"

He couldn't help thinking she sounded a little disappointed that today wouldn't be like yesterday. "Nope, so it's back to work and I need to put in a long day. Hook up after I get home?"

She looked so damn sleepy-pretty rolling onto her back. She wore a thin white cotton strappy thing and her nipples poked through the fabric. "I have the book club tonight at the café. I told them all I'd come, so I wouldn't want to let them down."

Shit, now *he* was the disappointed one. But he tried not to let it show. "See you afterward then?"

She nodded against the pillow. "Not sure how late it runs, but yeah."

"I'll probably heat up some leftover lasagna for dinner. There's plenty if you want some when you get here."

"I think Mary Beth serves sandwiches at the book club." Then a lascivious expression stole over her face as the corners of her mouth quirked into a decidedly wicked grin. "But I'll probably be hungry for something else entirely by the time we're together."

His dick perked to life in his jeans and he had a feeling he'd better get going before he ended up right back in bed with her. But then he heard himself uttering the idea that had been on his mind lately. Even as the words left him, he couldn't believe he was saying them—and yet at the same time, it seemed so damn easy. "Listen, it's starting to seem silly for you to keep a room at the inn since you're never there. So . . . if you want, just pack up your suitcase and bring it here tonight."

He saw her eyes change, her gaze brightening but then quickly turning a little doubtful as she pressed her head deeper into the pillow, a lock of hair falling over her cheek. "Rob—are you sure?"

He shrugged, trying to play it off as nothing—when it was actually the most enormous move he'd ever made with a woman. "Yeah. But only if you want. If you'd rather keep things like they are, that's cool, too."

She bit her lip as a slow smile stole over her face. "No. I'll pack my stuff up this afternoon."

"Good," he said simply, then turned to go.

And as he walked down the stairs, scratched King behind the ears, and made his way to the truck, he felt . . . light inside. It was a strange, new feeling he couldn't quite understand, but it was as if he'd been carrying a ton of weight on his back forever and it was suddenly gone.

As he drove past the canoe livery, he looked out on the water, covered with a pale sheen of mist this morning, and thought about the coming weekend—Memorial Day weekend, the real, true start of the season. He was looking forward to it because it would feel good to see Millie's business surviving and thriving. And because Lindsey would be there with him, making the whole situation a lot more like fun than work. And because Millie had *wanted* Lindsey there, and through all these strange twists of fate she *would* be.

Curving past the Moose Mart and the general store, he couldn't help thinking back to that rainbow yesterday and wondering, crazy as it seemed, if Millie *had* been looking down on them, if Millie had somehow orchestrated *all* of this. He still wasn't sure he believed in that kind of thing, but he liked the idea.

As he headed out of town toward Stanley Bobbins's place, he had the strange feeling that maybe he should turn around and go back home. That maybe he should still be with Lindsey. He wasn't sure why, but could only conclude it was about the big step he'd just taken in moving their relationship to a new, deeper place.

But that was pretty damn ridiculous. *You asked the girl to move in with you—that doesn't mean you have to be attached at the hip.*

So he drove on, following the main road for a few more miles before turning right. Stanley lived in a nice house way out in the woods, farther away than even Rob wanted to live from civilization. He liked his privacy, but he also liked being able to grab a gallon of milk or gas up the truck without going on a major excursion.

Winding his way across the twisting, narrow road, though, he still suffered a weird, burning feeling in his gut that he wasn't supposed to be going to Stanley's, that he was supposed to be back at the cabin with Lindsey. It was a stupid feeling, the kind that made no sense, so he kept driving—but it kept eating at him.

And the farther away he got, the more the feeling became almost a weird . . . sense of doom.

And Rob was a man who knew about senses of doom. He'd suffered them on more than one occasion. But he'd also always had a good reason. Tommy falling to his death. Being convicted of manslaughter. And each and every time he'd stupidly confided in someone about his past and then found out he shouldn't have. All damn good times to feel a sense of doom—so this was different than that; it came entirely without cause.

And he was a practical guy, far too practical to drive all the way out here only to turn around and go back for no reason.

Although maybe when he got to Stanley's, he'd borrow the phone, just call and check up on her, make sure everything was okay.

Of course, she probably wouldn't answer, still in bed—so he'd worry even more, despite how silly and groundless it was.

Damn it, you're acting like an idiot here.

After all, what the hell could be wrong? Maybe he was worried somehow, deep down inside, that she'd change her mind. That she'd examine the fact that she'd agreed to move in with him, an ex-con, and that the reality of it would hit home and that maybe, just maybe, he'd never see her again.

Shit, talk about paranoia. But maybe that was his past coming back to haunt him. He didn't believe for a second

Lindsey would bail on him—she wasn't the most grounded person in the world, but when it came to him, he *felt* her devotion. He knew she cared for him in a way no one ever had.

The farther he traveled, though, the clearer it became: If he went on to work, he'd only drive himself crazy wondering if something was wrong.

Even though he knew it couldn't be. Because he'd only left her twenty minutes ago and all had been right with the world.

Still, cussing himself as he did it, he turned the truck around and started back toward the cabin.

The sound of someone pounding on the door jarred Lindsey from sleep. Who the hell could be out there this early?

But she pushed her annoyance aside, recalling that not long ago *she'd* been out there pounding on the door. Maybe it was Carla. Or Eleanor, for some reason. Of course, Eleanor would probably call first. But then, Carla *had* called, last night, and Lindsey hadn't bothered listening to the message, so it was probably Carla. God, she hoped nothing was wrong. As she pulled on the dirty pair of blue jeans she'd shed last evening after hiking, she rushed to the stairs.

By now King was barking and she was saying, "Shush, King, it's all right," even as she hurried to the door with the dog hot on her heels.

Yanking it open, she flinched—it wasn't Carla. On the porch in front of her stood a man, around her age, wearing a simple button-down shirt and cotton jacket with stiff-looking khakis. His dark blond hair was cropped close and he might have been handsome if not for his eyes. He looked deeply troubled, like maybe he was the saddest guy on the planet, even as he smiled at her.

Her first thought was that, expecting Carla, she hadn't gotten completely dressed and was standing in front of him in a thin cotton cami without a bra. Her second was to be glad King stood at her side, acting protective in the same way he always did with Rob. And like Rob, she let her fingers rest in the thick fur near the dog's collar and she didn't tell him to shush anymore as a low growl echoed from his throat. She tried like hell not to look nervous. "Can I help you?"

"Lindsey," he said, his voice warm, overfriendly.

Who the hell was he? She still struggled to look in control of the situation even as she crossed one arm over herself, trying to cover her breasts. "Do I know you?"

"Sure," he said. "I'm William."

She searched her memory for a William. In Chicago, she might have come up with a few. Here, no—she didn't know anyone named William. She knew she looked confused. "Um . . ."

"William Tell," he clarified.

Oh God. WilliamTell1 from her blog.

He'd been commenting there for ages, and that had been fine—until now, until he was standing on Rob's front porch. "William," she said, trying not to look horrified. "Um, wow—nice to meet you."

He tilted his head, looking a little less troubled now, and it eased her fears a bit. "You're really pretty," he said. "Even more than in pictures."

Her fear returned, her chest tightening. "So—what brings you here?"

His smile relaxed a little and the disturbed look returned to his eyes as quickly as it had faded. "That, my dear Lindsey, is a long story, I'm afraid. But I want to tell you the whole thing if you'll come with me for a walk. It's a little chilly out—you should grab a jacket."

Her entire being froze up at his words. He thought she was going somewhere with him? What worried her most, though, were those eyes of his. She knew that quickly that he simply wasn't a normal guy.

"You know, William, I wish I could, but I'm expecting someone. I . . . only answered the door like this because

I thought you were someone else. I have plans this morning." Damn it, she sounded nervous now and she knew it.

William Tell, though, didn't sound nervous at all. "Who are you expecting?"

"Rob. My boyfriend. You probably read about him on the blog. This is his house, in fact." And for the first time it occurred to her to wonder how the hell he'd found her at Rob's place, for God's sake. And just as quickly, she realized she'd talked about it at the blog. When all the female readers had wanted her to dish more about him, she'd mentioned the big log cabin just up from the livery. She'd thought she'd been careful never to say anything *too* personal, but she realized now that personal stuff wasn't just *secret* stuff—it was stuff like the general location of Rob's house, too. She'd just never dreamed anyone would seek her out in Moose Falls, Montana.

"You aren't expecting Rob, Lindsey," William replied in that same weird, calm voice. "Rob just left for work."

This silenced her for a moment and she wondered how frightened she looked. "But he's coming back," she assured him. "He forgot his lunch. He called to tell me. I was just about to pack it up for him."

"Does Rob always knock on his own front door?"

She'd tried to think fast, but now she'd been caught in a dumb lie. She stood before him at a loss for words, her heart beating against her rib cage like a drum. So she took a different approach. "Look, William, maybe we can make plans for later. Would you like to meet at the Lakeside Café for lunch?"

"You're supposed to have lunch with Carla today."

Her blood ran cold. How did he know so much?

Then it hit her. Carla's phone call. Maybe she hadn't been calling to change plans. Maybe she'd been calling to warn her.

"Would you like to join us? I'm just . . . not ready to go out right now. I just got up and I need to shower."

His face changed a bit then and she could have sworn she saw compassion in his eyes. "You know, Lindsey, I don't want to scare you, and I can see that's what I'm doing." He shook his head as if to berate himself. "That wasn't my intent and I apologize."

She drew in her breath, at a loss for words. Maybe this was going to be all right—maybe he was going to leave. "Okay."

"But I really need you to come with me."

Her stomach twisted. "Where?"

"Just on a walk. There are some things I need to tell you."

She found herself wondering how much of an attack dog King really was and exactly what she'd need to do to make him attack. "I'm really sorry, William, but I just can't. I'd be happy to meet you later, though."

"No," he said solemnly. "Like I said, I don't want to scare you—but I can't take no for an answer. You have to come with me, Lindsey, and then, after we talk, you'll understand."

Finally realizing that reasoning with him wasn't going to work, Lindsey took a step back, ready to slam the door in his face and lock it.

He stepped forward too quick, though, and when she tried to shut the door, his body blocked it. King barked and lunged toward him, but William's knee came up, striking the dog's chest so hard that he yelped, and knocking him back so violently that it left King dazed.

That's when William pulled a gun from his jacket pocket. "Call off the dog, Lindsey, or I'll have to kill him," he said, only a little less calmly than before, even with his body jammed between the door and the threshold.

When King got to his feet, still looking ready to defend her, Lindsey had only a split second to make a decision. "King, heel!" That's what Rob said when King did anything he shouldn't.

The dog stayed in place, but still snarled at William, and Lindsey didn't know what to do. Maybe she should have taken her chances that King would be faster than William with a gun, but Rob loved that dog more than he loved himself.

"Okay then," William said. "Put on some shoes and a jacket and come with me." He'd worked his way inside the house now, although the door remained open.

"You're making me nervous, William," she said, trying to play on his sympathies, since he seemed to have at least a few. She was desperate now and it was all she could think of. "I don't like guns. Do we really have to bring a gun into this?"

"Apparently we do," he said. "Since you won't take a walk with me otherwise."

"I thought you didn't want to scare me."

"I don't. But you're forcing me to."

Uh-huh. Okay, if there was any doubt before, this sealed it—certified nut job.

When she glanced down and saw the only shoes around were her bright pink peek-toe pumps, which had gotten left by the door at some point a couple of days ago, she said, "I need to get my gym shoes from upstairs." Which would at least buy her a minute to think.

But he saw the heels on the floor next to the little table where Rob left his keys. "These'll do."

She lifted her gaze to him. "They're hard to walk in if we're going very far."

He looked skeptical. "You've always worn shoes like this before." Weird, if she didn't know better, she'd have believed he really knew her, not just her blog.

"Everything is different here," she replied, and meant it in so many ways she could barely fathom it.

Unfortunately, William just scowled, then pointed angrily toward the pumps. "Put those on. And a jacket, like I said."

Lindsey's legs felt rubbery as she stepped into her favorite shoes. A glance to the peg board on the wall revealed several of Rob's jackets but none of her own. She reached for a faded jean jacket he sometimes wore—only to have William snap at her. "You're not wearing *that*—nothing of *his*. Forget the jacket." He even yanked it from her hand and dashed it to the floor beside King—who looked angry, emitting a low growl, but still held his ground after that one solitary command. "Come on, let's go."

"What about the jacket? I'll freeze."

"You'll live," he said, and she realized she'd probably gotten all the sympathy from William Tell that she was going to.

Stepping outside the house as he held the pistol at his side felt surreal. She was so frightened that her legs would barely move—her limbs felt stiff and uncooperative.

"Come on," he said again, motioning for her to follow him down the steps onto the walkway that led to the road. Her chest heaved and her lungs hurt from fear as she numbly trailed after him. She looked around—the road, the driveway—for a strange car, but saw none. So, like her, William had walked here. From where? The Grizzly Inn?

Glancing back up to the porch, she found King's face in the large picture window, his nose pressed against the glass. Her gaze stuck on him for some reason—at this strange moment, he was the only one she could connect with in any way—and he started to bark; loud, pure German shepherd barks that could easily be heard from outside.

"Shut him up," William said.

"From out here? How?"

That one stumped William, and Lindsey kept looking back at the dog as she traversed the long stone path, thinking, *Bark, King. Keep barking.* Maybe it wouldn't help anything, but maybe someone would pass near the house and figure out something was wrong. She feared it was pretty much her only hope now.

"Just hurry up," William said, befuddled by the barking dog, and Lindsey tried to walk faster, but accidentally took a step off the path into the grass near the mailbox, stumbling in her heels.

"Hell—leave those here," William snapped.

She looked up at him. "And go back for my gym shoes?"

"No. Just leave 'em."

She sucked in her breath. It was cold out and she was already freezing, wrapping her bare arms around herself. "What about my feet? You can't expect me to go barefoot."

"We're not walking far. We're riding most of the way." Oh shit.

As William grabbed on to her arm with his free hand to keep her moving, her feet cut into the cool asphalt beneath them, hard and ruddy. She kept staring up at King in the window, who barked dutifully back the whole time they moved up the road in the early morning light.

This isn't happening. It can't be.

But the bite of the blacktop into her tender feet said it was real. Just like the goosebumps on her arms and the way her nipples tightened into embarrassingly tight beads in the brisk air. In that moment, it felt like King's bark was the only thing keeping her connected to safety, sanity. And so she watched him, watched him, looking at nothing else as she and William passed by the cabin, then the driveway, nearing the far edge of the big yard. She couldn't really see the dog's face anymore, but just watched the window and listened to the faint-and-getting-fainter sound of his bark—until the house disappeared from view.

The good news was—they were walking toward town. She spotted another car besides her own in front of the Grizzly Inn and figured it must be his. Late-model sedan, black, and looked like a luxury car. William Tell had money.

The bad news was that when they approached the boathouse, he steered her down onto the dock. Dear God. He was going to put her in a canoe? Going to take her somewhere on this lake and do God knew what to her?

Please, someone see me. Eleanor? Mary Beth? Anybody.

But everything was so still and it was barely light out. And misty, too, on the lake. She knew, sensed, that she was on her own.

"Put that blue canoe in the water," he instructed, and she thought, *Damn it.* If *he'd* turned his back to put in the boat, maybe she could have pushed him in, then run. But he'd thought of that, too, and casually, comfortably held the gun on her as she slowly did as he'd instructed. "Faster," he said.

"You know, William," she said, struggling to slide the heavy canoe into the water on her own, "you don't seem like the kind of guy who would normally do something like this."

He laughed cynically. "I'm not. If you only knew how much I'm not."

"Then—why *are* you?" She paused before letting the boat's bow drop from the dock and took her best shot at sincerity. "I mean, we can walk right over to the Lakeside Café and have breakfast as soon as Mary Beth opens, which should be soon."

He simply tilted his head and looked a little sad. "You know this has gone past that now, Lindsey. It's not that simple anymore. You're not even wearing shoes, for Christ's sake. Get in the boat."

She considered simply *not* getting in. She remembered hearing somewhere that you weren't supposed to let an abductor take you away from where you started, even if it meant risking death, because going somewhere with them almost *always* resulted in death.

"What if I don't?" she asked.

"I'll have to kill you," he said softly—but surely.

She nearly lost her breath. "You'd really do that, William?"

"I really would," he said. "I wouldn't want to—I'd hate it. But I won't be deterred from what I came here for, Lindsey—it's that simple. Now get in the damn boat," he added, voice hardening.

Lindsey got in the canoe. Because William seemed just crazy enough that he might blow her brains out if she didn't. Maybe it was the wrong move. But she was out of right ones.

She'd never felt more desolate as the canoe floated away from the boathouse, heading quickly deeper into the mist. She looked over her shoulder as Moose Falls grew smaller behind her—but she mainly saw William with his gun. He sat behind her, saying, "Row, Lindsey. Toward the center of the lake."

"Where are we going?"

"The island."

God, he even knew about the island. Had she blogged about that? Oh no—of course she had. She'd stupidly written about having sex with Rob there. She could scarcely envision a more isolated place. She couldn't even run from there if she got the chance.

As she paddled deeper into the lake, she considered flipping the canoe, but they'd taken no life jackets and she knew the water was dangerously cold. So what else? What could she do? *Stay calm. Think.*

"William?" she asked without turning to look at him. She tried to see the island through the mist but couldn't, and she tried to remember how far away it was, how far she had to go. Would it be possible to steer in such a manner that they'd miss it altogether and she'd buy some time?

"Yeah?" he asked.

"What is it you want from me?"

"To be honest, Lindsey, I've been enamored of you for a long time. But this isn't really about what I want from *you*. It's what I want from Rob that matters."

She jerked her head around to look at him, utterly stunned.

"From Rob? What are you talking about?" This made no sense—what did Rob have to do with this?

"Rob murdered my brother, Lindsey. And now I finally have a chance to make him pay. By taking something *he* loves."

Seventeen

Rob knew the second he hit the driveway and could hear King barking that his instincts were correct and something was wrong. What the hell was going on?

He ran to the house and inside to find the dog frantic, going crazy. "What's up, buddy? Where's Lindsey?" Was she hurt somewhere? Had she fallen down the steps?

He ran around the house looking for any sign of her. The bed was empty and unmade; the bathroom empty, as well. Where was she?

Rushing back downstairs, he noticed one of his jackets on the floor. And the little table where he usually put his keys had been shoved out of its normal spot. That's when he saw the light blinking on the answering machine and hit it. "Rob, this is Carla. Is Lindsey there with you? I really need to talk to you guys. There was some guy in the bar tonight, a guy from Lindsey's blog, and he seemed pretty creepy. He claimed he was here to hike, but he didn't seem the type and gave me a bad feeling. Eleanor just let him check in at the Grizzly because she was kind of afraid not to, and I'm going to call Dave—a cop I used to date over in Cedarville—when I hang up here, but I'm pretty sure he'll just tell me that until the guy does something wrong, you're on your own. So be careful, okay? And I'll be in touch tomorrow morning."

By the time the message ended, Rob's stomach had hollowed. There was a reason he'd felt that sense of doom, all right. Shit.

Yanking open the door, he stepped back out onto the porch. The guy had come here and taken her. That had to be what was going on. If King wasn't barking his head off, he might think otherwise, might think she'd just headed back to the Grizzly Inn or gone on a hike by herself or something—but things weren't right here. And he knew it even more when King followed him out, ran down the porch steps, then stopped and looked up at him anxiously, as if to say, *Come on.*

King led Rob down the front walk where, at the end, he found her dressy shoes, the ones she'd been wearing the very first time he'd met her. They lay tossed aside in the grass. *Shit, shit, shit*—this was bad. "Where the hell did he take her, King?"

And as if King had understood the question perfectly, he started up the road at a fast trot. Rob didn't hesitate to follow—King had always been a damn smart dog. "Keep going, buddy. Take me to her."

King kept heading up the road, barking intermittently and looking over his shoulder to make sure Rob was coming. But it surprised the hell out of him when King turned onto the dock. When Rob hesitated, the dog barked insistently, looking back and forth between him and the row of upside down canoes. Rob glanced from the dock's edge back to the cabin. He knew what the *opposing* view was, too—if you stood at just the right angle at the edge of the picture window, you could see part of the dock. King had seen someone bring Lindsey here. And if he wasn't mistaken, the last canoe he'd hauled in on Sunday, a blue one a couple of teenage boys from Cedarville had taken out, was gone.

Just then, he heard a car and looked up to see Carla's VW Beetle pulling alongside the dock. The passenger-side window lowered and she leaned over. "Did you guys get my message?"

"Call the cops," he said. "He has her. I think he took her in one of the canoes. I'm going after her."

"People don't understand me, Lindsey."

They sat on the ground near the spot where Lindsey and Rob had made love just last week. Today, though, the mist hung heavy over the island. She could see that the sun was out and starting to burn it off over the water, but the island remained shrouded in fog, making her feel all the more alone and frightened. Her feet were cold and sore, she was freezing, and the whole thing felt surreal. She didn't feel like she was anywhere near Moose Falls. She didn't feel like she was anywhere near . . . anything. She felt cut off, like he'd taken her a thousand miles away.

"Maybe *I* could," she lied gently. "If you let me. It's just hard to feel very comfortable around a guy who's pointing a gun at me." She no longer had any plans in mind. She was pretty much trapped here with him, after all. All she could do now was try to keep him at bay, try to appear as if she cared about him so that maybe he wouldn't hurt her. She was still trying to wrap her mind around what he'd told her on the ride here. He wasn't just William Tell from her blog. He was Billy, the boy who'd once been Rob's best friend, the maniac who'd promised to come after him after he got out of prison. The news had taken a horrendous situation and multiplied it times a hundred.

"You want me to put the gun down? Okay," he said, much to her surprise. "But stay where you are. Don't move." Then he got up, walked several yards, and placed the pistol at the base of a small sapling near the water's edge. After which he came back and sat down next to her, this time so close that their arms touched.

The very sensation of his flesh against hers made her nauseous, but she had to fight it—she had to act like it was okay, like she wasn't afraid. She looked out through the mist toward the shore, knowing Rainbow Lookout was somewhere up there. And she thought of Rob, and of how in love with him she'd fallen, and of how badly she'd messed things up here.

"You found Rob through my blog, didn't you?" she asked, just to confirm her carelessness.

He nodded easily.

"I never said his last name."

"It was the tattoo," he said. "I didn't know he had it, but it made sense." He looked at her then. "Have you found out who Gina is yet or do I get to tell you?"

"I know. His daughter."

"It surprised me, frankly. I wouldn't have thought he'd give a damn. But I guess he got lonely in prison, weak." He cast a weird little smile, as if the thought pleased him, and she wanted to slap it right off his face. But instead she took a deep breath and looked back out at the water and tried to forget how close he sat.

"He's suffered enormously over what happened," she said.

"Good, I'm glad. But it's not enough. He hasn't suffered as much as me."

"You might be surprised," she countered. "He's been mostly alone in the world."

"That's because he did something wrong and God or the fates or whatever runs this place is making him pay for it. The difference is, I didn't do *anything* wrong, but I ended up alone, too."

"Even so, you just said God is making him pay. Isn't that enough?"

William shook his head. "In the end, God always ends up going easy on the bad guys. And look, here you are, madly in love with him, so it proves my point. He gets *you*, and what do *I* get?"

"I'm sure there are lots of women who would be crazy

about you, William." *If you could get that disturbing look off your face.* "If you could let go of the past and look to the future."

"That's why I'm here. When I leave this place, I'll be able to let go of the past."

"That's great," she said. "How do you intend to do it?"

"With you," he replied, again turning to look at her, his face way too close for comfort. "You're the key. You make it perfect."

She blinked, caught off guard. "How do you mean?"

"I spent my whole adult life imagining that one day I'd find that son of a bitch and kill him. I envisioned all kinds of ways I could do it. Guns, knives, other alternatives that would stretch it out, make him suffer. But now . . . now, I don't even have to do *that.* I can kill him in another way—metaphorically, you might say. It'll be downright poetic. Do you read poetry, Lindsey?"

She swallowed. *Freaking psycho.* "A little."

"When I was younger, I wasn't the academic type, but since then I've discovered how beautiful poetry can be, and how it can intertwine with life almost cosmically. Do you know what I mean?"

She had no freaking idea. She only knew she was talking to a nutcase. "Kind of."

"I can kill Rob by taking what he loves."

Her blood ran cold yet again. "Rob doesn't love me. It's just an affair to him." After this morning, she was starting to think maybe Rob *did* love her, the same way she loved him, but Psycho here didn't need to know that.

"No," he said. "I don't believe that. Even just from your blog, I can tell you make him happy. I can almost feel it in the words. Rob's as in love with you as I am."

She gasped, and he smiled.

"That's right, Lindsey, I'm in love with you. That's the most poetic part. See? And now I'm going to show you how much, and at the same time, it'll rip Rob's soul out."

With that, he twisted toward her, his hands closing tight on both her arms—then kissed her, hard and insistent and sloppy. She instinctively turned her head away, her whole body going rigid, and William went still, too.

He whispered in her ear. "I'm not so bad, am I, Lindsey? I'm not a bad-looking guy. You have to give me a chance. You *have* to." His tone was more commanding than pleading. "I know I can make you love me."

"I love *Rob*," she blurted out, then wanted to smack herself. She'd said as much on the blog, of course, but it was a pretty dumb time to remind her captor.

His eyes went cold, confirming her mistake. *"Don't say that. Don't say it ever again."*

"Okay," she agreed, shivering in fear now, barely able to breathe amid her terror.

Then his eyebrows knit, even as his countenance turned calmer again. "I wanted this to be more civilized. I'd hoped you'd just be reasonable, take a walk with me, get to know me—and then you'd decide to leave him and come away with me." He shook his head. "But you messed up my plan, Lindsey. And now here we are, out on this island, and things aren't going to be simple."

He'd said something like that once before, and she wondered briefly now if she could convince him otherwise. "Maybe things *could* still be simple. Let's go back to the house. I'll make some tea and we can talk. I *can* get to know you better. Maybe . . . I'll feel differently then." She tried, with all her might, to lift her hand to his shoulder, to give him some small affectionate touch, but she couldn't do it.

And William was shaking his head anyway. "It's too late for that. And you don't want me. I can see it in your eyes—I never stood a chance with you. And that means . . ." He closed his eyes, sighed sadly. "That means things *can't* be simple. I have to *take* what I want to make Rob suffer. I have to *take* it."

His voice had grown angrier toward the end—and that's

when he pushed her to her back on the damp ground, pinning her wrists to the grass at both sides of her head.

Oh God! She hadn't even seen the move coming.

But she was going to fight. She was going to fight with everything in her!

She might not win, yet she would do her damnedest to stop him. Because the only man who should be touching her was Rob. She was going to think of Rob, and fight for Rob, and try to draw strength from merely knowing Rob—who was probably the strongest person she'd ever met.

And as William bent to harshly kiss her neck, making her blood curdle, she thought, too, of the island they were on—Misty Isle. As he released her wrists from his tight grasp, clumsily shoving his fingers beneath her shoulder straps, she remembered the story of the Indians seeing their ancestors in the fog and thinking it meant this was a *safe* place. She'd felt that here, too, with Rob.

When William wrenched the straps downward, she turned her head toward the interior of the island, peering into the deep, white swirling mist, just thinking, *Please, please, help me.* She was begging God, she supposed.

And for some reason, she kept her eyes open, just staring, staring into the fog, maybe hoping it would swallow her—and that's when she saw Aunt Millie's face forming in the mist like a ghost. She'd surely conjured the image herself, and even as the sight made her fear she was going crazy—it also shocked her so much that her adrenaline surged and she used every ounce of force inside her to heave William off of her.

He looked at her for a moment from where he'd landed a few feet away, clearly as stunned by her strength as she was. And he'd just gathered his wits about him enough to start back toward her—when she heard a dog bark and looked up to see King bounding through the mist.

The next few moments were a blur. King attacked William as Rob came hurtling behind the dog. Lindsey lay on the ground, not quite able to move, but she pointed to where the gun rested and said, "There," to Rob. He snatched it up, eyes dark and reckless, and she realized that just because he was here, this wasn't over—not yet.

A few feet away, King had pinned William to the ground, where he trembled uncontrollably, looking pathetic and almost pitiable. Weirdly, she almost felt sorry for him, but also found herself thinking, *How does it feel to be held down like that, pal?*

"Get away from him, Lindsey," Rob commanded, and as she found the energy to get to her feet and stumble away, closer to Rob, he said, "Heel, King. Heel." Then, "Good dog."

Good dog, indeed. Lindsey planned to keep him in Milk-Bones for life.

Now Rob pointed William's own pistol at him, cocking the trigger—which William hadn't done the whole time with Lindsey, only she hadn't known enough about guns to realize it until now. William's shirt was torn in front, his forehead bleeding.

She looked back to Rob in time to see the horror in his eyes as he slowly realized exactly who had abducted her.

"Jesus fucking Christ," he muttered. "Billy?"

Sitting up, William held his hands out to his sides. "Surprise." He still sounded weirdly smug, calm.

"What the *hell*?" Rob, understandably, appeared stunned.

"Took me a while," William said, "but I finally found you."

Rob shook his head in disbelief, his eyes glassy. "How?"

Her captor now glanced in her direction. "The Love Letters blog."

Rob clearly remained confused. For all the time they'd spent together, she'd only spoken of the blog in passing and she wasn't even sure if he'd ever seen a blog or understood how they worked.

"Lindsey led me right to you."

Lindsey's heart shriveled in her chest as Rob glanced over

at her, trying to piece it all together. But then he looked back to William. "It's me you want to hurt. Why drag her into this?"

That strange, slow smile crept back onto William's face. "I wanted to take what you love, just like you took what *I* loved. And I got so close—didn't I, Lindsey?" He looked to her once more, as if they shared a secret, before refocusing on Rob. "A few more minutes and I'd have had her, the same way you have."

At this, Rob's back straightened sharply and his eyes narrowed—his shock transforming back into anger. "I should blow your fucking head off," he said, and Lindsey tensed.

But William just kept smiling that sickly smile. "Go ahead, shoot me, end my misery. I'll die happy knowing you'll rot in another cell, you bastard."

When Rob said nothing in reply, just kept the gun trained on William, William's grin grew. "Maybe you need some incentive. Maybe you need me to make another move on your girl." With that, he pushed to his feet and cast a predatory glare in her direction.

"Jesus," Rob muttered, rushing to step between her and William.

And thank God, because she'd collapsed on the ground, physically spent, fearing she couldn't run if she had to. At least King was at her side and she knew the dog would leap to her defense again if needed.

"I don't want to shoot you, Billy," Rob said to his old friend. "I loved you once, man. But I'll rot in a fucking cell if that's what it takes, because I *sure* as hell won't let you hurt her."

William held his hands out to his sides again. "I'm not trying to hurt her. It's you I want to hurt. You took everything from me. *Everything*."

William's voice had just cracked, and now Rob's tone softened, too. "I never meant to. I had nothing to do with your parents' death. And I didn't push Tommy, I swear to God."

Rob's pleading words hung in the air—until William lunged toward him. Rob fired the gun, the shot blasting through the thick mist and making Lindsey scream. It hit nothing, but was enough to make Billy back off again, holding his hands up as if in surrender.

King barked and started to spring toward William, but Rob said, "*Heel*," sharp, quick—and Lindsey saw a whole new sort of fury in her lover's gaze as he held the gun tight on William.

"I thought you wouldn't have it in you, wouldn't shoot," William said, sounding at once incredulous but almost weirdly pleased, making Lindsey think that on some level he really did want to die.

"You forget where you sent me," Rob replied, his eyes steely, his voice cold, exacting, and confident now. "Prison can turn a normal guy into one mean fucking son of a bitch. And for anybody who crosses me now, that's *who I am*." He stepped forward, gun pointed, closing in on William and emphasizing each word he spoke. "*One. Mean. Fucking. Son of a bitch*."

Lindsey's heart was in her throat. Oh God. She'd never seen Rob like this. William . . . *Billy* . . . had pushed him too far.

"Hold it right there! Police! Hands on your head and drop your weapon." Lindsey flinched, then turned to see five police officers emerging from the fading mist. Three aimed guns at Rob and the other two held their pistols on William. "You, too. Hands on your head—now!"

Rob bent to lower the gun to a clump of grass near his feet, then slowly lifted his hands to the back of his head. William did as instructed, too—but Lindsey focused on Rob, who managed to look both strong and somehow broken. Because—oh God—they thought he was the bad guy here.

And it didn't help when William suddenly blurted, "He tried to kill me! He's a convicted felon—he murdered my brother and now he's trying to kill me, too!"

"No, it's *his* fault!" Lindsey cried, pointing to William. "He kidnapped me and the gun is his, and if Rob hadn't shown up when he did . . ." She shivered and didn't finish the sentence.

The tallest cop, in his late thirties, didn't even glance in Lindsey's direction, but said, "Stand back, ma'am. You may not know this, but if this is Rob Colter, he *is* a convicted felon. We did a background check on the way."

Oh God, no—they still thought he was the scary one here. This was a nightmare. Lindsey *didn't* stand back—instead, she took a few steps closer. "I know about Rob's past, but he's done nothing wrong!"

Only now did the lead officer look over at her—to speak kindly but firm. "Ma'am, I need to ask you to be quiet now. We'll get this all sorted out at the station over in Cedarville. Now step away from the two gentlemen."

Lindsey sucked in her breath, feeling helpless. If she couldn't speak up for Rob . . . She'd never felt so frustrated even as one of the cops, a woman, came to lead her away. She looked over her shoulder to see both Rob and William being handcuffed, behind their backs, and her heart burned for Rob even more. He so didn't deserve this! And what kind of memories must it be bringing back for him? Being shackled? In front of his onetime best friend? And in front of her, too. She looked quickly away—an effort to protect his pride—but not before she saw him shut his eyes, as if trying to blot it all out.

"Wait," Rob said quietly then to the cop cuffing him. "Can I at least give her my shirt?"

He didn't look at Lindsey as he spoke, but as the officer withdrew the cuffs long enough to carefully slip off the open flannel shirt Rob wore over his tee, she knew he'd seen how scantily clad she was.

And as she put her arms through the big sleeves and wrapped the shirt around her and let Rob's masculine scent envelop her, she drew strength from him. Even now, *she* drew strength from *him*.

Rob had been through this before. He wasn't surprised when the cops quickly separated the three of them, placing them in different boats to be taken back to town. Lindsey and William were being transported in the canoes that had already been on the island when the cops arrived; Rob and King were put in the small motorized boat kept in the boathouse. He'd never imagined he'd be riding in the very boat he stored for them.

When cops had found him and Billy arguing at the base of that water tower seventeen years ago, they'd done the same thing—gotten them apart, taken them to the station house separately for questioning. Today, as the little caravan of boats headed toward the dock, he saw three cruisers, parked at haphazard angles, lights flashing, and knew each would deliver one of them to the Cedarville Police Station, which served Moose Falls since the town was too small for its own force.

To see those damn blue lights, to have his arms wrenched behind his back in sharp, tight cuffs, felt unreal. Billy had found him? What were the odds? But then again, maybe it was karmic, destined to happen.

He'd already known about Lindsey, too—he'd said something about her blog, after all, and it matched Carla's phone message—so had he decided raping her would be good enough revenge? He gritted his teeth as the ugly word passed through his mind. When he thought of *that* he didn't even care what happened to him now—just as long as she was okay. He was pretty sure he'd gotten there in time, but he'd need to talk to her alone to make sure. And if that bastard had done anything to her, anything Rob didn't know about . . . shit, what kind of freaking monster had Billy turned into?

But then, maybe his eyes had answered that question. He looked much the same as he had as a kid—physically, anyway. Only he was cleaner cut as an adult, and his eyes—hell, his eyes had just looked plain crazy. *Did I do that? Did I drive Billy out of his mind?*

But then, no. Hell, sometimes it was hard even for *him* to remember that he didn't kill Tommy. So many people had held him responsible—sometimes it was easy to start believing maybe *he* was the crazy one and had somehow just remembered it all wrong.

He knew that wasn't true, but he also knew that—just as he'd told Lindsey—when it came down to it, he *was* responsible for Tommy's death. If he hadn't followed Tommy up onto that rickety old tower, he never would have fallen. Or he *probably* wouldn't have. Hell, there were no answers, but he'd suffered a lot of guilt any way you sliced it.

The boat that carried him, being motorized, reached the dock ahead of the others, and it was still early in the day, but Carla, Eleanor, Mary Beth, and Maynard all stood outside the Lazy Elk waiting to see what happened. Rob asked the cops escorting him if he could ask one of them to take his dog home.

"Hey, Carla!" he yelled a second later, and asked her for the favor.

She came scurrying over, weaving her way between the police cars. "Sure, Rob, of course," she said. Then dropped her gaze to the dog. "Come here, King, come here."

"Go on, boy. It's okay, buddy—go with Carla," Rob told him. King had never met her before, but generally had a good sense of who Rob trusted and who he didn't. "Door's open," he told Carla.

Her eyes were wide. "Is—is Lindsey okay?"

He nodded. "I think."

Her eyes dropped to his cuffs. "God, what happened? Is everything all right?"

At this, one of the policemen stepped between them.

"Carla, you gotta take the dog and go now. Quit asking questions."

She gave the guy a challenging look. "Dave, I know these people. They're my friends."

"Well, you can't talk to 'em now. In fact," he said, then raised his voice loud enough to be heard at the Lazy Elk, "you all need to go back about your business and let us do ours. Okay?"

So Carla took the dog. And the other folks from town slowly made their way inside the bar. And Rob was slammed into the back of a cruiser with a barrier between the front seat and the back, and just like the cuffs, it seemed all too familiar. He'd only taken one other such ride, but you didn't forget a thing like that.

And so, he concluded as the police car twisted and turned up the mountainous roads to Cedarville, this was how his life would go. Even here, where he'd thought he'd found peace, there *was* no peace. It simply wasn't meant to be.

Shit, that was a lot to swallow along with everything else.

But he had a feeling he'd better damn well start swallowing it. Everything he'd tried to build here had just fallen apart.

Eighteen

The next six hours were slow and grueling. Rob was put in a small room by himself with only an old wooden table and some folding chairs, but there was a window with a view, so when he was alone, he looked outside. He found a hawk's nest in a nearby pine. He saw some hoofprints—likely elk—in the soft earth not far from the window and wondered how long they'd been there. He tried to stay calm.

From time to time, people came to talk to him. Dave the cop, a detective named Corgill, another detective named Blanchard. Small, curly-haired Corgill was trying to be a tough guy, repeatedly bringing up Rob's past, but Blanchard was more decent. Good cop, bad cop. At one point, Dave—his arresting officer—brought him a ham sandwich, some chips, and a Coke.

As they all moved between Rob, Lindsey, and Billy, though, he could tell they were beginning to get the real picture of what had happened, beginning to realize he wasn't at fault here. And the last time the door opened, Blanchard was alone.

He was an average-sized guy, probably about Rob's age, with thinning hair, a tweed jacket that seemed too stiff for the Montana wilderness, and a worn gold wedding band that made Rob feel a little jealous of the nice, calm, happy life he probably led.

"It shakes down like this, Rob," Blanchard said. "We were able to verify that your boy, Billy, has indeed been under psychiatric care in the past, and he has a history of psychotic episodes, although not in recent years. However, he called his lawyer in Portland, who asked that we send him for mental observation, which is what we're doing—he's being transported to a hospital in Missoula. That's the lawyer's way of trying to get him off the hook for his actions today, but meanwhile, he's being charged with kidnapping and assault, so we'll have to wait and see how that all turns out. Your girl's story checks out with yours and—"

Rob couldn't help interrupting him. "Can you tell me if she's okay? Did he hurt her?" Corgill had refused to answer any of his questions, but he'd built a decent rapport with Blanchard—and he needed confirmation that Lindsey was all right.

Blanchard's eyes changed a little—he supposed a married guy could understand his worry. "Yeah, seems to be. She's shaken, of course—and we brought up a counselor from Whitefish to talk with her. But she said you got there . . . in time, she said. In time."

Rob nodded and his heart quit beating quite so fast.

"*Your* biggest problem," Blanchard went on, "is that you're a convicted felon who was in possession of a firearm earlier today. But we've hashed the whole thing out with the DA, and they're declining to prosecute. What that means is—you're free to go and so is Miss Brooks. In a few minutes, a couple of the officers will drive you both back home."

Home. What a concept.

But Rob couldn't let himself go there right now. He had to concentrate on today, now, on the fact that at least he was free and clear, at least Lindsey wasn't hurt, at least they could go back to the cabin and recover from this together.

"All right then," Blanchard said, "we'll get your paperwork finished up and you're outta here."

The detective started for the door, but Rob said, "One more question."

Blanchard stopped, his hand on the doorknob, and looked up. "What's that?"

"Do you know how he found me? I mean, I try to keep a pretty low profile. I keep my number unlisted and I've never been put into any of those computer databases that give people's addresses. I'm not the easiest guy to find, so I'm just wondering how I screwed up and let him locate me."

Blanchard's eyes narrowed and Rob didn't like the troubled look on his face. "*You* didn't do anything, Rob. It was Lindsey Brooks's blog that led him here. Both she and he corroborated that, so . . . I thought you realized it, too."

"No," Rob said, feeling a little strangled. "Billy said something about that on the island, but I didn't know what he meant and figured it was just crazy talk. I, uh, don't know what her blog says."

Jesus fucking Christ, what had she done?

He guessed he suddenly looked like a guy who was about to crumble, because Blanchard came back from the door and spoke softly, like someone who was breaking bad news, telling you someone had died. "Without meaning to, she dropped enough clues, like details about Moose Falls and a description of a tattoo, along with your first name, that Billy figured out it was you and was able to locate you. Turns out Billy had an online crush on her. He followed her blog religiously and just got lucky that the girl he liked had hooked up with his old enemy and talked about it to her readers."

"I'll be damned," Rob muttered. And he meant it. *I will be damned.* He *felt* damned. Damned to hell. A kind of hell on earth.

"Sorry it worked out that way," Blanchard said, adding, "Take care," and he was gone.

And Rob was left sitting there trying to absorb the news that Billy's ravings on the island were actually true, that Lindsey, *Lindsey*, had led Billy straight to him. After all these years. After he'd mostly stopped worrying about Billy's threat. Lindsey had caused everything that had happened today.

He leaned forward over the table, head in his hands. *Shit.* Shit, shit, shit.

The door to the room was open now and he wondered if people were waiting for him to come out. The policemen. Lindsey. But he couldn't get up yet. He had to wrap his brain around this. As if he hadn't had enough pure *shit* to wrap his brain around already today.

Lindsey had caused this. All of it. Lindsey had put both of them in danger. Lindsey had almost gotten herself raped. Lindsey had almost forced him to kill someone—really *kill* them this time. And because of it, the few people in town he'd begun to feel bold enough to call friends had seen him hauled away in handcuffs. And the authorities now knew all about his past. Which meant everyone else would, too.

He'd understood the enormity of today's events almost as soon as they'd happened, but he'd thought it was dumb luck, his past catching up with him. Despite the mention of Lindsey's blog, he'd never imagined she'd brought this upon him.

So he sat with his head in his hands, his anger battling with regret and sadness and heartbreak and everything else that came with it. Everything had changed today—*everything.* And there wasn't a damn thing he could do about it.

Get hold of yourself, man. Pull yourself together.

He had to walk out of here in a minute. He had to face people. He had to see Lindsey. And damn it, he *wanted* to see her. He wanted to see for himself that she was okay. He wanted to take her in his arms and hug her so damn hard, just to make sure they *both* knew she was safe.

Even though he also wanted to scream at her for being so fucking careless with his life.

But this is your own fault, pal. Nobody else's.

He hadn't erred by trusting her exactly—she was trustworthy. She was caring. She was amazing in so many ways.

But she liked to talk. To the whole damn world, apparently.

So, ultimately, *his* mistake had been the same as always—he'd fucked up simply by letting someone into his life.

Lindsey thought it might have been the longest day of her life. Even longer than the days after her breakup with Garrett. Compared to this, having embarrassing photos of herself plastered all over the Internet felt fairly uneventful.

She knew now, as she stood in the main room of the mostly quiet little police station, that everything was going to be fine. William had just been taken away to some hospital for mental observation and she'd been assured by Detective Blanchard that he'd either end up in a mental ward or he'd be found guilty of his crimes today and go to jail. Rob, on the other hand, had been cleared of any wrongdoing—thank God! What she didn't know was if he hated her. For accidentally bringing William here.

So she stood in her bare feet and Rob's big red plaid flannel shirt, waiting nervously—when Rob strode out of the little room the detective had left a few minutes before. He looked tired, his red T-shirt rumpled—but when his eyes fell on her, all she felt was warmth.

Thank you, God. He doesn't hate me.

He closed the space between them and pulled her into a snug embrace and she'd never felt anything more reassuring than those strong arms wrapping around her, than that hard male body she was suddenly pressed up against.

"Thank God you're all right," he whispered in her ear. "You *are* all right, aren't you?" He pulled back just enough to look her in the eye.

"I've had better days, but yeah, I'm okay. Thanks to you. And . . ." Oh God, where to begin on the next part? At a loss, she just kept it simple. "I'm so sorry, Rob. So, so sorry."

His expression looked sad yet understanding just before he kissed her forehead, then murmured, "We'll talk about it later. Let's just get home."

In the back of the squad car, they held hands but mostly didn't speak—she supposed they both felt the presence of the two officers up front, even if the police radio filled the car with other noise. And she started to fear that Rob seemed a little . . . distant.

Of course, she supposed the guy had a *right* to act distant. She'd had a scary, awful, draining day—but she hadn't had her worst nightmare dredged up and thrown in her face when she'd least expected it. And her worst nightmare didn't seem so bad compared to Rob's anyway. So if Rob was still upset, still shocked by it all, she was content to simply hold his hand and be there for him.

It was then that he glanced down at her feet. "God, you're barefoot," he uttered softly. "I didn't even notice before."

"Oh—yeah," she replied. They were filthy and kind of sore on the bottom, but she'd quit thinking about them much.

"Are they okay?"

She nodded. "They'll live."

Then he gave her a small, sad-but-trying-to-be-happy smile. "For a girl who loves shoes as much as you, this must be the worst thing that could happen to you."

She tried to return a gentle grin. "Well, next to abduction by a psycho and having my fiancé dump me while I'm naked in front of a camera—yeah, it's pretty rotten."

"Here," he said, tenderly drawing one foot up into his lap. She turned in the seat to accommodate the position—and found it hard not to purr as Rob sweetly, thoroughly massaged her dirty, aching feet. Sure, he could be gruff sometimes, but she knew that deep down he was the most caring guy alive.

"Thank you," she said. "That feels amazing."

Soon, the cop car rolled past Bob's Pizza and the general store—Moose Falls tumbling over the rocks on the opposite side of the road where they couldn't quite be seen—then rounded the bend to the lake. They were back in town, and everything looked normal again—you'd never have known that this morning there'd been a nut with a gun, a kidnapping, and a slew of cop cars racing to the boathouse.

"Would it be possible to stop at the Grizzly Inn for a minute so I can get some clean clothes?" she asked, leaning toward the front seat.

"Sure," the cop driving the cruiser said, then swung into the lot where her car sat. She wondered if the other car beside it was indeed William's, but didn't ask.

One of the cops found Eleanor and got a key to Lindsey's room—and as much as she loved Eleanor, Lindsey was glad she didn't come out herself, since she wasn't yet ready to face her friends and just wanted to be alone with Rob right now.

As she stepped into her quiet, woodsy room, grabbing up a comfy outfit—a clean pink cotton cami and bra, jeans, and fresh underwear—it occurred to her that she'd been planning to pack her bags and check out today. She didn't have the energy for that anymore—officially moving in with Rob would have to wait until tomorrow, even if her heart was already there. Despite the dirt on the bottom of her feet, she slipped on her black beaded flip-flops from the general store.

Walking into Rob's cabin a few minutes later truly *did* feel like coming home.

Inside, they found the house straightened—the jacket she'd tried to put on that morning had been hung up, her shoes had been brought in and set neatly by a pair of Rob's hiking boots near the door. "My peek-toe pumps!" Lindsey exclaimed in joy.

King barked a hello and rushed to greet them and they

both spent a few long minutes returning his affection. "You did good today, buddy," Rob said, taking the big dog's face between his hands.

Lindsey even bent to give King a hug, remembering the way he'd bounded from the fog to save her. "Thank you, King. You are officially the best dog ever."

"He led me to you," Rob said.

Her eyes went wide. She'd known the dog was good, but—wow. "He did?"

Rob explained then how King had practically ushered him to the dock that morning, and she couldn't resist hugging the big furry guy yet again.

A moment later, they found a note from Carla: *King's been fed. Let me know if you need anything. I hope everything's okay.*

"She's nice, Carla," Rob said, setting the note back on the kitchen counter.

"The best," Lindsey agreed.

And yet, despite the warmth of their homecoming, Lindsey thought Rob still seemed . . . far away. And she found herself wanting to impress upon him again how truly, deeply sorry she was for what had happened, but at the same time, she sensed Rob wasn't quite ready to rehash it all with her.

He shored up that suspicion when he said, "You want the shower first?" without even glancing in her direction.

"Okay," she answered like a mouse, slowly starting to feel more alone than together with him.

You're overworrying this, she told herself as she stood in the shower, letting the warm water blast down over her to wash off the day's grime—both literal and mental. They'd both been through a lot today, and he was surely exhausted. Things were fine. His hug had said so. And the way he'd massaged her feet in the cruiser.

Her thoughts turned, too, to what had happened between her and William that morning. Now it seemed almost like a weird nightmare that hadn't really happened. He'd scared the holy shit out of her—she'd really thought she was going to be raped. But Rob and King had shown up in time, and she was okay.

And she'd seen in Rob's eyes and heard in his voice that he cared for her—it was undeniable. So why was she so damn worried *now*, now when he'd wanted to come *home* with her, now that he'd hugged her and reassured her?

She exited the bathroom in fresh clothes with her hair half dried and falling in loose curls around her shoulders, feeling much revived. She found Rob sitting in the living room, King curled at his feet. It was dusky now, and the room was dark—he hadn't turned on any lights.

So *she* did, which made him look up.

She tried to smile brightly, tried to inject some normalcy in the moment. "Shower's all yours. How about if I heat up some lasagna?"

He nodded, but didn't smile. "That'd be good, Abby." Then he slowly pushed to his feet and headed up the stairs to the bathroom.

Well, at least he was calling her Abby again. That was something. Once upon a time, the nickname had annoyed her, but if he was ready to tease again, that was a step in the right direction.

So she listened to the shower run and put slabs of lasagna on two plates, then started heating them in the microwave. After which she used hamburger buns, butter, and garlic salt to construct makeshift garlic bread, sliding the pieces into the toaster. She turned on the radio, and more lights.

But when Rob came down a few minutes later, dressed in fresh jeans and what looked like a well-aged Seattle Seahawks T-shirt, his feet in thick, cozy socks, he didn't seem any happier. Even when he spied the steaming hot food on the table and said, "Smells good."

The only noise while they ate was the soft alternative music playing in the background and the sounds of silverware against plates. Despite her best efforts, Lindsey began to feel tense, and it got worse with each quietly passing minute, until finally she said, "Are you okay, Rob?"

He looked up, looked undeniably strong—but sad. "Not really, no."

A big *whoosh* of air left her as she sank deeper into her chair, hurting for him. And maybe for her. She had to tell him again, had to make him understand.

"Rob, you have to know how sorry I am. I've gotten used to being in the public eye and I've never had anything like this happen, so it just never occurred to me. I'm a sharer. I share. That's what I do. I can't help it. It's part of my personality, and so all this happened because I was just . . . being me—but if I could take it back, I would. I'm so sorry to make you deal with something so horrible, so sorry you had to see Billy again, and so sorry the cops thought you were guilty of something this morning. I'm just . . . sorry."

She'd blurted it all out without taking a breath, and when she was finally done, Rob simply put his fork down and said, "I guess we have to talk about this now," then got up and headed into the living room, taking a seat on the leather sofa.

So . . . he really *was* angry with her. And that was understandable.

Her heart beat a mile a minute as she, too, lowered her fork and stood up. Walking into the living room felt like walking to a sentencing.

But he'd asked her to move in with him just this morning, so . . . they'd deal with this, and they would come through it okay.

Taking a seat next to him, she pulled one leg up under her and turned to face him. "Rob, please tell me you know how sorry I am. I never dreamed anything I wrote in my blog could hurt you in any way."

He turned to face her, too, sitting cross-legged on the sofa—but his expression looked grim and his voice was more cutting than before. "You weren't aware I liked my privacy? You weren't aware, after I told you why, that I *needed* my privacy?"

That stung, and she let out another deflated breath. What was worse—he made a good point. "I just never dreamed my little blog could affect you. I never meant to bring back a nightmare from your past. I know I screwed up and I've learned my lesson—no more personal stuff out there, I swear. I can't imagine how hard today was for you, but I just hope you can forgive me and that we can move forward."

Music still played—the Weepies sang "World Spins Madly On"—but nothing in the room moved. Rob simply looked at her for a long while, until finally he said, his voice sounding strangely *kind*, "You don't realize what you've done, do you?"

She pulled in her breath. "I know I brought back something you never wanted to think about again, and I apologize from the bottom of my heart."

Yet he shook his head. "No, honey, that's not it. That part's over, and yeah, it sucked, and yeah, I was really pissed when I found out why all this happened—but that's not the issue. You don't realize what you've set in motion."

Now it was Lindsey who shook her head—helplessly. "What are you talking about?"

He simply sighed, shut his eyes for a second, then opened them back on her. "Lindsey," he said softly, "I have to leave here now."

She squinted her confusion. "What?"

"My life in Moose Falls is over."

What the hell was he talking about? "Huh? Why?"

He spoke calmly, almost slowly, as if trying to explain to a child. "The cops in Cedarville know my past now. They also know Carla and every other person in Moose Falls, I'm sure. I'm betting that right about now the news is starting to make the rounds and it won't take long—a few days, tops—before everybody knows. And guess what? Nobody wants to rent a canoe from a killer. Nobody wants an ex-con at their house building sheds or room additions or bookshelves or garages. *Nobody.* Take it from me, I know. Pretty soon I'll quit hearing updates from Eleanor on weekend reservations, and Bernard will quit meeting my eyes when I buy groceries or tools. Inside of a week I won't just be the unfriendly guy in town—I'll be the scary guy no one wants anything to do with."

Oh. Oh God. She hadn't even thought about that. She'd thought this was over now. Her immediate reaction was to assure him he was wrong. "Rob, no—maybe it won't be that way." A shame it came out so weak.

"Of course it will." He, on the other hand, sounded certain. "So that means I have to leave here, leave this one place where I've really been . . . happy. I wanted to stay here for the rest of my life, Lindsey, and now I can't."

Her lips actually trembled as she spoke, but she tried to believe in her words as she said them. "Maybe you could . . . weather the storm. They'll get over it in time, they'll realize you're a good guy."

But again, he was shaking his head. "Nope—they'd always be looking over their shoulders. And I can't survive without work. And I won't let Millie's business wither and die just because people are afraid of me. So I guess you got what you wanted in the end, even if it's only by accident. I'll be happy to let you have the livery now. And the house, too, if you want it."

Lindsey's mouth dropped open as all the blood drained from her face. She couldn't believe what he was saying, couldn't believe he was telling her she could have Aunt Millie's place now. She also couldn't believe how horribly *wrong* that sounded.

She started shaking her head profusely. "No, I won't take it. I don't want it anymore. It's yours—it belongs with you. Nothing else makes sense."

"Not anymore," he said solemnly. "So you'd better consider

taking it or someone else will get it cheap and I'd rather leave it with Millie's family."

The whole thing simply sounded unthinkable. "Rob, please let me help you work this out."

Next to her, he tilted his head, his eyes a mix of emotions, and to her surprise, at the moment the one she saw most prominently was . . . affection. For her. He even reached out and took both her hands in his. "Lindsey, honey—I'm crazy about you." Oh God, it was the first time he'd ever said anything like that. "And I don't really blame you—I blame *myself* for letting down my guard as usual, for letting someone into my life. And you . . . hell, you helped me feel alive again, and I thank you for that. But I can't stay here and wait for the fallout that's coming. And . . . I can't have you in my life anymore, either. I can't have *anyone* in my life—once and for all."

Her whole body felt heavy, weighted, with what he'd just said. He was crazy about her. But he was kicking her out of his life. Had she indeed heard that correctly? "So you're breaking up with me," she said, her voice strange, light, the words almost unclear to her own ears.

He simply looked at her, still calm, still sure. "If you want to call it that." He made it sound so easy.

Oh God. He'd just dumped her. And sure, she'd been worried about his reaction to all this earlier, stuck alone with no shoes in that dumb little room at the police station for hours. But after his greeting when they'd been released, she'd felt so relieved, and she'd had no idea this was coming.

This was nothing like the Garrett breakup—but it was harder somehow, even behind closed doors this time, because . . . she'd hurt him so badly and there wasn't a damn thing she could do about it. She'd ruined his life.

She knew he'd been through hell, various kinds of it, over and over—but she had to take one last stab at making him understand that she wanted to be with him, no matter what, that she wanted to help him overcome all this, that she'd do whatever it took. "Give me a chance to help you bounce back from this, Rob. I know I can. I want to be there for you. I . . ." She shook her head helplessly, searching for words. "I . . . don't want to go back to life without you."

His eyes filled with more emotion than she'd seen since they'd gotten home, and she knew that last part was getting to him. She hadn't said *I love you*, but pretty damn close.

And even so, even still, he finally said, "I can't, honey. I can't."

"But I'm *so, so* sorry, Rob." She wanted to cry, felt her chest heaving, her eyes stinging, yet managed to keep tears at bay. She refused to appear weak—because she wanted to be the strong one right now.

Yet her strength didn't change anything. When next he spoke, his words were harsh, and still somehow they came out sounding kind. "I know you're sorry, honey, but being sorry . . . doesn't fix anything."

So that was it. The end of it. The end of her "affair" with the guy she'd fallen head over heels in love with. The end of her simple, sweet new life with him. The end.

Feeling depleted—and done wasting words on a stubborn man who clearly didn't feel for her what she felt for him—Lindsey pushed to her feet and started rushing around the house. Upstairs, she found her overnight bag and went about collecting her things—the dirty clothes from today, a hair-brush from the dresser, a bra hanging over the foot of the bed that had gotten left behind a few days ago.

He didn't want her? Well then, he wouldn't have her. Not for one more night, not for one more hour, if this was how he felt. He could go back to being alone with King.

Moving briskly back down the steps with the bag on one shoulder and her lime denim jacket in her fist, she stopped by the door to cram her peek-toe pumps inside the bag. She was still managing not to cry even as she reached for the doorknob.

She hadn't even looked up at him as she'd passed through

the room, so it came as a shock when his hand closed around her wrist.

Flinching, she jerked her gaze to his face.

And—oh God—his eyes. They burned on her hotter than ever and even after the horrendous day she'd had, and the horrendous last fifteen minutes especially, one heated look like that from her burly lumberjack was enough to make her surge with moisture.

Of course, there was more than sex in the look, *much* more. There was *everything*—everything they'd shared together. There was sex and canoes and hiking and rainbows and photo albums and secrets and regrets and wishes. There were animal-print bras and Fish Festival trophies and the smell of rain. There were piggyback rides and pizza from Bob's and letters she'd thought he'd written to a secret lover and a pair of Keds. But—of course—mostly . . . there was desire. Hard. Pure. Needful.

With his hand still gripping her arm, he turned her toward him, leaned down to bring his face so close to hers that she thought she'd combust, and then he pressed his mouth to hers for the hardest, longest kiss she'd ever experienced.

At some point, her jacket dropped in a clump to the floor and soon her bag hit the throw rug by the door with a hard *plop.* Thank God he eventually put his arms around her or she might have melted to the hardwood herself. As it was, his tongue invaded her mouth, deeply, making her feel more taken by a man than she'd thought it was possible to feel without having sex.

When finally the kiss ended, leaving them both breathless, she panted, "What was that?"

"A kiss goodbye," he rasped, deep, throaty.

Goodbye, huh? It had felt a lot more like hello.

Even so, if he said it was goodbye, well then, it was goodbye. So in a last burst of strength, she drew back her arms—which at some point had circled his neck—and forced herself to back away from the male body that felt so perfect crushed against hers. She tried to pretend she hadn't noticed the hard bulge behind his zipper pressing so seductively against the front of her jeans.

That's when his hands closed warm and firm over her hips again and he looked down into her eyes before lowering his gaze to her mouth. Every nerve ending in her body was on red alert—her senses were telling her to go, that it was just wrong and plain dumb to stand around making out with a guy who was giving her the heave-ho, but her body definitely wanted her to stay a little longer, to let him touch her, kiss her, to let her breasts mold to his chest, to let the crux of her thighs move against his.

Neither of them said another word before he was kissing her again—more hard, slaking kisses that made her mouth feel deliciously punished as they echoed through her entire body. She couldn't help kissing him back, responding with her body, as well. A few seconds ago, she'd been ready to walk out that door, be a tough, strong chick—but she just loved him too much. Tough and strong had given way to achy and needy that fast.

Soon his hand rose to the side of her breast, making her moan into his mouth, and when his thumb brushed across the hardened peak through her clothes, she let out a high-pitched whimper of pleasure.

Then Rob's voice growled low in her ear. "If you don't want this, you'd better say so right now."

Nineteen

Be smart. Say so. Go. Because sex now, sex after being dumped—that couldn't be wise. You can't let that happen. You'll only feel all the more miserable later.

Only . . . "I *do* want it," she heard herself whisper. And it was more than just the heat of the moment. It was actually a conscious decision. It was needing one last physical connection with him. It was not being ready, or able, to let go. It was knowing it would be the very last time, and that she'd soak up every touch, every move, every sensation with an awareness she would take with her, that would help her remember how the best, most intense sex of her life had felt. And that would help her remember how the best, most intense connection she'd ever shared with a man had felt, too. Knowing the memories would soon be all she had to hold on to came with a reckless need to make still more of them, one last time.

Maybe it only made sense. They'd started out together as just sex; maybe they should end as just sex, too. Except now she knew that sex with Rob could never be "just sex."

She heard him blow out a hot breath that clearly meant *Thank God* as he took her breast full in his hand and pressed his tongue possessively back between her lips.

From there, things moved quickly, jaggedly. Kisses turned to something more like hot, hungry bites, wicked nibbles—his teeth gliding over her upper lip, *her* teeth closing over his lower one a few seconds later to make him groan. She arched into him, desperate to feel his erection against her, that supreme hardness that filled her soul with raw, naked want. One of his hands grasped tight to her ass, molding, pulling her to him, the other massaged her breast, his thumb teasing the nipple, making it more and more sensitive, forcing more frantic whimpers from her throat. They moved together in a hot grind that nearly made her come, that quick, as Rob peeled down one strap of her cami to reveal a pink bra underneath. He leaned in to lower a kiss to the curve of her breast and things slowed—just a little.

She watched him kissing her there, again, again, the soft pleasure expanding inside her, almost colliding with the harder pleasure from below. She could hear his ragged breathing as the stubble on his chin lightly chafed her skin.

He released her then—to get more clothes off her. He pulled down the other strap of her cami and helped her free her arms, the fabric dropping to her waist. He studied her breasts within her bra like he was studying some artistic masterpiece—until he reached for those straps, too, dropping them just enough that her breasts tumbled free. "Damn," he murmured at the sight of them, almost as if it were the first time, and then he curled his arms back around her, bending to take one turgid pink bud into his mouth.

She mewled her pleasure as it stretched all through her, making her wetter below. He kissed first, sucking gently, but then his ministrations turned more demanding, until she felt light-headed at the sensations barreling through her. As he switched to the other nipple, she found herself clawing at his back, needing his shirt off.

And when he helped, finally removing the tee and tossing it aside, the tattoo on his chest no longer made her feel threatened—now it only made her love him all the more. She found herself kissing it, kissing her way passionately across his chest. She pressed her palms there, soaking up the feel of his skin, the hard muscles beneath, the soft curling bits of hair. She flicked her tongue over his nipple and made him flinch and curse as he continued caressing her breasts.

Instinct led her downward, kissing her way over his stomach until she was on her knees. Which she hadn't quite planned on.

As she gazed on his zipper and the wonderfully large bulge there, she knew what would happen next was obvious almost to the point of feeling a little clichéd. She'd never actually given a guy a blow job on her knees before and up until this moment, she might have viewed it as too submissive a position to willingly take. But clichés and submissive positions all went out the window as she reached for the button on his jeans. Nothing really mattered but this moment, and pleasure, giving it and taking it, relishing every second, doing it all because this was her last chance to do *anything* with him.

She bit her lip as she unzipped his pants and pushed them open. His erection sprang from his underwear, which she also pushed down. Oh God, he was beautiful, and right now she needed to connect with him like she'd never needed anything before. Because—it just hit her—*this would be the last time for him, too.* For God only knew how long. If he was true to himself, maybe ever. She needed to pleasure him. She needed to give *him* something to take with him after this was over, too.

She licked a trail from base to tip and listened to his sharp hiss of pleasure. Then she wrapped her hand full around his length and took him in her mouth.

"Aw, God," he groaned through clenched teeth, and she sank deeper, simply giving, giving—giving him all that she could. His hands were in her hair and he was telling her she was beautiful, and good. "So good, honey. So damn good."

She moved that way on him until her mouth felt sore and stretched, and she released him from between her lips, peering upward. His eyes, as always when they were being intimate, shone fiery and needful on her. "Stand up," he whispered, helping her to her feet.

Then he kissed her again, but she felt it even more than before because her lips were so swollen. Her arms naturally looped around his neck and his around her waist, but this time her nipples pressed against his bare chest.

Soon she found herself taking his length in her fist again—exploring, massaging—and he reached to open her jeans, too. Once her zipper had been lowered, she helped him push them down and off—only to hear him groan when he saw her panties. She wore a leopard-print thong that totally clashed with her bra and the cami still around her waist—she'd grabbed them simply because they were clean and on top in her drawer. She hadn't even been thinking about his affinity for such fabric; she hadn't even been thinking about whether or not they'd have sex tonight after all they'd been through today.

"Jesus," he muttered. And then *he* was the one dropping to his knees.

First, he simply ran his fingers over her mound, sending little tendrils of pleasure ricocheting through her as her hands sank into his hair. When he delivered a kiss to the front, she trembled and her legs went weak. He'd kissed her there before—but she somehow felt it more this time.

When he kissed her there again, she sucked in her breath and nearly lost her balance—and Rob put his hands on her hips and leaned her back against the wall by the door. When she stumbled a bit on his hiking boots, he knocked them out of the way.

Then he parted her legs farther and pushed the leopard-print fabric aside.

He gently kissed her again—nothing between his mouth and her flesh now—and she shivered and moaned. Oh God, it felt good. So powerful, amazing. So . . . intimate. And loving. He was loving her with his mouth and she knew it.

He licked and kissed her with a slow thoroughness that filled her whole being. He pushed two fingers up inside her and said, "Damn, honey—so wet."

And all she could utter was a light, "Uh-huh," because she was overwhelmed with pleasure and heat and never wanted it to end.

At some point, she lifted her left foot up onto the table where Rob kept his keys. It was a stretch, but she need to open herself to him further, and he groaned when she did it, licking at her more feverishly. Leaning against the jackets and clothes on the peg board by the door, trembling with the intensity of the pleasure, she reached overhead to grab on to two of the pegs for balance. She tried to memorize the stark heat on his face, tried to memorize everything about how it felt, right down to the way her fallen bra rubbed against the undersides of her breasts as she moved against his mouth, right down to the way the edge of the table pressed into the bottom of her foot.

Finally, the pleasure got the best of her and she knew she would come. And as always with Rob, she felt free to beg for what she needed from him. "Don't stop. Please don't stop."

She moved against his mouth. She let herself stop thinking. She let herself feel nothing but pleasure for a few long, almost achingly surreal moments—until finally she exploded.

She held the pegs tighter, trying not to collapse as she cried out and thrust against his mouth, again, again, again.

When it was over, she nearly *did* collapse, but Rob pushed to his feet and caught her in his arms, whispering, "Put your arms around me—I've got you, honey. It's all right."

And they stood that way for a long, blissful, recovering moment, and he whispered some more. "You're so damn beautiful," he rasped in her ear, and then, "Honey, I need inside you."

"Yes," was all she said—because she needed him in her, too. She peered up into his eyes and was completely honest. "Do it hard. Make me feel you. I need to feel you hard."

His response was but a low growl and a look into her eyes that told her she'd just aroused the hell out of him. Next, he was turning her around, away from him, pulling down her thong, and leaning in from behind to help brace her hands on the key table.

And then he plunged inside. Oh God, he felt big this way—even bigger than usual. She yelled out and held the table tight since her legs remained weak.

"Okay?" he asked near her ear.

Her voice trembled, even as she said, "More than." Then, "Please."

And he didn't have to ask, *Please what*—instead he answered simply by pounding into her, deep, over and over, making them both cry out with every powerful stroke.

She never wanted it to end. At some point she realized he'd wrapped both his arms around her waist to help keep her on her feet, and the warmth of his body behind her only added to the things she wanted to keep, hold on to, never let go. They were both moaning, panting, filling the house with noises that had long ago drowned out the soft music from across the room. Nothing existed but their bodies connecting in the most intense way she could imagine.

Finally, he pulled out of her and she sort of wanted to cry, but she turned around to see him reaching for her hand.

His jeans were still on, hovering at his hips, but he stumbled over the loose fabric at his feet then and ended up bumping into the back of the couch—where he simply let himself slide downward until his butt hit the floor. His cock still stood strong and fully erect as he said, "Come ride me, Lindsey."

Her stomach contracted and she needed him back in her

like she needed to breathe. She wasted no time before straddling him on the floor and lowering herself onto him. Their eyes met as they both let out the low groans of reconnection.

And then she did what he'd asked of her, she rode him, slow and thorough, her hands on his chest, his on her hips. His eyes wandered down to her breasts, and lower, to where their bodies joined, but they always came back to her face.

She started kissing him again, because she couldn't help it, because she needed to feel his warm mouth beneath hers, needed to feel the delicious way his tongue stroked between her lips.

And through it all, she stayed aware during every second that this was the last time, this was goodbye sex. She'd never had goodbye sex before, but it was by far the most intimate encounter of her life.

Moving on him, she continued to absorb every detail of every sensation, the slick slide where their bodies were wet together, the hard muscles beneath her fingertips, the dark look in his eyes, the stubble on his chin, the music she could hear again now—everything.

"Come for me again, Lindsey," he said, soft, in his sure, prodding way—the way that told her he knew she would.

She knew it, too—she'd never been so orgasmic with anyone before him.

And because it was the last time, for everything, because there were no rules here or no propriety, because this was the last chance for pleasure, she lifted his hands to her breasts, molding them to her, and leaned to whisper in his ear, "Kiss them for me. Suck them. Make me feel it deep inside."

She pulled back in time to see his face change—a mix of heat and emotion. Because she knew that *he* knew she was letting it *all* out, letting herself go—maybe in a way she never had before, even with him.

He said nothing, but dropped his gaze to her chest as he squeezed and stroked his thumbs over her taut, sensitive nipples. Then he bent his head to suckle her breast as he had before, but harder now, harder, and she arched against him and felt the thick, gathering pleasure, felt it mounting, building—until the crushing climax hit, rocking her, jerking her whole body as it rumbled through her, stealing her control, stealing her senses, making her whimper and moan. And just like every other part of this, she soaked that up, too, knowing it was the last time with Rob.

"Aw, Jesus," he murmured beneath her then. "Me, too, honey." And as usual when they were in this position, his mighty drives lifted her from the floor, impaling her even deeper, and she cried out at the intensity as he groaned through every thrust he delivered.

Until finally they both went quiet, still, and she fell forward against him and they held each other for a long, silent moment.

Which was when King let out a dog whimper and they both looked up to see him staring at them from his rug across the room. "Hell," Rob said on a sigh. "We let the dog watch us have sex again."

Although, true as it was, it didn't fit the moment—it was simply too inconsequential compared with everything else. She replied softly. "It doesn't matter."

"I know," he said, sounding sad, like he already realized.

She looked into his eyes then, still straddling him, still joined in that most intimate way, and she wondered if maybe, somehow, he was feeling like she was—so connected to him that the idea of never seeing him again was clawing her heart out.

"Do you still want me to go?" she whispered.

He let out a heavy breath, and that quickly, she already knew the answer. "It's not what I want," he said. "It's what I need."

It was classic Rob. Classic, stubborn, loner Rob. So it shouldn't have surprised her—yet somehow, it did. *He doesn't love me.*

It surprised her and hurt her all over again—and made her desperate to get the hell out of there, now.

If he didn't want her, she damn well wasn't going to sit around crying about it in front of him. Nope, that part would come later. But for now, she just had to go.

Thrusting up off him, she reached for a handful of tissues from a box by the couch, not-very-delicately made quick work of tidying herself, then rushed into her clothes with her back to him.

Don't cry. Do not cry. Just stay mad—that will help. Stay mad at the stupid man for being so . . . stupid. And for . . . just plain not caring about you the way you care about him.

Damn it. Shouldn't have let herself think that last part. *Do not cry, Lindsey.*

After getting her cami readjusted over her bra, she thrust her arms into her lime jacket, picked up her bag, and reached for the doorknob—for the second time in half an hour.

She stopped this time, though, to turn back to him. He was just now getting to his feet, pulling his jeans up.

"I have two things to say to you," she announced. "The first one is—you should find your daughter. To discover there's a man out there who loves her so much might make her not care so much about the bad parts." *The same way I didn't care about the bad parts.*

"The second thing is . . ." She stopped, shook her head, still stunned—by this whole day, and this whole night. "I can't believe you're letting me walk out this door."

He stepped forward, his eyes glassy with emotion, and earnest. "I'm sorry," he said.

"Being sorry," she reminded him, "doesn't fix anything."

Twenty

Lindsey was going home. To Chicago. It wasn't that she wanted to exactly—it wasn't that it even really felt like home to her anymore, in a way. It was only that she couldn't stay in Moose Falls any longer and she had nowhere else to go.

"But I'm resuming my job next week," she told Carla and Eleanor over fuzzy navels—another first for Eleanor—at the Lazy Elk the following afternoon. They were the place's only inhabitants and sat at one end of the bar. "I called my boss this morning and told her I'm ready to start the column again. So that will give me something good to focus on."

"But you could do that here, too, couldn't you?" Carla said, looking sad. Lindsey was going to miss her, too.

"I could," she said, "but I can't. You know why."

She'd given them the short version of her breakup with Rob. Because of what had happened yesterday, they knew now about his stay in prison and why he was so gruff and antisocial—or why he had been before Lindsey had come along, and now probably would be again. They still didn't know who Gina was, though—only that the tattoo had drawn

William Tell here—and Lindsey didn't elaborate, figuring she could leave Rob one last secret of his own.

"Are you going to go say goodbye to him?" Eleanor asked, sipping her drink. "Maybe he'll have a change of heart after a little time has passed."

But Lindsey gave her head a vehement shake. "Nope, not Rob. I'm pretty sure he loves me, but with Rob . . . love isn't enough. He can't forgive me for drawing Billy here. And after me, he'll probably never trust anyone again, ever."

Next to her, Carla drew in her breath, looking pensive. "So you're just gonna leave? No goodbyes—nothing?"

"Well, I'm pretty sure we said our goodbyes last night." *With mind-rattling sex.* "But I wrote him a letter to tell him I was going. Just to . . . you know, give me a sense of closure and say a few things I didn't get to say last night. I put it in his mailbox before coming here."

"Are you going to buy the livery and the cabin from him?" Eleanor asked. "Because I like Rob, and if he leaves I'll be sorry to see him go, but I'd also be real happy to have *you* come back."

Lindsey could barely even wrap her mind around the concept. She knew it made sense—if Rob really, truly did leave, she should buy the place. That's what she'd come here to do, for God's sake. And she'd been happy here. And to her vast surprise, she thought she could even enjoy living here, soaking up the sense of community, the peace and quiet, the smell of pine trees and mountain rain—even if it meant her peek-toe pumps only came out of the closet for nights at the Lazy Elk. And certainly, if Aunt Millie knew all the circumstances, she would rather have Lindsey running the place than someone else.

But the thought she couldn't bear was taking the place from Rob, knowing in her heart that it belonged with him. She could buy it, own it, run it—but she'd always feel a little empty inside; she'd always know that wasn't how it was supposed to be.

Yet she couldn't explain all that to Eleanor, so she simply shook her head. "I can't think that far ahead. Right now, all I can focus on is going back to the city and rebuilding my life there."

That wouldn't be easy, either, of course. She'd have to face whatever was left of the local media scorn; she'd have to rebuild her social life without Garrett, probably under *more* media scrutiny; she'd have to figure out all over again who she was and what she wanted out of life. But all that would be easier than staying here with Rob only a stone's throw away.

"I still can't believe he broke up with you," Carla said, shaking her head so dramatically that Lindsey feared the drink was getting to her.

"Neither can I," she said quietly. "But I don't need a man too stupid to see how fabulous I am, right?"

"Right," the other two ladies repeated in unison.

"What I hate most," Lindsey mused, thinking out loud, "is being afraid he's right. Not about dumping me, but about . . . leaving. I tried to tell him people wouldn't judge him by his past, but . . . maybe I'm wrong about that. Am I wrong? Do you guys feel differently about him now? Are you afraid of him?"

Eleanor swiped a hand down through the air. "Afraid of Rob? Pshaw. Unlike that dog of his, his bark is worse than his bite, and I've known all along that deep down he was a nice fella. Only difference now is that I know where he got the bark from and I guess I can't blame him for being wary of folks."

Lindsey looked to Carla. "What about you? Honestly? If you needed repairs done here, would you still call Rob?"

Carla blinked. "Well, yeah. I mean, if he was brand-new in town and I found out he'd done time, maybe not. But now that I know him, sure I would."

"What do you think about other people? People who *don't* really know him. People who haven't spent any time with him."

Eleanor and Carla exchanged worried looks that tightened Lindsey's chest until Eleanor finally said, "Mountain people can be a little persnickety about who they trust."

Lindsey let out a heavy sigh. "It's just not fair. I don't want Rob to have to leave. It's not right."

Only when Carla's hand covered hers on the table did she realize she'd gotten emotional without warning. Maybe the drink was getting to her, too. Or maybe just the rank injustice of it all.

"Listen," Carla said, "I used to date Dave, the police chief over in Cedarville who you met yesterday. I don't know that it'll do any good, but maybe I could put in a word with him not to let the details about Rob's past get around. He generally does what I say."

Lindsey looked up, perplexed. "Why?"

"We're kind of . . . friends with benefits. And I can threaten to withhold benefits. Works every time."

Eleanor gasped.

And Lindsey smiled. "Thanks, Carla." Then she let out a tired sigh. "Let's go have lunch at Mary Beth's before I leave. I could use a last slice of her lemon meringue pie for the road."

Just then, the phone behind the bar rang, and Carla hopped up and walked around to answer it. "Lazy Elk Bar and Grill."

Lindsey and Eleanor watched her mouth drop open in pure shock as she said, "Uh-huh . . . uh-huh . . . hold on." Then she covered the mouthpiece with her hand and whispered frantically to Lindsey, "Oh my God! This is Garrett! He's tracked you down and wants to talk to you!"

Oh my God was right! As for how he'd tracked her down, she could only guess *he'd* been reading her blog, too.

"Do you want me to tell him to go jump off a bridge?" Carla asked. "Because I'd be happy to."

But no, Lindsey could handle this. She could handle a lot more than she could a few weeks ago. "Give me the phone," she said, then put it to her ear. "Garrett?"

"Lindsey," he said, clearly trying to sound warm. "Hi, sweetheart, how are you?"

"I'm fine—but no longer your sweetheart," she reminded him.

On the other end, he sighed. "Lindsey, listen—I need to talk to you. I need to tell you . . . how sorry I am."

She couldn't believe it. "You're not serious."

"Of course I am," he said, indignant. "I . . . made a big mistake breaking up with you, Linds. And I know I said some very regrettable things, but . . ."

"But people liked you better when you were part of a glamorous couple?" she guessed.

"No, it's not like that. I miss you. I guess you meant more to me than I realized."

"Wow, you really know how to woo a girl, you silver-tongued devil."

"Lindsey, please quit being sarcastic and give me a chance. I want to see you. I want to work things out."

When she'd first arrived here, Lindsey might have listened to him. Even as angry and hurt as she'd been then, she'd also come to Moose Falls feeling so adrift and confused and desperate that maybe, just maybe, she would have jumped at any sad chance to reclaim her old life. But that old life didn't look so grand anymore. She'd learned a lot about life, and love, and living since then.

And maybe that was why she couldn't help hearing *herself* in Garrett's words, hearing her apologies to Rob. Maybe Rob was right—being sorry *didn't* fix things. The big difference between her and Garrett, though, she understood then, was that she wasn't like him; she hadn't acted mean or ugly, and she had never intentionally hurt anyone.

For a moment, she considered telling Garrett that if he ever came near her again, he'd once more find himself wearing the nearest dessert she could get her hands on—but then she realized that she no longer cared enough about him to even be angry anymore. She felt no need for revenge, only the need to end the conversation. "Garrett," she said very sweetly, "I accept your apology. But you were right when you broke up with me. We're very different people and we don't belong together. Goodbye." Then she hung up.

Carla and Eleanor both sat gaping at her with wide eyes and open mouths until Carla finally said, "Why were you just so nice to that jerk?"

And Lindsey smiled—pleased with herself. "Because I'm so very over him."

Yep, her heart definitely belonged to another man now—even if that man wasn't going to make good use of it. And maybe it always would, like it or not.

As the ladies finished their drinks and stood to head over to the Lakeside Café, Lindsey remembered to ask, "How was the book club last night? I'm sorry I missed it—I'd really been looking forward to it."

"Oh," Carla said, "we decided to postpone since you weren't there, wait until a night you could come. So instead we just ate pie and talked about how much you've livened this place up and hoped that you and Rob were doing okay."

Lindsey wanted to cry, and she didn't think it had to do with the drink. "That's the nicest thing I've ever heard."

She knew in her heart of hearts that she really didn't want to leave. But she had to. As soon as they ate lunch, she had to lug her giant suitcase into her trunk and hightail it out of Moose Falls before she completely fell apart.

Rob had spent the morning sleeping. Or trying to. He'd had a shitty night, tossing and turning and having bad dreams he couldn't quite remember. So by the time the morning arrived, he needed more sleep—but it wouldn't come, so he mostly lay there thinking. Planning.

He'd tell Stanley Bobbins the whole truth about his past—since it was surely making the rounds already by now anyway—and find out if Stanley wanted him to finish the job or not, assuring him he wouldn't be offended if Stanley didn't want him back at his place. He had a wife and kid there, after all, and Rob was an ex-con. He'd talk to Steve Fisher, too—see if he'd prefer someone else do the finishing work on his room addition.

He'd also send word to Lindsey at the Grizzly Inn to let her know how much he wanted for the livery, cabin, and surrounding land—and he was planning on giving it to her dirt cheap. If she didn't want all of it, he'd split it up. If she didn't want any of it, he'd put it on the market, complete with furnishings—and just hope to hell someone came along who would really love and take care of the place, for Millie's sake.

Then he'd put King in the truck and hit the road until they found someplace new.

Shit—that sounded bleak. It *felt* bleak.

But it was like he'd told Lindsey. Nobody wanted to do business with a convicted murderer—he knew from experience, and he even understood why. If he'd led a more normal life, he wouldn't want to do business with an ex-con, either.

Trying to make himself get out of bed was hard. It was difficult to feel very motivated. In one day, he'd lost everything he valued. His work. His home. Millie's legacy. And Millie's niece, too. Still lying amid rumpled sheets, he closed his eyes against the sunny day outside the window and tried to block the pain searing through his chest. He'd gotten so fucking careless. He'd let himself . . . care. Way too much. He'd let himself believe, stupidly, that he could live a normal existence.

Now the idea of moving on, starting over, alone—except for King, of course—was challenging. And he wasn't even really mad at Lindsey for how it had happened. Lindsey was vibrant, alive, talkative—that's who she was. But that sure as hell wasn't the kind of person a private-for-a-reason guy like him could keep in his life. No matter how much it hurt to let her go.

Finally, around two that afternoon, he dragged himself

up, pulled on the jeans he'd dropped next to the bed last night, and slunk down to the kitchen. He found a few muffins Lindsey had brought over from the café a couple of days ago. A little stale now, but that hardly mattered. He took a few bites before realizing he didn't have much of an appetite. Glancing down, he saw King peering up at him uncertainly. The dog knew something was still wrong.

Rob scratched behind his ears and tried to sound reassuring. "Everything's okay, buddy. No worries—we'll be fine."

But King didn't look relieved.

When the phone rang, he didn't answer. He didn't want to talk to anybody. After yesterday, who knew who the hell it would be and what they would want? He'd muster the strength to deal with people soon, but not right now. And as the answering machine clicked on, a vision formed in his head: villagers with torches. He almost laughed. But not quite.

"Hey, Rob, it's Carla," he heard her say into the machine. "I've been thinking of putting a new roof on the Elk, but I have no idea what that would cost. Let me know if you have time to work up an estimate, okay?"

And then she hung up. And he stood there staring blankly at the phone.

He *knew* Carla knew. She had to. She was thick as thieves with Lindsey and well acquainted with Dave the cop, too. Maybe this was some sort of staged thing, something Lindsey had asked her to do. So for this moment, he was going to ignore it.

When the phone rang again, though, he picked it up—unthinkingly. "Hello?" he nearly barked into the receiver.

"My goodness, Rob, it's Eleanor, and you about took my ear off."

He let out a sigh. "Sorry, Eleanor. Bad morning."

"Well, after yesterday, I supposed you're entitled. But I'm just calling to fill you in on this weekend's reservations.

You'll want to have the livery open by Friday at noon because the summer crowds are officially rolling in and they're all asking about the canoes. The weather forecast is great, so Moose Falls' tourist season is booming."

He barely knew how to respond. Since surely Eleanor knew about him now, too. "Okay," he said numbly. "Thanks for letting me know."

When he hung up with Eleanor, life didn't feel quite so bleak. It was as if yesterday hadn't happened. People expected him to be renting them canoes this weekend. Eleanor's voice had sounded completely normal, not like a woman who was nervous around him now or thought of him any differently. Carla had sounded normal, too.

This couldn't last—all this normalness. So he shouldn't start feeling a false sense of security. But he was beginning to feel like maybe he could step out on his front porch without fearing an angry mob with tar and feathers.

Maybe he should get dressed and walk down to the livery, get a little fresh air. It would probably be good for him. Or maybe he should clear his head by doing a little work in the woodshop. Even when he sold the livery, it would be nice to leave the new bench behind. Millie would have liked that—she liked leaving things better than when she'd arrived, and he thought it was a good way to live.

The phone trilled again while he stood there thinking through all this, so he picked it up—but he tried not to snap this time. "Hello."

"Rob. It's Dave Baines from the Cedarville Police Department."

His lightening mood dissipated instantly. "Yeah?"

"Listen, just wanted to give you an update. Although it's too early for this to be official, word from the psych ward in Missoula is that Billy isn't competent to stand trial and will be committed to a permanent psychiatric facility. If he ever gets out, we have a laundry list of charges against him for which he'll stand trial, but for now this is all gonna die a quiet death. I hope it's not a disappointment—I'm sure you'd like to see the guy get what he deserves for his actions yesterday morning—but at least you and Miss Brooks won't have to deal with a trial anytime in the near future."

Rob let out the breath he hadn't quite realized he was holding. "No, that's not a disappointment at all. I . . . uh, don't need to have my past put on display in a trial, if you know what I mean. I suspect enough people will be hearing about it already after yesterday."

"Not if I can help it."

Rob flinched, taken aback. "No?"

"The way I see it, that's nobody's business. You've been an ideal citizen since your release seven years ago, and as far as I can see, you're an upstanding local business owner just trying to live a quiet life. If news of your past incarceration gets out in the area, it won't be from anyone in this department, and that's a personal promise."

Rob swallowed back his shock. "Uh, thank you. I appreciate that. More than I can say."

"No problem. And by the way, I don't know if Cedarville is too far of a drive for you, but I've got a little fishing pond out behind my house and I'm looking to put a dock on it. I hear you do good work, so I'd like to get an estimate if you're interested."

Rob leaned back against the arm of the couch, feeling light-headed. "Uh, no, Cedarville's not too far." For this guy, right now, he'd drive all the way across Montana. "If it's all right, I'll come over one evening next week and take a look."

Dave Baines gave Rob directions to his house and they decided to meet next Tuesday at seven. Rob hung up, feeling all the more stunned.

He stood there for another minute, just waiting to see if the phone would ring yet again—but it didn't. He was glad, actually, because he was already freaked out enough. And even though he knew Lindsey was surely behind all this . . .

was it possible? Could it be that he really *didn't* have to leave Moose Falls?

He knew it was far too soon to say, probably even too soon to start feeling hopeful—but hell, he felt . . . hopeful.

If nothing else, even if he still ended up having to move on, this restored his faith in people a little. A lot. Just having a few people not judge him by his past felt . . . amazing. Lindsey had been the first and he'd thought she was rare and unique and wonderful—hell, he still did. In fact, he was beginning to wonder how he was going to live without her. But maybe this meant she wasn't the only person who could believe in him.

Heading back upstairs, Rob took a shower and got dressed, deciding he'd head down to the livery. He'd been meaning to wood-treat the dock—maybe doing it before the weekend crowds came was a good idea.

As he stepped outside, fresh air hit his face, reviving him even more. And as he made his way down the walk, King tailing dutifully behind, he thought of Lindsey. Of how much he knew he'd hurt her last night. Partly in anger, partly in fear. It had seemed the only answer—letting her go, letting go of everything. Now, today, he wasn't sure—he wasn't sure of anything right now because nothing was making clear sense to him, nothing was going as he'd expected after yesterday.

He'd heard the mail truck pass by a while ago, so he opened the mailbox, surprised to see a package inside. On top were a couple of bills, but he reached underneath to find a small, neatly wrapped box—in shiny paper sprinkled with little brown bears, which he thought he'd seen for sale at the general store. An envelope was tied on top, with *Rob* written in a tidy script on front. What the hell could *this* be?

Taking the package in one hand and the bills in the other, he headed back up the walk and onto the porch, where he settled in the swing. King lay down near his feet and Rob set the bills aside to untie the bow holding the box and envelope together. He opened the package first—a throwback to childhood, he supposed. He didn't get many gifts and felt that childish urgency to see what it was, even before he knew who it came from.

Inside, he found a double frame holding the pictures of him and Millie that Eleanor had taken last summer. His heart contracted. And, of course, he already knew who they were from—he supposed he'd known the moment he'd seen silly bear-laden wrapping paper in his mailbox.

Laying the frame aside carefully to make sure he didn't drop or scratch it, he tore into the envelope, where he found a letter written on three sheets of Grizzly Inn stationery.

Dear Rob,

I never meant to bring so much havoc into your life. I know you feel like you've lost everything because of me, and I regret that with all my heart. I made a mistake and I'm sorry for it. But you won't forgive me. I would think you of all people might understand about mistakes and needing forgiveness.

I'm going home now. Because I can't bear to be near you and not be with you. And because if I leave, maybe you'll decide to stay. Even if you do leave, you can sell the place to someone else, because I can't take it from you. I just can't. It would cease to be Aunt Millie's place in my heart—it would only be the place I stole from the man I loved.

That's right, I love you. I never told you because I didn't want to freak you out. But since I'm leaving, I can tell you. I love you, Rob. I love you in a purer, more real way than I've ever loved a man. I love you in spite of your faults, even because of them. I love all that you are. And even though you think you've lost everything because of me, even though you think you have to start over somewhere new, alone, again—what you fail to see is that if you'd wanted me with you, I'd have been there. I'd start over with you if that's what you wanted. I wouldn't let you lose everything ever again, because no matter what happened, you'd have always had me.

I believe you love me, too, Rob. I've seen it in your eyes, heard it in your voice, and God knows I've felt it in your touch.

But I'm realizing that you just don't have forgiveness in your soul—it's not a part of you. You can't forgive yourself for Tommy and now you can't forgive me, either. So maybe you'll always be alone, and that breaks my heart, but maybe it's what you really want, or I wouldn't be about to get in my car and drive away from you forever.

I wish you happiness, Rob. And I hope you find it. I want you to find love. I want you to find your daughter. And mostly, I hope you find peace—and I'm sorrier than I can say if I truly took that away from you.

All my love,
Lindsey

God.

He'd never had a woman say things like that to him before.

Sitting there on the swing, staring down at the letter, his heart turned inside out. She loved him. All of him. Even with his faults. Even because of them. She loved him. Loved him. Loved him.

His throat felt like it was closing up. His stomach churned. She would have stayed with him. Whatever happened. She would have stayed.

And he'd been too ignorant to see that. Too ignorant to acknowledge the power of what she felt for him. And of what *he* felt for *her.*

Slowly, Rob stood up, gathered the frame and bills and wrapping and letter, and carried it all inside. He felt weird—wired yet also numb. Too much had happened in the last day and a half to make sense of it. Simply too much.

Just walk down to the boathouse. Get out the wood sealant. Spend an afternoon doing some mindless work in the sun. Clear your head.

So he set the items he carried on the kitchen table and walked back outside with King. Emerging from beneath the tree cover near the house, he reached the road and glanced toward town. And, through the pine branches, saw Lindsey lugging that big behemoth suitcase into her car.

Aw, shit.

What would it be like to watch her leave? What would it be like to wake up tomorrow morning and know she was far, far away?

He already knew there was more than one kind of prison cell. But now it hit him that maybe there were even more kinds than he'd realized. Maybe he'd turned Millie's cabin into one—just a different kind. But Lindsey had changed that, brought it to life, brought *him* to life.

And as she slammed her trunk and walked to the driver's-side door, he realized he couldn't let her go. He'd been a fucking idiot and he had to stop it—now.

Only—hell—how could he? She was already backing out, ready to pull away. There was no way he could reach her in time. But he had to. He had to.

So he began to run.

Up the road that rimmed Spirit Lake, past the boathouse, toward the roundabout.

He ran like a man possessed, watching as her car neared the roundabout, too.

And—damn it—his heart plummeted when he realized she didn't see him and despite how hard he sprinted toward her, he wasn't going to make it in time. She was going to leave Moose Falls—and him—behind.

Twenty-one

"Okay now, we just have to do this. We just have to drive away. From Moose Falls. From Aunt Millie's place. From Rob. We can do it. We have to. There's no other answer. And if Rob can start over time and again, so can we." Even if Chicago didn't feel like where she wanted to be. Even if being a jet-set, limelight sort of girl had lost a lot of its appeal over the last few weeks. And even if—oh boy, this was bad—she'd started talking to her car again as she drove away from the Grizzly Inn. And she hadn't even been drinking this time.

Lindsey hadn't realized leaving would be so hard, but she remained set on it. Even as she took one last loving glance at the Lazy Elk out her driver's-side window as she neared the roundabout, then flicked her focus to the road—where something big blocked her path! She slammed on the brakes, trying to focus.

It wasn't a bear this time. Oh God—it was Rob!

The car screeched to a halt and turned a little sideways in the road, the tires flinging up gravel, before coming to a stop just a few feet away from him. He stood before her with his arms spread wide. What the *hell*?

She threw the car into park, got out, and slammed the door. “Are you crazy? Is it not bad enough that I ruin your life, but now you want me to live with the guilt of running you down?”

Rob’s voice came unexpectedly calm, quiet. He said, “I love you, Lindsey.”

And she ceased being able to breathe. She just stood there, too stunned to speak.

“I love you and I need your kind of havoc in my life and I forgive you for bringing Billy here. I know you didn’t mean to—I know you’re a caring person. I forgive you, Lindsey. I forgive you.” His voice went softer then. “So can *you* forgive *me*?”

Lindsey opened her mouth, but still no words came. Her whole body felt weak and tears threatened. “I . . . I . . .” *Oh God, say something.*

“Can you forgive me for last night? For being so blind?”

This time she managed to nod. But still couldn’t get any words out.

And she didn’t have to, apparently. Because he was still talking—saying things she could never have imagined coming from Rob Colter. “Don’t leave me, Lindsey. I need you. I love you. You make my life better than it’s ever been. Better than I ever even hoped it could be. You . . . set me free.”

Holy crap. She set him free? Had he really just said that? No man had ever said anything so perfect to her in her life.

“Say you love me,” he said, stepping nearer, taking her hands in his. “I need to hear it. From your lips.”

“I love you,” she whispered, lost in his desperate gaze.

His mouth trembled now. “Say what you said in the letter. Say you’ll never leave me. No matter what.”

She could still barely speak and was trying not to cry, but she did her best. “I’ll never leave you, Rob. Ever.”

Rob pulled her to him then in a great, crushing embrace—an embrace she'd never thought she'd feel again. Oh God, he was so big and warm and wonderful—her arms locked tight around his neck as tears began to roll down her cheeks.

And when she heard a loud, dreamy-sounding sigh, she looked over her shoulder to see Carla, Eleanor, and Mary Beth standing on the front stoop of the Lazy Elk starting to applaud.

Epilogue

One year later

Lindsey checked the meatloaf in the oven—almost done. The mashed potatoes were mashed and the creamed corn was creaming. Almost time to put the biscuits in the oven and light the candles.

She'd had a busy day—well, heck, a busy year! In addition to resuming her Love Letters column to great success, she was still giving advice in her blog—although she'd cut out most of the personal stuff, having learned that when you loved someone, it came with responsibilities. Additionally, she'd also recently resurrected the *Moose Falls Gazette*. She wrote most of the articles herself, at least for now, but she'd made Eleanor the paper's official photographer, and the townsfolk seemed to enjoy having the little newspaper back in print. She'd spent time helping Carla institute a new tradition at the Lazy Elk—"New Drink Night," which took place every other Friday, and had even inspired Carla to start investing in fruit for wedges. And besides all that, she'd just been put in charge of picking the next book club selection for the ladies at the Lakeside Café, and after careful study of several of her favorites, she'd chosen *The Devil Wears Prada.* Since she did, too—even in Moose Falls on occasion.

Of course, this time of year, she was also busy helping Rob with the canoe livery—and she owned three pairs of Keds now! Because a girl had to have practical shoes that coordinated with her clothes, even if they weren't Jimmy Choos.

All in all, she just loved being a part of Aunt Millie's world, in both old ways and new.

Rob was just as busy as Lindsey—maybe even more so. His construction business was booming, so much that he'd hired a couple of carpenters to help him keep up with the demand. Rob also continued to work in his woodshop whenever he had time—after finding out about his wood-carving skills, the town council had commissioned a large moose for the roundabout, especially since Rob had agreed to do it cheap. As fond as people were of the bear, most were in agreement that it just didn't make sense, and the Moose Falls Wooden Moose Committee was born.

Rob had also, with Lindsey's help and Internet prowess, tracked down Karen, Gina's mother. It had taken a bit of prodding from Lindsey, but that's how their relationship worked—she prodded and he eventually realized she was right. Rob had talked to Karen on the phone, filling her in on where he was in life and asking her to consider telling Gina about him, and that he'd like to meet her. The call had been hard for him to make—he'd felt like he was going back on a promise and he knew what he was suggesting could be upsetting—but Lindsey had convinced him that having him in her life could be a wonderful thing for his daughter.

Although surprised, Karen had been reasonable about the request, and they'd learned that Gina *did* know she had another father somewhere. Karen and her husband planned to take a weekend trip to Moose Falls this summer to talk with Rob and Lindsey, and then decide if they were open to telling Gina that Rob wanted to meet her—and Rob felt that was more than fair. They'd also learned that Gina was a straight-A student with lots of friends and an interest in being a veterinarian, and Lindsey knew how happy it made Rob to find out his daughter was having a good life, with or without him in it.

Rob and Lindsey had married last fall, on the lawn by the lake, near the boathouse. At Rob's request, they'd kept it small, but Lindsey had gone all out on fashion, even managing to get her parents to bring a doggie tux for King from Chicago. And on their wedding night, Rob had shown Lindsey his wedding present to her, which he'd secretly snuck down to Kalispell for: He'd had *her* name tattooed near his heart, too.

Life had changed so much. Her peek-toe pumps didn't get much wear anymore, but she did still break out her favorite heels for certain occasions: book club night (because Mrs. Bixby seemed to enjoy Lindsey's shoes as much as Lindsey did), girls' nights out in Whitefish or Kalispell with Carla, evenings at the Lazy Elk—and nights like tonight.

When King stood up and let out a little bark, she knew Rob had just pulled into the driveway. Showtime.

She met him at the door, whipping it open wearing black platform pumps with leopard-print heels and a coordinating leopard-print apron that tied around the waist and covered her breasts with black lace cups. Of course, she wore nothing else.

"Dinner is served," she said in her sultriest voice, then licked her upper lip for good measure.

Rob dropped his lunchbox just inside and took her into his arms, eyes blazing with lust. "Who needs dinner when I've got you?"

"Mmm," she purred. "My kinda man."

"My kinda woman," he replied, then pulled back to give her a long, hungry once-over. "In my kinda apron."

"Your animal-print fetish is showing again, Mr. Colter."

And as he bent to kiss her, even as the heat of it moved all through her, she pushed him back to say, "Wait. We have to eat first or my fabulous, hardy lumberjack dinner will get cold."

"Get serious, Abby," he said, his eyes chiding her. "That's why God put a Warm setting on our oven."

Which they then used. And warmed each other up in a whole different way—not noticing until afterward that King was watching the whole thing from his rug across the room.